I stand and pull him to my couch, pushing him gently until he sits. Then, carefully, I sit on his lap facing him, wrapping my legs around his back, my arms around his neck.

"Mmmm," I say. "I'm warming up already."

I arch my back and lean in until my nose touches his. "You have four more things you must do for me."

"What are they?"

"Hold me."

His arms slide from his sides to my lower back and pull me closer to him.

"Nice," I say. "Very nice."

He pulls me even closer. "What is the next thing I must do?" he asks.

I flip a strand of hair out of my eyes. "Kiss me."

He kisses my forehead. "Like that?"

I shake my head. "Lower."

He kisses my nose.

I shake my head.

He kisses—a nice, soft, gentle kiss. "That's three things," he said. "What else?"

"Could you take me to your room now?"

Books by J. J. Murray

RENEE AND JAY

SOMETHING REAL

ORIGINAL LOVE

I'M YOUR GIRL

CAN'T GET ENOUGH OF YOUR LOVE

TOO MUCH OF A GOOD THING

THE REAL THING

SHE'S THE ONE

I'LL BE YOUR EVERYTHING

A GOOD MAN

Published by Kensington Publishing Corporation

the real thing

J. J. Murray

KENSINGTON PUBLISHING CORP.
http://www.kensingtonbooks.com

KENSINGTON BOOKS are published by

Kensington Publishing Corp.
119 West 40th Street
New York, NY 10018

All Kensington Titles, Imprints, and Distributed Lines are available at special quantity discounts for bulk purchases for sales promotions, premiums, fund-raising, and educational or institutional use.Special book excerpts or customized printings can also be created to fit specific needs. For details, write or phone the office of the Kensington special sales manager: Kensington Publishing Corp., 119 West 40th Street, New York, NY 10018, attn: Special Sales Department, Phone: 1-800-221-2647.

Kensington and the K logo Reg. U.S. Pat. & TM Off.

ISBN-13: 978-0-7582-7690-2
ISBN-10: 0-7582-7690-7

First trade paperback printing: April 2010
First mass market printing: February 2013

10 9 8 7 6 5 4 3 2 1

Printed in the United States of America

For Amy

Chapter 1

"**D**o you know where Dante Lattanza lives?"

The towheaded child on the wooden dock jutting off Turkey Island whizzes a long silver lure past the prow of my rented aluminum boat. "You talk funny, eh?"

It's because I'm from Red Hook in Brooklyn. At least I don't say "Eh?" after every sentence. "I'm from New York City," I say, not wanting to confuse him. "So, do you know where he lives?"

"Yeah."

This Canadian kid is obviously more interested in catching a fish than answering questions from a black woman in jeans, waterproof Timberlands, and a red and black flannel shirt. "Your outfit will help you blend in," Shelley, my editor at *Personality* magazine, told me. "I'll still be black in the Great White North," I had complained, "no matter what I wear." Shelley only rolled her eyes. She does that a lot whenever I'm around. I think she has a wandering eye. She never seems to focus on me when I talk to her.

"Um," I say, turning off the ten-horsepower motor and drifting toward the shore, "where exactly is Dante Lattanza's house?"

The kid's eyes stay glued to the lure sluicing through the water. "He lives in a cottage."

Cottage, house, what difference does it make? "Which *cottage* does he live in?"

The lure flies up from the water and zips immediately toward me, missing the stern of the boat by inches, er, centimeters, or whatever archaic units these Canadians use. "What time is it?"

I ask which cottage, and he asks for the time. "Almost four-thirty, but I really need to know . . ."

The kid reels in the lure rapidly, throws down his pole, and takes off up some stairs to a house, er, cottage. It looks like a *house* with a huge screen porch and some decking in front of another houselike section. "Where are you going?"

The kid doesn't turn or even acknowledge me. What? Is it time for his meds? Maybe he'll come back with some intelligence and some respect for his elders.

This is such a waste of time. I had gotten an anonymous letter last month telling me where to find the reclusive, elusive Dante "Blood and Guts" Lattanza, former middleweight champion and boxing wunderkind in the mid-nineties until he lost two bloody brawls to better, faster, and stronger fighters. "He's training at Aylen Lake, Ontario, from the end of August through November," the letter said. Retired for ten years, Lattanza was making a comeback just as *Personality* had named him one of the sexiest men alive based on a bit part he had in a recent *Rocky* rip-off called *Heavy Leather.* Normally, *Personality* magazine only chooses from the Hollywood ranks, but someone in editorial must have a crush on Lattanza.

It has been a slow year for sexy men. "The older ones keep dying off," Shelley had told me, "and the younger ones just don't seem to know anything about cultivating sex appeal." Except for Denzel Washington in 1996, all the winners since 1985 have been white, with Richard Gere, Brad

Pitt, and George Clooney winning twice. There has yet to be a single Italian winner, and I, for one, think Italians are very sexy.

Something about their eyes just moves me.

Shelley wants me to get a few good close-ups of Lattanza's face before Tank "The Lion" Washington, the current undisputed middleweight champion and the man who originally took Dante's title, splits it open, and generally rearranges it during their rematch this December. "We can't put bloody faced Italian men in *Personality*," Shelley had explained. "Oh, I suppose we can if it's a shot from a *Sopranos* episode or one of whosawhatsit's model boy toys."

I had to fly from LaGuardia to Ottawa and rent a car to drive 225 kilometers (about 135 miles) to this little strangely shaped lake through the towns of Kanata, Carp, Golden Lake, Killaloe Station, and Barry's Bay. It was kind of like escaping Red Hook, where I live in a renovated warehouse at Reed and Brunt streets with a lovely view of the East River, which my insane realtor called "Buttermilk Channel." It actually looks like buttermilk some days, but . . . It's the freaking East River! Calling it something else does *not* make it any cleaner.

Now, I'm floating on Aylen Lake in front of Turkey Island, feeling like a flanneled turkey and waiting for a blond-headed, freckled kid with selective hearing to—

Oh, there he is, and he's carrying a . . . stopwatch? Is he going to time the gaps in his synapses?

"Dante will be by here in a few minutes," the boy says.

"By here, as in *here*? He'll be by *this* island?" I take a weather-beaten paddle and dip it in the water, pushing the boat away from the shore.

"Yeah. He comes right by here, eh?"

I look around. I see no boats, canoes, or sailboats on the lake, not a single person other than Towhead out on a dock, not even any of the moose, bear, or loons I've read about cavorting on the shoreline. "Really?"

The kid points to a rocky outcropping bathed in sunlight and jutting off the northeast shore maybe a quarter mile away. "He's about to begin."

I look at the outcropping and don't see anyone. "Begin what?"

"The last part of his workout," the kid says. "He broke his record by twelve seconds yesterday."

I get my camera ready anyway, screwing on a telephoto lens. "You don't say? What exactly am I going to . . . see?"

Then I see a man diving off the rocks at least thirty feet above the water. He wears what looks like a parachute or a backpack on his back. *That's* Dante Lattanza? He's also a cliff diver?

The kid starts the stopwatch. "He'll swim across the channel to the point of our island, run across to the other point, swim the other channel to that cottage over there, run up the hill, ring a bell, run down the hill, and swim back."

I zoom in on a man's arms furiously cutting through the waves, his head bobbing up every ten strokes. "What's on his back?"

"Twenty kilos in a backpack," Towhead says. "He has weights on his wrists and ankles, too. It adds a total of thirty kilos."

This means absolutely nothing to me.

I snap a few shots of Lattanza's flailing arms, the sunny outcropping in the background. He is an extremely strong swimmer, cutting through the water like . . . well, like a man carrying an extra thirty kilos, practically disappearing underwater occasionally. These shots won't do. I couldn't sell these to even the most desperate tabloids. Lattanza isn't, however, exactly tabloid material. He's practically unknown.

And then . . .

Lattanza reaches the northeast point of Turkey Island, rising out of the blue green water like a cut sculpture, tanned and toned and looking like Carrara marble. He sprints down the somewhat sandy shore in bare feet. I click away on auto as he glides closer.

"*Ciao*, David," Lattanza says with a smile as he passes the dock.

"*Ciao*, Dante," David says.

I keep my finger on the trigger, so to speak, taking Lattanza in, keeping him framed until he dives off the other point into the water. I sit and review the pictures I've taken and see a man defying nature. Lattanza is forty-two but hasn't an ounce of fat on him, his entire body cut like one of Michelangelo's models. He has such dark eyes, dark eyebrows, dark stubble, and thick, wavy black hair. His signature high cheekbones make his smile even more effective because of his squint. I can't believe Shelley and the rest of the editorial staff only have him at number thirteen.

I'd, um, I'd put him in the top . . . seven. But then again, I've been single a long time. When was the last time? Who was I with? Who was president? Ooh, look at his—

"Hey," David says.

"Yes?" I look up briefly. Lattanza has a seriously interesting butt, as if he has two huge fists back there. Our readers will rejoice. I may rejoice a little bit later my damn self. He has a nice, muscular booty.

"Listen for the bell," David says.

"What bell?"

"Shh. You'll hear it, eh?"

I look at the southeast shore about another quarter mile away and see Lattanza rise from the water onto a dock, run up some steps, and disappear into the woods. . . .

A bell rings.

Then I hear shouts, "you-hoos," and car and boat horns honking. What's all this about?

"He's ahead of his record," David says.

"What was all that noise?"

David grins. "I'm not the only one timing him, eh?"

So at least the residents, vacationers, and cottagers on Aylen Lake know they have a celebrity among them. This must be the highlight of their day. Whoopee.

I see Lattanza bouncing down the steps to another dock and zooming off. Thirty kilos extra and he's flying like that. Tank Washington may be in for more of a fight than he has imagined. Lattanza will still lose, but maybe the fight won't be the bloodbath Las Vegas is predicting and HBO Pay-Per-View is counting on. They're already touting the rematch as "The Lion vs. the Legend—*Twice* in a Lifetime." The first fight was *Ring* magazine's "Fight of the Year" ten years ago. The two had combined for over eighteen hundred punches, eight hundred of which connected—five *hundred* or so to Lattanza's face and body. Most folks, though, don't expect a repeat performance, especially from Lattanza. The experts think he'll run out of gas after the third round.

I see Lattanza using his legs now—hairy things, strong kick, no letup as he comes back—silhouetted against the sun, powerful, virile, truly not number thirteen. I let the camera fire away. With that background, that face, and that body, he should be at least in the top five. I'll have to talk to Shelley about his placement. Unlike many on this year's list, every bit of Dante Lattanza is real and as God made him. He has no blond highlights in his hair, no calf implants, no caps for his teeth, and no sex appeal based on whom he's sleeping with, adopting children with, or dating. In addition, he doesn't need a personal trainer because he's his *own* personal trainer.

I am witnessing an atypical boxer's workout. My granddaddy fought in the amateurs, getting pretty far in the New York Gold Gloves, and he maintained a boxing workout throughout the rest of his life at Gleason's Gym, so I know boxing. Granddaddy ran in the morning, went to work, then picked me up after school to spend a few hours in the gym shadowboxing, pounding the heavy bag, popping the focus mitts, peppering the speed and double-end bags, jumping rope, and sparring whenever he could. Yet here's Dante swimming a total of a mile or so and playing a hunchbacked lifeguard on *Baywatch*.

Lattanza is on the island again, and he's not slowing down. He only nods at David, shoots—is that a grin?—at me, and again he's crunching down the beach to the point and flying into the water.

I check to see if I snapped the grin, and I did. It's a nice grin. I'm not sure if all those teeth are originally his, but . . . nice. The squint makes his eyes twinkle. On the other hand, maybe they just twinkle and the squint . . .

Listen to me. Daydreaming about a photograph.

Hmm.

Okay, top three.

David runs out onto the dock. "This is my favorite part."

I zoom in on the rocks, expecting Lattanza to stop to catch his breath. He doesn't. He literally leaps from rock to rock, handhold to handhold, almost hopping up that rock formation to the top where he rings another bell.

David clicks the stopwatch. "He beat yesterday by fifteen seconds!"

More noise, yelling—what is this "You-hoo!" business?—horns blaring.

"He's going to get that title back for sure," David says.

Not.

Lattanza turns, addresses the noise, and bows, sunlight drenching him in amber.

Damn. I forgot to keep shooting. I click one of him taking off the backpack and raising his arms into the air. It reminds me of a scene from *Rocky*. That scene gave me goose bumps.

I look at my arms. They are long brown goose bumps that end with nails that desperately need a manicure.

Well.

Hmm.

Lattanza's bow would have been a cheesy shot, but I wish I had taken it.

Hmm.

I may have to, um, make the interview last longer than my usual thirty minutes. You know, stretch it a bit. I need to make sure I probe this man and get to his essence. Except for *Heavy Leather,* Lattanza has been out of the spotlight for ten years. This is an important interview. Readers will want to know why he's been hiding for so long.

I also, um, have to check out his abs up close.

My last short-lived boyfriend, whose name still escapes me (Chuck? Howard?), had love handles, which turned simply to fat, and I quickly returned to a single life.

Dante Lattanza has love ripples.

I wonder what those feel like.

Chapter 2

Dante Lattanza is a throwback to another era, my grand-daddy had told me, a real "Rocky" in the mold of the Bronx Bull Jake LaMotta and Carmen Basilio. Dante is the same height as LaMotta (5' 8") was, and has a better winning (50–2) and knockout percentage (96%) than either LaMotta or Basilio ever had, but these Italian boxers each had their African-American nemeses that kept them from immortality. LaMotta's nemesis was Joe Louis, Basilio's nemesis was Sugar Ray Robinson, and Lattanza's nemesis was and will soon again be Tank Washington.

Lattanza just hasn't kept up with the times. For forty-seven fights, he put all his hopes into a thundering left hook. By the time he fought Washington, Lattanza and his left hook hardly ruffled hair. After his divorce and a ten-year layoff, Lattanza was making a comeback and blood-and-gutting his way to miraculous victories over younger, faster, better skilled and stronger fighters, often knocking them out in the last few rounds while far behind on points.

Thus, I was here in Canada to catch up *Personality* readers on the last ten years of his life.

Such fun.

At least he's nice to look at.

Shelley doesn't assign me any truly juicy stories. She won't allow me to trail pop singers who can't follow judges' orders and lose their children as a result. She forbids me from stalking starlets who use drugs and kleptomania to handle their fame. She wouldn't dream of letting me interview fashion designers who end up in West Virginia prisons, the "it" couple and what flavor of the human rainbow they are going to adopt this week, and heiresses sent to jail, not sent to jail, sent to jail, an appearance with Letterman—oh, the freaking horror! Other more seasoned and cynical writers get those scandalous stories. I get the human-interest puff pieces, the feel-good, gosh-ain't-this-a-nice-person stories, the ones that should give our readers hyperglycemia because of all the sugar dripping off the page.

Celebrities. We actually quote them, as if any of them have something interesting and original to say. Most of them read their lines and have to go through several takes to get those lines right in front of the camera, right? Yet, we splash their drivel weekly (which they often tell us *weakly*) as nuggets of wisdom. "It's so miserable to be rich and famous," they seem to say. "You should see the little ten *bazillion* square feet bungalow I live in with *only* an unimpeded view of the Pacific Ocean." They tell us how awful the paparazzi are—"I hope they at least get my good side, but what are you gonna do?"—and how simply devastating it is to have their personal lives put out in public for us to . . . envy? Shoot, give me $1.5 million a picture or $250,000 an episode and let me see how I handle the paparazzi for a day. I bet I'd . . . stay home and read or surf the Internet or bid on eBay for Brooklyn Dodgers memorabilia and old Johnny Mathis and Smokey Robinson recordings.

What? A modern girl can't go old school? Okay, okay, Mathis and Robinson are more "ancient school" than old school, but when you're lonely and pining for a man, whose voice would you rather hear caressing your ears— Keith Sweat and his nasal tones or smooth Smokey kissing your soul with "Cruisin'," "The Tracks of My Tears," "Being with You," and "Ooo Baby Baby"? You don't turn on some R. Kelly and all of his nasty baggage when Johnny's voice can snuggle up to your heart with "Chances Are," "A Certain Smile," "Misty," and "I'm Coming Home." Icons. I listen to icons. They never go out of style. They're immortal.

Johnny and Smokey are not famous for being famous like so many celebrities these days. What a vicious cycle. Fifteen minutes of fame (or infamy) translates into ten talk shows a year, maybe a guest appearance on a sitcom, and a bit (and often bitter) part in a movie. I don't hate the famous, but c'mon, now—they're *people*. They're not heroes. They're not role models. They're not saving the world. They're not going to end up in the *Encyclopedia Britannica*. They're only as famous (or infamous) as their last movie, album, show, or run-in with the law.

I once had an interview with a disco queen (who shall remain nameless) who had a few hits in the seventies and was making a comeback thanks to so many rappers sampling her beats. She was old news, yet Shelley told me to go "get the skinny." After waiting two hours for *not*-skinny Disco Diva's makeup artist to transform her fifty-something face into maybe forty-nine, she had absolutely nothing to say. *Nothing*. Yet I wrote it well, three paragraphs that said absolutely nothing. "Nice piece," Shelley said. "Of what?" I countered. "Toilet paper?"

I signed on to *Personality* to be a news reporter, not a gushing, exclamation-point-filled writer of the fantasy lives of unreal celebrities. *Personality* magazine is supposed to have an even mix of celebrity and human-interest stories, but I swear that celebrities fill more than half our pages. Our covers are also starting to mirror the *Enquirer* and *Star*.

I have never had a subscription to *Personality*, and I don't ever intend to get one.

I don't care much for the stories in the magazine. I don't care if that pop singer is watching herself do a pole dance on her latest music video. I don't care if that same pop singer thinks the world is "cruel." As John Wayne once said, "Life is tough. Life is tougher if you're stupid." You're stupid, Miss Pole Dancer. Get over yourself, honey. I don't care if a megastar bought a multimillion-dollar island for his children to grow up on so they can "live ordinary lives." What is ordinary about that? I don't care which celebrity is cheating on a celebrity spouse with another celebrity who's cheating on his high school sweetheart. I don't care who has rehab center frequent-flyer miles. I don't care what singers-turned-actresses (and there is a glut of those these days) wear under their dresses at the Golden Globes. I don't care if a magpie caused a singer/actor to pee himself on an Australian golf course. I don't care if the daughter of a well-known boozer and druggie can read Noam Chomsky.

So the freak what.

I knew the Dante Lattanza "sexy man" story would be at best a puff piece filling one-fourth of a page or less. I hate puff pieces so much that I don't even set out to write them when Shelley assigns them to me. I write in-depth, hard-hitting stories that often reveal the seedy underbelly of fame or even the insipid and lackluster nature of celebrated lives. Yet my stories, which you actually have to chew on before swallowing, get reduced to a few glossy pictures and a paragraph or two, lasting just long enough for the average person to read on the subway, in the bathroom, on the bus, or at a stoplight.

I hate that. I didn't go to Columbia and spend ten years chasing down stories for *The New York Times* to write puff pieces for a living. The pay is significantly better now, but the prestige isn't there. Puff pieces, which I define as "stories that the magazine's in-house lawyer *won't* need to read," are lifeless, flavorless, and controversy-less.

In other words, happy happy joy joy not.

All I need is thirty minutes to get Lattanza to answer a few soft questions, take a few pictures, and maybe get to know him (and his washboard abs) better. I want him to explain the town of Barry's Bay to me. Who is Barry, and where is the bay? I didn't see any water around that little town. I want to ask him why the boat rental person at a place called "the Landing" had charged me so much. Does he have a thing against black people or Americans in general? Why are there so many burly women on Canadian road crews? What's up with those logging trucks creeping uphill at 5 kilometers per hour and screaming downhill at 150 kilometers per hour? Do you have to wear flannel to be a Canadian citizen? Why do I understand the French words on the road signs better than I understand the English words? Why is the road to this lake unpaved? If I wanted to drive on a washboard, I'd get an ATV. Moreover, what's up with the Monopoly money these Canadians use? Who decided red was a good color for money?

I want to ask Lattanza why he chose this remote wilderness setting to train for a fight against a man he could never beat, and I especially want to know why Lattanza is even taking this fight in the first place. "Do you have a death wish?" I want to ask. Tank Washington is ten years younger than Lattanza is. What is the point? A payday? What payday, rumored to be in the seven digits, is worth your face or your ability to think and breathe in the future?

My research into Lattanza's life revealed a few interesting points. First, he had a normal, ordinary childhood in the Carroll Gardens section of South Brooklyn, where someone filmed *Moonstruck* a while ago. That, in itself, is interesting. He had a normal childhood in a neighborhood stereotypically rumored to have Mafia ties. He was never in any trouble with the law, and he was a good student at St. Saviour, even attending Kingsborough Community College after high school. An early article revealed that every weekday he jogged to and from St. Saviour, a distance of about two miles, wearing his school uniform. Second, he *still* has a following, an army of devout, devoted fans. "Rabid, rude, and raucous," one boxing analyst had said of them. In today's "fifteen minutes of fame" society, to have anything last so many years is amazing. When Lattanza lost his first match to Tank on points, Lattanza's fans had rioted, throwing chairs and even a few non-Lattanza fans into the ring in Las Vegas. Lattanza hadn't won a single round on any of the judges' scorecards, yet they rioted.

The next fight with Cordoza was even more lopsided— and bloody. Lattanza's eyes were almost swollen shut, cuts above and below both eyes. Finally, Lattanza simply disappeared until *Heavy Leather,* dropping completely off the map. Even Google had no record of his whereabouts for the last ten years. Now, ten years later, he's back, 3–0 with three knockouts during his comeback, ranked in the top ten by *Ring* magazine, and chosen by Tank Washington to take his last beating and bloodletting.

I could sense there was more to Dante Lattanza than I could see. He was a story waiting to happen. My normal philosophy of "There's nothing new under the sun" is in jeopardy. Lattanza is something so old school he's actually new. In addition, it wouldn't be as easy as detailing a man's simple desire to be a champion again. I could sense a tight, hard-hitting piece that could end up in newspapers across the country, a real scoop, a real human-interest story that could put my name up there with Red Miller or Jim Murray.

I could also sense a simple need deep within me to . . .

Okay, I'm busted.

I just want to see a real man up close before they start stitching up his face.

Is that such a crime?

Chapter 3

I pull-start the motor and cruise over to a dock to the right of the outcropping, seeing Lattanza's cottage sitting some sixty feet back from the precipice in a clearing surrounded by pine and birch trees. It's really a beautiful cottage, with two stories, a stone chimney, lots of picture windows, and plentiful decking. I shift the motor to neutral and float into an open area of the long dock, a fancy ski boat and a fishing boat tied on the left side, an old wooden boat beached on the shore, stone stairs climbing the hill to the cottage.

A seriously dark tan teenaged boy comes down those stairs to tend to my boat. This should be Dante Jr., and his features are more like mine. Full lips, short curly hair, a wider nose than his daddy has. I had never seen Lattanza's ex-wife, but she must have been an exceptionally beautiful black woman.

"Hi," I say.

He only nods and ties the front rope of my boat to a cleat on the dock while I do the same at my end.

"My name is Christiana Artis," I say, smiling. "I'm from *Personality* magazine, and I—"

He interrupts me with a burst of Italian that he shouts behind him. I hear my name and the word "personality" clearly, though the way Dante Jr. says it has some serious attitude. Another burst of Italian from a deeper and, I must say, sexier voice drifts down to us.

"My dad doesn't give interviews," he says.

"You're Dante Junior, right?"

"DJ."

"Um, DJ," I say carefully, "I know he hasn't given an interview in many years, but I thought if I made the effort, you know, came out to the middle of nowhere, that I'd—"

"You came out for nothing," DJ interrupts with a shrug.

I look up the stairs and see Lattanza toweling himself off behind some sturdy pine trees. You can't come down and tell me yourself, huh? You have to send the kid, right?

"I, uh, I watched part of his workout, and I was—"

"And took some pictures without Dad's permission."

I nod. I look up the stairs. Lattanza has put on a plain white T-shirt.

"I can always say I was taking pictures of that beautiful island," I say, "and he just happened to be in them, lucky me."

DJ frowns. "It would be a lie."

This isn't going well. I sigh. "Well, tell him he's been named one of *Personality* magazine's sexiest people alive." I hear a rustling up above. "Tell him I'll put the entire interview in his own words so there will be no chance for any lies."

DJ looks up the stairs. "*My* dad?"

Hmm. Why not? "He's only number thirteen."

"Tredici!" a voice thunders down from the rocks and echoes all around me. *"Impossibile!"*

I have struck a chord. I had heard that Lattanza was vain. Not being number one in anything for so long must be hard for him to swallow.

DJ laughs. "*My* dad?" he repeats.

"He's a handsome man," I say, and I mean it, though it is hard to see Lattanza through all those tree branches.

"You all are crazy," DJ says.

I nod. "I'd put him much higher, but I'm just a writer and a photographer."

DJ shakes his head. "Higher? I can't believe he even made the top thousand."

Another explosion of Italian echoes around us.

"Just kidding, Dad," DJ says, crouching in front of me. "Look, Dad doesn't like the attention, okay?" he whispers. "Especially from you. Reporters like you turned on him after he lost to Cordoza, and he has vowed not to speak to any more reporters."

I was afraid of this. I had written many boxing stories while at the *Times* since I told them—in a stretch of the truth—that I *trained* at Gleason's Gym with my granddaddy. It was just an excuse for Granddaddy and me to get in to free boxing matches at Madison Square Garden. I wrote the hell out of those stories, however, so no one ever questioned my knowledge of the sport.

"You said your name was Artis?" DJ asks.

"Yes."

"Weren't you the one who wrote that my dad never had any talent?"

I had written plenty of other painful things, but not that . . . exactly. "I didn't write that, DJ. I never wrote—"

DJ unties the front rope and tosses it into the boat. "Leave him alone, okay? And when you publish those pictures, and I know you will, don't disrespect him or make him look like a clown." He pushes off the front of the boat with his foot.

Since my end is still secure, I have to turn around to speak to him as the boat slides away from the dock. "Look, I came a long way, and I only need thirty minutes."

"To ruin my *papino* some more?"

This boy *really* loves his *papino,* er, daddy. How do I get through to him? "I'm not here to ruin your, um, *papino.* I'm here to set the record straight, okay? I'm here—"

I stop because I have to catch my breath.

Lattanza, sans blood and guts, is bouncing down the stairs with all his cuts and bulges and . . . oh yeah, he's pissed. Those eyes are not twinkling at me at all. Those are the eyes that other boxers look into when he fights them.

"Tredici? Non penso cosi!"

I take a deep breath. "Mr. Lattanza, I—"

Lattanza stomps to the end of the dock and sits, his bare feet dangling over the water, my boat swiveling farther away. "Call me Dante."

"Okay, Dante, I—"

"Why only thirteen?" he asks.

"I, uh, I don't—"

"There are twelve sexier than me?"

His voice is so damn hot. I can't explain it. It has passion in it, fire. It curls around my heart and pokes at it with hot fingers. "My, um, my editor—"

He shakes his head. "What do you think?" He raises his arms and flexes like a bodybuilder.

"Dad, c'mon," DJ says.

"Hmm?" Dante flexes even harder. "Is this the body of a thirteen?"

I notice gray hairs around his ears and some gray in his stubble, but he doesn't look a day over thirty. Fine white scar lines and some thicker scar lines crease his eyelids and eyebrows, the thickest scar below his right eye. "I'd put you in the top ten," I say softly, not looking into his eyes. "Maybe even the top three."

"Ha!" Dante says, springing to his feet. He directs a torrent of Italian at DJ, and DJ comes to the end of the dock, pulling the back rope until my boat returns to the dock.

"I know you," Dante says as DJ ties the rope to the cleat.

"I don't think we've ever met. I'm—"

"You are Christiana Artis," Dante interrupts.

How does he know me? "You can call me Tiana."

Dante shakes his head. "Christiana is a better name, a good name for *scrittore cattivo*."

I blink, expecting a translation. He doesn't give one. Bad scribbler? Wait. It probably means "bad writer." Yes, he probably knows me.

"You say you came all this way," Dante says. "You say you have made an effort. How much effort are you willing to make?"

I'm supposed to be the one asking questions, not him. "Look, I only need thirty minutes, maybe a few more pictures." I look up at the outcropping of rocks. "I can get a really good shot of you up there with the sunset in the background."

"Ha!" He crouches down, his calves bulging, a crucifix swaying from a gold chain around his neck. "So your caption can read, 'Dante Lattanza, washed-up boxer in the sunset of his life'?"

I wouldn't put it past some of my editors to do that, but . . . "No, of course not. It will, um, be sexy." I can't believe I just said that. "You know, sexiest men alive, sexy pose. You were, um, sexy in *Heavy Leather*."

Dante shakes his head. "No. No pictures. You are writing what you *giornalisti* call a puff piece, yes?"

He knows me, and he knows about our puff pieces. Hmm. "Yes, but I want the whole story for another article I hope to publish just before you fight Washington." Which I've just now decided to do. "Probably for *Sports Illustrated*." Or not. *Personality* might even run with it. Hell, we all work for Time-Life.

"Then no," he says with authority. "No interview. No puff piece. Use the pictures you already took. Use the lies you have been writing about me for years. Put me at thirteen,

non importa." He flies into more Italian, and DJ unties the
front of my boat again.

That rope is getting a workout.

"Mr. Lattanza, Dante, please," I plead. "I took a plane
out of LaGuardia this morning to Ottawa and drove all the
way on some very iffy roads just to see you. I have covered
a dozen of your fights. I grew up in Red Hook, right next to
Carroll Gardens where you—"

"I did not ask you to come here and interrupt things,"
Dante says, interrupting me. He looks in my boat. "You
have no *bagaglio,* no bags?"

I watch the prow of the boat spinning away from the
dock again and have to swivel in my seat to keep eye contact with him. "Like I said, I didn't plan to be here for more
than half an hour. I didn't bring a change of clothes because I planned to get on another plane—"

Dante laughs, and despite his anger, it is an unrestrained
laugh, a genuine laugh. "You thought you could show up,
ask your questions, and go."

I relax a little when I see his eyes twinkle. "Yes."

He stands taller. "You think you can capture me in thirty
minutes?"

I nod.

"Impossibile!"

So vain! At least his eyes aren't angry with me anymore.

"Look," I say, "I'll ask you maybe five questions, you
answer, I go away. End." What's Italian for *end*? *Fine*?

He arrests me with those eyes. "Five questions."

"Right."

"Non importa then. *Ciao.*" He turns to leave the dock.

So temperamental! "Dante!"

He turns.

"How do I capture you then?"

Dante stares me down, freezing me in my seat. I stare
back as long as I can but have to turn away. I hear more

Italian, whispered this time, the phrase "*corpo provocante*" said twice, and reach blindly to untie the back rope. When I look up, Dante is gone and DJ is once again pulling my boat toward the dock.

"Am I staying or leaving?" I ask. "That rope is getting tired."

"It's up to you," DJ says. "If you want an interview, a *real* interview, not a few questions and a picture, you must do five things."

That's . . . weird. "Why five?"

He, too, freezes me with a stare. "He says you ask five questions, you must do five things."

Mission *impossibile!* But I can't leave without this story. "Okay. It's fair. What do I have to do?"

He reaches a hand down to me, and I take it. I step out of the boat while he gathers my laptop case and camera bag. At least DJ has manners. I wonder who taught him. It couldn't have been his *papino*.

"You must go fishing with him in the morning," he says.

I narrow my eyes. "You're kidding. I haven't been fishing in years."

"And Dad takes it seriously, too. He'll want to leave at four-thirty, an hour before the sun rises." He nods toward the stairs.

"Why so early?" I ask.

"Tradition," he says, trying to sound like his daddy.

"Oh." I walk to the bottom step. "Um, where am I staying?"

"Dad says you can use the guesthouse."

How generous. "Does it have . . . ?"

DJ rolls his eyes. "It has a full, modern bathroom if you're worried, with running water and everything."

I wasn't worried. I'm used to roughing it. Some of the hotels I've stayed in, you wouldn't believe.

Okay, okay, I was worried. I like the great outdoors, I really do. I just do not want to do my business in an outhouse surrounded by those great outdoors and creatures that do not understand American.

I start up the steps. "What else do I have to do?"

He trails behind. "After fishing you have to climb Mount Baldy with us and help us prepare breakfast."

"That's two things," I say.

"Not to him. The catching, climbing, cleaning, cooking, and eating are all one thing to him."

Italians can't count.

I reach the top of the stairs and see two paths, one to the main cottage all lit up and glowing like Christmas by the sunset, another, narrower path to what looks like an overgrown shack with a small window facing me. "Back there?" I ask.

DJ nods. "After that, you must complete a full workout with him."

I get a vision of my body jumping off that outcropping and sinking straight to the bottom. "I know he's kidding now."

"My *papino* does not kid."

I get another vision of what the sky must look like from the bottom of a lake, fish swimming around my head—and talking bad about my hair. "I'll have to swim across and everything like that?"

"You look like you're in pretty good shape," DJ says.

"Did your dad say that?"

DJ looks down. "He said a lot of things about you, um, some of which I'm too embarrassed to repeat."

I stop on the path and smile at him. "Such as?"

He looks at my boots. "Most of it was nice. *Molto graziosa.* He thinks you're very pretty."

My heart thumps. "He said a lot of things down there. What else?"

He frowned. "He says you're *pericolosa.*"

I repeat the word slowly. "I'm . . . perilous?"

"Dangerous." He steps past me under a pine tree.

"What's, um, *'corpo provocante'* mean?"

DJ turns slightly. "Um, it sort of means sexy body."

My heart thumps again. Dante's right, of course. I am dangerous, and I do have a sexy body.

I can't believe he called me that in front of his son!

People have told me I have a cute face, that I don't look my age (thirty-five), that my eyes are penetrating. Below that, though, I have a smoking hot body and booty. I smile. *Pericolosa, molto graziosa,* and *corpo provocante.* I am a very dangerous beauty with a sexy body, which may make me a femme fatale to Dante Lattanza.

"So after this full workout that will probably drown me," I ask, "what's next?"

DJ stops in front of the guesthouse and opens the door, flipping on an interior light. "Then you . . ." He frowns. "I've forgotten the fourth thing. The last thing you'll do is go waterskiing. After that—"

"I have never been waterskiing in my life," I say, rooted in the doorway.

"Dad will teach you," DJ says. "He's a good teacher."

I get another vision, and this time Dante's strong hands hold me in the water . . . before the boat rips me through the water at a hundred miles an hour, my head the only appendage still attached after—

"After all that, you'll get your interview," DJ says.

Personality doesn't pay me enough to do this. "What if I, um, what if I fail?"

DJ turns away. "Then you'll know how he felt." He looks up at me in the shy way that teenaged boys sometimes look at *molto graziosa* women. It touches me. "I'm sorry. Just . . . try, okay? *Tenere provare,* he might say. It means to try it, to keep trying. He says it all the time to me.

That's all he really expects you to do. He doesn't expect you to succeed."

Now *that* was a challenge. "You're really protective of your daddy, aren't you?"

DJ nods. "He's my *papino*, my dad, you know?"

He flips on a light, and I see a nice guestroom with whitewashed furniture contrasting against dark pine walls. A queen-sized bed sits in a corner, a single lamp on the headboard, next to a huge wardrobe, the bathroom just beyond in the shadows. A massive eight-drawer dresser rests under the only window, a Sony TV on top. A phone on its own stand and a cozy-looking chocolate recliner command the corner closest to the window.

"Dad built it for my mama," DJ says. "She never likes coming up here, so he made it as modern as he could."

"Why *didn't* she like coming up here?" I ask, emphasizing the past tense.

He counts out on his fingers. "She doesn't like the bugs, the cold water, the lack of entertainment, the silence, the cold air, Barry's Bay, did I mention the bugs? Um, the weather, the fish . . ."

He's still talking in the present tense. She *still* visits? Maybe it's simply to be with her son. "Your daddy built all this?"

"Yeah. Red and I helped some."

"Who's Red?"

DJ smiles. "Red Gregory, Dad's best friend. You'll meet him at dinner." He opens the wardrobe revealing stacks of blue jeans, sweaters, sweatshirts, and several jackets and windbreakers. "Um, Mama always leaves a bunch of what she calls 'Canada clothes' up here."

Clothes she doesn't mind getting dirty, I suppose.

"They might fit you, I don't know," DJ says. "Dad said you could wear them." He points at stacks and stacks of sweatpants and sweatshirts. "You'll need to dress warmly when we go fishing."

I check a label on one of the pairs of jeans. Size six? Is she anorexic? If I hold my breath and butter my thighs, I might be able to wear them—for about a minute.

"Dinner's at six sharp," DJ says. "Don't be late." He nods once and leaves, shutting the door behind him.

I haven't worn a size six since I was in the eighth grade. They look worn enough, though, and if she didn't dry them in a dryer . . .

I pull the blinds and drop out of my size tens. I have a decent figure, but I prefer my clothes to be a little baggy. If I can get into . . . *geez*! . . . these tiny *little* . . . hold breath, zip, button . . . c'mon button! . . . exhale.

Whew.

I walk into the bathroom, standing on the toilet seat to see my butt in the mirror above the pedestal sink. Whoa. You could read a newspaper through these size sixes. I can't feel my toes.

I look over at the shower curtain, parting it to see . . . Damn. Is that a whirlpool tub? It's a two-seater with candles and potpourri already on the ledges. Maybe Dante's ex doesn't visit just to visit, and the two of them come out here to have some ex-sex.

I hope there's some Lysol somewhere. It looks clean enough, but I'm not taking any chances.

The top button of the jeans is cutting off circulation to my legs, so I remove the pants and put mine back on. My toes throb back to life. I take off my flannel shirt and put on an oversized black sweatshirt with a howling wolf on the front.

I check the time. Five-fifteen.

Time to prowl.

Chapter 4

I'm almost out the door when I remember Shelley. I should check in to tell her that I won't be back in New York tonight or tomorrow. I get my cell phone from my laptop bag, flipping it open.

No signal.

I wave it around the room, even returning to the bathroom to stand on the toilet seat again.

Nothing.

I glance again at the tub. Maybe if I stand in there I could . . . No.

I settle into the cozy recliner and look at the old-fashioned yellow phone. Hmm. Dante's number is listed right there below the buttons. I put his number in my cell phone. You know, just in case I need to check some facts with him later.

I pick up the phone, dialing a zero. I used to have a calling card, but who uses those anymore? After a pleasant chat with an operator who is *so* excited to place a call "all the way to Manhattan," I get a hold of Shelley, who had to be minutes from leaving her office.

"I'm here," I tell her.

"Where's 'here'?" she asks.

"Aylen Lake, Canada. I'm in Dante Lattanza's guest-house."

"Wonderful!" Shelley gushes. "Did you already interview him and he's letting you stay?"

I explain to her about my five tasks.

"Sounds like the seven labors of Hercules to me," she says. "That's so . . . strange. What are Italians doing in Ontario anyway?"

"I'm black and I'm not in Africa."

"True," Shelley says. "What's he like?"

How much do I tell her? Do I tell her anything she doesn't already know? "He's almost exactly like you told me. He's vain. He's temperamental. He's proud." He's hot, handsome, sexy, and probably still having mad whirlpool sex with his ex.

"All the things you are, too," Shelley says.

"I'm not that vain." Temperamental, yes. Proud, yes.

"Look, I need to see this ASAP, Tiana," Shelley says. "How soon can you send it?"

Deadlines, schmedlines. The "sexy man" issue won't hit the stands until late November or early December, and it's only the beginning of September. With computers these days, you can almost insert a story ten minutes before the printing presses run. "I ought to finish capturing him by midnight tomorrow. I'll send you some pictures as soon as I can." Do they have Internet service this far north? Hmm. "I may have to bring them in to the office. You'll love them. They're of him working out."

"Lots of testosterone, huh?"

"Yes." And sweat. And winks. And that cute little squint. "If all goes well, I may have a longer piece for you in December."

"Hmm, just before the fight," she says. "I like it. It might be the last ink Lattanza gets for a while."

I roll my eyes. "I'll give you the skinny for the sexy man

issue by Thursday and expand it later for the issue before the fight."

"I love to watch him fight, but I wince a lot," Shelley says.

That was so . . . random. A wave of garlic blows through the screen in the window. "Whoa. I gotta go. I think dinner's almost ready."

"Is there something you're not telling me, Tiana?"

She always thinks there's "more to the story." There is, but I don't have to tell her. I decide to be temperamental. "You know how I feel about these puff pieces, right?"

"Yes, but we all—"

"Have to start somewhere," I say, finishing her favorite line. "I know, Shelley."

"I could still have you writing obituaries," she says.

I growl. Six months I wrote advance obituaries for the richly famous and the famously rich. It's about as morbid a writing job as there is. I'm not as superstitious as my predecessor, who once wrote an obit for a rapper who died the next day. "I just like being busy, Shelley. I'm like any boxer who's been out of the ring for too long. My writing gets rusty if I'm not writing every day."

"Do you feel busy now?"

"Yes. I feel . . . professional, you know? Like I did at the *Times*." I add the last bit to threaten her, though I know she can replace me with a phone call. "They still want me back, you know."

I hear Shelley sigh. "Do you really want to go through that grind again, Tiana? All that racing around?"

"I miss the adventure, the grit." And the full use of my brain. How hard is it to ask a starlet how big her house is and does she have a vacation home that doesn't have seven and a half bathrooms gilded in platinum?

"You're in Canada, Tiana," she says, "the adventure capital of North America."

Hardly. The only adventure I've had so far is watching my boat swivel back and forth at a dock. But tomorrow . . . tomorrow should be interesting.

"Hey, before I forget, what do we have on Dante's ex-wife?" I ask.

"Dante, huh? You're on a first-name basis already?"

I sigh. "Do we have anything on her or not?"

I hear a series of clicks. "Nope. Nothing in the archives. You, um, trying to replace her, Tiana?"

"What?"

"You like him, don't you?"

"What's not to like? He's one of the sexiest men alive, right?" This year, anyway. I had a few fantasies about number seven last year, another Italian (go figure!) who had a minor role in a pirate movie and who has since married the princess of Slobobia or something.

"Just don't send me a 'he's the greatest thing since the toaster' article, okay?"

I bite off a curse before it hits my lips. "I never write those kinds of articles, and you know it."

"Well, it sounds as if you're getting involved," Shelley says. "You're at his guesthouse, aren't you?"

I describe it to her. She particularly likes the sound of the tub.

"Why would it have two seats if it was only built for her?" she asks. "Can you explain that?"

I can't, and I don't want to. "So she likes to prop up her feet or something, I don't know."

"I'll bet he still loves her," Shelley says. "That's how those Italian men are. They *possess* their women, even after they break up. You remember *Married to the Mob*. That woman, wasn't it Michelle Pfeiffer? That was before her lip implants, of course. Dreadful things, aren't they? Like two worms wrestling with each other. Anyway—"

"Dante is not in the Mafia, Shelley," I interrupt, "and they've been divorced going on ten years."

"A little possessive yourself, aren't you?" I know Shelley is smiling. She believes I should already be married and have a teenager by now.

"Shelley, I'm here to do an interview and that's it," I say. "He's only a job. He's only a paycheck. He's a handsome man, but he's obviously not over his ex. I'm not here to—"

"Keep telling yourself that, Tiana," Shelley interrupts. "You've always struck me as someone who wants something more. Dante Lattanza is definitely all that and then some. I wouldn't blame you in the least if you . . ."

"If I what?"

Shelley doesn't answer.

"I'll have the puffer to you in two days," I say angrily. "Good-bye, Shelley."

She thinks she knows me. She thinks she knows what I'm after. She thinks I'm on the prowl.

I look at the wolf on my shirt, a moon rising just above my left breast.

Maybe I am.

And if playing a she-wolf helps me to get a decent story, I will be the best she-wolf I can be.

Chapter 5

Islink or skulk or however wolves move from the guest-house through a canopy of pines to a side door. Opening it, I step into an amazing kitchen, pots hanging on hooks suspended from the ceiling over a massive butcher's block, top-of-the-line Sub-Zero appliances, a double sink big enough to swallow four turkeys, and . . . Is that a brick oven? It looks as if it belongs in a pizzeria or a bakery.

"Nice, isn't it?"

I turn and see a tall black cook in maybe his early fifties, with a shiny forehead dominating a head of tight gray and graying curls. He wears the requisite jeans, boots, and a stained chef's apron over a green sweatshirt. He's skinny as a rail, sports a few freckles under his huge brown eyes, and has shovels for hands.

"Hi, I'm—"

"I know who you are," he interrupts. "No introductions are necessary, Miss Artis. I'm Red."

This is Dante's best friend, and he's Dante's personal cook? "Where's Dante?"

"Answering his fan mail," Red says, rinsing several green and red peppers. "He still gets hundreds of letters, and he answers them all himself." He cracks open a green pepper with his fingers, removing the seeds. "You like linguini?"

"Sure."

He slaps the green pepper on the butcher block and dices it as fast as lightning. In less than a minute, he has sliced and diced three green and two red peppers. He places them in a huge pot on the stove, stirring them in. He pulls a plastic spoon from a cabinet and dips it into the sauce. "Let me know what you think."

I take the spoon, blow on the chunky sauce, and taste . . . heaven. "This is good. This is really good. What all's in it?"

He crosses his arms and nods. "You tell me."

I look down at the spoon. "Green and red peppers."

He rolls his eyes.

"Garlic. Sausage."

"What kind?" he asks.

"The good kind?"

He laughs. "It's fresh sausage from a farm near here. What else?"

"Well, tomato sauce, of course."

Red squints.

"Homemade tomato sauce with real tomatoes," I say quickly. "Um . . ." I only know one kind of tomato. "Roma?"

He smiles. "Right. Been cooking it since sunup." He leans in closely. "Let's get this out of the way quick," he whispers, handing me an apron. "I sent you the letter with this address, okay?"

I tie on the apron. "Why?"

"A few years back, you wrote some articles, including that op-ed piece where you said, let me get this right, 'too many champions are spoiling the soup of boxing.' Wasn't it called 'Alphabet Soup'?" He tosses me a head of lettuce. "For the salad."

I crack open the lettuce and let water run through it. "Yeah. I wrote that. I can't stand all those stupid acronyms."

Red nods. "WBA, WBO, NABF, WBC, IBF, IBA . . . BFD."

I laugh. "I read a *Ring* article that said it better. It said that there's only one world, so we should have only one world champion. I was trying to say that all those acronyms were metaphors for mediocrity. It seems as if every fighter has a belt. Isn't there a midcontinental something belt out there, too?"

"Yeah. Which midcontinent, no one knows." Red starts skinning several carrots at once. "I liked that line. Metaphors for mediocrity. I told Dante, and he liked it, too. He also liked three other articles you wrote. He has them posted in his room." He whips out a huge clear salad bowl from under the sink, setting it near me.

I start tearing the lettuce and dropping it into the bowl. "I'm waiting for the 'but.'"

"But," he says, dicing seven carrots at once with a weaponlike cleaver. "The last two you wrote . . ."

"They were kind of harsh." I drop the last shreds of lettuce into the bowl.

Red scoops the carrots into the bowl and begins chopping radishes. "But they were honest. Dante values honesty. Don't ever try to lie to him."

"I won't."

He waves the cleaver in the air. "Dante liked those harsh ones, too."

I keep both eyes fixed to that cleaver. "He couldn't have."

"He did. He said you have brutal honesty. He tacked them up in his room as well. I know he reads them every day and every night to motivate himself. What was that line? Oh yeah. 'Dante Lattanza is not just over the hill. He's at the bottom of the mountain and couldn't see the top even with a telescope.'"

I wince, wiping my hands on my apron. "I was just disappointed he didn't unify the middleweight title. That would have been the only unified title that year."

"I liked the way you worked in Simon and Garfunkel's 'The Boxer.' It was a classy piece," he says.

"Thank you," I say.

"It wasn't the usual boxing story, you know? It had a human element to it."

I still have it first in my professional writing portfolio.

"How'd you, um." He pauses. "You don't strike me as the type to cover boxing matches. You're a knockout, don't get me wrong, but . . ."

I explain about my granddaddy, and Red nods often. "I was also dating a guy back then who was really into boxing, so I had a bunch of working dates. Then I learned he was working one of the card girls on the side, so . . ."

"Hawaiian Tropic girl?"

Is this guy psychic? "How'd you know?"

"My girlfriend Lelani was once one of those, and she's really from Hawaii." He looks out the window over the sink. "She ought to be back from town any time now. She's getting more groceries. We eat a lot here." He frowns at the salad. "Mushrooms." He points to a closet. "In there, the portobello, sliced thick." He opens a drawer, takes out a knife, and lays it on the butcher block.

I go to the closet and find several varieties of mushrooms, one variety the size of my fist. I return to the butcher block and begin slicing the portobello.

"You and Lelani will get along," Red says. "You're almost as jaded as she is about boxing."

There's something strange going on here, but I can't quite figure it out. "Um, Dante knows I wrote those articles, yet he's letting me stay. I don't get it."

"I do. I knew you'd motivate him. Just you being here will do that."

"How? How will my mere presence motivate him?"

He smiles broadly. "You are, to put it bluntly, his *worst* fan. He's already trying to prove to you that he's not over the hill."

I push the mushrooms into the salad. "If he isn't careful with Washington, he may be under the hill."

He nods. "Keep saying stuff like that, Christiana. He needs to hear it."

"So . . . you knew he'd give me grief about the interview, but you also knew he'd allow me to stay."

He nods.

"You're pretty shrewd, Red."

"One of us has to be," he says. "For all of Dante's good qualities, and he has a ton of them, he's still a little naive. He thinks he can win by sheer willpower. We both know that's not the case these days. I believe that Dante is letting you stay because he wants to prove he's not only on the mountain but nearing the top again."

I look away from Red and roll my eyes. "You don't really think he's capable of beating Tank Washington, do you?"

He rests against the butcher block. "Boxing is a young man's game, and Dante has always been young at heart, but there's only so much heart can do for you in the championship rounds. If he's still standing after the final bell, that's a victory in my book."

Hmm. Even Dante's best friend has his doubts. "Tank has been on a tear, though. Seven knockouts in a row, all before the fifth round."

"Tank is fighting against inferior competition, and I think he's finally realized it. Though he beat Dante the first time, he really hasn't had a victory over an elite fighter since Dante."

I nod. It's true. Tank has been fighting the "almost" champions.

"Not one of Tank's opponents had any kind of heart," Red says. "Dante has heart enough for five men. But that's also the problem. He doesn't know when he's licked. He can't see that he doesn't have the skills necessary to be champion. Instead of covering up, he'll keep swinging and get his face peppered. You have never questioned his heart or his will to win in anything you've written about him. How'd you put it? 'If heart were all a fighter needed . . .' "

" 'Dante Lattanza would be the pound-for-pound best fighter the world has or will ever see.' " I look at the wood floor. "But I ended the piece badly."

Red nods. "'Heart just isn't enough anymore,'"

"Yeah." Yet, here I am, the one who wounded Dante the most with the truth and counted him out. I need to change the subject. "Red, how long have you been . . . What exactly do you do for Dante?"

"Check the bread, please." He hands me two huge white oven mitts.

I open the oven, the door as big as the hatchback for a car, and see golden brown Italian bread—what else?—resting on long wooden paddles, hot garlic wind rolling over me. "I think they're done." I pull out the first paddle and rest it on the butcher block where Red slices the loaves rapidly.

"Butter's in the fridge, top shelf, right side."

I find the butter and a butter knife and begin buttering the cuts in the bread.

"So what exactly do I do for Dante?" Red says. "I've been cooking for Dante during his comeback, and even a little before that. Just after the divorce actually. I'm kind of his cook, trainer, guru, and gopher. Mainly, I'm his friend. He lost all his friends after the Cordoza fight. His former trainers, excuse me, 'nutritionists,' fed him all that roughage and bran, like he was already over the hill and couldn't take a dump. All that bran slowed him down. And all that weightlifting Johnny Sears put him through at Gleason's Gym only tightened him up. He was strong, but he was slow. Pasta seems to speed him up. So does the air up here. He works out so hard that he's always three to four pounds around his fighting weight, so it doesn't really matter what I feed him. Happy stomach, happy man. Can you cook?"

This is beginning to feel like an interview. "Yes, I can cook."

"Do you own a microwave?"

"Only for popcorn and hot tea." And leftovers. I wince. There are leftovers in my fridge right now that I should have thrown out before I came here.

Red smiles. "Good. That . . . that woman never did cook."

I don't want to talk about the woman whose ass has been in my two-seater tub, maybe on both seats. "Red, I'm curious. Why did Dante hire you?"

He turns to me with a withering stare. "I can cook. He can eat. He pays well. What could be better?"

Oops. "I don't doubt you can cook, I mean . . . You're not exactly Italian, and here you are preparing an Italian feast."

He sighs. "I used to be one of his sparring partners a long time ago. Trust me, I had no ambitions beyond sparring. I'm too tall, too skinny, and I can't keep an ounce to stick to me. That was when I was trying to make a name for myself in Manhattan. I was working as a sous chef at the Four Seasons when Dante hired me away and brought Lelani and me up here."

I blink. "The Four Seasons on Fifty-second Street?"

"You know any other?"

I shake my head.

"Sous chef was as far as I got, probably as far as I *could* get. I mean, what restaurant would hire anyone named Red

Gregory from Brooklyn for its main chef? Unless I changed my name to, oh, Benito—and *only* Benito, mind you—and I somehow turned my Brooklyn accent into something Mediterranean, I was stuck. After . . . that . . . woman divorced Dante, he called me up, Lelani and I moved up here, and I've been cooking for him ever since."

Now that's a commitment. "Year round?"

"Yeah."

I shiver.

"It gets cold up here, right?" he says. "It's a cold that has teeth and clamps down on you. We usually take most of the worst part of winter off to go south. Dante has a place similar to this down in Virginia."

At least Dante isn't hurting for money. "So he's still, um, financially stable?"

Red nods. "Unlike some boxers whose promoters took unhealthy cuts from their purses, Dante has been in charge of his own finances from the beginning. He does all the negotiating, and he's good at it. He can afford to be generous. He built me this kitchen from my specifications. Brick oven, the right pots, the right tools. He also built our cottage next door." He checks a large pot of noodles, stirring them slowly with a wooden spoon.

"And the guesthouse."

Red sighs and shakes his head. "That was a *waste*. There's a carbon copy of it down in Virginia." He seems to shudder. "I don't want to talk about her. I don't want to live in the basement tonight. I'm going to live in the balcony, okay?"

A strange extended metaphor, but I get it. "Living in the balcony. I like it."

He nods at the lake. "You handle a boat well."

"Hey, I'm from Red Hook," I say. "It goes with the territory. My granddaddy taught me."

"You must have done some fishing in the Hook, too, huh?"

Not that I'd ever eat anything from the East River. "Yeah."

"Good. I hear you'll be fishing in the morning. Dante takes his fishing seriously."

"So DJ told me."

He holds me with his eyes. "You have no idea. Serious to you and me is silly to Dante. He is as fierce an angler as he is a boxer. And he believes that eating fish is good for him. There will be smallmouth bass filets on the table tonight, at *his* end. He eats them like most folks eat potato chips, so I wouldn't ask him for any."

"I won't." But I probably will. I like fish filets.

Red starts getting out real china plates, not paper plates. "You're just here for the interview, right?"

What a strange question. "Of course."

"Nothing more?"

"No."

He shrugs. "You just remind me of his ex, that's all, except without the claws and fangs."

Hmm. Red obviously despises this woman, and the way he keeps bringing her up, he obviously wants to discuss her. "What was her name?"

"Evil Lynn."

"Huh?"

"Evil Lynn is what I call her. She tells everyone to call her *Eve*lyn."

Still in the present tense. And what a pretentious name.

"You're Dante's type," Red continues, stacking the plates on the counter and rolling silverware in red napkins.

"And what type is that?"

Red smiles. "You're a force of nature. You exude power. Dante gravitates toward clout and muscle."

And, I have a *corpo provocante*. "He likes a strong woman. Is that what you're saying?"

He nods. "You hang around here long enough, and you might get something more than you bargained for."

There's that phrase again. Something more? I don't want something more. If I have to flirt my booty off to get Dante to open up and give me meat for a better story, I will flirt like a champion.

"Dante is . . . he just *is*, okay?" Red says. "There's no one like him. He's . . . he's an amazing person. He's as amazing as Evil Lynn is not, understand? When she visits, Lelani and I hit the road."

It's official. *Eve*lyn gets visiting rights, and maybe even conjugal visiting rights.

"And Dante lets her, that's what gets me," Red says. "'She will come back to me,' Dante says. 'She is my *portafortuna*, my good luck charm.' It's a complicated relationship and arrangement. They both raise DJ—she gets him for the school year —and DJ's turning out fine. But when they get together . . ."

I have to ask. "So they still . . ." I wince for good measure, as if wincing is the international sign for sleeping together.

"Conjugate?" Red says. "Get busy?"

I blush and nod.

"No. Not that Dante doesn't try."

Hence, the two-seater. Great.

"Christiana, Dante still thinks they're married," Red says. " 'No papers will dissolve what God has blessed,' he says. He's old school like that. And when Evil Lynn comes up here to visit, she complicates everything. She throws off his training schedule completely. He's far too generous with her, and she treats him like dirt. She has the ability to completely silence an Italian man without saying a word."

Frightening.

"She wouldn't even allow him to speak Italian in public or around DJ," Red says with a shake of his head. "'In English, please,' she says. When he was winning, she was only part shrew. He lost to Washington and Cordoza, she started losing interest, and she became all shrew."

Therefore, that means . . . "Evelyn is a gold digger?" I say her name like a normal person does.

"She was an RN making nice money," Red says, "I doubt she was ever a gold digger. I just try to stay away from her, understand?"

I nod. "Did she ever love him?"

"Oh, I'm sure she loved him in her own way," Red says. "But when the losses came . . ." He shrugs. "I used to think the losses were what made him such a legend. 'Blood and Guts,' right? He had no nickname before that. Forty-seven fights without a nickname. He was just . . . Dante Lattanza."

"When did Evelyn finally give up on him?" I ask.

"A month after the Cordoza fight and she gave up on him entirely. She moved back to Syracuse and filed for divorce the same day. As soon as he got the papers, he quit boxing."

"And DJ was what, six?"

"Yeah. It was such a tough time for him," Red says. "He's come through it pretty well. They've kept it cool. Visits anytime anywhere. Lots of trips together. Christmases down in Virginia or in Syracuse. It has been a fairly peaceful life for DJ, you know? Almost a regular life."

I don't know about that. "What changed? I mean, after ten years, he suddenly decides to start boxing again."

He sighs for the longest time. "It's mostly Evelyn's fault. Dante one day got it in his head to win her back by making a comeback. He even made a deal with her. For every win in this comeback, they go out on a date. Should he win the title, and he has an even shot if Tank's off his game, Evelyn has agreed to try again." He holds me with his eyes. "He's fighting to remarry the shrew."

Now *that's* crazy! "No way."

Red nods. "It's crazy. The way she treated him, and yet . . ." He shrugs. "That's Dante to the core."

I can't believe this. "C'mon, Red. He can't beat Tank Washington. Tank's in his prime. Dante's too slow, has no defense, and has nothing left in that left hook of his. He's never had a jab."

Red smiles. "Your granddaddy taught you about boxing, too."

I nod.

"Dante knows he's up against it. He probably knows he'll lose, too. He hopes the attempt will be enough to win her back."

Dante is dreaming the impossible dream here. "Is she, um, worth . . . No, I have no right to ask that."

Red shakes his head. "Is Evelyn worth the effort?"

I nod.

"She ain't worth a damn," Red scowls, "but there's no accounting for love."

Amen to that.

He looks behind me.

"You checking out my butt, Red?"

Red nods. "You fill out her clothes a whole lot better than she does."

I don't dare tell him these aren't her jeans.

"Go out there and ring that bell," he says, pointing at a bell hanging under the eaves of the front porch. "Let's get our dinner on."

Where, I hope, I can have some tasty conversation.

Chapter 6

The Italian food is tasty, but the conversation is foreign. Dante doesn't speak anything but Italian at the meal, which at first is sexy as hell but then becomes utterly rude. He and DJ talk at the other end of the table as if I'm not here. DJ isn't nearly as fluent as Dante is, and it seems as if Dante is correcting DJ every so often. DJ doesn't seem to mind, though. If it weren't so rude to me, I'd think it was charming the way father and son get along.

Red and Lelani whisper sweet nothings to each other for most of the meal, and I can tell they're still in love. I've never sat this closely to a real Hawaiian before, and she is stunning. Lelani has to be half Red's age. With her rounded cheekbones, jet black hair, and Asian eyes that I swear are purple with green accents, Lelani has an all-over tan darker than Red and me combined. She has no visible tan lines, so she has to sunbathe in the nude. I wonder where.

No, I don't. Life is embarrassing enough without the threat of accidentally stepping on a nude Hawaiian in the Canadian woods.

During the salad garnished with Red's homemade croutons, I catch a few phrases like *grazie* and *per favore* and *squisito* and *molto graziosa.* When Dante looks at me and says something something *cioccolata,* however, I get right upset. I'm not dark chocolate. I'm not even partially chocolate. I'm kind of average, run-of-the-mill, Crunch bar chocolate. I can't stand *not* interviewing the interviewee or at least breaking the ice for the real interview later. And there's something unseemly about the host excommunicating more than half of his dinner table.

I have to do something.

When I'm halfway through my pasta, I decide that enough is enough. I turn to Red. "Red, everything is so delicious. How's the bread, everybody?"

Silence reigns. Linguini twirling stops, spoons arrested in the air.

Direct questioning it is. "DJ, how is the bread?"

DJ looks first at Dante, hesitating.

Dante nods.

"It's good," DJ says, returning his eyes to his plate.

"Not too buttery?" I ask.

DJ lifts his head.

Dante nods.

"No," DJ says.

Hmm. The son has to get permission from his daddy to speak. I might as well try to give Dante whiplash.

"I wasn't sure how much butter to use," I say. "And how was the salad, DJ?"

Same routine, Dante's eyes receding to two little dark dots.

"Fine," DJ says.

I can't believe no one is talking about food at the dinner table. It's not normal. It doesn't fit into my stereotype of a typical Italian meal. Even commercials for the Olive Garden are noisy with conversation.

I stare into Dante's eyes. "May I try some of those fish filets? They look delicious."

Dante doesn't even blink. He had already eaten most of them, leaving two small pieces on the platter.

"May I?" I ask, smiling. "I want to get the full Canadian experience."

Dante still doesn't blink.

I smile at DJ. "DJ, could you pass the fish to me, please?"

DJ looks shaken. Sorry, big guy. I have to mess with your daddy. You just happen to be in the middle.

Dante eventually nods, but he *still* doesn't blink. My eyes would be completely dried out by now.

DJ hands the platter to Red, who holds it out in front of me.

"Grazie," I say, and I take one of the filets. I look up. "Does anyone else want this last little bit?"

Lelani's eyebrows rise slightly. I'll bet she has wanted some of these filets for years. I mean, she's from Hawaii. I'll bet she craves fish.

I dish out the last filet to her, and she gobbles it up the second it hits the plate.

I bite into the filet, and it is divine! Lemony, buttery, salty, and peppery—perfect. "You were right, Red. This is good. Bass, is it?"

Red nods. "Smallmouth that Dante caught this morning."

I flex my arms. "I'm feeling stronger already."

Red coughs.

After fifteen more seconds of silence, the forks and spoons resume their noise, but no one speaks English or Italian. I have silenced them with the simple "theft" of two small-mouth bass filets.

It is now time for shock and awe.

"So, Red, how is Dante's training going?" I ask brightly. "All I saw was his cliff diving and swimming exhibition."

Red stares me down.

I roll my eyes. I know I wasn't supposed to talk, Red,

but dinner isn't fun without some conversation. And if you haven't figured it out, I'm trying to get under Dante's skin. Some of my most effective interviews took off once I thoroughly pissed off my interviewee.

"His training is going well," Red says, avoiding Dante's eyes.

I dab my lips with a napkin. "Will he be ready to go all twelve rounds?"

Red bites viciously into a piece of bread. "He could go fifteen rounds if he had to," he says through clenched teeth.

Hmm. Dante doesn't seem to be fazed. I must not be pushing the right buttons yet. "So, for a boxer at his advanced age, would you say his stamina is poor, fair, or good?"

Red clears his throat and sips some ice water. "His stamina is excellent, Christiana."

Oh. Throw in my name, as if it will shut me up. "Does Dante have a jab yet?"

Dante's mouth drops open. Good. My words are getting under his skin. The jab is his soft spot. Cool. I'll be jabbing at him all night now.

Red seems to choke and has to drink some more of his ice water. "He's, um, he's working on it."

I wait for the silence to get louder. "So . . . he *doesn't* have a working jab yet. Don't you think he'll need it? Tank Washington didn't get his nickname from counterpunching. He roars straight ahead. Even a half-hearted jab slows him down. But then again, a half-hearted jab won't stop a man like Tank completely. He's good at wearing his opponents down. He's not very exciting to watch, but Tank is certainly effective."

Dante finally blinks. He shuts his mouth.

Red glances quickly at Dante, then back to me. "He'll need his full arsenal of punches to—"

"Is Dante getting any stronger?" I interrupt. "His left

hook isn't what it used to be. Sure, he knocked Avila out with it, but it wasn't a one-punch knockout. It wasn't even early in the fight. I think I counted *fifteen* left hooks over the first nine rounds before Avila hit the deck. But, Avila, what was he, fifty? He was way past his prime. What did he have, a hundred fights? I think Avila's grandkids were in the audience watching him."

Dante throws his head back and laughs, shoots bursts of Italian to DJ, and smiles.

Finally. Not exactly the reaction I was expecting, but at least it's a reaction. "What is so funny, Mr. Lattanza?"

Dante nods and continues smiling. "You will find out firsthand tomorrow, Christiana. *Firsthand.* I make a joke." He stands. "*Andiamo,*" he says to DJ, and the two of them leave, banging out the front door to the deck outside.

Red turns to me, grabbing my forearm. "What are you trying to do?"

I watch Dante, and sure enough, he looks back at me. "I'm just trying to stir the pot a little." I turn to Red. "I haven't even begun cooking yet, Red."

"I asked you here to motivate him, not to alienate him," Red whispers.

"I know what I'm doing, Red," I whisper back. We're being so clandestine. "And from the way he just laughed, I don't think I'm pissing him off too badly." I clear my throat and raise my voice. "What were, um, he and DJ saying about me?"

"You don't want to know," Lelani says. "Really."

"Oh, but I do," I say. "It's rude to talk about someone in *front* of their back, too." Which almost makes sense.

Red sighs. "They were comparing you to *Eve*lyn."

I smile. "How'd I do?"

"Until you opened your mouth, you were winning," Red says. "You were beating her on points."

"Really?" It's nice to be winning. "No knockout, technical or otherwise?"

Red gets up and leaves the table, joining DJ and Dante outside.

"Listen, Christiana," Lelani says, "I don't understand everything they said about you, but Dante hasn't smiled this much in a long time."

"He was smiling? All I saw was a man with his mouth open."

Lelani giggles. "It must be a European thing. I have noticed European males do that all the time."

"But he's from Brooklyn."

"There are still lots of Europeans in Brooklyn, Christiana, aren't there?" She squeezes my arm. "Whatever you're doing, just . . . keep it up."

"I plan to." I look around. "Did I talk too much for real?"

Lelani nods. "You could be Italian."

I guess there's a little Italian in every journalist. We don't talk with our hands, though. We couldn't write anything down if we did that.

"Why didn't *you* say anything?" I ask.

"This is a man's world," Lelani says, stretching and patting her stomach. "Except when Evil Lynn's around, but I don't want to talk about her, Christiana."

"Call me Tiana."

She shakes her head. "Here, you are Christiana. It sounds Italian. Dante seems to like saying it."

"Sheesh, Dante likes it. Dante this, Dante that. Is he the king or what?"

"Yeah," Lelani says.

"Well, I didn't vote for him."

Lelani giggles again. She stands and motions me to the kitchen. "This is his castle, he is the king, and we are his subjects."

But he's a king without a queen. At least until his ex gets here.

Lelani throws me a dishrag as I enter the kitchen. "You wash, I'll dry."

We are going to have a serious stack of dishes and plenty of pots to do. "That's not fair."

She fixes me with those purple mood eyes of hers. "I know where everything belongs, and if Red can't find what he's looking for in any of these cabinets, I'll catch hell." She sighs. "I do most of the dishes around here. It'll be nice to get a little break, okay?"

I turn on the hot water and wait for it to steam. Lelani adds Joy and a capful of bleach to the water. Then I wash the dishes as she brings them in from the table.

It's so *good* to be one of the king's subjects. I hold up a plate. Is this the king's plate? I had better clean it spotless for his highness.

Reporters should never do dishes.

After a lull and cringing at what the bleach will do to my fingers, I ask, "Lelani, how did you meet Red?"

Lelani groans. "Are you interviewing me, too?"

I flip a glob of suds at her. "Shoot. We're just two sisters talking while doing the dishes, and the boys . . ." I see Dante and DJ throwing rocks off the outcropping, Red fiddling with a pair of red boxing gloves. "Are they just . . . throwing rocks?"

"And talking," Lelani says. "They talk a lot more than anyone I know."

I smile. "Until you met me."

She wrinkles up her lips. "True. I just think it's sweet. They are so close, all three of them. Red is almost DJ's grandpa, you know?"

I grab a plate and dunk it in the water. "Now that we're close and they're far away, I have to know more about you and Red."

Lelani rinses a plate and immediately dries it. "You're curious how a Hawaiian wahine hooked up with a black brother from Brooklyn."

How alliterative for her to say so. "Well, yeah. What were you doing messing with the men from my neighborhood?"

She smiles. "Red and I met in a kitchen, but not like this one. The one at the Four Seasons. I was working as a hostess slash waitress slash you-name-it."

"Didn't you . . ." I mimic holding a round card over my head.

"Didn't I what?"

I take a few steps and turn, my hands still over my head.

"What are you doing, Christiana?"

I drop my arms. "Never mind."

"Anyway," Lelani says, "Red would fix me something special, new, and unpronounceable at the end of my shifts and offer it to me. When Felix wasn't around."

"Who's Felix?"

"Felix was the queen of cuisine, if you catch my drift."

"Drift caught." I hand her another plate. "Naturally you ate all these exotic dishes."

"Not at first, but eventually . . . yeah. The man can cook. Red won my stomach first. Back then I had been doing the card girl bit at Madison Square Garden—"

I raise my arms again. "I just asked you if—"

She laughs. "Is *that* what you were doing?"

I nod.

"Girl, let me show you how it is done." She rolls up her shirt, revealing the flattest stomach I've ever seen, and raises a plate in the air, her face one bright smile. She then circles the butcher block, thrusting her chest forward, shaking her hips wickedly, and posing in front of me at the end. "You just weren't doing it right." She puts the plate away.

"Oh." If I ever did that, the cops would arrest me for soliciting.

"Anyway, on a night I was to go out between the third, seventh, and eleventh rounds, I saw Red in Dante's corner." She shakes her head. "I felt kind of embarrassed, you know, me all in my almost nothingness, but there he was, his eyes never leaving mine. He had to be the only man in Madison Square Garden who *only* looked at my eyes that night." She rinses a few more plates. "A few days later at work, he told me he liked me." She looks at her hands. "He said he liked me. Since I was wearing a long coat and boots when he said it, I fell for him." She flashes those purple eyes at me. "He likes me for my mind."

"C'mon, *and* your body." And those eyes. She should be an eye model. Do they have those? "Did you ever do a Hawaiian Tropic calendar?"

She blinks. "That was ages ago, when I was twenty-five."

"Ages ago?"

"Girl, I'm forty."

I *hate* her! I hate her a *lot*. Hawaiians must never age. "I never would have guessed it."

"I love getting carded."

I rarely get carded! Life is so unfair. Forty! That's just not fair. She has the flawless skin of a teenager but without the acne and baby fat, not a single wrinkle or worry line, and her body is sculpted. Hey, wait a minute. "I've been thinking of having a breast reduction." Not. "Have you ever had any work done?"

"Like implants or Botox?"

I *knew* it! She brought up the B word, not me. "Yes."

"No."

I *hate* her! I hate her even *more* than a lot! Some women have all the luck. Wait. They're not married. Hmm. Maybe there's trouble in paradise. "So why aren't you two married?"

Lelani sighs. "After twelve years you'd think we'd be married, but we're not. We came into this thing with no preconceived notions of how a relationship was supposed to be. We were both raised by single parents, so we had no firsthand knowledge of what a good marriage was."

And neither do I.

Granddaddy raised me, and most of the couples I witnessed as a child in Red Hook were unmarried. They seemed to drift into a relationship, fight a lot during the relationship, and fight even harder to get out of the relationship. And even when the relationship ended, they *still* fought. I don't remember anyone so much as holding hands—during the day, now—in Red Hook. Edgar and Marion Moody were the only married people Granddaddy and I knew, and they lived just across the hall from us, where they fussed and fumed all week, slamming doors and probably each other. They only seemed to love each other on payday over a couple bottles of wine. Then Edgar would have one drink too many, Marion would remind him of the previous week's mayhem, and they were at each other's throats again, their screaming matches echoing long into the night. "Them sure are some *moody* people," Granddaddy used to joke, and it wasn't long before I associated marriage with moodiness and screaming matches. "I'm never getting married," I once told Granddaddy, "cuz I wanna be happy."

Lelani places another plate in the cabinet. "Red and I even have an agreement that if either one of us wants out, it's cool. No reasons or explanations necessary."

I don't know if I like the open-endedness of that. Just . . . poof! I'm out! Later! Gotta go! "But twelve years has to prove something to you, right?"

"I don't think I'll ever get tired of Red," she says. "And I guess, so far, he's not tired of me."

Red would be out of his mind if he ever tired of Lelani. They make the most handsome couple. "Didn't you ever want children?"

"I couldn't."

I shouldn't have asked that. "Oh, you can't have—"

"I'm sure I can. I just couldn't very well have a child if there were no guarantees her father would be in her life, right?"

Beautiful and smart. Lelani is a lethal combination. "So . . . Red doesn't want children." I am getting far too nosy, but I can't help myself. It's in my blood.

"Sometimes he does, and sometimes he doesn't. You see, Red's main loyalty lies with Dante, not with me."

"And you're okay with that?"

"Not completely, but, yeah, I'm okay with it. It's something I can count on in a world where there isn't much written in stone, you know? I can always count on those two being friends. Always. They have been through so much together. All those victories, those defeats, the divorce, the comeback. I'm just fortunate to be along for the ride." She smiles. "I have been to so many places with Red, so many . . ." She laughs. "So many restaurants. I think he chooses cities for their cuisine. We've been to New Orleans, Chicago, Miami, Boston, New York, Memphis, Toronto, Pittsburgh—"

"Pittsburgh!"

"For the Polish food. I am getting a North American education in food, and Red is my tour guide. We'll be going to Montreal sometime this month."

And she doesn't gain a single ounce. Have I mentioned that I hate her?

"I wouldn't trade my life for anyone's," she says. "I've been happy for quite a while, thank you very much."

"And to think Red said you were jaded," I say, handing her a glass. "You're anything but."

"Oh, I just don't know you yet." She bumps me with one of those teenager's hips of hers, and it hurts a little. I'll probably bruise. Does she work out, too? Geez! I need to get into shape just to do the dishes around here.

"I'm not going to be here that long," I say.

"Oh, you'll be here at least for two more days, right?"

I nod.

"I'll get cynical soon enough. I mean, here I am, a wahine ten thousand miles from home, a glorified gopher for the most brilliant sous chef in New York who's *not* working as a sous chef in New York because he's a boxer's gopher, best man, trainer, and confidant. The folks in Barry's Bay still think I'm a Chippewa Indian. How could I *ever* be jaded? I'm just a small town *kaikamahine* from Maui."

I bump her back, and I'm sure it hurts me more than it hurts her. I like Lelani's attitude and personality, but that forty-year-old body of hers needs a dent or something. And I bet that if she had even one kid, she wouldn't get a single stretch mark. "What's ka-ka-ma-he-nay mean?"

"It means 'girl.' A wahine is a lady or woman. I'm still just a girl." She tosses back her mane of black hair.

"I hate you," I say.

She laughs.

"Did I say that out loud?"

She nods.

"Don't you age?"

"I try not to."

I raise my eyebrows. "It must be Red's cooking."

"Yeah, he can cook." She bites her lower lip. "But I'd like to think it's more than that. Most of the Canadians I've met don't look their age. It must be all the fresh, clean air and water up here."

I may have to retire here if I can look like a teenager for the rest of my life. I may even get some purple contacts. I doubt I could ever grow my hair out as long as hers. What that must be like to take care of!

We finish up and go through the dining area into a great room filled with sofas and chairs semicircled in front of a huge stone fireplace, a flat screen TV attached to the stones above the mantle. A fire roaring, soft music playing, stars twinkling in the sky—this is one romantic room. But where are the men? I look past the dining area and see a screened porch where Red, DJ, and Dante are playing cards.

"What are they playing?" I whisper to Lelani, who drops onto a sofa and kicks up her long, toned legs.

"Cutthroat spades. It's all they ever play." She digs for and finds a remote control beneath the cushions. She clicks on the TV and tunes into the Food Channel. "I can some-times tempt Red away from the game by watching this channel." She looks at her man. "Probably not tonight. He must be losing."

I peer at the screen, expecting to hear French. Nope. As rustic as this place is, it definitely has all the comforts of home.

I'm in a snooping mood, so I browse a bookcase full of scrapbooks and photo albums, each with a date on the spine. I pick the one with the earliest date and curl up near the fire where I can shoot glances at Dante and keep my feet warm at the same time.

The first scrapbook contains some ancient black-and-white pictures of scary-looking Italians with thick mous-taches and serious-looking Mafia hats.

And those are just the women!

I'm kidding.

A little.

I think those are women.

I *hope* those are women.

Some of the men have bundles of rags on a cart. Others have carts filled with junk. There aren't any names or captions, so I assume they're some of Dante's ancestors. I can't tell where these people are, but it could be old New York City or Palermo or Rome or—

There is so much that I *don't* know about Dante Lattanza.

Ah. A baby picture. Dante was cute, squinting even then. His nose was actually straight once? Amazing. Those eyes of his were penetrating even then. A family portrait takes up the entire next page. His mother is a frail-looking thing, his father a beast with hairy arms and eyebrows, a tuft of hair billowing up from under his shirt. The man probably had to shave his chest.

The next page contains a picture of his father in a military uniform. I do some mental math. I'll bet his daddy served in Vietnam. Two more pictures of Dante and his mama follow. I flip through the rest of the book and see no more family pictures of any kind, just collages of Brooklyn scenes, some vaguely familiar. No brothers, no sisters, no aunts, no birthdays. Just . . . scenes. No more family portraits either. Did his daddy run off? Did he die in Vietnam? Did he stop taking pictures? What?

I smile at Dante's first boxing picture. His red gloves are as big as his head, and he is so skinny! His shorts pass his knees, and his wife-beater T-shirt is three times too big. But those eyes . . . I've seen those eyes before. Those little black dots. I chuckle. His left hand is at his hip. That man hasn't had a jab or any kind of defense from the very beginning.

I look up and catch Dante's eyes flitting away from me. Hmm. He has been checking me out. I had better give him more to see then. Leisurely and she-wolflike, I go to the bookcase to get as many scrapbooks as I can carry, almost clearing out a row, flexing my butt and getting a little hippy on my walk back to the couch. Lelani taught me well. As I sit, I feel Dante's eyes piercing me. That fire sure is hotter than it was a few minutes ago.

Is he still looking . . . ? No.

Fewer pictures and more clippings fill the next scrapbooks I open. I see Dante winning the Golden Gloves and . . . Is that the Olympic trials? I didn't know he tried out for the Olympic team. It's quite an honor just to be part of the trials. I glance from a picture of him at eighteen to the forty-two-year-old playing cards. He really hasn't aged that much either. The air up here has been kind to him as well.

The next scrapbook, thicker than all the others, chronicles his pro career. Clippings from *Ring, Newsday,* the *Times, Sports Illustrated,* and *Sporting News* abound and include some of my old articles. What do you know? I actually praised the man a few times. I also notice that I used the phrase "vaunted left hook" in three different articles. Well, it used to be vaunted. I must have liked that phrase, not that I'll ever use it again. I run a phrase through my head: "Undaunted and with a haunted look in his eyes, Dante wanted to flaunt his left hook. . . ."

Shelley would *taunt* that phrase to death.

Look at all these . . . Wait a minute. Where are his wedding pictures? I check the date on the spine. If DJ is sixteen, then there should be wedding pictures or at least a few shots of Evelyn in this one. Maybe there's a separate wedding album somewhere. I flip through and see nothing but clippings and articles. Maybe Evelyn has the album. Either that or Dante put it away after the divorce.

The last article is win number forty-seven, but the rest of the book is blank. I can tell his two losses were once in here, bits of tape covering newsprint in the corners. I'll bet my last few articles were in here once, and now they're hanging in Dante's room.

Hmm. I have to find that room. I may have to do a little recon . . .

The last scrapbook records his comeback. Three fights, pictures of his bloody face brooding in one corner while the referee counts down his opponent in the other. I count fifteen different articles after the third fight, one of which details his rematch with Tank Washington.

The rest of the book is blank, but stuck in between two pages is a picture of Evelyn and Dante. My heart flutters a little because it looks so recent. This might be a shot of one of their dates. I wish I could say Evil Lynn was anorexic with a white booty, no hips, bug eyes, bony arms, and a bad perm, but she's actually a nice-looking woman. She doesn't look anything like a diva or a shrew. Dante's eyes are only for her in the picture, and his smile is . . .

Damn.

He still loves her.

I've *never* had a man look at *me* like that.

Her eyes, though, are straight ahead, as if she's in charge of the universe. Maybe she is. She still seems to be in charge of Dante's universe. Coiffed and dressed to perfection, Evelyn is beautiful in a Dorothy Dandridge's skinny half-sister kind of way. Paparazzi wouldn't necessarily swarm this woman if she was an actress, and though I don't know her at all, I'm sure she'd have plenty of interesting things to say. I can see why she wouldn't like it up here. Other than present company, there's no one to see her, to walk behind her to hold her train, to bask in her queenly aura.

And Red says I remind him of her? Red needs glasses. I don't have a face like hers. When I turn sideways, people still see me.

I riffle through the scrapbooks again, and I get an idea. Dante's life would make a nice book, maybe an "as told to" autobiography. These pictures—well, maybe not the last one that's stressing me out so much—would be interspersed throughout, and these scrapbooks already form the outline of the book. It would be an easy write. He has to beat Tank Washington, however, for it to sell. If he can become champion again, it could be a best seller. It's a nice idea, but . . .

I put the books away, not she-wolfing it anymore as I replace them, and sit next to Lelani. "What are they playing to?"

"They play till the next fight and keep a running tally," she says. "They've been playing for close to two months now. Someone usually wins by hundreds, even thousands, of points."

"What does the winner get?" I ask.

"Bragging rights."

That's all? I fake a pout. "Don't they ever invite you to play, Lelani?"

"Me? I am strictly a poker player."

Figures.

"Whenever Evelyn visits unannounced—meaning that Red and I can't escape in time—they play partners," Lelani says. "Red and Dante—always—and DJ and his mama."

That also figures. "Who wins?"

"DJ and his mama." Lelani shakes her head. "I think sometimes Dante and Red lose on purpose, and now they're trying to make up for all those losses by playing cutthroat."

I make a power decision and stand. "It's time for me to play."

She blinks. "You're not going to try to take Evelyn's place, are you?"

"Oh no," I say. "I could never do anything like that." I smile. "I don't intend to play cards, Lelani. I just wanna play, you understand?"

"I dig," she says. "Go play."

I go directly to DJ and look over his shoulder. According to the scorecard, DJ is over nine hundred points behind Dante, who is around two hundred points behind Red.

"I bid . . . nine," DJ says.

No wonder this child is losing. He has a potential Boston in his hand. If he plays his cards right, he can take all . . . eighteen books. They're playing with the jokers, and he has *both* jokers and the ace and two of spades. Taking all eighteen is next to impossible in cutthroat, but with this hand, DJ has a chance.

"Do you play that the two of clubs leads?" I ask.

Red nods.

DJ has no clubs. This is perfect. I fan out DJ's cards and see a gold mine of spades. "You're a little too conservative, DJ, don't you think?"

"No coaching," Red says.

I put my nose on the top of DJ's ear and whisper, "Bid eighteen."

"What?" DJ says.

Red puts his hand flat on the table. "She said, 'Bid eighteen.'" Red takes his spades seriously.

"Goin' for a Boston," I say, smiling at Dante.

Dante doesn't smile. "We are not in Boston," he says.

I wink at him. "That's why we're goin' for one."

Dante does not appear to be amused. He pulls a tennis ball from under the table and squeezes it. Hmm. Keeping his hands strong. I like that in a man.

"We don't have to call it a 'Boston,'" I say to DJ. "We can call it an 'Aylen.'" I crouch next to DJ's seat, aiming my booty in Dante's direction. "C'mon, DJ. What do you have to lose? You're already dragging nine hundred points."

"I'll, uh, I'll take them all," DJ says softly.

Red squints at me. "I'll take . . . two."

"Uno," Dante says with authority.

"Let's set 'em both, DJ," I say, holding my breath.

Red throws out the two of clubs, and Dante tops it with

the ace, the card making a little slap. DJ trumps it with the three of spades. He can run them now! I point to the big joker.

"Now?" DJ asks, about to throw an ace of diamonds, which someone could conceivably trump.

"No coaching," Red says again.

"Who's coaching?" I say. "DJ, look at your hand, man."

"That is coaching," Dante says.

I shrug and hold out my hands and do a bad impression of Robert De Niro. "What? I just ask him to look at his hand. That is all. I do not tell him what to do with his hand. That would be coaching. I just ask him to look. Is that such a crime?"

I catch Red smiling. Dante only rolls his eyes.

DJ studies his hand. "Oh." DJ smiles. "Oh, yeah. They'll all—"

"Andiamo," Dante says.

DJ plays eleven consecutive spades, the ace, king, queen of hearts, and the ace, king, and queen of diamonds, collecting all eighteen books.

Take that!

Red smiles.

Dante scowls and says, *"Per caso."*

"It was just the luck of the draw, *Papino,*" DJ says softly.

"Where I come from," I say, "if you run a Boston, or in this case an Aylen, you win the entire game."

"We are not in Boston," Dante says again. He snaps up the cards and shuffles, the cards sounding like machine-gun fire.

I squeeze DJ's shoulders. "Don't ever be afraid to go for it," I tell him. "Just don't be afraid. *Tenere provare.*"

Dante blinks. Yeah, king of the house, I can speak your language. A little. I only remember the phrase because it sort of rhymes.

I linger for a few more hands, mainly hovering over DJ

and Red, and then I leave the screened porch and wander through the kitchen and up some back stairs. I look in the first room on the second floor and see a scary sight—it is a *clean* teenager's room. The wood floor is spotless, the bed is made, the clothes are put away, and the toiletries on a dresser (deodorant, shaving kit, Chap Stick) are lined up perfectly. I know if I open the dresser I'll see all of DJ's socks paired and lined up, his T-shirts and maybe even his boxers folded. DJ also has his own full bathroom. Where are the video games, the TV, the stereo, the pictures of rappers, and the uneaten food becoming science experiments? Where are the DVDs, CDs, and game magazines? This is so uncommon.

I go out into the hallway and see only one other door. I open it, thinking it's just a closet.

It isn't.

I pull a string, and a small room lights up. The walls are bare except for a crucifix, a few clippings—all mine—and a wedding picture of Dante and Evelyn cutting the cake. Once again, his eyes are on her while hers are elsewhere. He looks so fine in that tuxedo, and her dress had to cost a fortune. On the floor at my feet rest a sleeping bag and a pillow. There are no windows. There is no mattress. A single lightbulb dangles from the ceiling. Creepy. This is where Dante sleeps? All this relative opulence and he sleeps in a windowless, airless closet?

Or, is the guesthouse *really* where he stays, and he just threw this stuff in here because of me?

Wait.

The clippings are here. Red said the clippings were hanging up in "his room." Maybe it's a superstitious thing. Dante is an athlete, and athletes have superstitions. It feels so cramped, so claustrophobic. It's maybe one-third the size of a boxing ring. Why would anyone want to sleep in here for close to four months of training?

I am definitely going to ask him about this room.

I look again at the wedding picture. He uses this for motivation, too. Dante is so naive. He thinks he can recapture the past. He thinks he can have a successful rematch with the woman who dumped him. I'm sure it happens, but it has to be rare. What's the old saying about second marriages? Isn't a second marriage "the triumph of hope over experience"?

You'd think Dante would have learned from his mistake.

I close the door and return to the great room, the fire dying away to embers, Lelani snoozing on a couch. The game still rages on the screened porch, so I walk in and announce, "I'm going to bed."

No one speaks. How nice.

I look at Dante. "Um, four-thirty, right?"

"DJ will wake you at four," Red says while Dante only stares at me.

At . . . four? Is he kidding? "I'll be ready."

I leave the main house and go into the guesthouse, closing and—there are no locks. Why are there no locks? Hmm. I guess I'll be safe. After brushing my teeth and donning a pair of Evelyn's tight shorts and a tighter T-shirt, I snuggle under the covers and make some preliminary notes on my laptop:

> Dante Lattanza is misogynistic, arrogant, stubborn, headstrong, mean, authoritarian . . . "whipped" by ex . . . probably still in love with ex . . . juvenile, infantile . . . a sore loser . . . rude . . . nice abs . . . naive . . . has a tennis ball fixation . . .

He *is* a handsome man. He *is* sexy. The pictures will take care of that for me. I won't have to state the obvious in my article.

Lattanza had a humble upbringing, maybe father not around much, frail mother (dead? In a home? Wouldn't she be here?), loyal, devoted to son, handy, fit . . . all that hardness, those cuts . . . ferocity is a necessity for a boxer . . . fearlessness may make him appear vain . . . is vanity necessary for a champion? Or is he feigning invincibility?

I close my laptop, set it above me on the headboard, and turn out the light. Starlight streams in through the slats in the blinds despite the curtains on the window, but that's all right. I wonder what 4 AM *looks* like. I'm not usually up that early, even when I'm traveling a long way to do an interview. Even when I was younger and hit the clubs, I never stayed out past 2:30 AM.

The wind rustles the trees around me, and I hear their branches brush the roof. It smells so nice, like Pine-Sol on crack. This is so far from the "madding crowd," so peaceful, so still. Was that a loon's call? I hear they mate for life. . . .

I drift to sleep like the waves kissing the shore outside, dreaming of lonely loons, lightning lefts, and a *corpo provocante*.

Chapter 7

A soft knocking sound awakens me.

It has to be a tree limb rubbing against the guesthouse. It can't be 4 AM yet. I turn over.

There it is again. I sit up.

"Miss Artis," a voice whispers. "Christiana, we're leaving in half an hour."

It's still dark. The fish have to be sleeping.

"Miss Artis?"

I rise, wrap a quilt about me, and open the door. A blast of cold air hits me in the face. "I'm up. I'm just going to take a quick shower."

DJ smiles at my bare feet. "Right. Don't forget to dress warmly."

I shut the door. "Thirty minutes," I whisper. "What's so special about four-thirty? Are the fish only biting at four-thirty? Geez. Can the fish even see the bait when it's this dark?"

I stumble to the bathroom, flip on the light, and stare at the tub. There's no showerhead here. How can I take a quick shower if there's no showerhead? I've never heard of anyone taking a quick bath. It would take five minutes for the tub to fill up.

Wait.

I'm going fishing.

Who's gonna know if I'm stank?

Besides me.

The fish won't care.

While I search Evelyn's clothes for anything heavy, fur-lined, and Arctic, I tell myself to be as *not-Eve*lyn as possible today. DJ says she doesn't like it here. Maybe she absolutely loathes this place. Therefore, I have to act as if I can't get enough of this place. Yes. I have to suck up so Dante will open up.

I put on layers of clothes starting with shorts over my underwear, fleece sweatpants over the shorts, and—*geez!*—tight-ass wind pants over the sweats. I can barely bend over to tie my hiking boots.

I should not eat anything for breakfast.

I'm almost out the door when I realize I haven't brushed my teeth. I have no precedent in my life for this. I have never brushed my teeth this early before. When the icy water hits my teeth, they start to grumble.

And it's still dark.

I lurch through the birch and pine trees to the kitchen, where Red is already awake and cooking something on the stove. It smells delicious, but I can't possibly eat zipped up as I am. He sees me and points at a cup of coffee.

"Thanks." I take a sip, and my teeth settle down.

He flips a bun of some kind onto a plate and slides the plate down the counter. "It's called a Chelsea bun. You'll like it."

Good thing I'm standing while I eat it, and it is yummy. "Red?"

"Yes?"

"Why is it so dark?"

Red wipes at his eyes. "Dante likes to get up early."

I sip some more coffee. "So, is it dark because, hey, it's four-fifteen, or is it dark because Dante likes to get up early?"

"Both."

I see DJ walk through the screened porch wearing a floppy tan fishing hat. "Red, I need a hat."

He leaves the kitchen and returns with a Boston Red Sox cap, settling it on my head. "It fits you," he says, "in *so* many ways."

"I don't root for the Sox," I say, taking it off and setting it on the counter. "I'm a Yankees fan."

"So is Dante, the poor man," Red says. "I would have gotten you an *Aylen* hat, but I think this *Boston* hat says it much better."

I put on the hat. "Cuts him two ways, huh?"

Red nods.

I nod. Anything to infuriate Dante, especially since he got me up at the crack of freaking *doom* to go fishing.

Red pulls several circular Styrofoam containers from the refrigerator and places them in front of me.

"What are these?" I ask.

"Worms and leeches," he says.

Lovely. I shouldn't have asked.

Red wraps up several Chelsea buns, and then pulls several bottles of water from the refrigerator and puts them in a little cooler. "Remember," he says, "Dante takes fishing seriously."

I am tired of hearing that. I pull the cap down close to my eyes and frown. "Is this serious-looking enough?"

"Just catch some fish, okay? You have to replace the fish you stole from his stomach last night."

I roll my eyes.

"And don't talk on the boat. Don't even make a sound."

"It will be as if I'm not even there."

I carry the leeches, worms, and cooler down to the dock, a trillion stars still dotting the sky. Mist covers the water, and I can barely see Dante or DJ in the fishing boat. I get into the boat—without a word—and hand the containers and cooler to DJ. Dante unties the boat, backs us out, and we're on our way.

And it's freaking cold! It can't be much above freezing.

The wind bites the tip of my nose and my earlobes as we haul ass down the lake. I clamp the windbreaker's hood to my head, pulling the strings tight. My eyes start to water, so I close them, listening to my windbreaker ripple like thunder.

After what seems like twenty minutes, we glide into a spot and float a bit. I can barely see the shore, an indefinite sunlike glow threatening the horizon. DJ hands me a pole, and while I remove my hood, I watch him put a leech onto his hook. It doesn't look too hard. He hands me the container of leeches.

They're . . . swimming. I didn't know leeches swam. They're like overgrown black sperm. Ew. Which one, which one . . . that one. He's stuck to the container. I choose him, give a little tug, and bring him directly to the hook, spearing him twice with the barb. I turn and face the shore, firing a cast into the mist and the darkness. Not bad, not great. I can still do this. I have no idea where I just cast my line, but at least my overgrown black sperm is in the water.

"Rocks over there," DJ whispers.

Shit. How am I supposed to know? There aren't exactly any signs out here, you know? We're fishing in a black hole! I start reeling in faster when BAM! I must be stuck. I pull, and the line shoots off a different direction.

I'm not stuck. That's a fish! I wish I could see it! I mean, I hear it—

That was a splash. It jumped in all that mist, and now I'm fighting it.

DJ moves closer to me. "Big?" he whispers.

How the hell should I know? It feels big. I nod.

It takes me five more minutes to get the fish close to the boat as the sun's rays finally creep over the tops of the trees. Whoa. That is a big fish.

Dante, who has yet to get a line in the water, stands holding the anchor line while DJ gets a net. The closer I work the fish to the boat, the harder it fights. In my head, Granddaddy is screaming, "Keep the rod tip up, Tiana!"

After an interesting dance DJ and I have with him sliding around me a couple of times with the net, he leans over the boat and . . .

The fish is in the boat.

I caught that. Uh-huh. I do a little strut. Looky there, Dante. Huh? Huh? What you got that I don't got? Huh?

DJ removes the fish, drops it into the live well, and tosses my line back into the water. "You still have your leech," he whispers. "That one was at least *four* pounds."

I still don't know what I caught. I hope it was a smallmouth bass. Red will cook it up for *me,* and Dante will have to ask *me* for a few bites, which I *may* not give him. I need to fatten Lelani up, don't I?

I reel in my line a little bit and cast to the same spot again, this time seeing the leech hit the water. A split second later and I get another *BAM!*

Dante still hasn't moved. He's still fiddling with that anchor rope.

The sun peeking over the trees now, I take off my windbreaker while fighting—geez, this one's bigger!—and keeping my rod tip up. When the fish hits the surface, it starts to dance before crashing to the water again. At least *eight* minutes later, DJ and I do our little dance, he nets the fish, and I rest on a seat. He pulls a scale from a tackle box and weighs this one.

"Five pounds, three ounces," he whispers, his eyes as big as donuts.

I nod. I knew it was bigger. I roll my neck. Yeah. I'm bad. Uh-huh.

"You'll need another leech," DJ whispers.

Dante still hasn't gotten a line into the water.

Yeah, Mr. Get Up Early, I'm kicking your ass, aren't I? I straighten my Red Sox hat. Who's the champ now, huh? And who's the chump?

I put on a new leech and cast out to my spot. Dante finally gets with the program, ties off the anchor rope, and casts a long silver lure just to the left of my cast. Uh-huh. Going where the action is, huh? Trying to move in on my spot. Okay. We'll see about that.

Something swirls at his lure and misses.

Dante grimaces.

Ha!

Then something hits mine, maybe the same something that missed his lure, and I'm fighting again. This one is smaller, though, and I have no trouble bringing it in and netting it myself. I even take it off the hook and drop it in the live well with *my* other fish all by my damn self.

While DJ has to rerig after breaking his line and Dante watches in agony as fish swirl and miss a lure as big as they are, I make my fourth cast—and catch another fish.

I spin my hat around my head once, bending the bill slightly. This Red Sox player is four for four in less than thirty minutes. After netting this one and adding it to my collection, I remove my wind pants and windbreaker and turn my cap around like a catcher.

That's when I catch Dante smiling at me.

I like it when he smiles.

None of us catches another fish for over an hour, but I am content. The sun burns off the mist, and I have to take off my sweatshirt and sweatpants. There's something almost mystical about casting into a pool of sunlight, not a single ripple on the water, the only sound the gentle rocking of the boat, a loon calling somewhere in the distance.

"They have left," Dante says.

"Or Christiana caught them all," DJ says.

I bite my lips together. I want to say something so badly! I want to tell Dante that his huge chunk of metal scared the fish away.

Dante pulls up the anchor, and we cruise a short distance away to a sandy beach. DJ takes off his shoes, socks, and sweats, and hops into the water, pulling the boat up onto the sand. I leap off the boat holding my wind pants and windbreaker while Dante saunters over to the live well and looks inside. I catch his lips saying, "Wow."

Wow. I'll take that as a compliment.

I slip into my wind pants and zip up my windbreaker. The bugs haven't been too bad, but I'm taking no chances. When DJ hands me a can of industrial-strength bug repellant, I spray my hands, my clothes, and my hat. The smell is anything but feminine, but at least I won't be breakfast for something that buzzes, bites, or stings.

Dante drops off the front of the boat, zipping up his jacket. *"Andiamo,"* he says, nodding at DJ.

Andiamo, I say to myself. Let's go.

One task down, four tasks to go.

Chapter 8

DJ hangs back with me as Dante walks briskly down a path and into the woods, not a single glance behind him. He's either angry I skunked him and DJ, or that's just the way he normally hikes.

As we follow, DJ points up at a huge rock jutting out over the forest. "That's Old Baldy," he says. "It's only about fifteen hundred feet up."

Whew. When someone says "mountain climbing," I think of K2 and snowy peaks. This climb will be a cinch.

"That's where we're going next. Normally, we would have made a fire and fried up whatever we caught on the beach before climbing, but the ones you caught are too big. I'll clean them for you, and Red will cook them for us later."

Whew again. The last time I dissected something it was green, unpleasantly froggy, and extremely dead. Granddaddy cleaned any fish we caught, and though I watched Granddaddy do it, I doubt I could remember all the steps. And those were saltwater fish from the Atlantic. I'll bet Canadian fish require extra steps.

Dante keeps a blistering pace once we start our ascent,

bounding up the path. I barely keep up, fifty feet behind DJ, trying not to turn the burned-out stumps around me into grizzly bears. Only that thought makes me sweat, the ascent no more than a steady climb up a dirt path bisected by roots. Dante looks back occasionally, but other than brief glimpses of his eyes, I mainly get to watch his two "butt-fists" in action. Nice. Proportional. Definitely squeezable. Strange, they now remind me of the tennis ball he was squeezing last night.

I am sweating profusely and oozing bug repellant by the time we near the summit, but I don't care. As we near the jutting rock, the pathway gets rugged and narrow, and I have to use branches, roots, and even small pine trees to help me get to the top. Dante walks right out onto that huge rock and sits, seeming to brood over the horizon. I wish I had brought my camera. He looks as rugged as the scenery, and that shot would be sensational.

The view is breathtaking, though I'm a little nervous to be so far above the towering trees we passed. They're way down there looking like the ends of green party toothpicks. I follow DJ to another part of the slab, and he points out several little lakes to the north and west where he and Dante had fished before.

"That's Lake O'Neill," he says. "We call it Pole Lake, though. The one to the left is Wilkins. It was a pain dragging our old wooden boat back to them, but the fish were so thick you could just reach in and grab them."

I doubt that, but it's a nice image.

I take off my hat and let gentle breezes dry my sweat as I finger-comb my hair, the rest doing me some good. It probably isn't much later than 7 AM.

Dante still broods. I'll bet he's angry that I haven't given up yet, that he hasn't licked me yet.

I'm mad he hasn't licked me yet, too, but that's a whole other fantasy.

On our way back, Dante and DJ add small pebbles to a cairn of rocks just off the path. I balance a piece of white quartz on top of theirs, and we start our descent. I slide a few times on the way down, but I don't shout out, righting myself and continuing, never falling more than a few paces behind DJ.

Two tasks down, three to go.

When we get back to the boat, Dante pulls a cutting board and a wicked-looking filet knife from a bin and hands them to DJ. Then Dante grabs a plastic cup and wanders away down the beach.

"Um, I guess this means you have to clean them now," DJ says.

Joy.

I stare after Dante long enough for DJ to explain. "There's a natural spring down there," he says. "He drinks a cup every day he's up here."

"Superstitious?" I say, finally breaking my silence. That has to be some sort of record. I've been with them for nearly three hours.

"Delicious," DJ says.

He pulls the smallest fish out of the live well. "I can do them for you."

Yes!

But no. That would be a victory for my brooding host, and I intend to go undefeated today.

I sigh. "I really should do it. I caught them. But I'll need some help here." I step closer to him and whisper, "I have never done this before."

"It's not that hard," he says. "Just messy."

And slimy.

DJ hands me the smallest fish, still wriggling like a hoochie-coochie dancer, and I grab it by the lip. "You have to break its neck first," he says.

I grimace. "How do I do that?"

"Turn the fish over."

I do, and I am now staring at its whitish stomach.

"Put your index and middle fingers inside its gills," he says.

He's kidding. I look up. He's not kidding. "These gills look, um, sharp."

"They are," he says.

Oh, that's comforting.

"As you put in your fingers, slide your thumb to just behind his head. Then . . ." He pulls back his wrist. "It's like popping a pop top."

I don't want to do this, but *"tenere provare"* rings in my head. I slip my fingers in through those scary-looking red gills and slide my thumb back, pulling with my fingers and pressing with my thumb at the same time. The fish's tail jerks back and forth before I hear a sickening crack.

The fish goes limp, blood spurting from a little hose or artery—whatever. It's spewing blood, and it's not a beautiful sight.

"Now what?" I ask.

DJ talks me through the next few steps with the filet knife. I start the knife just below a little fin where its—gulp—anus is. I start my cut and bring the knife all the way back to where I broke its neck, the fish's guts flopping out like . . .

I don't have a metaphor for this. I don't ever want to have a metaphor for this.

The fish's guts spill out, and it's nasty.

He points to a spot with a hooked finger. "Just . . . get under all that, pull it toward you, and the entire head should come off at the same time."

DJ is an excellent teacher, and though my fingers will never forgive me, I now hold the fish in two parts. DJ takes the head and entrails and begins feeling something with his fingers. "Look," he says.

I don't want to look, but I do. I watch a little . . . lobster come out of a sac.

"It's a crayfish," he says. "Dad will want to know. He always asks what they've been eating."

How . . . delectable.

The rest of the cleaning process is much less grotesque. I slit either side of the top fins and pull them out. I peel back the skin to the tail on both sides of what's left. I slide the knife as close to the ribs as I can, and—

I have two okay-sized filets in my hand, nice white meat with little specks of green and blue.

DJ gets a roll of aluminum foil from the boat and wraps them up. "Now all you have to do are the larger ones."

Larger fish take longer, and by the last fish—the behemoth—my fingers hurt so badly. I have little scales and other nastiness under my nails, I have cut myself several times with the knife, and each fish surprises me with half-digested crap that DJ identifies with glee.

Dante returns with a burst of Italian as I'm wrapping up the biggest filet.

"*Papino,* the first one had a crayfish inside, the next two had minnows, and the last one had two crayfish, a frog, half a perch, and some bugs," DJ says.

Those were bugs? They looked like—

Again, I have no metaphors, no similes.

They were just plain freaking slug-nasty.

I hand the stack of wrapped filets to Dante while DJ cleans up the cutting board and knife.

I then remove my hiking boots and socks and march into the water, washing as much crap off my hands as I can. I even pick up some sand and rub my hands together. They look cleaner, but they smell like death.

"*Andiamo,*" Dante says to DJ while I'm still in the water.

I gather my socks and hiking boots and slosh to the back

of the boat, water soaking up into my sweats. I climb in
without either one of them offering to help me.

Andiamo.

Two tasks down, three to go.

Damn. I check my nails.

Two *nails* down—on *each* hand—only three to go.

Chapter 9

"You caught them all?" Red asks.

I haven't stopped scrubbing my hands with scalding hot water, antibacterial soap, and a Brillo pad for the last fifteen minutes.

"I could have stuffed two of these for dinner," Red says. "And the biggest was really five pounds, three ounces?"

I am scrubbing off skin now, but I don't care. That fishy smell is still there.

"You could have had the big one mounted," Red says, setting the world's largest cast-iron skillet on the stove and firing up a gas burner. "It's bigger than anything Dante has ever caught up here."

Really. So *that's* why he wasn't speaking. I not only outfished him, I caught a fish bigger—in only thirty minutes—than any fish he's ever caught in *years* up here.

"Christiana, why aren't you speaking?" Red asks.

I smile and turn off the water, smelling my hands. They still don't smell nice, but at least I know they're cleaner. "I'm just proving I can *tenere provare* without speaking."

"You didn't speak the entire time you were fishing and hiking?" he asks.

"Not to Dante," I say.

"Amazing," he says. "You had trouble breathing, didn't you?"

"Ha ha," I say.

"Come over here," Red says, "and I'll show you how to make my famous Lime Pine Batter."

Red's secret batter is fun to make. While I use an old-fashioned glass juicer to squeeze the juice out of six limes, Red adds two cups of flour, two teaspoons of baking powder, two pinches of salt, four egg whites, and a cup of water to a bowl. After I add my lime juice, he pulls a can of pineapples from a cupboard.

"The secret to the secret recipe," he says.

I smell my hands. They're kind of limey. Cool. They don't smell like fish anymore. My cuts sting like hell, but at least my hands aren't fishy anymore.

Red opens the can with an old-fashioned twist opener but doesn't remove the lid entirely, instead pouring the pineapple juice into the bowl and putting the can into the fridge. Then he mixes it until all the lumps are gone.

"Dry the fish," he tells me.

I hesitate.

"Use some paper towels," he says. "Just pat them dry."

Oh. I thought I'd have to do something more sophisticated than using a paper towel.

I dry the filets, patting them gently, and drop them into the batter. Red drops an entire stick of real butter onto the skillet, where it melts quickly and begins to steam.

"They're your fish," Red says, handing me a spatula.

"That's what I keep hearing," I say.

"Just let them get nice and golden brown."

I look at the clock. "When's lunch?"

He smiles. "When you say it is." He winks. "Just ring the bell."

I begin laying filets onto the skillet. "Is this all we're having? No chips?"

"We still have salad left over from last night," he says. "And we're not in England, Christiana."

I am suddenly so hungry! My mouth waters as I watch the filets cook, and as soon as the first little one browns, it is in my mouth.

That batter is orgasmic. Lime Pine, and I'm fine. Whoo. He should sell this stuff. I mean, I already have the jingle he'll need: "When on fish you want to dine, use Lime Pine and you'll feel fine."

Okay, so I'll never work on Madison Avenue.

Once they're all crispy and brown, I walk outside and ring the bell. I don't set a single plate on the table, merely transfer the filets to a huge platter I find. This platter is going in the middle of the table, so if Dante wants any, he'll have to move closer to me.

In theory.

In actuality, no one sits during lunch, all of us just standing around and chowing down. No one touches the salad, but with around seven pounds of filets, there is no room for salad.

I keep up my silent routine, and other than a few strange looks from Lelani, no one seems to mind.

And then it starts to rain.

Not in proverbial buckets or with cats and dogs. Niagara Falls breaks bad around the cabin, lightning streaking across the dark sky like skeletal fingers, sonic thunder booms rattling the dishes in the cupboards.

"No workout today," DJ says.

My hamstrings rejoice. The climb wasn't all that strenuous, but I'm beginning to feel it in my legs. No way I could survive Dante's boxing workout today.

"We will wait," Dante says, looking out a window at

what used to be the lake. It has disappeared, walls of rain obliterating any view of the water. Even Turkey Island becomes a dark green blur.

"It'll be muddy," Red says.

"It will make me work harder," Dante says.

"It might make you pull something," Red says. "We'll wait till tomorrow, all right?"

Dante isn't happy, but I don't care. I need all the rest I can get. Boxing in mud? I'd probably slip a disc.

While we wait . . . and wait—Canadian storms seem to be lazy and like to hang around—DJ and I start a thousand-piece puzzle of Raphael's *School of Athens*. In fact, most of the puzzles we have to choose from are famous pieces of art in a thousand or more pieces, from Michelangelo's *The Creation of Adam* to Picasso's *Ma Jolie*. We avoid a Monet—*St. Lazare Station*—since it has two thousand pieces of varying shades of blue and green. I don't want to go blind.

And then . . . we piece together a famous puzzle while Dante paces from window to window and the thunder rolls. DJ tells me he has put this one together before with Evelyn on just such a day, and I feel honored. He also tells me about every famous philosopher we eventually see as we work. I point at an old man lounging on the steps. "Who's this?" I ask.

"Oh, that's Diogenes," DJ says. "They nicknamed him 'the Dog.' He lived in a tub and walked around barefoot. When Alexander the Great himself told Diogenes he'd grant him any favor, Diogenes said, 'Please move out of my sunlight.'"

I like Diogenes. He could be from Red Hook.

After four solid hours of rain, Dante gives up and decides to go swimming. No one joins him, and I almost caution him about, oh, the lightning still flashing in the sky, the huge waves crashing into the dock, the drop in temperature, and the darkness. It's not my place to say anything, though, and I'm happy in my place in front of the puzzle.

More fish for dinner, more silence, more rain, more of that puzzle, this time with Lelani helping us. Just before nine, I place Michelangelo into the puzzle. I'll bet this Italian wouldn't go swimming during a thunderstorm. He only painted them.

After that, we all drift to our beds.

Kind of boring, yeah, but peaceful, and the steady drip of rain puts me deep into sleep in no time at all.

Chapter 10

Someone very nice lets me sleep in, and by the time I roll out of bed and get to the kitchen, it's close to lunchtime. Wisps of fog and mist dance on the water, fluffy white clouds barrel across the blue sky, and the pines outside sway in the stiff breeze of pure pine heaven.

I could get used to this place.

Red pulls a plate from the oven, and I chow down on a cheesy omelet and some thick slabs of bacon while Lelani flips through some fashion magazine. "Where is everybody?" I ask.

"Getting ready," Red says, sipping some hot tea.

"Is it time for Dante's workout?" I whisper to Lelani.

Lelani nods. "He wants to get an early jump and train longer today because of yesterday. 'I'm a day behind schedule!' he says."

She has one creepy Dante impersonation.

Red sighs and stares at me. "You sure you want to do this?"

No. "I'm sure."

He looks at my sweatpants and tight T-shirt. "Once this

wind dies down, it's going to heat up, so I'd get into some loose shorts and a much looser T-shirt if I were you."

I pose for him. "What are you saying, Red?"

Lelani reaches over and tries to pull the T-shirt's fabric from my back and can't. "I think he's saying that he's afraid that when you throw your first punch, you will come out of this shirt like the Hulk."

"Oh." I shake my head. "I'll be fine." I hope.

"You have any running shoes?" Red asks.

"No. Just my boots."

Lelani looks from her tiny feet to mine. "I have nothing that will fit you. I doubt Evelyn's 'Canadian' shoes will fit you either."

"I didn't come here to wear Evelyn's shoes," I say, taking one last delicious bite of omelet, cheese dripping onto the fork. "I'll do just fine in my boots."

I need those boots for the hike up the muddy hill behind the cottage to a clearing where a full ring and all the toys appear. They cut the ring right into the hillside. Heavy bags sway from tree limbs, and a speed bag and two long mirrors have been mounted directly to trees. It's so . . . Robinson Crusoe or something, so . . .

Okay, okay. It's not Gleason's Gym. It's just so rustic. If I were to take photos of his training area and publish them, Dante would become a laughingstock overnight. At least it smells nicer than Gleason's Gym, and that crisp breeze is heavenly. I look toward the lake and can't see even a single wave. The only way the paparazzi could get any shots of this place would be from the air.

Red talks to me while I tighten my shoelaces. "We always aim for fifteen four-minute rounds. The first five rounds are skipping rope." He hands me a jump rope.

No problem, chief. I got this.

Though DJ and Dante are more adept and efficient than

I'll ever be, effortlessly twirling their ropes to near invisibility, I ain't no slouch. I learned a thing or two on the mean streets of Red Hook. After a rough start, I feel the old rhythm and do tricks like cross crosses, front back crosses, leg overs, and side swings at a steady pace. I ain't crazy. This is only the beginning of the workout. I need to pace myself. I feel like chanting "Hello Operator" or "Down in the Valley," but I don't. This is serious work here. I used to do the Rump Jump but not anymore. At my age, I might not get back up.

After four minutes, Red says, "Time," and DJ and Dante stop.

Screw that.

I keep jumping at my relaxed, easy pace. DJ and Dante see me and start jumping again. I skip a little closer to where they are and face them doing a series of front back crosses and side swings. Red yells "Time!" four more times, but we don't stop for a second.

Dante is so intense! It's like a game. I do a leg over, and he does a leg over. I do a side swing, and he does a side swing. My legs are on fire, my arms are numb, my wrists are calling me names, and my lungs are screaming by the time Red hollers, *"Time!"*

I stop.

DJ stops.

Dante jumps for four more minutes.

I let him. He's the boxer, not me.

"You need to pace yourself more," Red whispers to me.

I bend over and try to find the air. It was just here a minute ago. Where did the air go? I know I just worked off breakfast, lunch, and dinner from yesterday.

"I'll be fine," I whisper. "What's next?"

"Three rounds of shadowboxing," Red says.

I watch sweat drip off my forehead.

Shadowboxing? No sweat.

Since there are only two mirrors, DJ and Dante go to work in front of them. I face Red and start throwing as Granddaddy taught me, left hand high, right hand tucked, jabbing mostly, dancing, circling, and ducking. Red calls time again, but I keep throwing. I add uppercuts and a couple horrible hooks and notice DJ and Dante kicking up dust behind me.

I am going to die here.

I somehow complete twenty minutes of nonstop jumping and fifteen minutes of shadowboxing. I must be crazy.

"Time!" Red hollers again.

I can't feel my back, my arms, or my shoulders. I feel blisters forming on my ankles from these hiking boots.

I wonder if they can just bury me here. I'd smell like pine trees for all eternity.

I see DJ and Dante move toward the heavy bags, wrapping each other's hands and sliding into white boxing gloves. Red hands me a wrap, and I wrap my own damn hands, thank you very much.

Red has to help me with the red gloves he was working on yesterday. It's scary, but they barely fit. I have some big hands.

"Six rounds," Red whispers, "and you better rest *every* time I call time." He puts on some big mitts and stands in front of me.

Six rounds. Twenty-four minutes with five minutes of rest. I doubt I can go twenty-nine minutes straight on the heavy bag, but I don't even have a heavy bag to hit. I don't want to hit birch trees or take potshots at Red.

I walk over to the other side of the heavy bag Dante is using and start throwing, trying to stay directly opposite of him. He knocks it to me, and I pop it back. It's as if we're playing tag and hide-and-go-seek at the same time. Red calls time after the first round, but I keep pounding, my shoulders threatening to secede from my body. Dante tries to get around the bag to me, but I'm too fast. He jukes right, and I go right. He feints left and goes right, and I nearly punch him in the stomach.

I only last two rounds before I rest a minute.

Not Dante. He continues to pop the bag.

I wearily move to DJ's bag and stay fairly still for the next four rounds, throwing jabs and overhand rights at the rate of, oh, one per minute. It's the strangest symphony. Dante's hands go *pop-pop-pop-pow-boom,* DJ's hands go *pop-pop-boom-pop-pop-boom,* and I merely go *pop.*

I look down at my chest and see my breasts staring up at me. I have sweated so much I look as if I'm in a wet T-shirt contest. I am seriously melting out here, and I'm giving Dante an eyeful.

And I don't give a damn.

We then remove our gloves and do one round of sit-ups—I do some weak-ass crunches instead—and then two rounds of push-ups, facing each other in a triangle. Dante's eyes lock with mine. If I go down, he goes down. When I come up, he comes up. If I hold my form, he holds his form. My triceps choose to die agonizing deaths after only twelve push-ups, and I flop to the dust in a sweaty heap.

Dante smiles.

Jerk.

And he does one *hundred* more push-ups before Red calls time.

"Last round!" Red calls.

My body rejoices.

"Ropes and stretching," Red says.

For some reason, the jump rope weighs a gazillion pounds. I can barely pick it up, much less swing it over my head. Dante and DJ begin windmilling like before, and though the breeze they give me is nice, I am embarrassed I can't even move the damn rope.

"Stretch," Red says.

I am usually a limber human being, and after I work out a kink in my lower back, I'm able to bend at my waist and grab under my feet.

Dante and DJ can do it, too.

That's not . . . normal.

I attempt a split and almost make it.

Dante and DJ do *full* splits.

That's just plain creepy.

I stand and pull a leg up over my head despite my tight shorts.

Dante does the same. DJ tries but loses his balance. Ha!

"Up to sparring today, Dante?" Red asks.

Dante nods, his leg still over his head. He lowers the leg. "I am up to anything today."

Jerk.

While he and DJ go into their wrapping routine and put on their gloves, I step closer to Red. "Wasn't that fifteen rounds?"

"Of exercise," he says. "Now we practice."

"He spars with DJ?"

"Sometimes with me, sometimes with DJ." He smiles. "But not today."

He begins wrapping *my* hands rapidly.

And I stupidly *watch* him wrap my hands. "You mean . . ."

He slides my sweaty gloves onto my hands, and I can't believe I'm not resisting. I mean, I'm trying to resist, but it's hard to resist when you can't feel your shoulders and your body is one large lead weight.

"You're kidding, right?" I protest.

He shakes his head. "You got anything left?"

I shake my head. "I had nothing left half an hour ago."

He tightens my right glove. "You're close to Tank's height. DJ and I are too tall. And no offense, but you're closer in weight to Dante than either of us."

"I am *not*," I hiss. "I don't weigh a hundred and sixty pounds."

"Close enough."

One forty-five, maybe one fifty if I'm a lazy ass, but this pisses me off! My shoulders are coming back to life, and my back quits complaining.

"Look, Christiana," Red says softly, "from the skills you've been showing me, I know you can hang with him for a round or two."

"One round?"

"Three rounds."

How did "a round or two" become "three"?

"Nine minutes," Red says. "We don't spar much to protect his hands and keep him from getting *dementia pugilistica*."

Punch drunk. Granddaddy told me that Jack Dempsey, Joe Louis, Willie Pep, Sugar Ray Robinson, Muhammad Ali, and Floyd Patterson all had it.

"Dante doesn't have any of the symptoms yet," Red says, "but he *has* fought fifty-two pro fights and had close to a hundred amateur fights. I don't want to risk it."

He fastens on an incredibly uncomfortable headgear that smells like motor oil.

"You don't think I can hurt him, do you?" I ask.

"No one has ever hurt him, Christiana."

Except *Eve*lyn.

Red holds out a mouthpiece, and I back away. "Don't worry. It's never been used." He places it inside my mouth. "Just jab him to death, okay?"

Suddenly, I don't feel so winded, tired, or sore. Red doesn't think I can hurt Dante. Red thinks I weigh 160 pounds. Red wants me just to jab him.

Well, Red doesn't know diddly.

I climb into the ring and pound my gloves together. "Let's get it on," I mumble through my mouthpiece.

Andiamo!

Chapter 11

I can do this.

I think.

I hope.

Ow. I have a cramp. In my entire body. Ow.

Feet comfortably apart, my weight on the balls of my feet, I am balanced. My knees are bent, but I'm not crouching. I stand slightly sideways, my left hand up, my right fist close to my chin, elbows tight to my ribs, my neck and shoulders relaxed.

Granddaddy taught me well.

DJ holds up an egg timer, turning it to three minutes. "Ding," he says.

Nice bell.

I circle Dante, who wears no headgear, several times, measuring him up, looking into his eyes. He throws no punches for thirty seconds, so I get bold. I extend my left foot and throw my left hand, rotating my fist and bringing it back. I have a decent jab, and I snap it close to his face, grazing his chin. I pop the jab again, thudding it off his chin. Geez, I just hit him hard! He doesn't blink, though, throwing a lazy jab of his own. I twist away from it, popping him in the nose with a short right. He throws a jab that falls a foot short, and I pop him in the nose again.

"I can see it coming," I mumble, popping him in the left shoulder with a jab.

He jabs and falls short again.

"I can time that jab with a calendar," I say, jabbing him twice on the right cheek.

I stick out my face. "Pop it."

He flails with a right and misses.

"Use your jab," I hiss.

He winds up and throws a straight right, but I duck and hit him with a right to the body, dancing away because the pain in my hand is excruciating. What is this man made of, granite?

He tries a right cross, but I duck under it and throw a right uppercut to his chin. Backing away, I chant, "Too slow, too slow."

"Time!" Red calls.

And just in time.

I'm about to throw up, collapse, and die.

I return to my corner where DJ has a stool waiting for me, but instead of throwing up, collapsing, and dying as I should, I stand and stare Dante down. I am amazed I still remember what to do. I am also amazed I'm not barfing over the top rope. I am *not* amazed I can't feel my right hand. I'll have to throw a lot more lefts this round.

"Ding!" DJ yells, smiling. At least someone out here is having a good time. I know that wasn't a minute just now! Geez!

I stalk Dante as best as I can, jabbing, circling, bobbing, and staying away from the left hook I know is coming. I check his feet, waiting for him to transfer his weight to his left foot. I see him transfer his weight! Here comes the hook! I step in close, the hook whooshing behind my head.

Since his right is down at his waist, I hit him with a right uppercut to his chin.

Backing out, I know I've hurt him. He has to be hurt. My right hand is one fused bruise. Why isn't he blinking or even wincing?

As he moves in on me—he is relentless!—I go into a peek-a-boo stance, both gloves covering my face, my elbows glued to my sides. He feints with another weak jab, then dips to throw a right to the left side of my body and—

I'm dying.

Oh, shit!

I cannot breathe. Who stole the air?

I know my ribs are broken, but I'm not going down.

"Time!" Red calls.

I stumble back to my corner and hit that stool this time.

"You all right?" DJ asks.

I nod, though I'm not all right. My kidneys and pancreas have congealed into one big blob, and my lungs are just now reinflating. I have no feeling from my waist to my neck. My calves are on fire. My pinkie toe is one large blister. One more round. I just have to stay away from him.

"Ding!"

Damn Canadians and their crazy units of measure! Was that a metric minute or what? Sixty seconds is *way* too short to rest.

I pop my jab and move away, dancing left and right, my legs lead weights, my arms and shoulders weeping with pain.

He pops me with a jab.

Ow.

Where'd that balloon on my face come from? It wasn't there a few seconds ago.

The word "better" forms on my lips for a millisecond but vanishes when he hits me with that left hook of his.

I now know what the interior of Halley's Comet looks like. I now know what is at the end of the tunnel. I now know what it feels like to have a hundred paparazzi taking my picture.

I stagger toward the ropes and hold on, my eyes filling with tears, my head pounding, my whole face swelling, a voice from a movie somewhere in my past exhorting me to "run to the light, children!" I'm not sure where the ground begins and the sky ends.

"Time!"

I slump onto my stool, my right cheek throbbing like a bass drum.

"You can stop any time, you know," DJ says, squirting water onto my face.

"Tenere provare," a voice says weakly. Hey, that was my voice. Why is it speaking Italian? Has Dante knocked me all the way to Palermo, or what?

"DJ," Dante says. *"Andiamo."*

DJ jumps into the ring.

"No," I say, and I stand, or at least I think I'm standing. I'm a few feet higher than I was before. That's the definition of standing, isn't it? I'm taller than the stool anyway. Why isn't my left leg working? I spit something from my mouth. Oh. My mouthpiece. I won't need it. They don't bury people with mouthpieces. "You haven't knocked me down yet, Dante."

Dante and three others who look just like him move a few feet away from me. "And I have not hit you hard yet," the four of them say. "DJ, *andiamo.*"

I take a step to grab DJ's shoulder, but I fall face-first to the canvas. I like gravity, I really do, but right now, I don't. Gravity is standing on my back. Both my legs won't work. Talk about a delayed reaction. Why is the world spinning counterclockwise? Am I in Australia? I thought I was in Palermo. I catch my breath and stand, my right leg shaking uncontrollably. C'mon, leg. Move. The other one is moving. Get your ass in gear.

Walking like the Mummy and dragging one leg behind me, I will myself toward Dante.

"I do not want to hurt you," Dante says.

"I'm not hurt," I lie. I wave him to me. He stalks to within an arm's length, and I throw out the weakest jab. I watch it fall onto his shoulder where it stops and rests. I try a right and it drops like a rock to my thigh. I fall forward and bang my head on his chest.

Ow.

"Okay, okay," I say. "I'm done."

Dante picks up my chin with his glove. "Who taught you?"

Even my chin hurts! "My granddaddy."

"He is a good trainer."

"Was," I say. "He died a few years ago."

"Mi dispiace. Come sta?"

How am I? Isn't that Spanish? I thought I was in Canada fighting an Italian. Or was it an Australian in Palermo? "I have a headache. How do you say that in Italian?"

"Ho mal di testa."

"Ho mal di testa." I put both gloves on his shoulders. "I haven't sparred in a long time. How'd I do?"

"Sto andando troppo forte. Andare lentamente."

I blink, but I'm not rude like Evelyn, and don't say, "In English."

"You are going too fast," he says. "You must pace yourself." He smiles. "You have had a long layoff, yes?"

I nod, focusing on his *chests* until the world stops spinning a little. "I didn't, um, hurt you, did I?"

"Your first jab, *sì. Pericoloso.*"

"Dangerous, huh?" Ha! "The uppercut didn't rock your world?"

"Certamente!" He smiles again.

I like this Dante. He smiles a lot. I just wish he didn't have two of them. No man should have sixty-four teeth in his head.

"But I deserved it," he says, guiding me to my corner. "I left myself open. I did not expect it. The unexpected ones hurt the most."

I sit. "I didn't see that hook coming either." The act of sitting clears my head a little. DJ squirts water into my mouth this time and helps me remove my headgear. "What's next?"

"Oh, you must rest now," Dante says.

"What's next?" I repeat.

"More shadowboxing," Red says.

Where no one can hit me. Unless shadows suddenly have developed lightning left hooks, I can do that. I grab for and latch on to the top rope, pulling myself to my feet.

"Are you sure?" Dante asks.

I look him square in the chest. *"Andiamo,"* I say. *"Andiamo."*

Chapter 12

We face each other in the middle of the ring.

"I will play southpaw," he says. "Shadow me."

I try to mirror him as best I can, my legs unsteady at first, but eventually I'm moving forward, backward, and side to side like him a full beat after him. He throws a right jab, and I throw a left jab. He throws a right hook, and I throw a left hook.

"Chin down," he tells me.

Ow. Even that hurts.

"Bene," he says, even though I'm not snapping my punches anymore.

"Molto bene," he chuckles when I nearly corkscrew myself into the canvas trying to throw a left hook.

While we literally dance, he says *"lentamente"* and *"ottimo"* and *"seta."*

"What's *seta* mean?" I ask.

"Silk," he says softly. "You move like silk . . ."

His voice is like silk, too.

He switches back to his normal, conventional stance, and DJ joins us in a game that reminds me of Twister. Red says, "Double jab cross," and we do it. "Right jab left hook . . . Chop some wood . . . Jab uppercut cross . . ."

"Time!"

I am beginning to love that word. It is a good word.

"Now, we rest," Dante says. "DJ, check the gas in the ski boat. If it is low, go to the landing and fill it up."

DJ nods and leaves. He is such a dutiful son.

Dante helps me with my gloves and starts sweeping pine needles and dust from the canvas with an old broom.

"I'll do it," Red says. "There's some fresh lemonade down there."

Sugar. I need sugar.

"Shall we?" Dante nods down the hill.

"Sure." I take a step. "*Andiamo,* right?"

He smiles. *"Andiamo."*

After I suck down several glasses of lemonade, Dante leads me to the outcropping, sitting on a bench made out of half a log and two stumps.

"Tell me about Red Hook," Dante says. "I am sure it has changed since I was there last."

"It's always changing," I say.

"From the beginning," he says.

"From the beginning . . . of time?"

He smiles. "Your time. Since you were *femminuccia,* a little girl."

"Oh." He wants my life story. I guess that's okay. "Well, I grew up on 'the Front.'" The Front is the nickname for Brooklyn's largest housing project. Over half the residents of Red Hook live there.

"You lived in the Red Hooks?" he asks. "Wasn't that *pericoloso?*"

"For most of the time I lived there, it wasn't so bad," I say. "I lived on Lorraine, what folks called 'Peyton Place.' The village raised the kids back then. Irish, Italian, Puerto Rican, and black families made sure we were safe and inside for dinner, to do homework, to get to bed early." I sigh. "That was until the late eighties when crack exploded onto the scene. Before crack, the cops used to play with us on the ball fields. Afterward, they only watched us and arrested us." In 1988, *Life* magazine ran a story about Red Hook ice-cream trucks dispensing crack and candy stores selling drug paraphernalia. "It was an ugly scene and the reason I did everything I could to get out."

"I had heard it was getting better," he says.

"Well, most of the grass is gone," I say. "Lots of concrete and walkways going everywhere like a labyrinth. Unemployment is still around thirty percent, the schools are near the bottom in achievement for all New York City schools, most families barely make ten grand a year . . ." I shake my head. "We still only have one McDonald's and one bank for eleven thousand people, but . . . murders, robberies, and assaults are down considerably, so I guess things are getting better." I smile. "I don't live on the Front anymore. I live on 'the Back.'"

"Ah, you are on the waterfront," he says. "So you like it up here at Aylen Lake then?"

"Very much." And I'm not just saying this to suck up to him anymore. I do like this place. It's rough, raw, and incredibly beautiful.

"I remember going to Red Hook as a boy," he says. "It was all cranes and old red brick, gray wood, narrow cobblestone streets, arched windows and doors."

He has Red Hook down pretty well. "It's still all that, but we have culture now."

"Really? There is culture in Red Hook? I have been away a long time!"

I ignore his sarcasm. "A few years ago I went to see Puccini's *Il Tabarro* performed outside on the *Mary A. Whalen,* a tanker at the Marine Terminal."

He knits his eyebrows together. "They performed Puccini outside on a boat?"

"Yes. Seagulls were hovering over the performers' heads for most of the night."

He smiles. *"Pericoloso."*

"Definitely." I finish my lemonade and set the glass on the ground.

"What else can you tell me?" he asks.

"There's so much to tell."

He touches my hand. "I miss Brooklyn, okay? I have not been home in ten years. You have just been there, what, yesterday? Tell me of my home."

I look at my hand, and *his* hand is still there. Then, I start to ramble about Red Hook. I tell him about the carousel horses made of scrap metal, cherry tomatoes at the Red Hook Community Farm, barbecue smoke rising on Old Timer's Day, and the imploding sugar factories and other brick castles making way for the "Great Blue Wall of Beard Street" (aka the Ikea furniture store).

"It is really a great blue wall?" he asks.

I nod, watching his hand slide away. *Come back!* I whisper in my head.

"Who would think of such a thing?" he asks.

I describe a particular German shepherd–pit bull I often see searching for food on the Erie Basin. "If there's any animal on earth, that animal represents Red Hook best."

"I do not understand," Dante says.

"He's a mutt, a big mutt, and somehow he's surviving in a less than nice place."

"Oh. Yes. I see."

I remind him of the brine, the smell of diesel, the natural gas fumes drifting over from Bayonne, New Jersey.

"Make me hungry," he says. "Tell me of the food. What does Red Hook taste like?"

It is the most amazing question anyone has ever asked

me. "It tastes . . ." I turn to face him. "Red Hook tastes like day-old cookies sold two-for-a-penny at Larsen's Bakery."

"Ah. Day-old. The best kind."

"Red Hook tastes like *moussaka* from Mazzat, *venduras relleno* from Alma, spicy brownies from Baked, the Red Hook Burger from Hope and Anchor, and a Swingle"—a frozen mini Key lime pie dipped in chocolate—"from Steve's Key Lime Pie."

He holds his stomach. "You are making me hungry."

"Red Hook *is* an Italian hero from Defonte's."

"Oh, you are killing me." He laughs. "Please continue."

I smile. "Did you ever go to Red Hook Park on a weekend?"

He grabs my hands fiercely. "*Sî*. The vendors! I ate so much, and so cheap!"

I grab *his* hand this time. Then I remind him of the *baleadas, mixto ceviche,* and huaraches the Central and South American vendors serve to long lines of people from all over New York every summer.

"I remember watching softball and eating *pupusas,*" he said. "The line was so long I was afraid they would run out!"

I throw out a series of names like Fuentes, Carcamo, McCann, Novakovich, Lopate, Jerard, O'Connell, Lam, McGettrick, Hellerstein, Masri, Balzano, and Hammer. I tell him about Markita Nicole Weaver, a ten-year-old who was making snow angels in a snowbank near PS 15 when a snowplow killed her.

"So sad," he says. "So tragic."

I talk to Dante Lattanza, my long-ago neighbor from Carroll Gardens, for thirty minutes straight, and he listens the whole time, sometimes grabbing my hands, sometimes talking with his hands. He focuses, you know? He isn't just asking questions to be polite. And the way he grabs my hands with those big ol' mitts of his . . .

"Why don't you go back?" I ask.

"I don't know."

"I mean, just before the fight," I say. "Go for a walk-through like the politicians do."

He shakes his head. "No one will recognize me."

"Are you kidding?" I say. "They'll have to close the streets."

He only pats my hands this time. "You are too kind."

"You're still a hero in Brooklyn, Dante," I say. "I mean that."

He looks out over the water. "Maybe I was once."

I am looking at the perfect shot for *Personality*. "Um, don't move, okay?"

"Okay."

I run to the guesthouse, wrestle my camera from its bag, and return, snapping away before Dante knows I'm there. When he turns, I stop. There is sadness on his face I haven't seen before.

"Um, could you walk out there?" I say. "The, um, the sky is . . ."

He stands and drifts to the edge of the outcropping. I keep firing away, capturing him from his waist up, that vulnerable, sad look in his eyes, his body framed by the bluest sky I've ever seen.

"You do not have to swim across the lake with me," he says.

I stand next to him, peering over the edge. "How far down is that?"

"Twenty-five, thirty feet."

I can see the bottom! "How deep is it?"

"The same. Maybe deeper."

If I can survive the jump, I know I can make it across. *"Andiamo,"* I say.

He looks me up and down. "But you are not dressed."

Shit. I don't have a swimsuit. I hope Evelyn has one in

there. I cringe inside. If she does . . . Oh, man. I can't wear another woman's swimsuit! I mean, I can wear her clothes, but her drawers?

"Are *you* ready?" I look at his shorts and T-shirt.

He nods. "I just need the weights."

"I'll be right back."

As I run to the guesthouse, I realize something: I haven't gone swimming in years.

That left hook must have knocked me senseless.

Chapter 13

The only swimsuit I can find is too small. It would almost be like wearing a thong, not that I've ever worn one. I know I'd look behind and see my crack smiling up at me, and in front, I'd see my breasts squirming to be free. What did I do when I was a kid? Oh yeah. I wore an oversized T-shirt to cover me.

I look at what I'm wearing. A T-shirt, bra, and shorts. They'll just have to do.

When I return to the outcropping, Lelani and DJ have joined Dante, who now wears the heavy backpack.

Lelani's mouth drops when she sees me. "You're going with him?"

"Sure," I say. "How much is in that backpack?"

"More than sixty pounds," DJ says.

Whoa.

Lelani pulls me aside. "You have any idea how cold that water is?"

"I'm in Canada, Lelani," I say, straightening up my T-shirt. "I'm sure it's very cold."

"Girl," she whispers, "it's the kind of cold that can stop your heart. Are you crazy?"

I nod. "I'm from Red Hook."

I leave her and stand next to Dante.

"It is a long way down," Dante says. "You must jump feet first."

I pray that the lessons I took at Sol Goldman Pool will come back to me. "Feet first? *You* dive out."

He smiles. "I tried jumping in, and the weight took me very deep. I dive out so I do not sink."

I look down again. If I jump feet first, this T-shirt will fly up over my head and strangle me, my bra will fly off, and the shorts will shoot up my crack and become a thong. I take a deep breath and look at Lelani. "Maybe I should use a life preserver or something."

Lelani nods and takes my arm. "I'll get you one." She pulls me toward the stairs.

I pull away. "I'll wait up here."

She ducks her head close to me. "You can't dive or even jump off wearing a life vest."

"Why not?" I ask.

"Ever use a bobber when you fish?"

I see a bobber hitting the water and popping up to the surface in my head. "Yeah. So?"

"At that height, the life vest could strangle you or at least make your girls very uncomfortable."

I like my girls. "I'll, uh, I'll just swim around then, huh?"

She nods. "Come on."

Down at the boat, she fits a life vest to me. It's snug, but I feel a lot more confident now. She points around the out-cropping. "Swim around to the bottom, but watch out. You don't want an Italian landing on you."

Oh, but I do. Repeatedly. "I'll try not to drown."

I dip my big toe into the water. Ow. It's so cold I wince. Instead of wading in, I drop off the dock feet first. The second I hit the water, my heart skips several beats. Lelani wasn't kidding about the cold. I check myself for anything missing, feel one breast bobbing out of my bra, secure it, and start to swim around the outcropping. As I turn the corner and look up, I hear a bell ringing, see a flying Italian, and hear an ear-splitting splash, as if a whale's tail just struck the water.

"Are you all right?" Dante asks, swimming beside me.

"Yeah. *Andiamo.*"

I keep pace with him for about ten seconds, eventually settling in to a decent freestyle rhythm. I just want to finish. I look up and see Dante's arms flashing in and out of the water like dolphins, well, really *fast* dolphins. He gets to the island first, but instead of sprinting across to the other point, he waits for me.

How sweet. He has stopped to watch me drown.

"Go on!" I yell.

He shakes his head and beckons to me.

I pick up the pace, cruising up to him with my lungs on fire, my toes ten icicles demanding to be thawed. As I come out of the water, I look down at my toes, expecting to see fewer than ten. They're all there.

"*Andiamo,* Christiana."

As we pass David and his trusty stopwatch, he says, "You're way behind yesterday, Dante."

Dante throws his head back and yells, "I have extra weight today."

Ha ha. "Don't wait for me."

He gets to the other point and waits. "It is okay. You worked me out good today. I need to slow down."

Then . . . we swim *together* to the other side, my body so numb it isn't cold anymore. I know that makes no sense, but that's how it feels. He helps me up onto a dock, we take some stairs, ring another bell—

No "You-hoo" today. Hmm.

We swim back at a snail's pace, and I can barely stand

when we reach the point a second time. I stagger with him down the beach.

"You aren't going to beat Tank Washington with times like this," David says.

"I will beat him anyway," Dante says. "You will see."

I am so tired I can barely put one foot in front of the other. "You go on," I tell Dante. "I need to catch my breath."

"I will send DJ back with the boat," he says.

He points across to the rocks. "The rocks are tricky. They would hurt your feet."

I won't feel the pain.

We get to the other point of the island. "You are shivering," he says.

I hadn't noticed. I thought I was just having a seizure.

I look across. What is that, a hundred yards? It's not that far. Okay, it's far, but I didn't come this far to quit now. I didn't fish, hike, clean fish, cook, work out, spar, and swim to stop three hundred feet from my goal. "How far is it?" I ask.

"Hmm, maybe a hundred meters," Dante says.

I step into the water, and for some reason, it feels warmer. "It's warm."

"Sì," he says. "The air temperature is dropping. It is best to be in the water."

So . . . I start swimming to the rocks as the sun starts to set, mainly doing the breaststroke, occasionally floating on my back. He helps me navigate the rocks, boosting me higher and higher. At the top, I want to fall flat on my face and die, but his strong hands hold me up.

"Go ring the bell," he says.

I peel off the life preserver and ring the hell out of that bell, using that little string to keep me vertical. I return to the outcropping to survey the distance I just traveled. I had to be completely out of my damn mind to do that, to do any of this. I should be in traction.

Dante raises my right arm and says, "You are the champ."

I raise my other arm about halfway and stare into the sunset. I am Nike, goddess of victory. Hear me roar!

All I can manage to say, however, is a feeble, "Yay."

But when I turn and look at Dante's face, at the sun shining off him and those dark, dark eyes, I know I am looking at a god.

I sneak a peak down at the prodigal breast and find it's out and now has a twin.

But Dante isn't looking at my breasts. He's looking into my eyes.

I am now a nearly naked, frozen, exhausted goddess.

I see his hand in mine as he lowers his arm.

I'm holding hands with a god.

This . . . I could get used to this.

Chapter 14

"Now, we ski," Dante says, squeezing my hand and barking commands in Italian to DJ.

I pull his hand, and Dante turns. "You have to be kidding."

He shakes his head. "I do not kid. I am from Brooklyn."

Lelani wraps me in several towels and a quilt for the ride back down the lake to the beach below Old Baldy. While DJ and Lelani ready the boat and the ski rope, Dante helps me into a fancy ski vest and the skis as we stand in three feet of water.

"I've never done this," I say.

"It is easy," Dante says. "I will be with you in the water."

He slides behind me, putting a bright yellow handle in my hands, the rope stretching off toward the boat.

"The key," he says, "is to stay crouched and let the boat pull you up."

I feel his hands moving down my sides.

"I will hold you as long as I can," he says. "Until Lelani is ready, you can lean back."

I lean back and feel all that granite. I also feel his frisky hands cupping my buttocks.

"Sorry," he says, and he moves them to my hips.

Put them back! "Um, Dante, what if I fall?"

"You fall," he says. "It happens."

I have to see if he's noticed my wandering breasts. "I mean, I'm afraid I'll lose what I'm wearing if I fall. My bra was not made for swimming."

"I have noticed," he says.

My wandering breasts, um, pucker up when he says that.

"The vest will keep everything on," he says.

I turn my head slightly and see his lips. "I'm not worried about my top."

"Oh," he says. "But it is getting dark. No one will see if that happens."

The ski rope tightens, and both Dante and I float away from shore, his hands firmly holding on to my thighs.

"Ready?" he asks.

"I guess."

"Just hold on and let the boat do the work." He moves his hands to my hips again, yelling, "Hit it!"

The first time I fall isn't as bad as the *fifth* time I fall. On tries one through four, I wasn't even close to getting up, the handle flying away from me and me biting the water face first. Dante would swim out to me, hold me again, and I'd . . . I'd fall again. The fifth time, though, I am still in my crouch and almost standing when the right ski just . . . flies away behind me.

I do a spectacular cartwheel.

And lose my shorts.

It is an interesting feeling to be floating in a cove without one's shorts on as the sun sets completely. I'm sure my plain white underwear most likely leaves nothing to anyone's imagination. Although I am glad that I shave down there, I am sure young DJ doesn't have to see a strange woman's, um, bald chicken under her sheer white panties. Yet when

Dante swims out to me, I don't tell him I've lost my shorts because I sort of want him to discover that on his own.

"One more time?" he asks.

"Sure," I say. I am so sore and achy my body is going to file for divorce from me, I just know it.

I feel his hands go down my thighs, I rotate my hips just enough, and . . .

"Oh," Dante says. "Your . . ."

"Yeah," I say. "I don't think I should make another attempt."

"What should I do?" Dante says, his hands gone from my body.

"Just bring the boat over," I say, taking off my only ski.

Dante signals for the boat, and Lelani drives it to us. "Tired?" she asks.

"Yeah, um . . ." I look at Dante, who quickly looks away. "I'm going to need one of the towels."

DJ points to the ladder at the back of the boat. "Just climb in."

"Um, I will, Lelani," I say, widening my eyes, "just as soon as I get that towel."

Lelani mouths, "You lost your . . ."

I nod.

She throws in a towel. I wrap it around my waist tightly and slowly climb the ladder onto the boat.

As soon as I sit, I see my shorts floating nearby. "Dante," I whisper, nodding toward the water.

He looks, takes an oar, hooks onto the shorts—

I guess there's no discreet way to rescue one's shorts from a lake without everyone on the boat and several folks out on docks knowing it. Dante raises the oar, and those shorts flap a little like a flag in the wind.

They're still laughing about it at the dinner table ninety minutes and a long hot bath later.

"You were supposed to let go, Christiana," DJ says. "When you're flying like Superman—"

"Super*woman*," I interrupt. "And Lelani drove the boat entirely too fast. We don't go faster than thirty miles per hour in Brooklyn."

"I was only doing twenty," Lelani says. "What I don't get is why your, um, bottoms didn't go to the bottom!"

"Yeah. Nice dinner conversation." I bite into a leftover filet. "Why don't we talk about these fish and how I caught them all? That would be fun to talk about."

DJ turns to Red. "Dad couldn't even get his line in the water, she was bringing them in so fast."

Dante looks away, but I can see a smile. "I was busy with the anchor. It had a tangle."

"Tangle, my eye," I say. "You were stunned. Admit it."

"Why should I be stunned?" Dante asks. "You are a Red Hook girl. Fishing is in your bones." He turns to Red. "She is also crazy. We are stopped for an instant, it is pitch dark, she cannot know where to cast, she throws into the fog, and over rocks." He shakes his head. "She is crazy."

"I prefer 'fearless,' thank you very much," I say. "Dante, there's something I've been meaning to ask you. Why do you use a lure bigger than the fish?"

He scoots his chair closer to mine. "I only want to catch big fish. Big lure. Big fish."

I smile. "Little leech catch big fish yesterday."

"Because I take you to the right spot at the right time," Dante says. "Fishing is about timing, always timing."

I look at Red. "Like I timed that weak jab of yours today."

"Oh, weak, you say?" Dante stands and waves a filet at me. "I was holding back."

"So was I," I say. "Like you said, I've had a long layoff. Give me four, five weeks, and you'll see."

"What will I see?" he asks.

I have him *so* bad. "Oh, that's right. You're old. You can't see the punches coming anymore. I guess you *won't* see."

Dante laughs and sits. "How is your face?"

I ignore him. "Five pounds, three ounces. Isn't that a record for this cottage?"

He shakes his head. "Luck."

"Skill and fearlessness," I counter. "Is that why you use a top-water lure? So you don't get stuck?"

"It is where the fish feed at five in the morning." He taps the table.

"Not yesterday morning they weren't," I say. "How big was that little minnow you *almost* caught?"

Dante smiles. "Again, how is your face?"

I throw a crust of bread at him, he throws it back, DJ adds a little lettuce, and Lelani hits me with a cherry tomato.

Dinner is a success.

Red pulls me into the kitchen to help with the dishes, and though I just want to curl up on a couch and sleep for a few months, I help him by scrubbing the platter.

"You've certainly brought the table back to life, Christiana," he says. "I've always thought there was something wrong when there was no conversation at the table."

"Amen."

"When Evelyn is around, it's even quieter than it was last night."

That's hard to imagine. "Why?"

"Because," he whispers, "she is not of this earth. She has the ability to freeze mouths in midsentence and minds in midthought. 'Dinner is for eating,' she used to say. 'Dinner is only for the finest conversation.' It's good to have noise at that table again."

"Sorry about the bread," I say. "I couldn't resist."

He leans on the counter and looks at the ceiling. "Nope. We have never had a food fight up here before."

"It was an unfair fight, though," I say. "Lelani hogged the salad bowl."

He taps me on the shoulder. "Go on. You earned your interview. We're all leaving for the night."

"Really? All of you?" Where can they go?

"DJ has a Risk tournament on Turkey Island, and those usually go all night. Lelani and I are going to repair to our cottage for a quiet evening at home."

"Repair?"

"I read it in a book once. Anyway, you'll have your privacy." He raises his eyebrows.

"Are you insinuating something, Red?"

"How shall I say this? Hmm." He looks down at me. "I watched my best friend's eyes today, and though he seemed focused on his workout, he couldn't keep his eyes off you."

Whoo.

He turns me toward the door. "Now you go and get your pen and paper, and when you come back, you and Dante will be all alone."

In the guesthouse, I take stock of my situation. I have just completed four tasks out of five, not necessarily with flying colors, but I finished them. I outfished a fisherman, kept up on a hike, cleaned some fish well enough to eat for two meals, lasted three rounds with a former middleweight champion, survived a left hook, swam a mile, skied for the first time, lost my shorts, and started a food fight at the dinner table.

All in a day's work.

And now I learn the subject of the interview I've earned has been making goo-goo eyes at me all day. I know he has seen my breasts, felt up my booty twice, and likes to be behind me for some reason.

Oh yeah, he hit me. It still hurts. An ordinary journalist would sue his ass.

Not me.

I just want to *squeeze* his ass.

Chapter 15

After writing a few questions in my notebook, putting on some strangely oversized black sweats, and finding some fluffy brown bear slippers that almost fit, I return to an empty great room, a roaring fire in the fireplace. I curl up on the couch and wait for Dante.

It is finally time to capture this man.

I hear Dante coming down the stairs, and my heart flutters a little. I know it's silly. I know I'm just here to interview him and go. I know nothing can come of this. Still it's nice to—

What's he doing in the kitchen?

I flip through the notebook, completely ignoring the soft questions on the first page. This will not be a puff-piece interview. This is going to go deep.

"You like lots of sugar or a little sugar in your tea?" he calls out.

He's making me tea. How sweet. "Two teaspoons!" I yell.

A moment later, he brings in two mugs of tea, the tea bags still floating inside. "I put in three teaspoons by mistake," he says. He wears a black sweatshirt and gray sweatpants, his feet bare.

"A mistake?" I say.

"Okay. I put in extra because you lost a lot of sugar today. I do not want you to pass out."

How . . . almost sweet. "Um, DJ said you wanted me to do five things, and I can only count four."

"Oh," he says, "but you did five things. You fished, you hiked, you worked out, you skied, and"—he smiles—"you made me do this."

"Do what?" Though I know. I'm a Columbia graduate.

"You made me smile."

I feel all warm and fuzzy. Whoo. "Well, are you ready?" I wave the pen in the air.

He sits in front of the fire, his back to a brick ledge. "*Sì.*"

"Okay . . ." Should I go with the flow or start with a humdinger? This is such an intimate setting. A comfortable couch, a glowing fire, darkness and stars lapping at the big picture windows. Hmm. Let's drop a hammer. "Why do you sleep on the floor in that closet?"

He blinks. "You've been to my room?"

"I snoop, Dante," I say, taking a sip. Nice. Red Rose. Good stuff. "It's what I do. So, why do you sleep there?"

He rolls his neck from side to side. "Why do you sleep in a bed?"

"Because it's comfortable," I say. Uh duh. "It's normal. It's where civilized people are supposed to sleep."

He pulls a tennis ball from his pocket and starts to squeeze it with his left hand. "It is exactly the opposite of why I sleep on the floor. It is not comfortable, though it is good for my back. It is to remind me of hard times."

"But all this beautiful scenery and no windows?"

"I choose to have no windows to remind me of my ancestors who were imprisoned for fighting against Mussolini. I have no bed to remind me of my *nonni* coming to America and having to sleep on the floor, pick rags, and sell junk thrown away by others. My family has been through many hard times. They made sacrifices to come to America. I make sacrifices, too. I do not get soft. I stay hard."

What a fantastic quote! Especially those last three words. A girl likes to hear those three magic words. "Um, why are my clippings on your wall?"

"Oh," he says quietly. "You have seen them, too."

"They're hard to miss."

He squeezes the ball hard with his left hand. "Motivation. That is why they are there. They represent my greatest failures."

"And the crucifix?"

He begins to squeeze the ball with his right hand. "More motivation. Greatest sacrifice ever."

"And . . . your wedding picture?"

He bounces the ball and catches it. "It is why I am fighting." He squeezes the ball again with his left hand.

I feel the need to probe him. "Your marriage could be considered another great failure."

He looks away. "We . . . divorced. I was not winning. It was my failure, not hers."

Oh, it's like that? Damn. "Wasn't she the one who left?"

"Because of my failure."

"And now?"

He turns to me and arrests me with those eyes. "I will win Evelyn back. I am fighting for love."

This is beginning to sound like a bad romance novel. "You mean *lost* love."

He switches hands with the ball. "We are still in love."

"Really?"

"Yes. I will win her back when I defeat Tank Washington." He sighs. "But I do not want you to put any of this in your story."

But this *is* the story! "Why not?"

"It is my wish."

"And this is an interview, which I earned today, right?" I not only earned it—I'm going to pay for it for days. "It is my *wish* to use this material."

"Please do not."

I shake my head. "C'mon, Dante. It's romantic." Okay, it's cheesy as hell, too, but . . . "It's sexy—"

He crushes the ball and holds it. "And if I lose, I will lose much more if this is known. I have gone away for ten years in shame. If I lose, I lose Evelyn. I lose all respect. I will disappear forever." He releases his hold on the ball. "I know it is your job, but this is my life. Think of what will happen to DJ. 'Your father lost twice when he lost that fight,' they will say. 'What a fool your father is!' I do not want this to haunt him for the rest of his life."

He has really thought all this through. "But I thought you were sure you were going to win."

He tosses the ball back and forth. "As you have said, I do not have one-punch knockout power anymore. And I do not have much of a jab. And since I do not have these skills, Washington may beat me on points like he did last time. He is a warrior. He is relentless. He puts on much pressure. There is no telling with judges. I bleed. Washington does not seem to. Blood earns points. I must wear him down until he falls. If he gets up and finishes the fight, I could have a knockdown and still lose."

These are all valid points, but . . . "But consider who I work for, Dante. My editors would want the human side of this story. Fighting for love is human."

"No. Please keep why I fight out of your story. Keep Evelyn out of your story."

"I can't guarantee it," I say, and I can't. Shelley will howl if I keep the "fighting for love" angle out of this.

He looks at the fire. "Paper burns. You could, how you say, withhold this information until after the fight."

I could, but . . . "Few people will believe it afterward, Dante. Think about it. Oh, by the way, he was fighting for love and he won. I forgot to mention that before. See how much more special that makes his victory?"

"I will not beg you."

"I'll think about it." For about a second. "Fighting for love" has to be in the first paragraph. It may even be the title.

"Grazie."

I look through my questions. "Why do you train up here?"

"You have already asked more than five questions," he says, and he sips his tea.

I take a sip of mine, too. I hope this doesn't mean the interview is over. "I want to capture you. I can't *possibly* capture you in five questions."

He smiles. *"Bene."*

I smile back. "So . . . why train up here?"

"No distractions." He looks at the ball. "Except for you. You are a major *distrazione."*

"Grazie. Why else?"

He takes the deepest breath. "The air is pure, you know? Clean. Has a flavor. The water is pure. Clean."

"And ice cold," I add.

"Ah. You would get used to it. Most of all, it is a place where I can focus. It is a place where DJ and I can be together all the time. It was where I went on my honeymoon."

"Oh?"

"Not at this place. Friends of ours have a place on the other shore. It was so beautiful that I bought some land and built this place."

I look at him slyly. "You're very handy."

"Grazie."

He doesn't get the hint. Oh well. "So, how did you and Evelyn meet?" Though I really don't care, a reader might care.

"She was a 'fight doctor,' so to speak. She was the nurse who stitched me up one evening after a fight. She was in the emergency room."

How romantic. Not. "Was it love at first sight?"

"Is there any other?"

I certainly hope so! He is such an Italian. "Did you ask her out while she was stitching you up?"

"Yes."

I laugh. "You didn't."

He shrugs. "She said no. She said she did not like boxing. 'It is so brutal,' she said. I did not give up. I sent flowers to her. Many flowers over many months."

While he didn't exactly stalk her, and flowers are nice, um . . . "Where did you propose?"

"In the emergency room. She was on break, and I asked." He bounces the ball. "In front of everybody, she said yes. Later, not in front of everybody, she said no."

That should have told him something. "But eventually . . ."

"I wore her down, with flowers, visits after every fight, no matter where I fight. 'You are my personal doctor,' I told her. She kept my face together. I tell her she is my *portafortuna,* my good luck charm. I cannot win without her. Eventually, she said yes."

Some of this is quotable, but . . . "Um, I hate to have to ask this, but why did your marriage end?"

"I already told you. I lost. I was no longer champion."

An unlikely story. "You mean she lost interest."

"No. Because I lost. Next question."

He's squeezing the hell out of that ball again. I better back off. "Did you . . . no." I'm not here to back off. "Did Evelyn ask you to retire after you lost to Washington?"

He drops the ball, and it rolls away. "How did you know that?"

"Woman's intuition. But you didn't retire, did you?"

He stands and retrieves the ball, squeezing it furiously. "How could I retire then? I was in the prime of my life. I could not. I wanted a rematch right away. Johnny Sears, my trainer, he wanted me to fight Cordoza first. 'To have another knockout under your belt,' he said. I made a deal with Evelyn. I will fight Cordoza, win, get a rematch with Washington, win, and retire. She says my record is good enough. She says my legacy is good enough. I say, I want to go out a champion. She says, 'You could get seriously hurt.' Back and forth . . . It was a long argument."

His losing didn't end their marriage. This argument ended their marriage. He had the gall to disagree with her.

I need to get this interview away from Evelyn for a spell. "Were you ever in love before Evelyn?" I ask.

He sighs. "Twice. With the same girl. I was nine. At mass. She was beautiful."

So cute. "What was her name?"

"Bettina. She was *cioccolata*. I had never seen such beauty before. Her face shone like the sun."

Bettina? Hmm. I haven't heard that name before. "Did you ask her out?"

"At nine, no. I saw her again when I was eighteen, a brand new pro boxer."

This is strange. "You only saw her twice?"

"*Sì*. She did not attend mass so often. She was probably not from Brooklyn." He sighs. "She was even more beautiful, so small, such small hands. But she was holding another man's hand. I never talked to her."

Loving from afar.

"I have learned that she died on nine-eleven."

So sad! How do you follow up on that? "So, um, would you consider her your first love?"

"I never spoke to her, but . . . I suppose I loved her. I was young."

He has such a sweet spirit! "So, have you always had a thing for black girls?"

"Yes." He holds me with his eyes. "I have always thought black women were beautiful. Their eyes shine so bright, like angels. And their shapes . . ."

My shape is sweating. I must have used too much lotion.

"Very athletic," he says. "They are put together like *scultura,* like sculpture. Silky black hair that also shines. Yes, to me, beauty is a black woman. No equals."

I wish more men had this attitude. Madison Avenue, too. We *do* have no equals. "What do you like best about black women?"

"Their eyes," he says, penetrating my eyes with his. "They do not seem to age. They are always bright."

This could be chancy, but . . . "What about the rest of her?" I stand and turn slightly sideways. "Do you like fronts or backs better?"

"Fronts or backs?" He smiles. "You mean, do I like breasts or booty better?"

I shouldn't have worn these sweats. "Um, yes."

"I like proportion. As much front as back."

I sit, my proportional front and my back rejoicing. "Didn't you ever want a nice Italian girl?"

He looks at the tennis ball. "They did not want me. I was skinny. And poor."

They didn't know what they were missing. "How about any other kind of girl who could cook like your mama?"

"Black women are *tremendo* cooks. Red's mama taught him everything he knows."

"Could Evelyn cook?"

He blinks and looks away. "It is why I have Red."

Evelyn couldn't cook. For some reason, this also makes me rejoice. "Did you ever have any, oh, flings?"

"Flings?"

"Before you were married, you know, one-night stands, weekend rendezvous, that sort of thing."

He looks confused. "Like a crush?"

"Um, no." I don't know why I'm stuck on this. "It would have been purely sexual."

"No. I have had no flings. I believe love and sex must go hand in hand. No love, no sex."

He made that perfectly clear. "But if there's love?"

"Yes. It is natural because of love."

I wish he had a ceiling fan. I am burning up! I had better change the subject. "Um, what have you been doing for the last ten years?"

"You have seen it. Fishing, traveling, staying in shape."

"Why do you fish so much?" I ask.

He nods. "A good question. I think I fish to teach myself more patience. When I was young, I rushed to my opponent and tried to beat him early. My opponents hit me a lot. Since I have been fishing, I have learned much patience. I am learning when to strike and when to fight. It is a way to calm me down."

Hmm. That quote is okay. It might go better in *Field and Stream,* though. "Why did you disappear?"

"I have not disappeared."

"Yes, you did," I say. "For ten years, the world has known nothing about you."

He shrugs. "What was there to know?"

Here's a strange question for a celebrity: "Was it easy to disappear?"

"It was easier than you think. Not many recognize me wearing clothes and without my boxing gloves."

I think I would.

"It was okay to be anonymous," he says.

Back to Evelyn. Discussing her will cool me off even

more. "Over the last ten years, did you ever try to rekindle your romance with Evelyn?"

"It is what I am doing now," he says. "More flowers, lots of visits. She says to stop the flowers. I send more. The waiting room in the emergency room at University Hospital is always so beautiful."

I'll bet. I'm sure they appreciate all those dying flowers rotting in their emergency room. "Why are you making a comeback now?"

"I have already told you. To win Evelyn back."

There has to be more to it than this. "Are you financially strapped?"

"No. I have made good investments. DJ is set for life."

I sigh. "Dante, you have to help me out here. If I don't tell people the real reason you're making a comeback, I'll need to tell them something else, something reasonable. You *will* be making a lot of money for this fight."

"I do not fight for money. I have never fought for money."

I know . . . he fights for love, yadda, yadda, yadda. "Why *else* are you fighting then?"

"What other reasons are there?"

He *really* doesn't know! "I don't know. Say you needed a challenge. Say you were bored. Say you have a grudge against Washington. Say you're having a midlife crisis. Something like that."

"Oh. I see. Hmm." He dribbles the tennis ball around his back. "Tell them I wanted to be a hero to my son. Be a good father. Give him someone to look up to."

"That's better," I say.

"It is true, too," he says.

I believe it. I flip back a few pages to my notes. "Um, where is your mother?"

"Heaven."

That was a quick answer. "What was her name?"

"Connie, but her friends called her Con. What does that have to do with me now? It has been many years since she died."

I shrug. "Just background, you know, in case my editor wants to know. When and how did she die?"

"Before I turned pro, when I was eighteen. She smoked a lot. Lung cancer. Dead at thirty-seven."

That sucks. "Did she get to see you at the Olympic trials?"

"Yes. She saw me lose in the semifinals. Then she died."

In that order. Geez, I'll bet he blames himself for her death. "Do you still feel guilty about that?"

"A little. She was very sick. She should not have been traveling. Next question."

I can't leave this line of questioning alone. This is crucial. "What kind of a woman was your mother?"

He smiles. "Best cook. Worked at Monte's Venetian Room. Never learned English. Never needed to learn. Carroll Gardens was like that. Sitting out on the stoop, she could talk to anyone. That was a long time ago. The neighborhood has changed. Cammareri Brothers Bakery is gone. Not so much Italian heard on the stoops. Mama would not like it as much."

Good stuff. I underline this quote. "What about your father?"

"I do not speak of him."

"Is he still alive?"

"I do not care. *Non importa.*"

He's not getting off that easily. "When did he leave?"

"I told you. I do not speak of him. Next question."

I think of the hairy man in the picture. "Did he serve in Vietnam?"

Silence.

"Did he die there?"

"No. That is all I will talk about him. What does he have to do with me?"

It could mean a lot from the attitude he's giving me. "His absence doesn't motivate you in any way?"

"No."

I will definitely have to research his father. Right now, though, I need to calm Dante down before he breaks that ball. "You're a wonderful father, Dante. I've been meaning to tell you."

Silence.

"I mean, you're DJ's older brother, friend, confidant, trainer. . . . It's a rare thing."

"It is the right thing."

That will be in any story I write about this man. "I agree. Do you get to spend as much time with him as you want?"

"I see him often enough."

"No, I mean when he's away. He spends the school year with Evelyn, right?"

"I have an apartment in Syracuse. I see him often."

Two houses, okay, *cottages,* and an apartment. Dante isn't hurting for money. "Do you see him as often as you'd like?"

"No. I am working on that."

Dante is a psychologist's dream. He seems to be trying to reunite his current family because something tore his old family apart. I decide to change the subject again. "Why boxing?"

"Che?"

I don't mean to confuse him, but I find I'm most effective if I use no transition—or logic, sometimes—when I'm interviewing people. This method often catches people off guard, and they say things without thinking. "Of all the sports in the world, why did you choose boxing?"

Dante's eyes light up. "I was skinny." He moves over to the opposite couch. "I was the smallest boy at school. There was this *bravaccio* named Franco. He chased me like dogs chase cars."

Very cool quote. "So you jogged to school."

"I *ran* to school. I was small, but I was *rapido*. Franco was *obeso*. He could only run so far. At school, though, it was not so easy. Very narrow hallways."

"So . . . you started boxing to stand up to Franco?"

"At first." He smiles. "I hit him only once in his *stomaco*. He left me alone. This was before Gleason's Gym."

Which begs the question . . . "When did you start training at Gleason's?"

"I just showed up one day after school. I was thirteen. Two miles to school, four miles to Gleason's, three miles home, nine miles a day I run."

Geez, that's over . . . two *thousand* miles a year! "You must have been exhausted!"

"I do not get tired."

I believe it. "Why Gleason's?"

"Gleason's is the best. Jake LaMotta, Rocky Graziano, Floyd Patterson, Muhammad Ali, Joe Frazier, George Foreman, Roy Jones, Pernell Whitaker, Carmen Basilio, Arturo Gatti—they all trained there. They were the best. I wanted to be the best."

Gleason's was also where Clint Eastwood trained Hilary Swank in *Million Dollar Baby,* a "best" picture. "Didn't you help out with Give a Kid a Dream?" Give a Kid a Dream is a program aimed at giving disadvantaged kids a chance to box.

"Yeah. I miss that. I should go back and help them train. Gleason's gave me a chance, so I should give back. There is a new generation of tough Brooklyn kids out there that could be champions. They are already running the streets. I'd like to make sure that running counts for something."

This man is rare, and these aren't just empty words. He is already one of the biggest contributors to the program, even though he hasn't stepped foot in Gleason's in ten years. I believe Dante *will* go back, not just say he will go back. I star these quotes for my longer piece. "Why aren't you training at Gleason's now?"

"I am not a champion."

In other words, he's embarrassed to show his face there. "Plenty of former champions train there."

"I do not like that word 'former.' It diminishes me. Once a champion, always a champion."

"But a champion without a nickname," I say. "Why do you think it took so long for you to get a nickname? I mean, you were the reigning champ for nearly six years."

"My fans, they tried. They called me the Carroll Gardens Brawler. It did not stick."

"Gardens . . . brawler. Kind of incompatible." If he were from Red Hook, just one neighborhood over, he could be the Left Hook from Red Hook. I wonder if anyone ever thought to call him Dante Inferno Lattanza. He's certainly fiery enough. "Um, how frustrated were you that it took so long in your attempt to unify the title?"

"It was an outrage," he says, his face getting red. "They always had some excuse. They wanted more money, they wanted a different ring, they did not like the referee, they wanted to use different gloves, they would rather fight in Las Vegas or Atlantic City, they had injuries. They were afraid of me in my prime. They were not true champions."

"At least you tried," I say. "You are one of the few who tried. How did you know . . . *When* did you know you were any good at boxing?"

"I still do not think I am that good," he says.

Vain one minute and humble the next.

"I am not like those champions," he continues. "I am, as you said, not as skilled. *Sangue e budelle.* Blood and guts.

I have always been this. When I was little, I asked to fight the biggest fighters. They laughed at me but gave me a chance. I went home bloody, but no one ever knocked me down. No one. No one ever will."

I can't dispute that. "What was your greatest moment?"

"Holding Dante Junior for the first time," he says immediately.

I will use this quote, too. "I meant . . ."

"I know what you meant. Is not all about boxing with me. Boxing put money in my pocket to put food on the table, have a place to live. Is a job. *Occupazione*. Is all about writing for you?"

Well . . . yeah. For the most part. I can't tell him that, though. "No. I get to travel, meet interesting people, and learn about life." Pop crayfish out of fish carcasses, get popped in the face . . .

He leans forward. "What was *your* greatest moment, Christiana?"

Ah. He's probing me now. I decide to be coy. "I haven't had it yet."

"A wise answer. DJ says you are *saggia*."

"What do you think?"

He moves over to my couch and sits at the other end. "I think you are sneaky. You are flirting with me, yes?"

The fire is hot, but his words are hotter. "A little."

"*Bugiardo terribile.* You are a terrible liar."

"Maybe." I moisten my lips. "You, um, keep getting closer to me. Have you been flirting with me?"

"*Sì.*"

I shouldn't have worn these sweats. I'm, um, sweating. "Why? I thought you were fighting for love."

"I am."

Doesn't he see the obvious contradiction? "Yet you flirt with me."

"I have a good reason to flirt," he says. "I did not flirt

with *giornalisti* in the past and they wrote lies about me. I flirt with you so you will tell the truth. Agreed? Is this why you flirt with me? To get me to tell you all my *pensieri segreti*, my secret thoughts?"

For some reason, I think this Brooklyn boy is working me instead of the other way around. "Maybe."

"Ah. *Saggia*."

"And maybe I'm flirting because . . . you . . ."

Stop right there, Miss Artis.

You do not want to go here.

This man is still in love with his ex.

He is *pericoloso, sì*, but you have more sense than this.

You cannot get involved.

Oh, sure, this is a romantic spot, he's just a few feet from you, he's looking sexy, you're sweating. . . .

"Because I what?"

Don't answer.

Be *saggia*.

This has happened to you before.

Several hot celebs have come on to you like this, one while his sleaze of a girlfriend was sitting right there. He probably wanted a threesome.

You can do this, Christiana.

Don't give in to those eyes.

He moves closer, less than an arm's length away.

But he's hot, and I'm hot for him. He isn't married, right? She's not around. We're alone. We're consenting adults. Red vacated the house just so this would happen, didn't he? Go with the damn flow!

I sigh, shut up the journalist in me, and put down my notebook.

"No more questions?" he asks.

I shake my head. "I'm finished."

"I'm not," he says, scooting even closer. "You did not answer my question."

"Because I shouldn't answer your question, Dante," I say. "Really. It's *non importa.*"

"My question or your answer?"

Shoot. "My answer. It won't mean anything."

He slides next to me, our legs touching. "Try me."

Can he feel my sweat? "Okay. For what it's worth, Dante, I find you . . . you're . . . you."

This has to be the *dumbest* thing I have ever said.

Dante laughs. "You cannot speak? Ha!"

Deep breath. "What I meant to say is . . ." He's nudging me with his leg. I like it. It is a sexy leg, and he has another one just like it. "What I mean to say is that I like you."

He sits back and squints. "You like me?"

"Yes," I say more confidently. "I like you."

He frowns. "Do you normally like who you interview?"

I laugh and shake my head. "I hardly like *anyone* I interview."

He turns away and crosses his arms. "And yet you do this for a living?"

I know it makes no sense. "Yes."

"Hmm." He nods. "Why don't you like the people you interview?"

A fair question. "Because they're usually fake."

"Ah." He turns to me smiling. "So I am not fake."

"No," I say. "Like I said, you're you." Ah. Now my other quote makes sense.

He nods. "Hmm." He squints at me again. It is so cute! "This is not some new trick to learn all my secrets?"

Damn, he's sharp! I take a deeper breath, because I'm getting deeper into this man. "No. I came to write a story about you, and . . . I, um, like I said . . . I like you."

"What do you like about me?"

The tips of my fingers are sweating. They usually don't sweat like this unless I'm finishing an awesome story. "You're . . . you." Quit repeating that, Christiana! "I mean, you don't change. You're not fake. So many of the people I interview put on a show for me. You don't."

He nods. "Oh, but I am stubborn, yes? How can you like that?"

I laugh. "I'm pretty stubborn, too."

He squeezes my leg. "I have noticed." He reaches by me and takes my paper and pen. "Now I interview you."

"What?"

"*Che.* When you do not understand, say '*che.*' "

I blink. *"Che?"*

"Bene." He licks the top of my pen.

I feel a bit moist.

"First question: What is your favorite color?"

He's so cute. "Green."

"Ah. *Verde.* The color of money."

I shake my head. "The color of life."

"Oh. Better." He writes it down on a blank sheet! "How tall are you?"

"Five seven."

He squints. "I thought we were the same height."

I smile. "You slouch."

"True." He writes it down. "Your weight?"

"What?"

"Say '*che.*' "

"Che?"

He smiles. "I want to know your weight. I held you in the water, but water makes you weigh less. I'm thinking maybe . . . one thirty, one thirty-five."

In my dreams. "You're right."

"Bene." He writes it down. "What is your degree?"

So formal! "I have a BA in journalism from Columbia."

"*Impressionante.* Impressive. You are very athletic. What sports did you play?"

I want to play some sports right now, and they don't involve his hands on that tennis ball or his tongue on the tip of my pen. "Um, none really. I trained with my grand-daddy. I work out when I can." Which is practically never.

"You are very fit."

"Grazie."

He stares at me. "How old are you?"

"Guess."

"Stand up."

I do.

He looks me up and down and all around, even instructing me to turn around once. "You may sit."

I sit.

"You are twenty-five."

I hate to burst his bubble. "I'm thirty-five."

"No," he says. "I have already written it down. I cannot change what I have written." His eyes become slits. "No more than you can change what you have written."

Whoa. He got me good.

"You are now twenty-five. You do not wear a ring." He pauses. "This either means you are not married or you have taken off your ring to flirt with me."

"I'm not married," I say quickly.

"Bene. Are you seeing anyone?"

Just the man in front of me. "No."

"Have you ever been married?"

"No."

"Close to being married?"

"No."

He sighs. "What do you have against marriage?"

So direct! "Nothing. Really. It just hasn't worked out that way for me." Geez, I am so unquotable. A journalist should never do an interview.

"What was the name of your last boyfriend?"

I think a little and catch glimpses of a guy, but . . . . "I can't remember. Howard something."

"It has been that long?"

It's been so long I'm not sure what a penis looks like up close. "Yes."

"But you are *bellissima,* so *erotica.*"

He's messing with all my *erotica* zones right now. "I've been busy."

"Oh. So your career is most important."

Dante would make an outstanding journalist. He's already catching me in little contradictions. "I've been at it for almost fourteen years, so right now it is."

"Hmm." He studies the notebook. "Where is your mama?"

Nice transition. "Heaven."

"*Tristissimo.* Your father?"

I know I opened the door for this, but . . . "I don't want to discuss this."

He sits back. "Oh, but you expect me to. I like you, too. I want to get to know you."

He says it so matter-of-factly. "You . . . like me?"

"You are likable. Now tell me about your father."

A pain shoots into my chest. "Only if you go first."

"Ah," he says, like the psychologist that I used to see when I was little. "So much *resistenza.*"

Resistenza? It was more like futility because I didn't see the point. I had drawn a stick-figure picture of a scarecrow around Halloween, and my teacher had rushed my drawing to the principal the second I finished it. The principal then called me into his office and asked me, "Who's this?" I told him it was a scarecrow, adding, "It is Halloween, you know." He pointed at one of the scarecrow's hands. "And what's this in his hand?" I told him it was the scarecrow's magic wand. "It's not a man holding a knife?" he asked. I shook my head. The principal then sent me to a shrink so I could deal with my "repressed issues." I was five, happy and thriving with Granddaddy, and because of a badly drawn scarecrow, I had to listen to that asshole psychologist say "Ah" fifty times in half an hour, twice a week, for three months. I didn't think I had any issues. I just couldn't draw very well! "Are you sure it's not your . . . *father* . . . holding a knife?" I shook my head until my neck hurt.

But I don't want to think about any of that right now.

"My father," Dante says. "Also not for story."

"Fine."

"My father never came home. He did not die in Vietnam, but he never came home. Mama waited for him. That is all I know."

That's it? "You never wanted to find him?"

"No." He leans forward. "He is not where he is supposed to be. I do not need to find him. Now you."

I don't want to talk about this. I don't want to talk about the *other* scarecrow in my life. How can I answer this without begging another question? "My father is in heaven, too."

He looks down. "Both your parents are dead?"

"Yes."

"How did they die?"

I put this behind me so long ago, and now this man is bringing it all back. "Look, I'd rather not say, Dante. Please. Change the subject." I ball my hands into fists.

He puts his right hand on top of my fists. "How old were you?"

I can't breathe, my heart is thudding, and I have to get out of here. "I was . . . I was two."

He brings his other hand to my fists. "You do not remember them?"

"No, I don't!" I shout. I jump to my feet and run outside to the outcropping under the stars into the cold and I'm holding myself and weeping and rocking and I'm all alone again and I'm two years old and there's no one to hold me—

Dante's hands reach around me, holding my stomach gently. "*Mi dispiace.* I should not have asked."

I turn into him and put my head on his shoulder. "I don't remember them at all, Dante."

"Shh, shh. It is all right."

He holds me for several minutes while I calm down, whispering, "Shh, shh, *bella,* it is all right."

I wipe my face on my sleeve. "I only had pictures." I tore up and threw away those pictures one very bad day when I was twelve. "And I didn't know how they died until I did a research paper on them in high school."

Which is a very long time not to know.

"Granddaddy told me not to research them. He said it would only give me pain, but I had to, you know? I went to the library and found a single article buried in the back pages of the *Times.*"

My legs buckle, but Dante holds me up.

"The headline read, MURDER SUICIDE IN RED HOOK. My daddy killed my mama."

Oh, God! Why now? Why here? Why?

"You do not have to tell me any more. Let us go inside where it is warm."

He takes me by the hand and leads me back to the fireplace, placing me on the floor with my back to the fire. He hands me my tea, and I take a shaky sip.

"I wish I had not asked," he says. "I am sorry."

I put down my mug. "It's okay. It's obviously something that I need to spill out of me." I wipe my eyes on my sleeve. "I still don't know why he killed her, even after all this time. I researched and researched, and I asked around, and I asked my granddaddy, but he wouldn't tell me anything."

"He was protecting you."

"I needed to know the truth, okay? The police officers and detectives I interviewed didn't know a whole lot either. My daddy killed my mama and then killed himself. That's all I know. As painful as that was to know, I still wrote it all up, footnoted it, and presented it in a detached, clinical way." I close my eyes. "And I got an A. I got an A for writing about my daddy killing my mama and then himself."

Other kids were researching crack, or rap, or legalizing marijuana, but no, I had to reach into the darkness and bring up some demons.

I look at the hands that typed that paper. "My teacher told me—with tears in *her* eyes, not mine—she told me, 'If you can write about that, Christiana, you can write about anything.'"

"You are good at what you do." He sits next to me and puts his hot hand on my neck. "You are strong because of it."

"Trust me, I'm not. It's all an act."

He wipes away a tear. "It is not an act. You are *coraggiosa*."

"I'm not . . . courageous. When you asked me yesterday where my bags were, and I told you I didn't have any, I lied. I have plenty of baggage."

"Ah. But no more than anyone else." He rubs my back, and it feels so good. "You have a very strong back."

What about my front? I want to ask. Oh yeah. He's already seen it, up close and personal—and dripping wet.

"Strong legs. Strong mind. Strong tongue." He leans closer to me, his breath hot on my ear. "Carrying your baggage all these years has made you strong. You are a strong woman. You are not just a *corpo provocante*."

I rub my back against his hand. "Don't stop."

"Ah." He slides behind me and massages my shoulders.

I am now officially wet. And hot. Though he's blocking the fire, I am feeling fire spreading through my entire body.

"I do not want you to leave tomorrow," he says.

I will never leave if you keep doing this. "I have to go, Dante. My flight leaves tomorrow night, and I have to drive to Ottawa first, and—"

"Stay." His hands slide to my lower back where he starts kneading my sore, sore muscles through my sweatshirt. I'm surprised he can't feel my sweat.

"Only if you don't stop doing that."

He laughs. "You should be sore. You used muscles today you have not used in a long time." His hands circle lower and lower, and when he gets to the top of my booty, I actually start to pant.

Against my horny judgment, and despite the tingling in my stuff, I get up and sit on another couch, a cool couch, the couch furthest away from his fiery hands. "So, Dante, if I stay, what will we do?"

He looks at his hands. "Did I do something wrong?"

"No. I'm just afraid I might do something wrong if I let you continue."

"Ah." He puts his hands together in his lap. "It was not just a massage to you either."

To me *either*? Why the hell did I leave? He could be grinding his hands into my booty right now! "So, um, what will we do tomorrow?"

"We will rest. We will go into town. We will shop. Swim. Relax." He flexes his hands. "Maybe a nice massage, too."

I smile. "You must do five things if you want me to stay," I say in a deep voice.

He blinks. "And they are?"

God, I miss his hands on my body. "First . . ."

I grab his hand and drag him out of the cottage to the guesthouse. I throw myself facedown on the bed. "You must massage me until I say stop."

I close my eyes.

I feel hands. I feel two hands. They rub gently over my shoulders and down my sides to—

He's pulling up my sweatshirt. I feel hands, hot hands, two of them, on my skin. They circle and caress and—

Thumbs dig into me. Am I groaning? I am. My voice sounds so . . . needy.

"What else do I have to do to get you to stay?" he whispers.

I look up at his eyes. Those eyes . . . those eyes would never hurt me. "I'll let you know tomorrow." Because when your hands are doing that, I cannot think!

"So you are staying?"

I nod, turn my head, and close my eyes.

"Where should I massage most?" he asks.

Whoo, what a question. "I am sore in so many places."

"So . . . anywhere?"

I nod. "Especially my legs."

I sit up slowly and remove my sweats, avoiding his eyes, fully forgetting that I am showing him the same underwear I was wearing when I was skiing. I had to dry them with a hair dryer. Because I'm sweating, I'm sure they're soaked . . . and thoroughly revealing. Damn. A man is looking at my crack. Whoo.

I have to say something. "I, um, I like the way your hands feel on my skin." I quickly hit the pillow and close my eyes.

He touches my calves. "Are you sore here?"

"*Sì*." Damn. Just saying "yes" in Italian is hot.

"And here?" He rubs my hamstrings.

"*Sì*." Check that—*oh sì*.

"And . . ." He brushes my booty so gently I get shivers, but his hand ends up grabbing my *foot*! "Here?"

I turn. *"Che?"*

He touches my face with a rough knuckle. "I, too, am afraid I will do something wrong if you let me continue."

But I *want* you to! Don't I?

I bury my head in my pillow, biting at the fabric Evelyn probably picked out. I pop up and rest my head on my hand. "All better."

He leans in and holds my face with his hands, kissing both of my cheeks. "Rest, Christiana. Tomorrow we play *turisti*."

I sit up and take his face in my hands. "May I at least kiss you good night?"

His jaw muscles tighten. "If you must."

I must, I must. I lick my lips and put a soft kiss on his . . . nose. I let go of his face and settle back onto my pillow. "Good night, Dante."

He smiles, grabs my foot again, growls a little, and leaves the bed. When he gets to the door, he turns. *"Ciao."*

"Ciao, Dante."

The door opens, I check out his ass one more time, and the door closes.

Oh, God, what a man.

I can't believe I revealed so much to him. What have I known him for, thirty hours? I've already told him things I've never told *anyone*. I've also dropped my sweats for him, let him kiss my cheeks, kissed his nose, and allowed his hands to hold my booty.

I've had a busy day.

But here I am *not* getting busy.

This is crazy.

I know I'm vulnerable, but . . . He's not fighting for *my* love. I have to keep telling myself that. He's fighting for another woman, the woman he built this guesthouse for, the shrew *Eve*lyn. I'll never be able to convince him that he's only fighting for the *memory* of another woman.

My booty is still tingling.

And so is my foot. What's up with that?

He doesn't want me to leave. That has to mean something. I hope it means something. If I really had to leave tomorrow, I don't think I could.

I slip out of my sweatshirt and bra, turn off the lights, and worm under the covers, wondering why I'm not dead to the world right now. I have never worked so hard in my life. He should have had to carry me in here.

Maybe that can be one of his five tasks.

Sì.

I was so close to having a booty rub and then some tonight, and then he grabs my foot? "I am afraid I might do something wrong," he says. Why did I even say that in the first place? I was getting some nice back in front of the fire, and I jetted away from him.

And I surely didn't want him to leave just now, so why didn't I just kiss him soulfully on the lips, rip down his sweats, and—

I *scream* into the pillow this time.

All better.

Not.

A loon echoes me out on the lake.

I know how you feel, buddy.

I know how you feel.

Chapter 16

After waking to sunlight instead of darkness, I take another nice long, hot bath, putting my booty fully on *both* seats in the tub. That's right, *Eve*lyn, another booty is moving in. I swim around with my bra, washing it with a bar of Lifebuoy. When I get out, I dry it with a hair dryer, but I don't put it on once it's dry. The underwires might still be too hot.

I walk naked to Evelyn's dresser before I remember where I am. I do this all the time at home. I look at the window and shrug because I am *coraggiosa*. I open the top drawer and see a few pairs of cotton underwear. I am not putting my same drawers on for the *third* straight day. I pull out a gray pair, put my heel in the back, and stretch that size six to a size ten. The elastic is still tight as hell, but at least my booty fits. I touch the underwires and find them to be cool. I put on my bra, and it is snug, too. I'll bet the hair dryer shrunk it.

I feel so buxom.

I choose a blue Nike running suit and a light blue T-shirt before I realize—damn. I can't wear boots with these! Oh, shit. I have to go Canadian today.

I size up a pair of size six jeans. I ought to be slimmer than I was yesterday. Maybe if I stretch them like I stretched her underwear . . .

Jean material is cruel and unforgiving, but I somehow manage to squeeze in, the metal button looking dangerously afraid. "Hold on, little buddy," I tell it.

It holds on.

I slip on a black T-shirt and a blue and black flannel shirt. If I had a string tie and a ten-gallon hat, I could be a Texan. I empty out dust, pine needles, and sand from my boots, and before I put on a pair of Evelyn's footy socks, I examine my feet and find two nasty blisters on both heels and one on my left pinkie toe.

Yee-haw.

I use three Band-Aids on each blister, slide on the socks, ease into the boots, grab my camera case, and walk gingerly to the kitchen.

These jeans are so tight I must look like I have a pinecone stuck up my ass.

As soon as I hit the kitchen door, Red hands me a cup of coffee and slides me a plate of bacon and eggs.

I don't dare eat. The little button is crying. I sip my coffee instead, waiting for Red to start the conversation.

Red says absolutely nothing for the longest time before he sighs and pours himself another cup. "You packed?"

"No." Not that I have anything to pack.

He frowns. "Why are you all dressed up then?"

This is dressed up? Red needs to get out of Canada more often. "These are Evelyn's clothes. I'm staying another day."

He blinks.

"Dante has asked me to go to town with him."

"No shit," he says, his mouth a giant O. "I mean, no kidding." He squints at me. "The interview went *very* well then."

I smile. "Yes. Much better than I expected."

He looks away. "You two didn't . . . did you?"

We could have if I hadn't been so skittish. "We didn't do any conjugating, Red. We just . . . talked. We did some conversating."

"If you just talked, then why . . ." He shakes his head. "He asked you to town."

"Yes."

He starts to say something but stops.

"Is anything wrong, Red?"

"Dante asked you to town," Red says in a monotone.

"Yes." Now I'm getting as frightened as the button on my pants. "Is, um, is town so bad?"

"Oh, no, no. It's a nice town. Really." He starts to laugh.

"What's so funny?"

He looks to the stairs and then back to me. "Dante only goes to town when Evelyn's here," he whispers.

"I had no idea this meant something," I whisper.

"It does," Red says. "It means everything."

Lelani enters the kitchen and kisses Red on the nose. She looks at me. "All packed?"

"Are you two trying to get rid of me?" I ask.

Red pulls Lelani to him. "Dante and Christiana are spending the day . . . in . . . town."

"No," Lelani says.

"Yes," Red says.

She turns and looks at me with the biggest eyes. "You didn't, um—"

"Geez," I say. "Is that all you two think about? No. We did not sleep together."

Lelani shakes her head. "That's not what I was going to say. I was going to say you didn't finish the interview."

"Oh." How embarrassing. "We did. I'll probably take a few more pictures while we're out."

She looks again at Red. "Dante asked Christiana to town."

Red kisses her forehead. "Yep."

Lelani looks up at Red. "Doesn't this sound like a date to you?"

"It certainly does," Red says. "Unless DJ is going." They both turn and look at me.

"Don't look at me," I say. "I have no idea if he's going or not."

I hear a speedy clomping down the stairs, and Dante appears all fresh and so clean in a nice pair of jeans and a big black sweater. "DJ is still at the island."

I immediately wonder how much he just overheard. I hope he didn't hear—

"How did you sleep, Christiana?" Dante asks.

"Very well," I say.

"Good." Dante grabs an apple from a fruit bowl and polishes it on his sweater. "They did not finish their Risk game. DJ will be at Duels' cottage for the day with his friends." He touches my elbow. "You look very nice."

"So do you." I see Red and Lelani watching us. *"Che?"* I say with attitude.

They fade into the other room, as they should. They know the power of *che.*

Dante moves a strand of my hair off my forehead. "Are you ready to go?"

I haven't had a man touch my hair like that in forever, and I suddenly feel so shy! I suck down the rest of my coffee. "Yes."

He offers his arm.

Now I'm blushing. Geez! I take his arm. *"Andiamo,"* I whisper.

The ski boat whisks us to the Landing where we get into a cavernous blue and white Toyota Land Cruiser, but I am too far away from Dante on the passenger side once we begin traveling up the dirt-and-gravel road.

"Is this new?" I ask.

"Oh no. It is three years old." He points at the odometer. "We have put one hundred and seventy thousand miles on it."

Geez. That's a lot of roadwork. "Where have you been driving to—California and back?"

"Trips," he says. "From here to Syracuse. Trips from Syracuse to Virginia and back."

Trips to see Evelyn, whose clothes I'm stretching to death. And from the number of miles, lots of trips to see Evelyn. "How often do you visit, um, DJ?"

"As often as I can," he says. "Every other weekend, sometimes every weekend."

Weekends with his kid. In Syracuse. Keeping his ex-wife in check. Keeping her from having a social life, too? Anything's possible, I guess.

"I should get me one of these," I say as we bounce along. "So clean."

"Do you have a car?" he asks.

"I've never had a car."

"I did not have one for many years," he says. "Now I cannot see how I lived without one."

A long gray animal shoots across the road. "What was that?"

"A gray fox," he says. "A rare event. They are so secretive."

I smile. "They're so . . . . foxy."

"Yes."

He doesn't say anymore. He was supposed to say, "Foxy, like you." I don't pout, though. I'm going to town with a man.

And my hands are sweaty.

Once we hit Highway 60, he flips through some CDs in the console between us. "You like Sinatra?" he asks.

"Sure," I say. I can name maybe two of Sinatra's songs. "Who doesn't?"

"Which of his songs do you like best?" he asks.

"'My Way,'" I say quickly. The only other one I know is "New York, New York."

He pops in a CD, hits a few buttons, and we listen to "My Way."

When the song ends, he turns down the volume. "You did not sing along."

"Oh, I, uh, I don't sing. At all."

He shakes his head. "Everybody sings."

"I, um, I sing silently."

"Ah. Who do you like best?"

I tell him about Johnny Mathis and Smokey Robinson. He presses a few buttons on his satellite radio receiver. After a medley of Spinners' songs, Smokey's "Cruisin'" comes on.

And Dante sings along flawlessly in a mellow tenor.

My jaw is in my lap.

"What?" he says. "I cannot know this music? It is almost opera to me."

I am beginning to like this man a lot. He doesn't sound a bit like Smokey, but hearing "Cruisin'" with an Italian accent is a panty dampener.

Before we descend into Barry's Bay, we have to stop for construction. A huge machine seems to be chewing up rocks and laying them down behind it as pavement. Unlike construction crews in the States, this work crew includes mostly women.

"Why are there so many women on Canadian construction crews?" I ask.

"I have wondered the same myself." He smiles broadly at a woman holding a walkie-talkie.

"No flirting."

"I smile at everybody." He turns and smiles at me.

"So you flirt with *everybody*."

"*Sì.*"

I frown.

"Oh," he says, "but I will try to only smile for you today, okay?"

Right.

We cruise through Barry's Bay (population twelve hundred) to a stop sign. The main drag reminds me of Van Brunt Street in Red Hook for some reason, only there are no gaping holes in the pavement and ample street parking. We go through the stop sign past Etmanskie's Shell and park on the sidewalk beside what looks like an old train depot.

We get out and cross the road to an antique store full of homemade furniture and art. I marvel at all the handmade you-name-it—chests, chairs, shelving, mirrors, walking sticks, clocks, and assorted yard art. African masks fill the walls, and carved wooden giraffes cavort with lions, tigers, and bears among the end tables. I see a stuffed moose—so cute!—that I just have to have, and Dante buys it for me.

"An early Christmas present," he says.

I immediately name the moose Dante. He'll keep me company in bed tonight if the real Dante doesn't. I compare Dante the Moose's nose with Dante's nose.

Dante the Moose wins.

But not by much.

We continue along the sidewalk and pass a bank and the post office.

"We will stop there last," he says.

"To collect all your fan mail?"

He smiles. "Yes."

"Do you ever get any, oh, naughty pictures?"

He nods. "All the time."

I take his arm. "Are any of them . . . *pericoloso*?"

"Sometimes."

I squeeze that rock-hard bicep. "As dangerous as me?"

He looks straight ahead. "No. But I have yet to get the mail today."

I punch his arm.

Ow.

He doesn't even flinch.

We cross the street at the stop sign and go into Yakabuski's Home Hardware to look at fishing supplies. Though Dante has enough lures to last him and his great-grandchildren for a hundred years, he buys several more.

"I do not have this color," he says, pointing at a shade of yellow green I can best describe as "phlegm."

A few doors down is Steadman's, where he purchases several packs of playing cards.

"The cards have been cruel to me since you have arrived," he tells me. "DJ was on a hot streak after the Boston."

"So . . . you're superstitious?"

"Not really. I spilled soda on the cards, too."

"Oh."

He shrugs. "Maybe you can play with us sometime."

That is the best kind of tug on a girl's heart. "I'd like that."

Back across the street, we go to Lorraine's Pharmacy for vitamins. I show him the over-fifty version of some brand.

"Very funny," he says.

"Just looking out for you," I say.

He takes them from me. "I will get them for Red." He pulls some children's chewable vitamins from the shelf. "These are for Lelani."

I think he's joking, but he adds them to our handbasket.

"Um, Lelani is forty, right?" I ask.

"Yes, but she looks like a child." He shakes the children's vitamins. "And she likes the taste of these."

He stops in front of a massive candy display. He looks at me. "Choose."

I do the only reasonable thing. I take one of every candy bar on that display and put it in the handbasket. "I have a sweet tooth."

We carry our bags and Dante the Moose to Palubiskie Variety, a typical package store to me, where Dante buys more leeches, several packs of hooks, at least fifty sinkers of all sizes and shapes, and another filet knife.

"Pretty confident, aren't you?" I say.

"You can never be prepared enough," he says.

"Ooh," I say. "The fish are scared, Dante. I can feel them trembling at the lake from here."

"We might go out later, and I will show you," he says, leaving the store and crossing the street again.

"What will you show me?" I ask, but I don't think he heard me. He is way too intent on making these errands.

I feel like Billy from *Family Circus*. We've been going up the street, crossing back, backtracking, crossing the street again—there seems to be no plan.

Oh yeah. We're *turisti*.

Back across the street, we go to a trendy little place called Steve's Sports. Inside, I browse some expensive outdoor clothes that I know I couldn't find in Red Hook. I find a fur-lined dark brown leather jacket I really like. I try it on in front of a mirror, and the jacket makes me look as if I have triple Ds. I see Dante watching behind me, so I do a little modeling.

"Pericoloso," he says.

I must have this jacket. I check the tag . . . *ouch.* "Expensive," I tell him, and I hang it back up. I browse some more and find a red, white, and green—how Italian!—flannel shirt. It's extra large, but it is so soft! I take it to the front and see the chest-increasing leather jacket on the counter in front of Dante.

Dante pulls out some of that funny Canadian money.

"It's okay," I tell him. "I don't really need the jacket."

He slides over the flannel shirt and pays the clerk. "A gift. I missed your birthday, didn't I?"

That's so sweet. And thoughtful. And . . . Damn. It's just plain nice. I don't get "nice" like this on any basis.

Let's see . . . We're now carrying a stuffed moose, lures, playing cards, leeches, sinkers, hooks, a filet knife, a flannel shirt, and a fur-lined leather jacket.

I am in danger of becoming a Canadian.

We cross a street and go into Greenfield's ValuMart. We push two carts through the store and fill them with fresh meats, cheeses, four kinds of pasta, ten pounds of tomatoes, bottled water, fresh fruit, and some microwave popcorn.

As Dante pays, I look at all the bags. "Um, Dante?"

"Yes?"

"The truck is a long way away."

"Yes."

We push the carts outside. "I can wait here while you bring the truck down."

He shakes his head. "Load me up."

"You're kidding."

"Load me up. I must still train."

I start handing him bags, and in three minutes, he looks like a white plastic Christmas tree, his arms and hands laden with every bag we have.

I pull out my camera and take several pictures before he notices.

"Hey!" he says, smiling.

"This isn't for the story," I say. "It's for me."

I let him take the lead so I can see his butt working, and I snap shot after shot of his struggles through Barry's Bay. He smiles at or says *"scusi"* to every person who crosses his path.

He stops behind the Land Cruiser, not a single bead of sweat on his forehead. Doesn't this man sweat? "In my back pocket," he says, "are the keys."

I step closer to him. "You want me to put my hands down your pants?"

"Yes," he says. "To get the keys."

I . . . take . . . my . . . time getting those keys.

He puts our booty into the back while the warmth of his booty fades from my hand. "Are you hungry?" he asks.

Very. But not for food.

We stroll arm-in-arm to the Barry's Bay Dairy, an old-fashioned diner with low prices and far too many choices. I get a plate of fries, Dante an ice water with lemon.

"That's all you're having?" I ask him, munching on my fries.

"I could say the same to you," he says.

I look down at the button on my jeans. The button is eyeing me warily. Don't worry, little buddy, I won't have any ice cream.

"I have a problem I must tell you about," Dante says. He pulls out a Sweet Marie candy bar and breaks it in half, handing half of it to me. "I am addicted to these. You will not tell Red?"

"Never."

He peels back the foil and takes a bite. "Mmm. I like *cioccolata*."

And I like that he likes *cioccolata*. "How much?"

"Che?"

"How much do you like *cioccolata*?"

He licks his lips. "I could eat it every day."

I smile. "They say dark chocolate is good for you."

He shrugs. "It is too bitter for me. I prefer sweet *cioccolata*."

"So if you only had one food on earth to eat for every meal, you'd pick . . ."

"Fish," he says.

I nearly fall out of my chair. "Fish?"

"Yes," he says. "Like the fish you caught."

After our little snack, we enter the early September sunshine. "Two more stops," he says.

We go back to the place where I got my moose, this time browsing necklaces. He picks out a simple gold cross.

"That's nice," I say.

He puts it around my neck before I can protest, not that I would have.

"I'm not very religious," I say.

"But you are spiritual," he says. "This is an empty cross. Jesus is in heaven. It will remind you of those who are in heaven. This is a symbol of hope."

Hope. I don't mind having hope hanging around my neck. Such a simple purchase, maybe thirty dollars Canadian, but—and I'm not just saying this because I want to get with this man—it's probably the nicest gift I've ever gotten.

"Grazie," I say.

I like that word.

At the post office, he gets a box full of letters from all over the world. He lets me carry the box to the Land Cruiser, and I see quite a few letters that say, "Photos: Do Not Bend."

I get in the Land Cruiser. "I'll bet these have nasty pictures in them."

"I am sure they do," he says. "You should not open them."

I hold the box as far away from me as I can. "Yeah." They might need to be sprayed with Lysol first.

He points to a letter marked "Photos" on top of the pile. "Open that one."

I carefully open the letter and see pictures of a naked white woman with an Italian flag tattooed way up her thigh. I've always wanted some kind of tattoo, but that one is only a half inch from her vulva. I hope she and the tattoo artist were friends.

"Not my type," he says, making a U-turn and heading back through town and out onto Highway 60. "It is why I throw out letters with photos without looking. Evelyn did not like me getting this mail."

I can see why! The lengths these women go to get Dante's attention.

Okay, I've come pretty far, too, but I would never do anything like this. I mean, a picture may be worth a thousand words, but no picture has any heart behind it. You can't feel heart—or love—from a picture.

"Did you ever get anything like that in your mail?" he asks as we eventually turn down the dirt road.

"No, and I've never sent anything like them either." I know how these kinds of pictures can just "show up" whenever, say, a woman wins the Miss America pageant.

"I am glad," he says.

"Why?"

"I believe beauty . . . and you are beautiful," he says with a wink. "I believe beauty should only reveal herself to one whom she loves, not share it with a world that does not love her or know her. That is why I am glad."

"Do you ever get any, um, fan mail from men?"

"Yes. Most want tickets. Some want to be sparring partners. A few have wanted to just be partners." He shrugs. "I have sex appeal. What am I to do?"

Only in America.

We cross the bridge over a dam, where he slows to a stop and rolls down the window. "I use mail for kindling in the fireplace. I started last night's fire with yesterday's mail."

Interesting use of one's fan mail.

He breathes deeply and smiles. "This is the place DJ

caught his first fish, a little perch." He shakes his head. "He thought he had caught a whale. Nothing but little fish there now." He squints up at the sun. "The weather this year is crazy. It should be colder this time of year. It is almost warm enough for swimming."

"Swimming, as in swimming, not racing to the island."

"Yes," he says. "Soaking. Letting the water soothe our cares away."

I sigh. "It sounds like a plan."

My plan, of course, is to put on my sheer white underwear, no shorts, no bra, and only an Evelyn-sized T-shirt. Once in the water, I will complain vociferously about the cold. Dante is a reasonable man. He won't want me to get hypothermia. He'll swim over to me, hold me, and warm the very cockles of my heart—whatever cockles are.

Once I wade in up to my knees, however, I realize that no amount of cockle warming is going to restart my heart if I submerge my body in this ice bath. "It's as cold as it was yesterday!" I shout.

Dante, who has already dived off the dock, only smiles and splashes water at me. "It is warmer today than yesterday." He swims toward me. "If you stay near the surface, you will be warmer."

I look and check my nipples, comparing them to the goose bumps on my arms. The goose bumps are bigger.

He floats on his back a few yards away. "See? I am in a warm spot."

I try to block his view of my nipply breasts. "No, I don't see."

He reaches a hand to me. "Come. You will get used to it."

Though I am already hypothermic below the knees, I take his hand . . . oh shit, it's freakin' cold!

"Float on your back," he says.

I have never been able to do this. "I'm not built to do that, Dante," I say, teeth chattering. "My booty weighs me down."

He dives under me, and in a moment I am in his arms, my legs and arms stretched out, just my booty in the water supported by one of his knees.

"Is this better?"

I put my arms around his solid neck. "Yeah. A lot better."

"I love this water," he says.

I can tell.

"It is so clear," he says. "I can see so much."

He's checking me out. It warms me up, but just a little. "What can you see?"

His eyes drift to the T-shirt clinging to my stomach. "I have never seen so many goose bumps on a stomach before. I see them everywhere through your shirt. Are you that cold?"

I don't want to leave his arms. "I'll be okay."

His eyes drift to my legs. "They are everywhere." He looks directly at my breasts. "So many." He looks into my eyes. "What will happen if I try to warm up your legs?"

I'll probably have an orgasm. Either that or I'll get even more goose bumps. "I don't know. Why don't you try?"

I watch his hand moving along my leg and nearly jerk out of his arms.

"My hand is cold, yes?"

"Yes!"

"Hmm. We must keep swimming to stay warm then." He turns me toward the rocks. "We will swim around to the other side. There is a rock in the sunlight we can rest on."

He releases me into the water, and I swear my nipples are audibly tearing the fabric of the T-shirt. Instead of swimming alongside him, I latch onto his back, and he swims us around the corner from the dock and to the rocks.

As soon as I step out of the water, my booty hits that warm rock, and it says, *"Grazie."*

"This is much better," I say. "The rocks are warm."

He scoots next to me, his legs touching mine. "Much better. I may have a tan for my fight, yes?"

I laugh. "I doubt it." I put my arm next to his. "You'll have to use a tanning bed to catch up."

He shrugs. "I do not tan very well, so I do not worry about it." He picks up my hand and compares it to his. "You have big hands."

"Thanks."

"I mean that in a good way," he says. "You see, my mama, she had big hands. They helped her make bread. They also helped her keep me in line."

"She spanked you?"

He nods. "Why my *sedere* is so rough today." He smiles. "I deserved every one of them."

I can't believe this choirboy was ever a bad boy. "You were bad?"

"I was a boy," he says. "I did boy things my mama did not like. I only do them once and . . ." He pantomimes a swat. "I learned very quickly."

I let my shoulder touch his. "What lessons did you learn?"

"So many! In the playground, I was very small, maybe three or four, and I hit a little girl in the back. I don't know why I did it, but . . . Mama did not move from her bench. She said, *'Vieni qui.'* I knew I was in trouble. She only said 'come here' when I was bad. She spanked me in front of everybody."

How cute!

"I have not hit a girl since." He grabs my hand. "Oh, but I hit you."

He should be spanked, but if I did spank him, I'd probably break my hand in six places.

He touches my cheek. "How is it?"

"It hurts," I pout.

He winces. "I am still so sorry."

I look at him with what I hope are puppy eyes. "And it still hurts so badly."

He looks down. "I wish I could take it back. It was instinct."

Instinctively, I lift his chin with my hand. "You could . . . maybe, you know, kiss it, make it feel better."

When he raises his head to kiss my cheek, I turn and kiss him softly on the lips.

Then, for whatever reason, I start to shiver. I mean, I'm out of the water. I'm warming up in the sun. I kiss him once on the lips, and my legs start quivering.

"You are shivering," he says.

"I'm . . . I'm not cold," I say. "I'm excited." And I want to kiss him again.

"Oh," he says. "Oh." He leans forward and holds his legs. "Another reason I like it up here. Cold water keeps me from thinking about . . ."

"About what?"

"About sex. I do not have sex in training. It will weaken my knees. My knees are old. All that running around the streets in Brooklyn, all the jumping, all those fights. I must protect my knees."

And I thought I jumped to conclusions easily. "It was just a kiss, Dante."

He drops his eyes. "I have not had a kiss like that in over ten years. It was not just a kiss, Christiana." He slips into the water, sighing heavily. "It meant something."

Did he just . . . ? No. Not from a single kiss. No man . . . well, maybe a man who hasn't had sex or a nice soft kiss in ten years . . .

I think I've just kissed a man who's harder up for sex than I am!

I slide into the water and shiver for real, again draping my arms over his shoulders and leaning on his back. "Take me back."

He swims us to the dock, turns, and lifts me onto the dock with ease. I take a towel and begin drying my hair and covering up my rock-hard nipples, but Dante stays in the water.

"Are you getting out?" I ask.

"In a moment," he says, breathing deeply.

My God, he *did*! He still is! The water *is* clear up here. Dante is pitching an underwater tent right here in front of me. Wow!

"Christiana, I am sorry."

I'm not. Make it dance!

"Why don't you go dry off, put on warm clothes," he suggests. "I will be up in a minute."

He's still, um, up. "Okay." I can't take my eyes off it.

I turn and let the towel fall off my booty, pulling up my T-shirt and wringing it out in front of me. I know he can see my crack perfectly. I glance back.

Yep. The water sure is clear here. That's at least a two-man tent now, for sure. I hold my T-shirt higher, exposing my stomach up to the bottom of my breasts. I look down at my underwear and see, um, mostly what my gynecologist sees.

"Dante?" I coo. Yeah, I'm milking this for all it's worth.

He moves closer to the dock so I can't see his tent. "Yes?"

"Um . . ." I let him look right up in there. "Will you make us a fire?"

"I will, um, make us a fire, yes," he says.

I sit and splay my legs out around him, wringing out my T-shirt even more. "Is there anything I can do to help?"

He spins completely away. "No, Christiana. I will build

a fire for us. You just . . ." He waves his hand toward the cottage.

I stand. "Okay." I start up the stairs, where I grasp the railing tightly with each step. Doesn't he know he's already made a fire inside me?

Inside the guesthouse, I ransack the drawers for the silkiest underwear I can find. None of it fits, but that gives me an idea. I just won't wear any. Since I don't see any kind of fuzz down there, I don't have to shave. The lake water, however, has turned me into serious ash. I lotion my entire body—twice—and pull on some easy-access drawstring sweats. Ignoring my bra entirely, I put on a wifebeater T-shirt that forms to my form deliciously. I decide to go barefoot (more lotion) and let the fire dry my hair naturally.

I want to look wild.

I want to look hungry.

I am *so* hungry.

And if he has a tent, I am going camping.

Chapter 17

I slink up to Dante, who wears far too many clothes, working on the fire and stuffing his mail under the grate. He wears baggy jeans, boots, and a T-shirt under a gray sweatshirt.

They will be my prizes later on.

I hope.

"Red and Lelani have gone out on the town tonight," he says without looking at me.

Good. "Where are they going?"

"To a little restaurant in town. Polish food. Red says it is good. They will not be back until late. Are you hungry? There's some leftover linguini."

Am I hungry? Are most bears Canadian? "Um, where's DJ?"

"The Risk game continues," Dante says. "He will again spend the night at the island."

I sit on the arm of the couch nearest the fireplace, dangling my legs. "Aren't you going to be a little hot?" I ask.

He turns and sees me. He turns back to the fire, poking at the logs with an iron poker.

And yes, I watch him work that poker, and yes, it makes me wet just thinking what he can do to me with *his* poker.

"I am already a little hot," he says.

"Take off your sweatshirt," I say.

He pulls it off without turning and tosses it on another couch.

Prize number one.

He puts the screen in front of the fire and backs away slowly, his leg brushing mine. I was worried I hadn't stuck my legs out far enough.

I grab his hand and fake a shiver. "I'm cold."

He gets the sweatshirt and holds it out to me.

"No," I say.

"Oh."

I stand and pull him to my couch, pushing him gently until he sits. Then, carefully, like a she-wolf, I sit on his lap facing him, wrapping my legs around his back, my arms around his neck.

"Mmm," I say. "I'm warming up already."

I arch my back and lean in until my nose touches his. "You have four more things you must do for me."

"Yes," he says. "What are they?"

"Hold me."

His arms slide from his sides to my lower back and pull me closer to him.

"Bene," I say. *"Molto bene."*

He pulls me even closer, my nipples brushing his chest. "What is the next thing I must do?" he asks.

I flip a strand of hair out of my eyes. "Kiss me."

He kisses my forehead. "Like that?"

I shake my head. "Lower."

He kisses my nose.

I shake my head.

He kisses my chin.

I shake my head.

He kisses my lips, no tongue, just a nice, soft, gentle kiss.

He pulls back. "That is three things. What else?"

It is time. "Could you take me to your room now?" My nipples have popped and probably bruised his chest. My juices are hot, heavy, and swirling. "I want to read my articles."

He lifts me off the couch, but I don't let go with my arms or my legs. "Oh yes," he says. "The articles. We must go read them."

"For motivation," I whisper.

"Yes. For motivation."

By the time we reach his room, my wife-beater is somewhere in the wind, my sweats down at my ankles. Inside the closet, he starts to pull the light string, but I stop him and put his hands on my breasts.

"Squeeze them hard," I whisper.

Oh shit, that feels good.

I tear off his T-shirt, and he begins to suck on my neck. I unzip his pants and worm my hand . . . He's not wearing underwear either! His pants fall to the floor while I stroke him, butting the head of his penis against my stomach. He lifts my right breast and sucks on its nipple, squeezing my left breast to bursting.

Then he crouches in front of me and immediately licks my clitoris with a hot tongue. I can barely stand, so I hold on to his head, pressing his nose against my stomach, while his tongue sets me on fire.

"Figa deliziosa," he says, looking up.

I don't know what he said, but that's all it takes for me to orgasm. I buck against his tongue until my spasms subside.

I grab his head and pull him to his feet while I drop down, gripping solid granite and kissing the tip of his penis. I let my tongue linger on the tip before taking him as far into my mouth as I can, stroking him to orgasm in a matter of seconds. He pulls my hair and cries out in a burst of whispered Italian as ten years of frustration come pouring out of him.

Daa-em. We could have doubled the population of Canada just then.

I pull him to the floor, his penis still throbbing, pushing him onto his sleeping bag and mounting him, digging my booty into his thighs, taking in every inch of him. Everything about this man is hard, and I find myself having difficulty squeezing his chest.

He sits up and kisses my nipples, whispering, *"Capezzoli dolci,"* nibbling them until I scream.

Then I have thundering orgasm number two, an orgasm that shoots out like lightning from my nipples to my toes.

I keep grinding him as he tries to separate my booty from my body.

"I don't want to hurt you," I say. Everywhere I touch is erect, smooth, sweaty, and hot.

"You cannot hurt me," he says. "Do not stop."

So I start bouncing up and down on that magnificent piece of granite between my legs, his hands squeezing my breasts to bursting, my fingers teasing my clit until I squeeze my booty together and come *again*. This time he joins me, and for the first time in my life, I feel like a fucking goddess. It's like I'm flying over Red Hill Park, a kite with a very thick string attached to me, and I'm high above the earth, the heat of the sun on my face, releasing and free-falling into his arms.

We roll over, still joined, and he kisses me with the sweetest tongue, sucking out my breath as he pumps me again, and again, and again . . . deeper and deeper . . .

I chew on his ear, feeling almost like Tyson biting Holyfield, and whisper, "I can't believe you're still hard."

Oh, God, that piston is still pumping!

"I am hard because you are *l'immersione bagnata*. You are soaking wet, Christiana."

I'm so wet I'm drowning.

I stand him up and push him against the wall, Evelyn's picture just to his right. I want to tear it down or at least turn it over, but then again I want her to "watch." I want her to see how a real woman makes love to a real man, how a real woman satisfies a real man.

I back into him, smacking my booty hard into his hips, probably bruising the hell out of my cheeks. He grabs my hair and thrusts, little by little moving *me* across the room to the other wall and away from Evelyn's picture. He raises my hands up high on the wall and fills me completely, thrills me entirely, slamming me into that wall while I scratch that wall before reaching back to spread my cheeks wider to take him all the way home.

"I want all of you, Dante," I pant. "All of you."

"Un bel culo," he says, biting the back of my neck.

We come together again, but this time, we fall to the floor on our sides, our eyes locked in the semidarkness.

"Where's the light coming from?" I whisper.

"The fireplace," he says. "The cracks in the floor. The boards are not so tight."

I place his left hand on my crack. "This crack isn't so tight anymore either."

He laughs softly. "This will not be in your story either."

"Why not?" I smile, not knowing if he can see it or not.

"Who would believe it?" he says. "You are *fantastica,* Christiana."

I slide my right hand over his chest. "You're more than *fantastico,* Dante. You are the ultimate lover."

He kisses my shoulder. "No. You are *amante ultima.*"

I take his viselike left hand in my right. "This is one of my greatest moments. No. This *is* my greatest moment. *Grazie.*"

He places my hand on his chest and runs his left hand down my side, leaving behind goose bumps wherever he touches. *"Fantastico corpo celeste.* Like *scultura."*

I don't know what he's saying, but his hot hand feels wonderful.

"I want to turn on the light to see all of you," he says.

I want to see all of him, too, so I rise, turn on the light, and see Adonis, David (the sculpture), a freaking *god.* I have never seen a body so well proportioned, so solidly built. His muscles have muscles. His ripples have ripples. The veins in his arms pulsate with life.

He looks me up and down, turning me slowly. *"La mia Venere dolce. Perfetto."* He reaches around and touches my smooth pussy. *"Levigato."* He spins me around as if I weigh an ounce, dropping and kissing just above my clitoris. "Ah. *Lentiggine."*

He is working me up again. *"Che?"*

"Freckles." He kisses them, his lips moving lower. "Tiny little *lentiggine."*

"Kiss them all," I wheeze, and in seconds, his tongue is all up in me again. This time I use my fingers to tighten my clit, and I come even harder than before.

Has anyone ever died during an orgasm? I mean, besides old men who marry twenty-year-olds for "love."

I lie on the bare floor while Dante traces circles around my nipples with his fingers and his tongue. The floor is cool on my skin, his fingers become flames, and his tongue keeps my nipples as erect as he *still* is.

I love Canada. They have natural Viagra in the water.

He rolls over onto his back, only our fingers touching now. "I have broken training."

I roll over, kissing his chest and resting my sweaty head on his shoulder. "I don't know. I'll bet we worked off that candy bar just now." I look down and see his granite penis waving to me. If they made a cast of that, the Dante Dildo would be the best-selling dildo of all time.

He strokes my hair, kissing me on top of my head. "We also worked off lunch, breakfast, yesterday's dinner. . . ."

"I like this room," I say.

"I will never look at this room the same way again."

I let my hand wander to his abs. "A window would be nice."

"It was originally a closet. I could maybe put in a skylight."

I drift my hand below his navel, tangling and untangling his pubic hair, occasionally brushing his shaft with the tips of my fingers. "A skylight would be nice."

"Yes, it would."

I grip his granite, moving my hand up and down.

"Christiana," he whispers.

"Make love to me, Dante."

I shiver as he enters me, and my hands find his ass, gripping those fists of his back there. He bends me so my feet rest on his shoulders, and then he plunges in and holds it there.

"Make love to me now," he says. "I will not move."

I squeeze, grind, and practically stroke his penis with everything inside me, speeding up until he comes and calls out my name.

So much for slower and less rushed.

He turns me over and begins rubbing my back. "Have I done all five things yet?"

I must be crazy. "No. Only four."

He squeezes my shoulders, working out the kinks in my neck, his penis growing harder and harder. I feel it slipping between my cheeks.

"I feel you, Dante."

"I cannot help it, Christiana," he whispers. "I cannot get enough of your *bel culo*."

Oh shit. Oh shit. I've never done it this way before. Oh shit . . . "Lower," I say.

"Sorry."

Whew. His penis is back inside me correctly, but if anything, he's bigger than before. If he goes any farther, I'll crack in two.

His sweat drips onto my back. "The best what?"

Oh, now the shaft, it's so fucking deep inside me. "The best massage . . ."

He thrusts it all the way in, and I thrust my ass back at him, and damn if I don't have the Northern Lights shoot through my entire body!

After he pulls out of me, I turn and grab him, holding him tightly.

"I did not hurt you, did I?" he asks.

"No." How do I tell him that I just had the all-time greatest orgasm any woman anywhere in world history has ever had?

"You are *dea del sesso.*"

"What's that mean?"

"You are a sex goddess."

"And you are a sex god." I reach down and feel his hardness. "Did you take Viagra or something?"

"No," he says. "You make me this hard. When we were on the rocks, I was this hard. When we got back to the dock and I looked at your . . . *figa,* your . . ."

"I'm a big girl."

"I looked at your pussy after I lifted you onto the dock and your *culo* as you walked away. I could not leave the water until it had gone away. Now that I am so close to you, I do not want it to go away."

He reaches over and grabs the sleeping bag, unzipping it quickly. He helps me inside and somehow zips us in. I hold his penis in my hands as the sweat starts to build.

"I want you again," I whisper. I want to possess this man.

"But you must be tired. . . ."

I put my finger on his lips. "I'm not tired, Dante." I pull him inside me as sweat drips from his forehead. I reach around to his ass and pull it closer.

The rest of him slides inside thanks to more sweat and our juices. I grab his booty with both hands and guide him deeper. The pain and the pleasure are exquisite.

He finds his rhythm, I scratch his ass, and then he fucks me. I'm not talking making love, making whoopee, or having sex. Dante Lattanza *fucks* me hard until I scream.

And it's good. It's the way a god and goddess are supposed to go at it.

"You have to be tired," I say, stroking his face. I have lost count of my orgasms and have totally lost track of the time.

"I have much stamina," he says.

I notice a light under the door. "Look how light it is out there."

"It is the sunrise," he says. "We have made love all night."

All night long.

"Dante, we weren't exactly making love the whole time."

"I am sorry," he says, his eyes looking sad. "I got carried away."

I grasp his face with both my hands. "No, no, it's all right. All of it was all right. You made love to me passionately, and when I wanted you to fuck the shit out of me, you fucked the shit out of me."

"It is a vulgar word," he says.

"What is?"

"Fottere."

I graze his booty with my fingernails. "You're very good at *fottere.* In fact, it was the best fo-tear I ever had."

He laughs. "Fo-tear is not a word." He stretches his back and groans.

"Oh, how are your knees?" I ask.

"Stronger. And how is your . . ."

"Both my *figa* and my *culo* are sore."

He sighs.

"But," I add, "they are happy and wanting more."

He stares at my breasts. "I thought I would break you in two."

I nod. "You did, but then you put me back together again." I sit up. "Damn, I'm hungry."

"Me, too," he says. "I would like some fish. Would you like some fish?"

"Didn't we eat it all?"

"Hmm." He rubs his eyes. "Yes. I will go catch us some fish. You go and bathe."

I need to soak my *figa* and *culo* for a while.

"By the time you are done, I will have two nice bass for us."

I smile. "You're going to cook for me?"

He shakes his head. "You do not want me to cook for you. I turn everything I cook black and crispy. I will clean them, though."

I kiss his cheek. "Okay."

He helps me to my feet and hugs me. "*Buon giorno,* Christiana."

I hug him back. "*Buon giorno,* Dante."

I . . . could . . . get . . . used . . . to . . . this.

Ow.

My booty . . .

Chapter 18

I soak in the two-seater, my feet propped up on the other seat, and let the hot bubbles soothe my aching thigh muscles, my poor *figa,* and my bruised *culo.* Bubbles and jets tingle me instantly, and I start to think about him inside me. In seconds, I set an all-time personal best for orgasms in a *month.*

In less than ten hours.

Buon giorno, indeed.

If just the *memory* of his body gives me an orgasm, I will be having waking wet dreams for weeks!

I throw on some more of Evelyn's sweats, once again with no underwear. I drift into the kitchen, make myself some Red Rose tea with extra sugar, and curl up in a chair looking out the picture windows at Turkey Island and the lake. Fall colors only an impressionist painter could duplicate. Peaceful waves, a pink and orange sun. It's as if God used a sponge and pressed colors into those mountains.

My hands are still sweaty. Geez, I'm fifteen again and have a crush on a cute guy.

Red comes in. "Are you leaving today?"

Is this his only concern? "Good morning, Red."

"Sorry. Good morning, Christiana."

I stretch. "No. I may never leave. I like it here. I have a bunch of vacation days saved up. I can work on my stories, maybe do a little more fishing . . ."

"Conjugate some Italian verbs . . ."

I smile. "Does it show?"

"It doesn't have to show. Sound travels around here."

"Che?"

"I'm sure we weren't the only folks to hear you two."

Oh my goodness! "You . . . listened?"

"We couldn't help hearing you," Red says. "Lelani's jealous."

I thought that closet was soundproof!

"I'm really . . ." I sigh. "I am so embarrassed right now."

Red sits in a chair next to me. "Don't be."

I replay last night and this morning. How loud were we? Did the sounds of our lovemaking echo around the lake?

"I have some news," Red says, looking suddenly serious.

"Is it good news or bad news?" I ask.

"It's just . . . news. Take it whatever way you want to." He exhales a long time, forcing a tight smile. "Evil Lynn is on her way here to pick up DJ a few days early."

"On her way . . . from Syracuse?" I feel a tinge of stress, but just a tinge.

"No."

The tinge becomes a pull. "From Ottawa?"

"She drives up, comes through the Thousand Islands." He looks at me. "She's driving through Barry's Bay as we speak."

The pull becomes a panic. "Holy shit!" I sit up. "But school doesn't start till after Labor Day, right? She shouldn't have to come up till Saturday or Sunday."

"She likes to surprise us."

What a . . . *shitty* surprise! I just get some, and here *she* comes. She has to be past Barry's Bay by now. I hope she gets stuck behind all that construction on 60. Maybe the pavement-eating machine will mistakenly chew her up. Shit! She's going to be here in less than half an hour!

"What am I supposed to do, Red?" I ask.

He smiles at me. "Want to surprise her back?"

"How?"

"Go with me to the Landing when I pick her up."

"No." I stand. "I have to clean up the guesthouse." I look at the sweats. "And I'm wearing her clothes! And the ones in the guesthouse smell like . . . They smell like Dante, Red."

"Lelani is taking care of all that," Red says. "Relax. Lelani will do the laundry, and we'll somehow sneak it all back without Evelyn knowing it. Don't worry. Sit. Finish your tea."

I sit. "Should I leave?"

"What for?"

Oh, I can think of several reasons, chief among them . . . "The queen is coming back to her castle."

He rolls his eyes. "Does Dante want you to leave?"

"He better not." Not after last night and this morning and, damn, I wanted more of him later today and tonight and tomorrow morning, too.

"So," Red says, "you've decided to stay."

"Yes."

"Good," Red says. "Just don't be too surprised if you see some changes in Dante. He's a whole different person whenever she's around."

"Why would he change? I mean, after last night . . ."

"Maybe you've broken her hold over him," Red says. "I hope you have. I would love to see him happy for a change."

I sigh. "Maybe I *should* go. You told me there's a lot of drama when she's around." I don't want any drama from DJ's mama.

"And until now, there's been no one to stop her," Red says. "Christiana, Evil Lynn is Salome, Jezebel, the Wicked Witch of the West, and Mata Hari all rolled into one. Someone has to be here to stand up to her. She's Dante's albatross, his Sisyphean stone, his—"

"You read a lot, Red."

"I have lots of time to do it up here." He looks out over the water. "Christiana, *you* are what Dante needs. He doesn't need her."

"What do I do?"

He throws out a jab. "Take it to her, champ. Show her who the boss is."

"While wearing her clothes?"

He shakes his head. "While wearing the *hell* out of her clothes." He bites his lip. "Lelani recommends you wear as little as possible so you, um, so you can let it all hang out. Her words, not mine."

I like the sound of that. "How cold is it out there?"

"About forty-five."

Damn. "Is what I'm wearing going to be enough?"

He turns away. "Doesn't leave much to the imagination."

Oh yeah. I have no drawers or bra on. "Isn't that good?"

"What's good for Dante is good enough for me," Red says. "But Christiana, brace yourself. Evil Lynn is not stupid. She will know what's up the second she sees you in her clothes. You think you can handle her?"

"I hope I can."

I mean, after all, I'm a middleweight, and Evelyn's only an itty-bitty flyweight.

Chapter 19

While Red tears off in the ski boat to get Evelyn and I fight off panic attacks on a couch in front of the fireplace, Lelani slides through the great room with a suitcase.

"You're not leaving, are you?" I ask.

"Didn't Red tell you?" she says. "When Evil Lynn's here, we go. By the way, you'll have to return her clothes to her. You wore so many, and I had to wash one pair of sweats twice."

Oh, that's just great.

"Your clothes and her clothes are in the dryer at our cottage. I didn't find much in the way of underwear, though. I wonder why." She giggles and gives me a hug. "Thank you both for last night."

"Che?" I seem to be saying that a lot lately.

"It was kind of like listening to porno, you know? Fired Red and me right up. You have to *come* around more often."

I am so embarrassed. "You were listening to us the whole time?"

"Let's just say that when I finally wore out Red, and he

went to sleep, I, um, had a little fun out on our couch while you two were humping." She raises her eyebrows. "You must be gifted or something, Christiana. You worked him *good*, girl."

I'm more than embarrassed now. I am mortified. "You can't leave, Lelani."

"I have to."

"Why?"

"*Eve*lyn has always been trouble, and the two of you will be nothing but more trouble. I don't want no trouble. It'll be much quieter in Montreal."

I grab her arm. "Lelani, you can't leave. I'll have no one to protect me."

"DJ will protect you."

"He's not here now," I say, squeezing her arm. "He's still over at the island."

"He'll show up, and he will protect you." She looks down at my hand. "You have huge hands."

I withdraw my huge hand from her arm. "Why would he side with me over his own mama? No child would do that."

"C'mon, girl, DJ likes you. I'll bet he even has a little crush on you."

"How do you know?"

"I watched some of your workout, and DJ couldn't take his eyes off you. And Dante is genuinely happy. I doubt DJ has seen him this happy *ever*."

That might be true, but . . .

"You are also so much more the mother DJ wishes he had. You have encouraged DJ more in two days than Evil Lynn could do in two years. She never goes fishing or hiking with them, and there you were, catching lots of fish and climbing a mountain. Evelyn also doesn't want DJ boxing at all."

The witch! "Why not? He's a natural. He'll probably be better than his father."

She looks around. "I wouldn't say that too loudly if I were you."

You're not me. "Has she said as much to DJ?"

She shrugs. "It's mostly in the face she makes whenever DJ works out with Dante." She makes a severely mean face, her eyes fierce. "She wants him to become an accountant or lawyer or doctor or something."

I shudder. The doctor and lawyer wish I can understand, but an accountant? What sixteen-year-old boy wants to push numbers his entire life?

"Where's Dante?" Lelani asks.

I smile shyly. "He's out fishing for my breakfast."

"Very cool."

"I know." And then I realize that whatever we catch, we'll probably have to share with Evelyn.

Lelani's eyes are dancing, and she won't stop grinning at me.

"How can you be so happy and so calm about all this?" I ask. "The enemy is coming!"

"Let's see," she says. "Hmm. Well, there's really only one reason."

"And that is?"

"It ain't happening to me. *Ciao*."

I follow her to the dock, where she places her suitcase next to a duffel bag. Lelani is really leaving. I suddenly feel so alone. We both look across the lake and see a boat approaching.

"There she is," Lelani says.

I can't see Evelyn, but I can sense her evil presence. It's as if I'm in a horror movie waiting for the final showdown with the Shrew from Syracuse.

"Nervous?" Lelani asks.

"Yes." I can't keep still.

"She'll be nervous once she sees you in all your . . ."

"My what?"

She steps closer. "Girl, I can see every part of you through those sweats. She will be able to see every part of you, too."

"I don't look like a hoochie, do I?"

She laughs. "Maybe a hoochie is what Dante needs."

"Che?"

"I'm joking. You look fine." She hands me a piece of paper. "This is Red's cell number. Just don't use it tonight, okay?"

I stuff the number into a pocket. "I won't."

"I intend to put a hurting on my man," Lelani says, "and I don't want to be interrupted."

The ski boat coasts into the dock, and I catch the front, expertly tying the boat down while Red ties the back.

A figure rises from a seat, clutching a Coach bag and wearing jeans, boots, and a heavy winter parka with a furry hood. Either she's huge under that coat, or Evelyn is anorexic.

"Hi," I say cheerfully. "I'm Christiana Artis from *Personality* magazine."

Evelyn steps out of the boat. "I was not aware that Dante was giving interviews."

"We finished our interview last night," I say.

Evelyn blinks at Lelani's suitcase. "And now you're leaving."

This is priceless! "No. Lelani and Red are leaving."

Evelyn turns her head slowly toward me. I get a vision of that girl in *The Exorcist*. I hope Evelyn doesn't projectile vomit on me.

I smile. "How long are you staying, *Eve*lyn?" Saying her name is a chore, but I'm trying to be polite. For now.

Evil Lynn blinks again. She must have something in her eyes. I watch her eyes narrow to little dots as she focuses on my sweats.

"Oh, I hope you don't mind if I borrowed some of your

clothes," I say as genuinely as I can. "Dante said it would be all right. I wasn't planning to stay overnight two days ago, so I didn't pack any clothes. They're a little tight, though. I hope I didn't stretch them too much. I'll be sure to wash them before I go."

I expect her to say, "The nerve!"

Evelyn shows more restraint than I would have. "And when will you be leaving?" she asks.

If school starts on Tuesday, then Evelyn would have to leave on Monday at the latest. "Monday night."

Boom. Take that.

Evelyn's mouth moves in an attempt to speak. Once again, she turns to Red, who quietly pulls her bags from the ski boat and puts Lelani's suitcase and his duffel bag into the boat.

"I've been staying in the guesthouse," I say. "It's really nice."

Evelyn's little eyes pop. I have to be winning this round. What must be going through her head!

"Oh," I add in my sad voice, "but I'll be staying at Red and Lelani's while they're gone." I step closer to Evelyn. "Do you need any help with your baggage?"

Her eyes pop again. Man, I am good with the jabs.

"I think I can manage, thank you," she says.

Red's eyes cut toward the lake. He wants to escape. Lelani is already in the boat and untying the back.

"Red, I hope you and Lelani have a wonderful time." I pick up two of Evelyn's bags. "I don't mind helping."

Red starts the boat while Lelani unties the front. "Good to see you, *Eve*lyn," he says. Then he backs out the boat and takes off across the lake.

Once the boat is out of range, all I hear are the waves tapping the dock.

I hold up Evelyn's bags, and they are seriously heavy. "Ready?"

She picks up the remaining bag and smiles. "I always overpack for up here. Sorry."

I swing them around and head to the stairs. "No problem."

I carry her bags up the stairs. I am surprised I can even walk up the stairs at all because my booty is so sore. I take the bags directly to the guesthouse while she lags far behind. I snicker. Evelyn's out of shape. Ha! I open the door and smile. Lelani has returned the room to exactly the way it was when I got here. I set Evelyn's bags on the bed, looking for anything Lelani might have missed. I only brought a laptop case, camera bag, and myself, so . . .

Evelyn walks into the guesthouse, blocking the door, mainly with her puffy coat. If I sneeze, she might fall over.

"I'll leave you to freshen up," I say.

She doesn't move. "I don't mean to be rude, but what exactly is going on here?"

She's getting out her claws. I check my nails. Hmm. My claws need some work. "Why does there have to be anything going on? I came to interview Dante for our sexyman issue. I only planned to be here for a day, but Dante asked me to stay a while longer."

She almost drops her bag. "Dante asked . . . you . . . to stay?"

I take a giant step toward her and stop. "Yes." I look at her boots. Nice boots. "You're just here to pick up DJ, right?"

She unzips her coat, revealing . . . Where's the rest of her? She can't weigh more than ninety pounds. She puts the *pet* in *petite*. And she wears a size six? Maybe she's lost some weight. Is there a size zero? Or even a size *negative* one?

"I am also here to see my husband," she says, finally dropping her bag.

I take a baby step this time. "Ex. He's your ex-husband."

She removes her coat and tosses it on the chair under the window. "If Dante beats Tank Washington, we are getting remarried. I'm sure he told you."

I squint. Either she isn't thinking straight, or she doesn't yet see me for the threat that I am.

"He *did* tell you, didn't he?" she asks.

"Yes."

She smiles, but I can tell it's a shaky smile, worry lines creasing her forehead. "We've been planning this all through his comeback." She pauses. "You aren't writing any of this down."

Huh?

"You're interviewing me, right?" she asks. "For my side of all this. For the story you're writing."

Well, I guess I could interview her, but I'd rather try to disarm her. "I hadn't planned to." It ain't all about you, *Evel*yn.

"Maybe later." She goes to the bed and unzips a bag.

Maybe never. "Didn't you just say '*if* Dante beats Tank'?"

She doesn't answer right away. "I thought I said 'when.'"

"You said 'if.'"

She sits on the bed. "It's quite a long shot, right?"

"You want him to win, don't you?" I ask.

She nods. "Of course I do."

"Well, Dante *will* beat Tank," I say. "There's no 'if' about it."

She shakes her head. "I hope you're right." She looks out the window. "Where is he, by the way?"

He's fishing for my breakfast. "Fishing."

She smiles. "Oh. The man sure loves to fish. He'll be working out later, though, right? I like to watch him work out."

This is *not* going the way I want it to. She's actually a nice person—so far—and I'm not scoring any points. I want to tell her all about Dante's training and his long workout last night with me that only ended a few hours ago. I want to say things that will clamp her little mouth shut. I want to tell her Dante is out fishing for *me*.

"Um," I say instead, "I have some batter to prepare. I'm sure he'll catch something."

"You're cooking for us? How sweet."

Yeah. How sweet.

I leave the guesthouse, letting the door slam behind me. What the hell just happened? I'm dressed in her clothes, I'm wearing said clothes so much better than she ever could, and I'm obviously overstaying my welcome. Is she that clueless? Or is she playing with me? I need to put the bitch down for the count, but how?

While I make a smaller batch of Red's famous Lime Pine Batter, I frown at myself. After my conversation with Evelyn, I'm not sure who the worse bitch is, her or me. I wish she had cussed or used improper English. I wish she had stuck her nose in the air. I wish she had growled at me—something. She probably doesn't know how, being from Syracuse and all. Syracuse must be a quiet place.

I look out the window over the sink. "C'mon, Dante," I whisper. "Come home."

I am getting so domestic, but I want this. I can see why DJ and Red protect Dante so much. I mean, he's lovable. He's a lovable man who just happens to be a boxer. He's a boxer and a gentleman. That might make for a nice movie. Dante is a hero to his son and to so many other people. He's nothing but a possession to Evelyn. I just cannot believe she actually said, "If Dante wins"! What kind of a woman says that about the man she plans to remarry?

"C'mon, Dante," I say to the big iron skillet. "I'm hungry. It's time for you to come home."

Dante is a man to me. A man. There are damn few of them around these days. It's not just his rock-hard abs and everything else that rocked my world until the sun rose today. He is a man I can—

I have to grasp the sink.

Dante Lattanza is a man I want to cook for, and for the rest of my life.

Not only do I want to take Evelyn's place, I want to take Red's place as well.

What did Shelley say? That Italian men want to possess their women? I want to *own* Dante Lattanza. I want to possess him. I want to say to the world that he's mine. Hands off, ladies, the boy is mine.

I hear a boat motor!

Finally.

I run out to the outcropping and wave at him, a big old goofy smile on my face. He smiles and holds up two fingers. Yes! Two fish! Which *he* will clean. Yes again!

Then his smile changes, his eyes darting to my left. I look behind and see Evelyn waving one of her sticks—I mean, one of her hands. I step back to her and see she has changed into a nice sweat suit. She has absolutely no chest, an okay figure, but not much of a booty. She is nowhere near a *corpo provocante,* though she does have a cute face framed by shoulder-length hair.

Dante and boat vanish from our sight, the motor throttling down. I start for the stairs. I have no idea what I'm doing. There is so much I want to say to Evelyn to slow her roll, to let her know that her man and I rolled around all night, that I left scratch marks up in his room, that I—

The boat motor cuts off. I let her get by me and see the fishing boat drifting into the dock. I look down at Dante. Damn. I've never seen him grimace like that before.

I follow Evelyn down the stairs at a leisurely pace. I shouldn't have to hurry. I am almost in total control of this situation. When I get down to the dock, I say, "Show me what you caught, Dante."

Dante reaches into the live well and pulls up . . . two fat females. How fitting. For one of us anyway.

Though I don't really want to, I say, "Hand them to me, and I'll start cleaning them."

He hands me the fish. "On leeches," he says.

"See," I say. "Little leeches catch big fish." I look at the bigger fish. "How much did this one weigh?"

"Only four pounds," he says. "Not as big as yours."

This is going so well. We have effectively ignored Evelyn, and we're talking about fishing, something Dante just loves to—

"I decided to surprise you, Dante," Evelyn says.

Dante looks at his feet. "You are early." He hands the cutting board and filet knife to me. "But it is a nice surprise."

Say what?

"I checked the weather report," Evelyn says. "It's supposed to be warm through Sunday. I thought we could do things together as a family, while the weather's still cooperating. We could go for a hike after lunch, couldn't we? And maybe later tonight you, DJ, and I could do a little fishing."

"We will see," Dante says.

Oh. So *that's* how she's going to play it. She can't compete with me physically or sexually, so she's focusing on reuniting the family unit. Evelyn hiking or fishing? *Impossibile!* Hmm. Maybe they could use her for bait if they run out of leeches.

I go to the shallow end of the dock, kick off my boots, roll up my sweats, and drop into the water, laying the cutting board on the dock. I hold up and break the neck of the first fish while Evelyn watches. A beautiful spray of blood spews into the air.

Evelyn looks away. "Why don't you get out of the boat, D?"

D? He's Dante. What is this "D" shit?

Dante hesitates. I would, too. There are two women on his dock. The woman he just slept with holds a filet knife. The other cut out his heart once. Dante may be in that boat for a long time—

Dante gets out, gives Evelyn a brief hug, and returns to the boat, unloading his bait and fishing poles. Just a "she's the mother of my child" hug. Didn't last more than a second. No kisses. Good.

I focus on the fish in front of me. I'm getting better at this cleaning stuff and have the first fish's guts out on the cutting board in no time. I squeeze a sac that is probably the fish's intestines, and out pops what's left of two little crayfish. "*Dante*, this one had two crayfish in her stomach."

Dante nods. "I lost two bigger ones on my top-water lure."

I smile. "Were they really bigger than the lure?"

He nods. "A little bigger."

"I wish I had gone," I say, shooting glances at Evelyn. We're ignoring her again, and it's so cool.

Dante sighs. "Christiana, when is your flight?"

I peel back the skin from one side and freeze. Is he trying to get rid of me? He had better not be. "Oh, I've decided to stay through Monday evening. If it's all right. I'll be at Red's while they're gone. I hope you don't mind."

Dante steps out of the boat in front of Evelyn. "How was your drive?"

I say "I hope you don't mind" and he gets out of the boat and asks Evelyn how her drive was. Doesn't he know that when someone says, "I hope you don't mind," the proper response is, "No, darling with the *figa delizioso,* I do not mind at all"? Doesn't he know he's supposed to ask me, "Will you mount my throbbing, granite penis now?"

"My drive was pleasant," she says in a mousy voice. "Hardly any traffic. You look good, D." She kisses his cheek.

I grip the filet knife tighter. Doesn't she know I'm armed? I flash the reflection of the filet knife across her face, but she doesn't notice.

"You look *really* good, D," she says.

"Thank you," he says. He doesn't say, *"Grazie."*

Red was right. Dante is changing before my eyes. I wish I knew some black magic to counteract her spell.

While I finish the first fish and start butchering the second, Dante gathers up his poles, tackle boxes, and the worm and leech containers. I can't catch his eyes. What's going on? What is going through his head right now?

I need him to look at me. "Dante, do you still have any aluminum foil in there?" I ask.

He tosses me a roll of foil with the briefest of glances.

"Grazie." I say it for him. I wrap up the filets and announce, "Well. I have to get up to the kitchen and start cooking. I think we have enough here for three."

Evelyn seems to shudder. "Oh, I don't eat fish from this lake."

I smile. "More for us, then."

Dante doesn't smile at me. He barely even looks at me. "We'll be up in a minute," he says.

"Sure." I hand him the cutting board and knife, searching for his eyes. "Take your time."

I strut up those steps, my booty swinging left and right to a bongo beat, willing myself not to look back. There's nothing going on behind me, nothing at all. He's mine, and that's what he's telling Evelyn right now. "Evil Lynn," he's saying, "I am much in love with Christiana, so it would be good of you to shrivel up and die now."

I look back. They're embracing for more than a second.

I look away.

Well.

Isn't that a pretty kettle of fish?

I sigh. They *do* have a child together. They're just friends. That's all. It's a friendly little hug. That's all it is.

I look back from the top of the stairs.

She is still hugging him. Dante, though, has his hands at his sides. I guess that's something.

At the top of the stairs, I giggle because she has to smell *me* on him. He didn't take a shower before he left. She's hugging on him and smelling *me*.

I can relax.

She didn't have him inside her just three short hours ago. She didn't have him counting her freckles down there. She wasn't stroking him and kissing him and—

Geez, I'm making myself wet again.

No. I have nothing to worry about.

Because the skillet is already hot, the filets sizzle in the butter as soon as they land. I pour only two glasses of orange juice and prepare only one plate.

Dante and I are going to share.

I can't believe Evelyn didn't ask even *once* about DJ. She came all this way to get him, and then she doesn't even *mention* his name. I wish she didn't have radar, though. I wish she didn't have whatever it was that made her wake up this morning and say, "I'm going to mess up Dante's life again." The second that Dante is finally happy, she drops in to spoil it.

But, I think, smiling, she didn't count on me being here, did she? Either this day is going to suck for our little *Eve*-lyn, or it's going to suck even more.

I look at the sizzling white filets in the big black pan.

I smile.

Everything I look at this morning reminds me of last night.

Chapter 20

The filets, however, get cold by the time Dante comes inside alone, sips his orange juice, and has one little filet without even sitting at the table.

"Are you okay?" I ask.

"I will be fine." He finishes his juice. "Her timing is . . . unfortunate."

I nod, leaving my seat and moving closer to him. "You've hardly eaten anything. Are they too cold?"

"I am not hungry," he says. "Maybe later." He takes a few steps away from me and toward the kitchen. "I am going up the hill to work out."

That was obvious. "Um, do you want some company? Someone to help you sweat?"

"I will only do a light workout today."

In other words, no, he wants to be alone. "I'm up for a light workout," I say. I want to be alone *with* him.

"You rest, Christiana."

I want to hug him, kiss him, something. "You seem so far away." Literally. For every step I take toward him, he takes a step away from me.

He looks at the bottom step of the stairs. "I will only be up the hill."

I take two giant steps before he can move, putting my hand on his shoulder. "I meant that you seem distant, you know. Far away."

He looks out the window in the kitchen door. "She has that effect on me."

At least he's aware of it. "Why? Why do you let her have that effect on you?"

He shakes his head and sighs. "I wish I knew." He steps away from my hand and trudges up the stairs. A few moments later, he comes down wearing shorts, running shoes, and a tank top.

"I'll, um, I'll just . . . rest then," I say.

"Bene," he says, and without a kiss, hug, or smile, he leaves through the kitchen door and is out of sight.

What have I gotten myself into here? Should I stay?

Tenere provare. I can't leave. I can't give up.

I take several deep breaths.

Tenere provare.

While Evelyn naps or restores her evil powers in the guestroom, I make a few casts off the dock and catch nothing but sun. I look up the hill behind the cottage every so often hoping to see Dante coming back from his workout. They say a watched pot never boils. Well, a watched Canadian hillside never spits out Italian boxers.

I quit fishing and take a walk down a narrow path past Dante's cottage, occasionally hearing the sounds of popping leather. It's no light workout at all. He's up there pounding the leather. I want to sneak up to watch. I want to run up there and wrestle him to the ground. I want him inside me again and again and again . . .

I can wait. I'm a big girl. This will all work out. I just have to stay busy.

I go inside Red and Lelani's cottage and rescue Evelyn's clothes from the dryer, folding them neatly and trying hard not to fall asleep. I hang up my clothes above the dryer, clipping my underwear and bra to a hanger as well. I return with the stack of Evelyn's clothes, setting them on a couch. If she wants them, she can come get them. I am just going to lie down and rest for a few minutes. . . .

I start dreaming the second I fall asleep, and at first, it is a very nice dream. Dante is there, of course. We're getting busy, oh yes, and he's thicker, longer, and harder than anything I've ever had inside me before. For some reason he is fascinated by a little tattoo on my thigh. I even have an Italian flag tattoo between my breasts. Suddenly, I notice Evelyn standing over us holding a steno pad and a pencil and taking notes. "No," she says, "not that way." She tries to pull my leg over my head, but I don't bend that way. "Here," she says, pushing Dante off me, "let me show you." While I watch, I see Dante wrapping Evelyn's stick legs behind her head and plunging deep inside her. She turns to me with a wicked smile and says, "You don't know what you're doing."

Even though I wake up wet, it is by far the worst dream I've ever had.

After changing into another pair of sweats, I notice the time. Three-thirty? I slept through lunch. I listen for any sign of Dante and hear nothing but the wind whooshing overhead. I pad into the kitchen to see what I can cook to knock Dante's clothes, I mean, socks off again. Leafing through an overstuffed three-ring binder of Red's recipes, I find one for pizza titled "The Dante Special."

Yes. We will have homemade pizza from scratch.

I chop three kinds of peppers and sweet onions, brown some sausage, and create a tasty pizza sauce using Roma tomatoes, tomato paste, and a heavy dose of oregano. I use my big hands to make and roll out the dough into two huge rectangles, mounding the dough with the toppings and at least three pounds of mozzarella. I hope the wind will carry the aroma through the pine trees up to Dante.

I don't see a single soul while the pizza is cooking. Not Dante. Not Evelyn. Not DJ. I am more of a guest than Evelyn is, yet here I am in the kitchen. I want to cook for this man, but I don't want to be *her* cook, too. I set the dinner table and keep the pizzas warming in the oven.

I may be the only one who sits at the table and eats.

When DJ finally returns around four-thirty, he is starving.

"Did you win?" I ask.

He shakes his head. "David and his brother made a secret deal to annihilate me, but I lasted a long time. Did you meet my mama?"

I nod. I have to restrain myself here. I can't have this child hating me for hating his mama.

"I wonder why she came up so early. I wasn't expecting her till Sunday." He shrugs. "What smells so good?"

I load that child up with six slices of pizza, but instead of sitting at the table, he carries his plate and a soda up to his room.

Alone again.

What am I doing here? Where's Evelyn? Does she take five hours to recharge her venom or what? And why is Dante taking so long? It's been close to seven hours!

Time for another walk.

I don't get five steps out of the house when I hear a splash. I stand at the top of the stairs and see Dante swimming and Evelyn sitting on the edge of the dock wearing that stupid winter parka and dangling her toes in the water. That's . . . bizarre. They don't seem to be speaking to each other, but the whole scene looks comfortable. It's as if this is part of some custom, some routine they have. I watch as he soaps himself up, dives under, and repeats the process with some shampoo a few feet from her dangling toes.

The bitch is watching Dante take a bath.

I don't want the bitch to watch Dante taking a bath.

I throw open the kitchen door and yell, "I made some pizza! Anybody hungry?"

Only Dante answers. "We will be right up."

An *hour* later (time doesn't fly in Canada when you're horny and confused), they join me at the dinner table for some warmed-up filets and the pizza. Evelyn says nothing, and she doesn't eat her crusts. She is so wasteful. I try to engage Dante in conversation, but he only gives me short answers and nods.

"How was your workout?" I ask.

"Okay," he says.

"It sounded as if you were working heavy," I say.

"Yes."

"Are you planning on fishing in the morning?" I ask.

"I don't know."

I can only blame Evelyn for his reluctance to speak at his own table. She is a damper, a shut door, a toilet seat, a padlock on his lips. He hasn't said anything in Italian since she's arrived, hasn't had a single twinkle in his eyes, and hasn't smiled even for a second. Why did he ever marry this bitch?

It is the longest, quietest dinner I've ever had.

Luckily, DJ bounds down the stairs for more pizza. "Any left?" he asks.

Evelyn turns her face toward him, and DJ plants a peck on her cheek.

Ooh, I feel the love.

I jump up and serve DJ some of the second pizza, now golden brown in the pizza oven. "Didn't you eat anything over there?" I ask him.

DJ smiles. "I think we ate everything in their cottage."

I pat his stomach. "Where do you put it all?"

He gets all shy again. "I have a high metabolism, like Dad. At the rate I'm growing, I won't be a middleweight."

"You'll be a heavyweight then," I say, staring hard at Evelyn.

"Oh, I dunno," DJ says. "I don't want to be fat and slow." He is so cute!

I put an extra gooey slice on his plate. "Are you going to join us?"

DJ looks past me at Evelyn and Dante. "Maybe later."

And up he goes.

I'd escape this mess, too, if I could, DJ.

The second I sit, Evelyn gets up and takes Dante's plate, even though a full slice of pizza rests on it. "You have to watch your weight, D," she says. She glances at my plate. I still have two slices to go. "Oh, you're not done, are you?"

Bitch.

She smiles at Dante. "I'll do the dishes, D. You just rest."

She collects his half-full glass as well and goes into the kitchen.

"Dante," I say, not whisper, "what are you thinking about?"

"Many things." He sighs. "Many, many things."

"I hope I'm one of those things." Though I ain't no thang.

A glimmer of a smile almost lights on his face. "Yes." His eyes travel to the kitchen. "I just wish . . ."

"We had more time?"

He nods.

"Dante, believe me, I didn't mean to cause so much trouble." Which is really a way of asking *if* I'm causing any trouble, right?

"It is not you," he says. He looks toward the kitchen again. "And it is not Evelyn. It is me. I am causing the trouble." He turns to me, whispering, "My mind is going many ways all at once. I hope you understand."

"My mind is kind of fried, too," I say, looking toward the kitchen. "But I would really like to come visit you tonight."

He looks at me sharply. "Oh no."

Oh yeah. DJ. "Would you rather come visit me?"

"I should be alone."

I smile. "I wore you out, didn't I?"

"No. I mean, I should be alone until the fight."

I get a serious chill. "We could just . . . snuggle, hold each other, and maybe sweat a little."

He leans closer. "That would . . . complicate things."

Not for me! "How?"

"You want me to be with you when Evelyn is so close by?" He looks again toward the kitchen. I want to grab his head and make him look me in the eye. "It is far too . . . complicated now."

I slide over in my chair, making damn sure to make a lot of noise. "Nothing seemed complicated last night. Everything made sense, yes?"

He looks away.

"Look at me, Dante."

He looks back at me but not in my eyes.

"Didn't everything make sense last night?" I ask.

"Yes," he whispers quickly. "Yes. Last night. It is not last night anymore. Things have changed."

Red was right. This cinches it. "I'll, um, just stay at Red's then, all by myself. I don't want to complicate things."

"How can you complicate things more than you already have?"

Che? That hurt! "Wait a minute. If she weren't here, would we be upstairs banging the shit out of each other right now?"

He gets up out of his chair. "Not so loud. We will talk outside."

I follow him to the outcropping. This is so fucking ridiculous. He can't even talk to me in his own house!

"Answer my question," I demand. "Would we be upstairs rattling the floorboards if she weren't here?"

"That is not the point. She *is* here. *That* is the point." Now he's looking back at the window over the sink.

"I'm over here." I sit on the bench.

He doesn't join me.

"Dante, don't you want to break away from her?"

He stands behind me. "She is the mother of our child. I can never break away from her."

I hate the word "never"! "I don't expect you to do that, Dante. I just want you to be happy."

He doesn't respond.

Maybe he doesn't want to be happy. If I were Irish, I'd say my Irish was up. "Why do you kiss her ass so much?"

"I do not do such a thing!"

Finally, some passion. I stand and face him. "Yes, you do. You've been kissing that flat ass of hers from the second she got here."

"A woman should never curse." He walks to the edge of the outcropping.

I walk up behind him. "Shit. Fuck. Damn. Motherfucker. I know a few more. Want to hear them? I'm from Red Hook, where Al Capone got his scar and became Scarface. I know a bunch of bad words. You should know quite a few, too. You *used* to be from Brooklyn."

He turns and shakes his head. "You are far too angry right now to be talking to me. We will talk again after she leaves."

"And when will that be?"

He looks down at the water. "I do not know."

"Dante, please," I say, softening my voice just a little. "I'm not really angry." Yet. If he dismisses me like that again, though, I'm going to be seriously angry. "I just want to know why you bow down so much in front of her."

"I do not bow down before her."

"You do," I say. "You're not yourself at all. You hardly speak, you don't smile, and you definitely don't act Italian."

"I always act Italian," he says.

"You know what I mean," I say. "I love to hear your other language. It's hot. I want to learn it."

He moves a step away from me. "I love to speak it."

"Then speak it!" I say louder. "Be yourself. You're not the same man now that you were last night. You're definitely not the man I had a magical night with."

"I am the same man," he says, setting his jaw. "You have only known me for one night. Evelyn and I had seven years together."

Oh, please. "And how many nights with her were like last night with me?"

"It is none of your business."

That sounded like a dismissal. I am officially angry now. "She divorced you, gave up on you, quit you when you needed her most. She didn't even try."

"And I have promised to win her back. I will keep that promise."

No fucking way! "After sleeping with me? Wait. We weren't sleeping, Dante. We were devouring each other. I have never wanted anyone as much as I wanted you last night, and you sure seemed to want me just as badly."

"But we cannot, Christiana, we cannot."

This shit isn't happening. "This is no fling, Dante. We talked before, during, and after sex. We cuddled. We woke up smiling together. It happened. It's happening. *We're* happening. I want it to happen, Dante. Did I complain about the fishing in any way?"

"No."

"Did I complain about climbing the mountain or training or skiing?"

"No."

I point at the kitchen window. "Hasn't Evelyn been one long complaint that never ends?"

"I have not heard her complain," Dante says.

Oh, geez! "She doesn't have to complain out loud, Dante. She is a silent complainer. If she likes something, she says nothing. If she doesn't like something, she is so silent she's deafening. You understand?"

"No."

"The witch doesn't say a positive or nice thing to anyone, not even to you!" I yell.

"She said I looked good," he says softly.

Only to mess with me. "Listen, Dante, you have fun with me. You can be yourself around me. You can speak your mind around me. You can argue with me. I'm good for you. There isn't anything you do that I wouldn't try. And I'm a pretty decent sparring partner, aren't I? I can take a punch. You hit Evelyn with a little jab, and she'll fall over and die."

I expect him to laugh a little, but he doesn't. "She is tougher than you think. She has a tough job in the emergency room. It takes guts to do what she does."

He has a point. I get a little light-headed just cleaning a fish. "I meant that I'm physically tough and she's not."

He looks far out into the distance. "In my mind, she is still my wife, Christiana."

Oh, for the love of . . . "She's not . . . your . . . wife . . . anymore."

"I must make it work."

This is too much! "Only *you* work. Only *you* are trying to make it work. You send the flowers, and she says to stop. You have to win a boxing match to get a single date. You have to win a championship belt to win another chance at taking her down the aisle. Shouldn't that tell you something?"

"A woman should always be treated like a queen."

Geez! "While your life goes to shit?"

He doesn't answer.

"I'm beginning to figure all this out now," I say, and I am pretty sure, too. "You feel guilty about last night, don't you? You feel like you've cheated on her. She divorced you ten years ago, but the first time you sleep with another woman, you feel guilty. Admit it."

"You do not understand," he says.

"I think I do," I say.

"Marriage is forever," he says. "The law, those papers— they don't change that. When I win the fight, we will try again. I have promised, and she has promised."

Evelyn made a promise? "When did she promise?"

"Today. While I was swimming."

I should have gone swimming. "You mean, she didn't promise you *until* today?"

"She said before that she was giving it serious thought. Today, she has made her decision."

He is so naive! "Dante, she's only promising because I'm here. Don't you see that?"

I've never seen him look so agitated. "What does it matter why or when she promised? She promised. That is good enough for me."

Here we go again. "Didn't she once promise to be your wife?"

"I let her down. I was no longer winning. I was a loser. I was not a champion anymore. She had every right to leave."

"What about for better or worse?" I ask. "What about that?"

"So we are still in worse," he says. "After I win, it will get better."

"And last night means nothing now?"

He closes his eyes. "Yes. I mean, no. I am so confused." He turns and looks at me, his eyebrows knitted together.

"You mean much to me. I did not think I could ever care for anyone else. I did not think I could ever make love to anyone else. You are everything a man could want. I close my eyes and I see you."

Oh, this is much better. I like where this is heading. "Am I naked?"

"Yes."

"And are we together? Are you inside me?"

"Yes. No. I *cannot* want you, don't you see? I should still want Evelyn."

If he mentions her name one more time, I'm going to hit him below the belt. "You don't want her. If you close your eyes and see me, you cannot want her."

"Like I said, it is complicated."

I am so confused right now! "So what am I to you right this second?"

"I . . . I do not know."

That clears up a bunch. Thanks, Dante.

"You are honest," he says. "You are fair. You have deep beauty, inside. You have made me smile. Your body is . . . You are perfection."

I am not going down without a fight. "I give you pleasure, don't I?"

"Very much."

"I kept you up all night, right?"

"Yes."

"You know I'd share every part of your life with you, don't you?"

He almost smiles. "I think you would."

"You know I believe in you, right?" I ask softly.

"Yes, Christiana. I know you believe in me."

I squeeze his hand and hold onto it. "Dante, I know in my heart that you can win this fight. She doesn't. She will only remarry you if you win. That *has* to tell you something."

He worms out of my hand. "It is her way of motivating me."

He dropped my hand. Shit. "But she gives you pain. How is that motivation? She has a separate life from yours. She does not believe in you. She is most likely praying that you will lose so she won't have to break your heart again."

He squares his shoulders in front of me. It's almost as if he's bucking at me! "How do you know all this? You have known her for less than a day."

Nice opening. "I knew you for about the same time before I chose to give you my heart."

Shit.

Shit shit.

Did I say that out loud? Shit. I did.

And now he's completely silent.

Damage control? Or just go for it? I have to go down swinging. "I'm giving you my heart, Dante. Freely, and with no reservations. It's yours."

That actually felt right. Thirty-five years I've waited to give my heart away, and here it is, on an outcropping at Aylen Lake, Ontario, Canada, to a man whose ex-wife is watching us from the kitchen window.

My timing for life's big moments really sucks.

"But I cannot give you my heart, Christiana," he says. "Not now."

I close my eyes. My timing just sucks all around, and what he just said just about seals it. I take both of his hands anyway. I'm a big girl. I've been through my share of rejection and heartache. I know when to walk away from a fight I can't win. "I know you can't give me your heart, Dante. But I need to know what I have to do to earn it. How can I capture your heart?"

"I do not know. If we only had more time, I could figure all this out."

Ah. The old "I need more time." He needs space, time, and distance. Oh, shit. I'm starting to tear up. "You want time? I can give you that." I try to smile, but my bottom lip won't cooperate. Oh great. Now I'm trembling all over. See what you started, lower lip? "I'll give you all the time you need. I'm . . . I guess I'm leaving."

"*Che?* But it is getting late. You said your flight is not until Monday morning."

I lied. "I can always get a flight out tomorrow. It's no trouble. I need to sort out a few things myself. The drive will help me clear my head."

"You leave tonight? It is so late. The roads are dark."

I punch him playfully on the shoulder while my heart breaks into a trillion pieces. "Hey, don't worry about me. Worry about Tank Washington kicking your ass."

I walk past him to Red and Lelani's cottage. I strip out of Evelyn's sweats and put my own clothes on. I find my laptop and camera case on a love seat and start for the door.

Dante blocks it. "Are you always this . . . *impetuosa*?"

"Yes. I am." I kiss him hard on the lips. "It's one of the things you like about me." I try to push past him.

"Do not leave. Wait. In the morning, I will be able to think more clearly."

I shake my head. "Maybe I can clear things up for you." I poke him in the chest. "You need me. You do not need her."

"And in the morning, maybe I will see this."

I sigh. "The only way you'll see that is if I go away and ignore you for a while."

"*Che?*"

"You want some time, I'm giving you time."

His eyes widen. "But that is not fair!"

"Life ain't fair, Dante," I say. "I thought you knew that." I push past him.

"She will tire of this place," he whispers behind me.

I whirl on him. "Why are you whispering?"

He starts to speak and stops.

"You can yell your damn head off with me," I say. "You can howl at the moon all you want with me. Half the lake heard us fucking last night."

"Shh, shh," he whispers.

"See? With her, you have to whisper." I turn to face him. "With me, you can yell. That's the difference between Evelyn and me. Do you want to whisper your way through life or yell your head off?" I walk to the outcropping for one last look. I pull out my camera and take several shots of the sunset with the island in the foreground.

"Evelyn will leave on her own in no time," he says softly. "She always does. She is here to get DJ. They will go, and then we can figure this out."

I put my camera back in its case. "Dante, you're sweet, but you are about the most naive and gullible person I have ever met. Evelyn will stay as long as I stay."

"You do not know her like I do."

I start for the stairs. "I think I do. She never had any competition before, right?"

"This is not a competition."

I stop at the top of the stairs. "Uh, yeah, it is. Unless you haven't been paying attention today, two women want you. I want you, and Evelyn seems to want you." If only to keep me from having Dante. "I think I have better reasons than she does, but what do I know? I am only a *scrittore cattivo.*"

He steps in front of me with his arms crossed. "What are these reasons?"

"I've been telling you my reasons, Dante," I fume. "Haven't you been listening?"

"Tell them to me again," he says.

"Okay, I'll break it down for you. You don't have to *do* anything for me." I look at Evelyn looking at me from the screened porch. The bitch probably walked out there so she could hear us better. "You don't have to win any titles for

me!" I shout. I turn and kiss his cheek. "I have to go now."
I start down the stairs.

"I do not want you to go, Christiana."

Whatever.

I jump into the rental boat, laying my cases on the middle seat. I go to untie the front rope, but Dante's hand blocks me.

"When this is all over . . ." he says.

"When *what* is all over? I thought it *was* all over." I push his hand away and untie the rope.

"When this is all over, I would like . . . I am confused now. In my heart. You have . . . You are in my heart."

Just "in." I don't own a thing about this man. So much for possessing him. "But I don't *have* your heart, right?"

"There is a difference?"

I roll my eyes. "Uh, yeah. But don't sweat it. A few more days with Evelyn, and I'll be a memory." I go to the back rope and untie it, the boat floating a few inches away from the dock.

"You could never be a memory, Christiana. Never."

I shouldn't do this, but . . . it's ultimatum time. "Then choose. Right now. This second. Her or me."

"You cannot expect me to make this choice this second."

I shake my head slowly and close my eyes. "You've already decided then, Dante. Good-bye."

He drops to the dock and kicks out his legs, hooking them over the side of the boat. He pulls it back to the dock. *"Pericoloso."*

"That's right, Dante, I'm dangerous," I say. "Twenty-four hours a day, seven days a week. That's what I am, man. You handled me pretty well last night, but could you handle me for the rest of your life? I doubt it. You're too soft for me. I can go the distance. Can you?"

His hands fly into the air. "Please stay. She will be gone in two days, three at the most."

"I don't want to wait." I turn and give the motor a pull. Nothing. Figures. "You know, you could ask *her* to leave."

His eyes pop. "You want me to ask *her* to leave?"

I tap my head. "That would be the best solution. *Saggia.* Out with the old, and in with the new."

"But I have promised—she has promised. If I win . . ."

This is so futile. "*Please* don't start repeating yourself. I know all that. I made a promise, blah blah blah. She has promised, yadda yadda yadda. All you have to do is tell her that you've changed your mind. Tell her to go kiss her own ass for a while."

"I cannot do this! Not when I am confused like this. It's so, it's so . . ."

"Complicated," I say, and I give the motor another pull. Nothing. I adjust the choke. "Dante, you are wasting your time with her. You deserve better than Evelyn. You deserve me."

He drops his chin to his chest. "I do not even deserve you."

True. It's kind of sweet, but now it's time for some tough love. "I know we were made for each other. We may even be soul mates. And maybe if you take the time to think about it, you'll see it, too."

He looks up at me. "Made for each other?"

"Do you know any other women who know as much about boxing as you do?"

He looks at the sky, then at me. "No."

"You know any women who can outfish you?"

He laughs. "You fish one day and get some big ones. This does not mean—"

"Whatever," I interrupt. "You know any women who can do what I did to you all night long?"

"No," he says softly.

"You know any woman who would share every bit of your life with you and be content with every bit of it?"

His eyes become little slits. "But, you have a life away from here, just as Evelyn has a life away from here."

Now he argues? *Now* he makes some sense? Geez, I'm in the fucking boat! I am within one successful pull of leaving this place forever! "I thought I had a life, Dante. I did. Now I know that there's a big hole in my life, and you've filled it. You fill all the holes in my life, and very well, I might add."

I am still so hot for this man. And why won't this fucking motor start? Shit. I click the gear level to neutral. Uh duh. It won't start in forward, genius.

"Dante, I've been wanting you inside me all day. Has Evelyn ever wanted you that badly?"

"She did once. But then I lost. I failed."

"Oh, please don't start that shit again," I say. "Dante, I'd want you if you never fought a single fight. I'd want you if you lost every fight. In fact, if you wanted to make love to me right now, I'd let you, right there on that dock."

"You . . . would?"

I start unbuttoning my flannel shirt and expose the tops of my breasts. I'm about to unzip my pants when his eyes drop. Whoa. I have really forced him into a crisis. I button up my shirt.

"Maybe it would be best if you went," he says.

Ouch. That was a good punch. "Dante, do you really mean that?"

He doesn't answer.

"You can't mean that." I move close to him, tears welling in my eyes again. "Please say you don't mean that."

Tears fill his eyes, too, punching another hole in my heart. "I do not know what I mean anymore, Christiana. Evelyn is my *portafortuna*, my good luck charm. She is—"

I take his hands and put them on my heart. "I could be your porta whatever-it-is."

"But she has already *been* my *portafortuna*."

"Enough. I give up." I push his hands away and go back to the motor, giving it a pull. It chugs to life and dies. Close. Next pull and I'm out of here. "I wish you well, Dante. I hope you win." I look up and see Evelyn on the stairs holding a big plastic bag.

"D?" she calls. "Did you buy these for me? They're very nice."

Dante doesn't speak.

"They're mine," I say, locking eyes with Dante. "Go get them," I whisper, "or do you need her permission first?"

He goes up the stairs, gets the bag, and returns to me, putting the bag in my hand. Evelyn, looking all smug and stupid in her stupid winter coat, still lingers stupidly at the top of the stupid stairs.

"Will you be at the fight?" Dante whispers.

Holy shit! What an asshole thing to say! "You don't need me there, do you? She's your portable tuna, right?"

He moves closer. "Please. I would like you to be there."

"Maybe, um, maybe it would be *best* that I *not* be there."

That shuts him up, only for a second. "It is too dark out. You do not know this lake very well."

"I'll manage." I pull as hard as I can, and the motor roars to life, smoke filling the air. I push in the choke and the smoke subsides. "I got here all by myself, didn't I?"

"Give me your phone number," he whispers. "I will call you."

Geez. *Now* he asks for my number? And in front of his soon-to-be-ex-wife-turned-wife? What the hell. I scribble it on a scrap of paper in one last show of defiance in front of Evelyn and hand it to him. "*Ciao,* Dante."

I don't listen for his good-bye, backing out and hauling ass across the lake as the sun sets. It is a teary ride, and I narrowly miss hitting a little island that gets in my way. I get to the Landing, beach the boat, put fifty dollars Canadian in an envelope, and slide it under the rental-office door. The rental car, a Ford Focus, starts right up, and I bounce up the long hill away from Aylen Lake.

At the bottom of that first hill, I stop on the bridge over the dam.

And I weep.

I hit the steering wheel with my fists.

I weep some more.

It serves me right. I got involved. I had every chance not to, but I went ahead and did it anyway. I lost my focus.

I am a fool.

I search for a radio station to calm me down, and all I can find are country stations.

Perfect.

I pound the steering wheel again.

I should go back and throw Evelyn over the outcropping. Yes. Her skinny body would hit the water with a tiny little *zoop*.

Wait. She wouldn't sink. She'd float. Do witches sink or float? I can't remember. She'd probably skip across the water like a skinny little rock.

I could sneak back to his room and . . .

No.

That will just have to be another of my fantasies. I have a lot of those. When you can't have the real thing, the next best thing is a bottle of wine and a fantasy.

I put the car in gear and bump along the road.

What a perfectly fucked-up life I lead.

Chapter 21

Because of several wrong turns, it takes me four hours to get to Ottawa. I bypass going to a hotel and sleep in the rental car.

I may never be able to sleep in a bed again.

I don't sleep much, but when I do, I dream of water, sun, and a talking birch tree.

I must be exhausted.

Birch trees don't talk. They only peel.

After dropping off the rental just after sunrise, I go into the airport, secure a seat on a plane bound for LaGuardia, and begin the puff piece, which is really a glorified list. People who read *Personality* love lists. It makes life more bite-sized and easier to swallow.

Name:	Dante Lattanza
Age:	42
Status:	Single
See him:	In *Heavy Leather* and on HBO Pay-Per-View at Madison Square Garden December 7 fighting for the middleweight title
Why he's sexy:	He's ageless, making an amazing

comeback after ten years. He's a great dad, training his son, Dante Jr., an up-and-coming boxer. He fights not for glory but "to put food on the table." He's *very* good with his hands, speaks fluent Italian and English, and has washboard abs.

I never asked Dante for his middle name. It's probably something fiery. I also never asked him his favorite color. He asked me. I should have returned the favor. Hmm. He's not quite single, but "trying to win back his ex-wife's love" is too much information for a simple list. See him (don't blink!) in that movie! Sexiness is so relative. What I think is sexy, just about everything about this man, just won't cut it. Shelley will delete the "very" and change "handy" to "He built his cottage in Canada by hand." Depending upon her mood, she might even redline "amazing" and "washboard abs." Though true, his abs might be a little too titillating for our readers. *Personality* magazine seems to be shifting away from the surface of the man to what makes him a man. Oh sure, the pictures will take care of the sexiness for me.

I look through the pictures again, and the unguarded photo from town with Dante carrying all our bags is sexy as hell. I'll have to blow that one up and put it over my bed.

Since I have time on my hands, I rewrite the puffer the way *I'd* want to read it:

Name: Dante "Blood and Guts" Lattanza

Age: 42 (but looks 25)

Status: Single (but should be hooking up with *Personality* writer and photographer Christiana Artis)

See him: In *Heavy Leather* looking sexy as hell and on HBO Pay-Per-View at Madison Square

Garden December 7 winning the middle-weight title

Why he's sexy: He has an educated tongue and knows just how to use it. He is solid granite in all the right places. He knows how to nibble nipples. He's very good with his hands and fingers. "I stay hard," he says, and it is true. He has stamina enough to go fifteen rounds of hot, sweaty lovemaking and still be erect, I mean, standing. He speaks fluent Italian, which is the hottest (by far) language to hear when some-one is pumping your booty. He is so delicious even his washboard abs taste good.

I have to cover up the screen from the prying eyes of the old woman next to me. I almost hit the delete button out of embarrassment but instead save it to the GP (for "Guilty Pleasures") folder. I have quite a few GP files, and I have to name this one GP33. Most are, well, pornographic. You know, things I would like to do to some of the men I've interviewed. One day, I may publish them, changing all the names, of course. Until then . . .

I send the original puffer to Shelley and start counting. If she's at her desk—she ought to be there by now—I'll be getting a call on my cell phone in three minutes or less. What a job. You work forty-eight hours on something that takes three minutes to read.

My cell phone vibrates.

"Yes, Shelley?"

"I love it!" she gushes. "I absolutely love it. I might have to tinker with it a bit."

Here it comes.

"What did you mean by 'good with his hands'?" she asks.

He knows how to work a booty. "He built his own cottage in Canada."

"Any other reasons?"

He knows how to squeeze the life into breasts. "No."

"Nice plug for HBO."

Gee, thanks.

"We've moved him up to number nine."

This is good news on an otherwise shitty day. "Really?"

She sighs. "Number ten was picked up for drunk driving and called Romanian people 'Transyl-vestites.' "

I chuckle. That's actually an intelligent pun. Mean, but . . .

"Number eleven was quoted in some little magazine years ago as saying New Yorkers don't know quote 'class from ass' unquote," Shelley says. Shelley doesn't curse unless she can "quote-unquote" it. "A blogger saw it and posted it online, and now the story has spread like a virus around the world."

Class from ass. At least it rhymed.

"And number twelve," Shelley continues, "well, his pictures didn't turn out very well. The lighting must have been terrible or something."

Oh no, not that!

"Are the pictures you've taken of Lattanza really sexy?" she asks.

"Yes." But the sexiest one is mine. I may just print out a small version for my wallet or tape it to my bathroom mirror. "I haven't loaded them into my laptop, or I would have sent them to you."

"You've been too busy to do that?"

"Yeah." Busy getting busy, mainly.

"I'm still worried about number eight," Shelley says.

"He seemed to be on some sort of bender when McBain interviewed him."

Number eight wears long sleeves at the beach. He's what I call a "track" star. "He was strung out again, Shelley."

"His pictures looked nice, though."

Oh, geez. He has nice pictures but has a habit he can't kick. "Shelley, trust me. If Dante Lattanza were ten years younger, he'd be on the cover."

"He's sexier than Clooney or Connery? Sean was always my personal favorite."

"Much sexier."

"And do you have firsthand knowledge?"

Firsthand, first-tongue, first-lips, first-*figa*, first-*culo*. "They're calling for my flight, Shelley. Gotta run." I shut my phone.

My flight isn't for another forty-five minutes, so I check all my many notes, numbering the quotes in the order I want to use them. I flex my fingers, then space down, leaving room for the first paragraph, something I always write last.

Now.

How do I capture this man in one thousand words or less?

Especially when he's just dumped me for a shrew?

And I miss him already?

What is wrong with me?

Chapter 22

<TITLE>:

<GRAPH 1>:

Lattanza had a quiet, "old-school" upbringing in the Carroll Gardens section of South Brooklyn. He was raised by "the best cook," his mother, Connie, a single mother who never learned English.

A nd he has been cuckolded by a noncook who still *requires* him to speak English. Whoever said boys tend to marry women who remind them of their mothers was full of shit.

"Carroll Gardens was like that," Lattanza says, a twinkle in his eye. "Sitting out on the stoop, she could talk to anyone. That was a long time ago. The neighborhood has changed. Cammareri Brothers Bakery is gone. Not so much

Italian heard on the stoops. Mama would not like it much."

I doubt Connie would approve of Evelyn at all. "Cannot cook? So skinny! Doesn't like fish? Not good enough for *my* boy."

Lattanza ran to and from school as a child. "I was skinny," he says. "There was this *bravaccio* who chased me like dogs chase cars. I was small, but I was *rapido*. I hit him once in the *stomaco*. He left me alone."

I know how that *bravaccio* feels. Dante hit me in the heart, and now I have to leave him alone.

At thirteen, Lattanza showed up at Gleason's Gym, where champions like Jake LaMotta, Rocky Graziano, Carmen Basilio, Arturo Gatti, Muhammad Ali, Roy Jones, Joe Frazier, and George Foreman trained. "They were the best," Lattanza says, his dark eyes bright. "I wanted to be the best."

Lattanza blossomed at Gleason's. "I asked to fight the biggest fighters. They laughed at me but gave me a chance. I went home bloody, but no one ever knocked me down. No one. No one ever will. Blood and guts. I have always been this."

Except when Evelyn's around. His face drains of blood and he becomes gutless. Just one little half-jab would cave in her mousy face. Hell, even a swing and a miss might blow her over.

Despite his nickname, Lattanza has given back to his community, contributing to Gleason's Give a Kid a Dream program. "I miss that. I should go back. Gleason's gave me a chance. I should give back. There is a new generation of tough Brooklyn kids out there that could be champions. They are already running the streets. I'd like to make sure that running counts for something."

Dante does have a good heart. I'll grant him that. I can't take that away from him.

Running nine miles a day, Lattanza gave his mother many proud moments before her sudden death when Lattanza was eighteen. He had high marks at St. Saviour, was the New York Gold Gloves middleweight champion, and was invited to the Olympic trials.

Lattanza's greatest moment? "Holding Dante Junior for the first time. It's not all about boxing with me. Boxing put money in my pocket to put food on the table, have a place to live. It is a job."

And this is my job. Though I had my greatest moment in the closet, my writing pays my bills and gives me a place to live. Writing about a man is my job. Stalking a man is not.

Lattanza takes his fatherly duties very seriously, involving his sixteen-year-old son "DJ" in every aspect of his training. He is DJ's older brother, friend, confidant, and trainer. A rare

thing? "It is the right thing." Dante fights, he says
with pride, "to be a hero to my son, to be a
good father, to be someone he can look up to."

"To win back his lost love," I want to write, but I don't.
I made a promise, and promises seem to be of utmost im-
portance to Dante. So far, I've kept out Evelyn and Dante's
father. And I'm also gushing here and there. I'll delete "a
twinkle in his eye" later. I guess I better grind out the rest
and put a hold on my gushing.

Lattanza, aided by his longtime sparring partner, friend, and personal cook, Red Gregory,
trains for fights far from the madding crowd up
at Aylen Lake, Ontario. He built the cottage
where they live in the summer and late fall far
from what he calls "*distrazione.*"

Until I showed up. Was that all I was? A distraction?

"The air is pure, you know? Clean. Has a flavor.
The water is ice cold. Pure. Clean." He squints. "It
is a place where I can focus. It is a place where
DJ and I can be together all the time."

I fight back a tear. I will never forget that place.

Lattanza's training regimen includes fishing,
mountain climbing, hiking, and swimming, atypical of most boxers today. He also sleeps on the
floor.

I'll never forget that place either. I hope he doesn't sand
off the scratch marks.

"It is not comfortable, though it is good for my back. It is to remind me of hard times. I choose to have no windows to remind me of my ancestors who were imprisoned for fighting against Mussolini. I have no bed to remind me of my *nonni* coming to America and having to sleep on the floor, pick rags, and sell junk thrown away by others. My family has been through many hard times. They made sacrifices to come to America. I make sacrifices, too. I do not get soft. I stay hard."

Yes, indeed you did, Mr. Lattanza. I will never forget that hardness as long as I live. It's making me a bit damp just thinking about it.

Now, do I mention the clippings, the crucifix, and the wedding picture? Well . . . two out of three will just have to do.

On the walls of his closetlike bedroom, he has clippings of his losses to Tank Washington and Felix Cordoza to motivate him. A crucifix reminds him of "the greatest sacrifice ever."

Recently named one of the "Sexiest Men Alive" by *Personality*, Lattanza has kept a low profile for the past ten years, "fishing, traveling, and staying in shape." Other than a bit part in *Heavy Leather*, he's been virtually invisible.

"It was easier than you think," he says. "Not many recognize me wearing clothes and without my gloves. It was okay to be anonymous."

If Lattanza should beat Washington in their long-awaited rematch on December 7 at Madison Square Garden, he won't ever have a chance to be anonymous again.

I am so frustrated. There's *so* much more to this man than this! But this is what we give the public. It's never enough. As vain as he appears to be, he's about the most humble athlete—or man—I've ever met. Sure, he's misguided, gullible, and naive, but so are most people.

Me most of all. I can't believe that I was naive enough to think I could muscle in on Dante and steal him away from the mother of his child. Two days cannot undo almost seventeen years of a "relationship"—and I use that term loosely.

I think the tone of the article portrays Dante's humble nature without me saying it. I want to tell the world how gentle he is, how much of a gentleman he is, how much he *isn't* the stereotypical conceited "warrior," how generous he is, how tender he can be, how his "Blood and Guts" nickname fits him and doesn't fit him. I want readers to know he's something more than a wicked left hook and a smile. I want them to know how crazy he is about his son.

I still don't have a first paragraph. "Dante Lattanza is not your average fighter" just doesn't cut it. "Dante Lattanza is a man" is a bit too grandiose, even though it's true. If I tell the world he's fighting for love, I'll break my promise to him.

But I'll have the ultimate opening. I'll have a paragraph that will yank the reader into the rest of my story.

I'm going to let this percolate for a few days over the weekend while I get properly drunk and cry a lot. I know I will. I'm already going through withdrawal.

There's my flight.

I wonder if I can start my pity party early with a glass of wine on the plane.

Chapter 23

They don't have any alcohol on the ninety-minute flight to LaGuardia, so I begin my pity party with some stale peanuts, sour orange juice, and a weak cup of coffee.

I catch a cab from the airport (on *Personality*'s tab, of course) and reread the serious article. I barely broke seven hundred words. The Evelyn/Dante's father info would double it easily. I just can't get past how much I gushed when I wrote it!

It's obvious I'm in love with him.

Shit.

I'm in love.

I spent, what, almost three days with this man and I'm in love? I have never believed in love at first sight. "Is there any other?" he said. Maybe he's right. But I've never let myself get this involved with anyone, even the boyfriends who put up with me more off than on. Love to me has always been just another word in musicals, in date movies, in soap operas, and on the radio.

I look up. We're just now hitting the Grand Central Parkway? Geez. Why don't you all move to Canada? There's plenty of space up there.

I need to talk to Dante. I need to apologize. I just need to hear his voice. It's a little after ten. If he went fishing, he'd probably be back by now. I find the cottage number in my cell phone's directory and make the call.

"Hello?"

Why is Evelyn answering the phone? "Um, hi, Evelyn. It's Christiana Artis. I, uh, I need to check a few things for my story with Dante."

Silence.

"So, um, I need to speak to Dante."

"He's sleeping," she says.

She's lying. The man never sleeps. "Well, please wake him up. My editor has to have my story by noon today." She lies, and I lie. It's a vicious cycle.

"I don't want to interrupt his dreams," she says.

"Che?"

"What?"

"That's what I said. *Che* means 'what.' Weren't you married to this guy once? Didn't you learn any Italian?"

"He only spoke English around me," she says.

Because you took away his ability to be Italian. "How do you know he's dreaming, Evelyn?"

"Because I'm looking at him."

Where is he? He can't be . . . But the only phone I saw was in the guestroom. Did he sleep there last night? No! She has to be lying, but how can I know for sure? "Please wake him. It'll only take a minute."

"He needs his rest," she says. "He was *very* busy last night."

You . . . . What's worse than a bitch? An itch. Evelyn is an *itch* from now on. Wait. She's talking in a normal voice. If she's in the guestroom, and *he's* in the guestroom . . . "Why aren't you whispering?"

"Dante can sleep through a hurricane," she says.

Itch! Witch! "Look, I really need to speak to him now."

"I'd really rather not wake him. I can take a message for him if you like."

No, I would not like. "I'll . . . I'll just call back later."

I slam shut my phone.

This is bullshit. She's lying. He wasn't "busy" last night, not with her. And she is nowhere near Dante now. He probably went fishing this morning to get away from her, and now he's down at the dock cleaning fish. Yeah. She's up in her little palace of a guesthouse while he cleans the fish she couldn't possibly eat. That phone was the only phone there. He wouldn't dare—

She has to be lying.

Oh, God, I hope she's lying.

Maybe if I call back, he'll answer this time. Not likely, but . . .

I hit the redial button.

No answer.

Why doesn't Dante have an answering machine, voice mail, something? Why won't he join the rest of us in the twenty-first century? I know he's old school, but there are things you have to have in the modern age.

I press all the numbers this time, hoping the phone misdialed the first time.

No answer.

She has obviously left the guesthouse. I'll bet that's it. She's left her little palace to go find Dante. He's not there with her. If she were there, she'd answer because she couldn't resist talking to me again, lying to me again, getting me all worked up.

But if Dante were getting busy with *me*, *I* wouldn't answer the phone for anything, even a hurricane.

Shit!

Okay. Get a grip. You can't go to pieces over this. You're from Red Hook, Brooklyn. We don't fall apart over things like this. Oh sure, we fume about something every second of every day, but there have been worse things that have happened to us, like 9/11, the Mets *"el foldo"* of 2007, the Knicks since Walt Frazier, the Dodgers leaving for LA, the Jets since Broadway Joe Namath. . . .

I fish in my pocket for Red's cell phone number. I know he's in Montreal, but maybe he can get through for me or at least give Dante a message.

Red doesn't answer either, but at least he has voice mail.

"Red, it's me, Christiana. Things didn't go too well, and I left last night. No one is answering the phone at Dante's cottage. Please have him call me as soon as you and Lelani get back from Montreal, okay? It's urgent. Bye."

I sigh. There really isn't much more I can do. Red will give him the message, and then Dante will call me.

I hope.

The cab stops. I pay him. I get out. I'm home in Red Hook, where everyone has to hang tough.

The Dutch, who obviously couldn't spell, originally named Red Hook (population eleven thousand) *Roode Hoek*. Red Hook is the former home of tough Brooklyn dockworkers and was once the stomping grounds of NBA star Carmelo Anthony, who lived here until he was in the third grade. The Knicks could certainly use him. Creepy horror writer H. P. Lovecraft grew up here. That should tell you something about Red Hook. Rocky Marciano's trainer Charley Goodman, *Wiseguy* actor Ray Sharkey, and real wise guy "Crazy Joe" Gallo were all Red Hookers, too. Gallo was shot up in Little Italy at Umberto's Clam House on his forty-third birthday while eating scungilli. Red Hook is also the site where that knucklehead floated his homemade wooden submarine, which looked like a floating brown egg, too close to the *QE2* and got arrested, a tallboy beer in his hand.

A sign on a Red Hook door says it all:

NO MENUS
NO CIRCULARS
NO ANYTHING
NO EVERYTHING

Or, as I overheard one night at Sunny's Bar, "Red Hook is like a hot chick in coveralls."

I'm no hot chick, and though I live in a pre-WWII warehouse near the intersection of Van Brunt and Reed, I own no coveralls. I open my black steel door and see twelve hundred square feet of "space" in my studio apartment, for which I pay only sixteen hundred a month plus utilities—a legal steal these days. I share this building with artists, designers, writers, and other bohemians like me, none of whom seem to have regular working hours. I know. Some of them work long into the night, hammering, banging, and generally being industrious. I have a beamed ceiling, a full East River view through an arched window, shiny hardwood floors, a tiny kitchen, a bathroom about the size of Dante's room, and lots of open space. Carnival Cruise ships appear, blast their horns, and disappear from my window, all of them sailing away and leaving me behind, and on a clear evening, I can catch Lady Liberty's glowing head.

Not tonight. New Jersey must be on fire again. Are those white caps on the water? New Jersey blows, too.

I hit my bed without undressing. It's not as stiff as the floor in Dante's room, but it sure is comfortable. I prop myself up on two pillows, listening to the *ding dang dong* of the buoys and checking out my "space."

I have turned my space into an eclectic mix of whatever strikes my fancy. I have a long green sofa from the sixties, above which hangs *Brown Skin,* an acrylic by Darlene F; *Twins,* a black and green painting by Olivia Rose Jackson;

and *Red Hook,* a series of color photographs by Scott A.
Ettin. All are framed, and none of them matches each other,
the couch, or anything else for that matter. Splashed
through my space are old movie posters, framed and un-
framed photographs of old Brooklyn, menus from defunct
Brooklyn restaurants, ancient magazine covers from *Col-
lier's,* playbills of plays I've never seen, and a postcard col-
lage of places I've never been. I have not spent much for
any of it, shopping so often at Main Street Ephemera (on
Columbia Street—don't ask) they know me by name. A
neon clock that rarely keeps the right time hangs over the
window and my Indo Nouveau sun lounger and side table,
the only truly expensive pieces I've bought. Whenever I
hold my laptop on my lap—where a laptop is supposed to
go—the sun lounger becomes my office. Scattered here
and there are TwigCraft lamps made from New York City
street trees and bamboo candleholders holding white
waxen nubs. Loads of shelving crammed with books, most
of them dusty hardbacks and other unique finds from Free-
bird Books & Goods, surrounds my space. A framed page
from *The Book of Changes* hangs opposite my "dining room"
table, an old library table surrounded by mismatched chairs
and stools, all gathered on an L-shaped rug remnant I bought
from a neighbor for five dollars.

My favorite places within my space are shrines to boxing and the Brooklyn Dodgers. Granddaddy had collected
a few boxing items over the years, and when he died, I in-
herited his collection. A glove signed by Joe Frazier dangles from a nail in between a black-and-white autographed
photo of Ali training at Gleason's and an ancient autographed photo of Kid Gavilán. A 16 x 20 photograph
signed by both Joe Louis and Jake LaMotta hangs above a
green Everlast robe on a hook. I sometimes wear the robe,
which Frazier wore in the fight against Jerry Quarry after

Ali beat him in the Garden, whenever I feel the need for a comeback.

I ought to put it on now. Maybe later.

I get up and hook Dante the Moose's tag to the nail. Wow. I've added to my boxing wall. I should have had Dante autograph the moose's nose.

My Brooklyn Dodgers wall is just to the left of my bed. All those heroes have gone away. I have Duke Snider climbing the Bulova watch sign, Maury Wills's number-thirty jersey, a lithograph of Ebbets Field with a real piece of brick attached at the bottom, and team photographs from the fifties. Jackie Robinson keeps stealing home, Pee Wee Reese keeps fielding the ball and throwing it to Gil Hodges, and Don Newcombe is forever winding up on the mound. I even have a globe containing a miniature Ebbets Field that plays "Take Me Out to the Ball Game." I want to buy an actual Ebbets Field chair, but I don't have the seven thousand dollars (!) it would take to add it to my dining room chair collection. I never saw the Brooklyn Dodgers play, but Granddaddy brought them to life for me, and he talked about them as if they were friends of his. "When Campy had a good day, there was no stoppin' 'em," he'd say. Now we've sent a Yankee manager out to LA to coach the "other" Dodgers. Serves 'em right.

Some people think my space is an indoor yard sale.

I just call it home.

I used to have friends who called Red Hook home, but they've all gone away. LaKeisha, Kimberly, and Kayla were the girls I used to jump rope with a *long* time ago on "the Back." I haven't seen LaKeisha since graduation. She was the one who wanted to be a dancer so badly. She was always teaching me different moves and dances that I could never quite master. She also had the ugliest toes I have ever seen, all gnarled and callused. I hope she's made it some-

where. Kimberly got pregnant during high school and
dropped out. She supposedly lives over in Queens with a
few more kids. I doubt I'd recognize her. Kayla is the only
one I've talked to in the last ten years, and that was just in
passing as we waited for the F Train at Rockefeller Center.
She's a senior analyst for some Wall Street firm making
"crazy money" doing arbitrage or something extremely
dull like that. She looked so corporate, dressed in a blue
pinstriped power jacket and skirt and carrying a dazzling
attaché. And this was the girl who wore baggy clothes and
skateboarded everywhere she went in ninth grade. She
seemed happy, though, and she promised to keep in touch.

I haven't heard from her in at least five years. Once
folks leave Red Hook, I guess they never come back.

I'm hardly home anyway, and leaving Red Hook daily is
a hassle and a half. The Mass Transit Authority (MTA) says
I have several choices, and each choice stinks. I can take
the 61B bus to Smith Street and take the F Train to Rockefeller Center roughly ten miles away. Sounds reasonable,
right? Well, the Massive Trauma Assholes are planning to
close the F and G lines any day now for up to a year, not
that I'll miss the Smith/Ninth Street station. "Derelict" is a
compliment for that station. The paint doesn't peel—it
reaches out, grabs you, follows you home, and asks to spend
the night. The escalator *might* have worked in 1965, and it
rains *inside* the station, too. This bus/subway method costs
me about an hour a day each way and roughly a hundred dollars a month. Some folks are skipping the Smith/Ninth Street
Station entirely and going on to the Borough Hall Station.
If they close the F and G lines, I'm looking at a ninety-
minute bus ride to work.

That would suck big time.

I can also take the New York Water Taxi to Pier 11 on
Wall Street and ride the Seventh Avenue Local to Times

Square at about, oh, two hundred fifty a month. It'd be cheaper to take the M6 bus from the pier, but I don't like buses. If I had my own boat like Dante's, I could cruise past the Statue of Liberty to work every day on the way to—I have no idea. Somewhere over near Thirty-fourth Street, probably, where I'd have to pay extortion rates to dock my boat, and I'd still need another mode of transportation from the dock to Rockefeller Center. I suppose I could buy a car.

Sorry. I lost my mind for a moment. I'm from Brooklyn. I don't drive. Someone or something drives *me*.

After all that good exercise with Dante, I guess I could bike it. I get out my trusty Lonely Planet New York City map that has been unfolded and folded so often that streets have vanished from most of the creases. I trace a relatively direct route with my finger. If I ride by Red Hill Park and pick up Clinton Street, I can cross the Brooklyn Bridge.

Hmm.

Crossing the Brooklyn Bridge at night? In the rain or snow? It does give one pause. Once in Manhattan, I could zip by City Hall Park and eventually go up Sixth Avenue. Yikes. That gives one several pauses. But even if I dog it or walk my bike through traffic, I'll get to work in half an hour and save up to three thousand dollars a year. I'll also be in better shape . . . and arrive at work sweaty. Yeah, I'll be sweaty, and if it snows, I'll be in trouble. Unless they sell snow tires for bikes.

Maybe I can combine the water taxi with a bike—the water taxis have bike racks. It's only about five miles from Pier 11 to Rockefeller Center, and I could be at work within forty minutes.

I need a damn helicopter.

I get out of bed and stand at my open window looking out into the daylight. I have never quite gotten used to Red Hook's smell. It's nothing like the fresh, clean air in

Canada. I also miss the silence, the lapping waves, the crackling fireplace, the pine breezes, even the icy cold water, the sunsets, Dante's sweat. . . .

Sigh.

I need a few days off to recover, so I call in "sick," buy a bottle of Cavit Pinot Noir (2002), put on my new red, white, and green flannel shirt, drink two glasses of wine, and pass out.

I sleep almost twenty hours, my cell phone on and charging a few inches from my pillow.

No one calls.

I finish the bottle and toast Lady Liberty with an awful, made-it-up-without-thinking, I'm-sorry-Emma-Lazaru poem:

"I am so tired to the core
My still sore ass is yearning for Dant-ee
There's wretched refuse oozing from the
     Jersey shore
Send *him;* I'm homey-less, cross, and horny
I lift my glass . . . hey . . . I'm on the floor."

And I pass out again.

Sorry, Emma. Your poem is still the bomb. I am just a lightweight when it comes to drinking.

Late Sunday, the day before Labor Day, I call Dante one last time, telling myself that if he doesn't answer, it will be a sign. I hold my cross to my lips, and . . .

I let it ring fifty times.

Maybe I misdialed . . .

The *second* time, I let it ring only ten times.

Shit.

I call Red's cell phone again. "Red, Christiana. Maybe you didn't get my message before, and maybe you did. Whatever. It is vital I speak to Dante. I, um, promised that I'd check over the story with him, you know, check the facts." That was weak. "If I don't hear from him by . . ." I check the neon clock. Hmm. "If I don't hear from him by midnight tonight, I will have to run the story without his, um, approval. Bye."

I never ask anyone to approve one of my stories. Not even Shelley. She just cuts them.

I drift off to sleep. . . .

At 11:43, my cell phone rings. I grab it and say, "You're cutting it close, Mr. Lattanza."

"It's me, Red."

Shit.

"I had to drive almost to Barry's Bay until I got a signal," he says. "How are you?"

This isn't about me. "Where's Dante?"

"He won't be . . . It's just me, Christiana."

My heart sinks.

"I gave him both of your messages," Red says, "but he doesn't want to talk to you."

I sigh. "Did he say anything?"

"Not much. He's not talking much to anyone these days. I told him you needed to check your facts, and he said he trusted you."

Wonderful. "That's all he said?"

"That's all."

I have to know. "Are he and Evelyn . . . ?"

"He wouldn't talk about that either."

So there's hope? "What do you think?"

"I don't know, Christiana. I just don't know. I don't want to tell you the wrong thing. I want to get my facts straight, too."

I don't blame him. "How long did Evelyn stay?"

"I didn't ask. She wasn't here when we got here last night."

That was unhelpful. "Why won't he answer the phone? I've been calling and calling." When I've been conscious.

"I don't know, okay? As I said, he's not talking to anyone. He's training like a maniac. I know he's underweight by at least six pounds."

"You had better overfeed him, then, right?"

"I'm trying."

I don't want to say this. "They're going to get back together, aren't they, Red?"

He sighs. "It seems that way, but like I said, I just don't know."

Shit.

"But you can't give up on him just yet, Christiana," Red says. "As I said, he's not speaking to anyone. He's brooding more than usual. He's definitely not himself, and Evelyn isn't around. Just . . . give him some time, okay? You affected him in a good way."

"Sure." Why don't I believe him?

"Really. I saw it. Lelani saw it. He is, as they used to say, so in to you."

Right. "He hurt me, Red. He's hurting me now. He chose her."

"You don't know that, Christiana. Just don't give up—"

"Too late," I interrupt. "Too late."

I click off the cell phone, then turn it off entirely, booting up my laptop. I pull up the longer piece, the one without a title or a first paragraph. I type "Fighting for Love" as the title. Yeah. Fighting for the love of a shrew of an ex-wife. Then, I write the first paragraph:

> Dante Lattanza is "fighting for love," trying to recapture the middleweight title and the love of his life, his ex-wife *Evelyn*.

Then my fingers fly as I detail his loss to Washington, the argument he had with Evelyn, the "deal" he has struck with her—*everything*. I include his lack of a father, his generosity to Red and Lelani, and a more detailed look at his training habits, including the outdoor gym and that stupid tennis ball.

But mainly, I splatter Evelyn all over that story, and it isn't a pretty picture.

Dante wants to do the impossible, and it's interesting and futile at the same time. People like reading about futility. It's the Don Quixote in all of us, I guess. We all cheer for the underdog, the flawed person who fights to the finish despite impossible odds. "Fighting for Love" is a great title for that kind of story. Shelley might even move it forward in the issue. It could be a cover story. It has human interest, drama, a celebrity—and it's a bona fide exclusive.

Dante says that if he loses, he'll lose twice, and everyone will know it. But he hurt me. He threw his best punch, but I'm still standing. He's a big boy. He can handle it. He's a public figure. He knew I was interviewing him. He knew this could happen.

But win or lose, I lose.

And damn if I don't miss the living hell out of him.

Chapter 24

I show Shelley the new and improved longer piece at the end of September, and she loves it so much that she sneaks it into the first October issue, six *weeks* before the sexy-man puff piece and almost three *months* before the fight.

"Shelley, it should have run closer to the fight," I argue in her meticulously organized office at Rockefeller Center. It's so orderly that even those who practice feng shui leave her office out of harmony, out of synch, and out of touch with reality.

Most of the folks leaving her office are writers, so they essentially leave the same way they come in.

"It's a scoop, Christiana," she says, looking at the magazine I had thrown onto her desk. "It's romantic."

I remove a paper clip from a little red box and place it an inch from her Rolodex on the opposite side of her desk. Shelley puts the paper clip back.

"It's already in the top ten all-time, Tiana," she says.

I take the magazine and close it, exposing the cover. "Mainly because of these exclusive pictures of megacouple's bambino. What'd we pay for these? Three million? Four?"

"Only two million," she says. "This is their second child, not their first."

I work for the criminally insane.

"We'll have to change Lattanza's sexy bio, too," she says. "How about this: 'Why he's sexy: He's fighting for love.' Isn't that romantic?"

Fighting for love blah blah blah. "Shelley, this could ruin him."

"We've moved him up to number nine. That should make you feel better."

It doesn't.

She sits back. "Well, you wrote it."

"I wrote it to run closer to the fight," I say. "There would have been less time to ruin him then."

"It doesn't really matter, Tiana. As long as he wins, he isn't ruined, right?" She snatches the magazine from me and opens it to my story. "By the way, his picture looks great. How did you ever get that shot?"

It's of Dante standing in a T-shirt on the outcropping in front of a purple and red sunset. "We were talking, and there it was."

"It's so strong, so masculine." She smiles. "And I especially like the caption George wrote for it: 'Dante Lattanza fights for a dream in the sunset of his life.' Sheer poetry."

I skulk to my office, close the door, and try to hide. ESPN has been calling me nonstop for an interview. Several *Sports Illustrated* and *Times* writers want to talk to me. Every sports talk show on TV and radio is boosting it up. Interviews with other boxers and Dante's old trainer, Johnny Sears, appear daily in newspapers in New York, Connecticut, and New Jersey. They're all painting Dante as a fool. This morning, Tank Washington was on ESPN saying, "Well, at least *I'm* fighting for the championship."

I call Dante again. No answer. I call Red to leave another message, this one simply for Red to call me, but Red miraculously answers.

"How's he taking it, Red?" I ask.

"Why, hello, George. How's my big brother?"

He can only get a signal in town, so . . . "Are you in Barry's Bay?"

"Yes, George."

This kind of thing happened once to me before. I was checking my facts with an informant when the man he was ratting on walked into the room. "He's standing right there, isn't he, Red?"

"That's right . . . you're so right, George."

Damn. "Um, how'd he take the story?"

A pause. "Yeah. We'll be going *down* to Virginia soon. Yep. *Way* down south."

Shit. "So he's taking it badly."

"You said it, George."

"Shit."

"My sentiments exactly, George."

This sucks! "When are you leaving for Virginia?"

A long pause. "Lelani and I are heading out this afternoon, Christiana," he whispers.

"Where's Dante?"

"Getting his mail for the last time. Giving them a forwarding address. You want it? It's only a P. O. box number."

"Sure." I write down the address of a P.O. box in Radford, Virginia. "When is Dante leaving?"

"He'll be pulling out late tonight."

Geez. I have to hurry. "How did he get a hold of the article, Red? I mean, it just came out two days ago down here."

"It's on the Internet, too."

Oh shit. I had forgotten about that.

"Pictures and captions and all," Red adds.

I have broken so many promises to this man. Shit. And

to DJ. I all but promised I wouldn't make his *papino* look like a fool. "I have to come see him, Red."

The longest pause. "That would be a good idea, George, but I'm not sure if Uncle Don would like it very much. You know Uncle Don. Pretty stuck in his ways. Hard to change his mind once he gets a thought in his head."

"I don't care if Dante likes it or not. I'm coming," I say. "Wish me luck."

"Good luck, George. Bye."

I march into Shelley's office. "I am going to see Lattanza for a follow-up. I'll need to get on the next available plane to Ottawa."

"What's to follow up?" she asks.

Oh yeah. That. A real reason. Hmm. Aha! "I never really did get a chance to talk to Evelyn about how she felt about all this." I sort of did, but . . . "For all I know, she might not want to be with him whether he wins or loses." This is my greatest hope. "The story is only through Lattanza's eyes. I want to get her take on it. Wouldn't that make a great story?"

Shelley nods. "She'd be one cruel woman to hurt him again, so I doubt she'll tell you the truth."

Ain't that the truth.

"But on the other hand, if she only confirms what *he* said . . ." Shelley frowns. "You can just call her, can't you?"

Damn. "You know I prefer face to face, and I'll need pictures of her, right?" I'll shoot her with a wide-angle lens, superimpose a shrew over her face, and—

"But why go to Canada, Tiana? Lattanza's ex doesn't live there, does she?"

Damn damn damn, Shelley. Stop thinking. Be your usual self. "I have a source who has told me that Evelyn read the story and has gone to visit him."

"So call his house."

"It's a cottage," I say quickly. "And don't you think I

have been calling? I've been calling night and day, and no one answers the phone."

"Because the whole world wants to interview him." She smiles. "Either that or he's not even there."

Shit! "Look, Shelley, I'll level with you. The source is his friend and trainer, Red Gregory. He's the one who told me where to find Dante in the first place." Forgive me, Red. "I just got off the phone with him, and he told me Evelyn is up there with him as we speak, and they're not answering the phone."

Shelley bites the end of a pencil. "Why aren't they answering the phone?"

Think it through, Shelley. It'll come to you.

"Oh." She blinks. "You think they're . . ."

I nod. "Yeah. I'm sure they're conjugating."

"My. Those kinds of shots *would* make a nice spread."

She has an amazing way with words.

Shelley swivels to her computer. "I'll have your itinerary ready in a jiffy. You have a telephoto lens, right?"

I nod, but I know I won't need it. Evelyn is in Syracuse with her son, Red and Lelani are leaving soon, and only Dante will be at his cottage tonight.

I hope I can get there in time.

Five hours later, I arrive angry, tired, and worried. Freezing rain over Ottawa delays the flight. Customs is especially invasive, asking me why I don't have a single bag with any clothes in it. Enterprise refuses to give me anything bigger than a Chevy Trailblazer even though the roads are going to be treacherous. I slip and slide on the wet, icy roads while ice-laden pine trees bend their heads toward me.

And now, I'm standing at the Landing waiting on Joe, the only one on earth working here, to mount a motor on a boat.

"I tore down the boat the day after you brought it back," Joe says. "I don't normally have people renting boats this time of year, not with ice in the water."

Oh joy.

"How much ice are we talking?" I ask.

"Nothing like what sunk the *Titanic*," he says.

And that's all he says.

I have a new definition for "cold comfort."

It is a slow, cold, bumpy (what was that?!) boat ride to Dante's cottage, snow flurries gliding into my hair and sticking to pine trees all over the lake. Dante's bass boat rests nose-up on shore, the dock already torn down. Otherwise, I would think I was too late. No true fisherman leaves his fishing boat behind. Someone has boarded up all the cottage's windows, no smoke rises from the chimney, and there isn't a single light on.

Dante's cottage is in lockdown mode.

I knock on the door and enter, my breath preceding me, stamping my feet for good measure. The sound echoes throughout the cottage. I hear noise upstairs. Climbing up, I find Dante packing a huge duffel bag in DJ's room, a coarse black beard on his face.

He has to know I'm standing here, but I watch my breath for a few moments to be polite. "Hi," I say eventually.

Dante glances at me, then returns to his task.

That was a virtual cold shoulder. "I know I'm probably the last person on earth you want to see right now."

"You have come a long way for nothing," he says. "I am leaving soon."

"For Virginia?"

"No. First I stop in Syracuse to see DJ and Evelyn for several days." He glares at me. "Then I join Red and Lelani in Virginia."

That certainly makes where I stand much clearer. "Well, I came to tell you something in person. I've been calling you, but—"

"I boarded up the guesthouse and turned off the ringer to the phone the day Evelyn left."

Boom.

He sighs. "She only stayed one night and took DJ with her the next day."

Shit. I could have stayed. But if I had, I just *know* she would have stayed longer. "But when I called that morning, you were asleep in her bed."

"I did no such thing," he says with a wave of his left hand. "I have never slept in that bed. I sleep only in my room before a fight. On the floor. You should know this."

I sit on the edge of DJ's bed. "She said you two got busy." Okay, she said *Dante* was *very* busy. So what?

"We did not. We argued all night about you. I did not sleep at all. When did you call?"

They argued about . . . me?

"When did you call, Christiana?"

I look at my hands. "Around ten."

"I was still out fishing. A five pounder. Not as big as yours, but it was a nice meal. Just DJ and I went out one last time. A tradition. It is a promise I make to him. I keep my promises."

I deserved that. "Did you . . . What was the argument about exactly?"

"As I said, you."

I take a deep breath. "Did you tell her we slept together?"

"Yes."

I blink. "You did?"

"She asked, and I told her. But what does it matter now?"

I don't like this new tone in his voice. It sounds ominous

and foreboding. I shouldn't have believed her lies. "I'm, well, I'm just sorry." I stand and move closer to him. "You certainly look rough and ready for anything."

"I am ready."

I move even closer. "I'm planning to be at the fight. I can't wait till you—"

He whirls on me, his eyes fierce. "Why did you tell the world that I fight for love? Christiana, why did you do this?"

I take a large step back. "Yeah, about that, I'm really sorry. I wrote it, um, twice. The first time I kept my promise. But after talking to Evelyn, I was angry with you. You have to understand. I thought you had used me or something. I thought I was just a fling. You understand, don't you?"

"No. I do not."

Everything is so "yes or no" with this man. "But the article wasn't supposed to come out until the second week in December."

"And that makes it better?" he growls. "You broke your promise. I told you what not to write, what I preferred to keep away from the public, and you wrote it anyway. The world did not need to know about my father. The world did not need to know about why I am really fighting this time, but now it knows. If I lose, I lose twice. The world will laugh at me forever."

I want to explain how short most people's attention spans are, but now is probably not the time. I need to humble myself before him. "Like I said, I was . . . angry, you know? I thought you . . . I thought you slept with her."

"I am not that disloyal," he says without growling. "I tell you that you are in my heart. I do not say such things lightly."

"But you slept with me even though you were dating your ex."

He sits on the bed and begins rolling socks. "Evelyn and I have had three dates in ten years. She did not . . . she *has* not had my heart for a long time. If you had waited another day, just twenty-four hours, you would know this. But now, because of your words that are flying all over the place, I cannot turn on the TV without hearing this. I cannot listen to the radio without hearing this. Now I must fight and win to get her back. You have helped me make my choice."

"That's bullshit, and you know it!"

"Is it?"

Yes! "Dante, if *I* had stayed, *she* would have stayed."

"You do not know this for sure."

"No, not for sure, but would you have argued with her if I were still here?"

"Yes," he says with a nod. "I am good at it. She would have left, and you would have stayed with me."

I feel so stupid. "But I have a job, Dante. I couldn't have stayed long."

"Long enough." He zips up his duffel bag. "But now, it does not matter." He lifts the bag and carries it to the hallway, returning with an equally large empty duffel bag.

"Don't you care about me?" I ask.

"I did. For a moment. It was a great moment." He opens a closet and begins pulling out hangers containing pants and shirts. "One of my greatest moments." He stuffs the pants and shirts into the bag without folding them. "But it is gone. Before, I was unsure. After the article, I am sure. I will fight for my love. Is that clear enough? Make sure you write it correctly. This is another interview, is it not?"

"No," I say. "It's not. I came to apologize. I came to see you. I want to be with you. I have been miserable without you." I stare into his eyes. "I love you."

He leaps from beside the bed to within inches of me. "How can you say that? By saying I fight for Evelyn's love, you doom yourself. If I win, she gets me, not you. I do not understand."

"I don't understand it either," I say. "It's why I'm so miserable."

He closes his eyes. "I have been miserable *because* of you. Love should not be so miserable." He opens his eyes and returns to the duffel bag. "Love should not be *doloroso*."

"No, it shouldn't."

He begins pulling out drawers, all of them empty. "Love should have smiles in it like eaten watermelons."

What a wonderful quote.

"It should have *risata*, laughter, in it."

I step close enough to touch his arm, but I'm afraid of what he'd do. "Sometimes it has pain, too, Dante. Maybe this is one of those times."

He turns and nearly knocks me down. "No. It cannot be love if I feel so miserable. *You* can be miserable in love. I cannot." He slams shut all of the empty drawers. "So as you can see, we do not have as much in common as you once thought. We were not made for each other. We are not soul mates." He grabs the bags. "It gets dark soon. I am leaving."

I follow him out, grabbing his sleeve before he reaches the top of the stairs. "Dante, if you don't win . . . No."

He turns and puts down the bags. "No . . . no what? You will be there if I lose? You will be there to put me back together again? You will be the second prize? You want me to lose?" He picks up the bags and starts down.

I stay at the top of the stairs, afraid to go down. "I'll be there for you whether you win or lose, but in my heart, I know you're going to win, Dante." It's about time I cried. I need something warm on my face. "I don't want you to win because I know what that means, but I know you will win."

He slides the bags across the kitchen floor and turns. "How do you know this?"

I start down the stairs. "It's your heart, Dante. Your heart is big enough. It's always been big enough. Forget what I wrote before. Heart *is* enough to win the big fights. You *will* be the champ." I stop on the last step and rest my hands on his shoulders. "Just do me a favor."

His eyes soften some. "What? What is this favor?"

"Please throw fifty jabs per round."

He smiles (yes!). "It will weaken my hook."

I throw a left jab, which he blocks with ease. "It will keep Tank away from you. The only way he can hurt you is if you let him get inside. He is a *bravaccio*. He wore you down in the last fight with all those body shots. You must jab and work *his* body to keep him off you."

He puts my hand on his chest. It seems harder than before. "I am in the best shape of my life. I can take a punch. You should know this."

"Fake him out then. He knows about your left hook." I start to throw a lazy left hook. "Make him look for it all night. Keep his mind occupied by feinting and just keep jabbing." I let my fist gently touch his cheek. It's a new feeling, all that hair there.

"You want me to *box* him, Christiana? I have never done that in my life. It is not my style."

I hug him, and he doesn't push me away. "I want you to box him and out-fox him. You are the teacher, and he is the student."

"I am the teacher."

I lean back but hold onto his neck. "Yes. And I don't want him to hurt this face." I let my hands slide down that block of granite. "He can never hurt you unless he cuts you. Like I did, with that article, with a bunch of my articles. If you don't bleed, the judges will be fairer. You know that." I kiss his lips lightly. "And protect these, too." Oh

God, my heart hurts. "You'll, um, no." I can't make myself say, "You'll need them after the fight." I drop my hands and take a deep breath. "That's really what I came to say."

He nods. "You promise to be there?"

"Yes. I promise." With every breath of my being.

He nods again. *"Bene. Andiamo."*

On the "race" to the Landing, which his boat wins with ease, flurries the size of half-dollars hit and melt on my face, mixing in with my tears. I help him winch his boat to a trailer hitched to the Land Cruiser, even wading into the icy water to lend a hand.

I give him a long hug, kiss his cheek, and take his hands. "When I first got here, Red told me you were an amazing man, and I confess I didn't believe him at the time. I thought you were . . ."

"What?"

"A jerk."

He laughs. "I had you fooled then."

"But I was wrong, Dante. I believe." I pull the necklace out and kiss the cross. "I do this a lot now."

"I have rubbed off on you."

I nod. "In the best way." I hug him again, and his arms surround me and lift me into the air.

He kisses me gently on the lips.

"Just . . . stay amazing, okay?" I ask.

"You, too. Stay *pericolosa.*"

"I'll try."

He looks into the sky. "The snow is getting thicker. I will follow behind you until I turn right at the Shell station."

"Grazie."

I check the rearview mirror often to see if Dante is still behind me. Snow clings to the sides of the road now, and as we coast through Barry's Bay, all those memories come back. I stop at the stop sign, putting the Trailblazer in park.

I get out and go to his window. I can't think of anything to say. I just want to look at him one last time, just the two of us. I reach in and squeeze his left shoulder. "Jab," I finally say. "Don't forget."

He nods. "*Ciao,* Christiana."

I start to choke up and can't say good-bye. I run to the Trailblazer, get in, and weep across Ontario all the way to Ottawa. This is twice I've done it now. I should write a travel book called *Places to Drive When You're Weeping.* Ontario is okay. There isn't anyone to see you but the moose.

What did I just hit? I look in the rearview. Ew.

Check that. There isn't anyone to see you but the moose and rabbits with very big feet . . .

. . . and very flat heads.

Chapter 25

Back to my old life.
Heavy sigh.

I had a fling, it was nice, it ended, and I'm home. I was barely home before, putting so much time and energy into that story, looking for a way to get back to Dante—before I got back *at* him. I was here for weeks without really being here. I was just spinning my wheels waiting for . . .

I don't know what I was waiting for. An escape, maybe. A way out of here. I guess I'm just plain stuck here in Red Hook, a place everyone in New York says is "in transition." They've been saying that for a long time.

Maybe I've been in transition for a long time, too.

Being in transition sucks most of the time.

As is usual when I am depressed, I don't feel like cooking. Instead, I order takeout from Good Fork, a cozy eatery run by a carpenter/actor and his gorgeous tattooed Korean wife. Tonight I eat a roast mission-fig salad with *prosciutto di Parma,* Gorgonzola, and reduced balsamic dressing while I wait for my laptop to boot up. I'll save the fettuccine with lamb Bolognese and *parmigiano reggiano* for later.

Damn. I never order the fettuccine. I guess my brain is telling me, "If you can't *have* the Italian, you can at least *eat* Italian." I sample a taste. It's not as good as Red's but is infinitely palatable and more than enough to last me all weekend.

I toy with playing online spades (cutthroat, naturally) for a few seconds, but I decide instead to research Lelani, of all people. I'd like to write an article on her simply because our readers will also be amazed that the wahine is forty. Who knows? I may even use her in an article titled, "Card Girls Gone Good."

I know it's silly, but I need something to do to take my mind off Dante and my monumental mistake.

I guess I could start by changing the background of my opening screen. It's the shot of Dante carrying all our bags that day in Barry's Bay. I look at it and smile every time I see it.

I'll keep it. I can always use a smile.

I first go to the Hawaiian Tropic Web site but find the pageant photo archives only go back to 2003. I type in her first name in Google and freeze.

I don't know her last name. Why didn't I ask?

I guess I had tunnel vision. I had focused too much on Dante's dark eyes, those little tunnels of darkness. They practically disappeared at first in the closet. And then when he had my sweats down—

Stop.

Save him for your dreams.

Okay.

I look back at the screen. Hmm. How many people named Lelani can there be? It's not exactly a common name. I start my search.

And I see a crap load of sites.

I learn that *Lelani* (or *Leilani*) means "heavenly lei."

That fits the Lelani I know. I mean, she's a flower. And Red does seem happy with her. Maybe she *is* a heavenly lei.

Let's see . . . There's a stripper in California who goes by *Leilani*. She looks like a Joan. Don't ask me why. Her turn-on is "the perfect kiss." Mine, too. Okay, you don't look like a Joan anymore. You look more like a Kelly.

Again, don't ask me why. It might have been her freckles, her *lentiggine*.

Dante liked my *lentiggine*. He located and licked every single—

Stop.

Later, Christiana.

Okay, okay.

Here's a minor actress named Lelani Sorenson, who had bit parts on *Perry Mason* and *Leave It to Beaver.* I don't believe this. She received a film credit for simply being on a *poster* in Beaver's room. I knew actresses were two-dimensional, but come on.

Wait a minute. I am getting horny. Lei. Stripper. Beaver. You get the picture.

Stop.

Sorry.

Let's see . . . Lelani Kai, women's wrestler, won her only title in 1985. She doesn't look Hawaiian at all. She could be from Beard Street. I look closer. Hmm. Maybe not. She has a Bronx look about her.

Again, don't ask me why. I just *know,* all right? Gimme a break.

It's getting warm in here. Lei. Stripper. Beaver. Wrestler. Dante's beard—

Later, Christiana. Under the covers.

Okay.

Hey now. "Lelani" is a level-sixteen Blood Elf Rogue who has a talent for assassination, herbs, and mining in the World Warcraft game. I wonder if Lelani knows this.

There's not a whole lot sexual about that. I mean, it's not like Dante will send flowers, I'll strip, we'll wrestle, he'll mine my beaver with his beard, and I'll get lei-ed, right?

I should have bought a bottle of wine. I can get through this if I pass out.

Shh, Christiana. Later.

Okay, I'll click on the next Google page, and if it makes me horny, I will quit this right now and get under the covers with my fantasies.

Who's this? Lelani Drakeford, actress. This sounds safe. Let's see what—

This is freaky. Lelani Drakeford has only one credit, for a movie called *Dottie Gets Spanked*.

Yeah. Um. Well. Dante hits hard, you know, so . . . Hmm. Not that my booty couldn't handle it, it's just . . .

I finish my salad and start a new, hopefully less erotic search for Dante's father, who may also be the subject of a future article, especially if Dante wins. Maybe the article itself could become a catalyst for reuniting the two. I stare at the cursor and curse the cursor. I didn't ask Dante for his daddy's first name either. What am I good for? I type "Lattanza" and . . .

Ah. *Bene. Perfetto.* Pictures of Dante. A couple fan sites I've already visited. I can't let myself be distracted, but he is a nice *distrazione*. He hasn't aged a bit. I click to the next page and see more of him—and pictures of his bloated cheeks and bloody brows that accompanied my "over the hill" *Times* article ten years ago. That means someone has finally made the connection between the two pieces and—

I click on one of the old pictures. Yep. There are my two articles, ten years apart and side by side. Wonderful. At least I didn't use "vaunted left hook" in my most recent article.

Back to reality.

I switch to Web mode (no images) and find an Antonio Lattanza, who arrived in New York in the 1880s and settled in South Philly. Hmm. That's not exactly Brooklyn, and Dante said his ancestors battled Mussolini. Maybe they came to Brooklyn after WWII. Again, I didn't ask.

I let my journalism skills go all to hell in Canada.

There are plenty of folks named Lattanzi here and there. Let's try "Lattanzi" in the search box. Ah. Lattanzi Ristorante in Little Italy. Giuseppe. Paolo. Chloe. Barbara. Giovanni. Nicola. Wait. Barbara? Um, there's Matt Lattanzi, ex-husband to Olivia Newton-John. He's okay looking, in a boy-toy kind of way.

All this lusting leads me to look up *Heavy Leather,* at best a half-star movie with a laughable premise. A father pushes his son into boxing, then fights his son in a heavyweight championship bout. How, um, *not* bloody likely. Dante was onscreen for maybe three minutes, sparring with and bloodying up the son before the father steps in saying to Dante, "I'm-a gonna teach-a you a thing or two about boxing." Funny I remember that line. I also remember Dante ducking and running from the slower, portly father who somehow connects and dazes Dante.

Also not bloody likely.

Who thinks up this shit? A father fighting his own son? A beer-drinking, crotch-scratching has-been changing over-night into a heavyweight contender? And when he has his son dazed and confused and going down in the last round, the father suddenly relents and lets his own son knock him out. Great applause, lots of hugs, dinner at Sardi's, roll the credits.

I feel a strong need to go rent this movie, but Hole in the Wall Video is two miles away, and I don't feel like doing anything tonight.

I don't feel like doing anything at all.

At . . . all.

I don't even feel like surfing the Internet anymore, which is about as much nothing as I usually do when I'm recovering from an assignment.

I could always get under the covers with Dante, so to speak, and let my imagination and fingers run wild. Whoo, just the thought . . .

I've had a few erotic dreams with him, and they always leave me sweaty and even hornier in the morning. My all-time favorite has us in a scene in *From Here to Eternity*, only we're in a sleeping bag as waves crash over us. A lesser favorite, though extremely hot, has him hitting my booty from behind while we ride the F Train. Yeah, I am all over that F Train by the time we're—

Stop. Christiana, you're recovering from heartbreak. You need to get up, get out there, and get moving. You can't dwell in your sensual past. You have to start over. Now.

But I don't feel good. Am I lovesick? Is that even physically possible? Is it possible to be sick of love or be sick *from* love? Is this what withdrawal feels like? I type in "lovesick" in Google.

Lovely. There is such a thing.

I have some of the symptoms. Am I mentally ill? Well . . . maybe. I do live in Red Hook. Am I pale? No. Am I dry? Ashy, yes. Are my eyes hollow? I go to my mirror. No. Do I feel anxious? Yes. Am I tearful? Only when I'm driving through Ontario. Do I have insomnia? Only when I can't sleep. Do I have trouble concentrating?

Um, what was the question?

Do I have OCD? Do I check the phone for messages, watch the phone, or hold the phone waiting for it to ring? Sometimes. Am I obsessed over an object of "superstitious" value? Dante the Moose and I are very well acquainted, but I won't take him everywhere I go. Okay, I'll probably wear the flannel shirt he bought me until I can see through it. Is my stomach upset? A little. I blame the Gorgonzola. Do I feel dizzy or confused? Sure. I'm an American. Is my serotonin level dropping? What the hell is serotonin? Oh. It helps control my mood. If it's too low, one Web site urges me to eat sweets and complex carbohydrates like pasta. Hmm. So Italians have high levels of serotonin, and the more linguini I order from Good Fork, the better.

I chuckle over some of the ancient "cures" for lovesickness. Baths. I have a stand-up shower. I suppose if I duct-tape the glass . . . No. Conversation. "Well," I say, "I can always talk to myself." Music? Smokey and Johnny will help. Poetry? Not. Wine? I'll need more. Travel? I'll go to work. Therapeutic intercourse? Only if it's with Dante Lattanza.

Am I going to start over?

Nah.

Not when I'm feeling inert. I wonder if inertia is a symptom of lovesickness, because I certainly feel inert. Yep. That's it. I'm an inert gas, and I'm not going anywhere.

What was that sound? Hmm. Maybe not all of my gas is inert. Again, I blame the Gorgonzola.

I am just going to stay in my "space" and float. In fact, I am going to do absolutely nothing and do it well. I'm going to do it so well that I'm going to write a book about it. I'll call it *Doing Nothing and Doing It Well*. It will be kind of a self-help book for people who have fallen in lust at first sight, an it's-okay-to-be-depressed-about-fucking-up book. "You lusted, you lost" will be the first sentence. "Sucks, doesn't it?" will be the second. It will probably sell well. I mean, look at *Seinfeld*. That show was about nothing, and America ate it up and asked for seconds.

Then the phone rings, and I find I have a problem. Well,

it's not really a problem. It's a conundrum. If I get up and answer it, I will be doing something, breaking my vow of doing nothing. If I *don't* get up and answer it, I will also be doing something, albeit in an apathetic, who-gives-a-shit kind of way. Which, then, is *less* nothing to do?

Decisions, decisions . . .

Chapter 26

I answer it, rationalizing that it's probably nothing. "Hello?"

"Tiana, you have to go out to the left coast."

Oh, it's only Shelley. She'll understand my quest for nothingness. It's kind of a requirement for her job, too. She edits nothing all day, and someone higher up actually publishes that nothing. "I'm taking some days off, Shelley. I'm beat."

"Toby McBain lost his house and car in a wildfire out there, and he has three more sexy men to do, so . . ."

I want to laugh (Toby is gay), but that would be doing more than I want to do right now. "So Toby can still do his damn job, Shelley. He doesn't need a house to do an interview at someone *else's* place. Don't tell me his ability to call for a cab or rent a car was burned up, too."

"He's very distraught," Shelley says. "He can't find one of his dogs."

Now *that* sucks. I like dogs. Unless they're purebred lap dogs with names like Mr. Bubbles or Mrs. Fancy Pants. I prefer mutts with names like Come Ear and Shithead.

"I wanted you to do those interviews anyway," Shelley says. "You'll write them better than Toby any day."

Not if I'm wallowing in self-pity. "Look, Shelley, I just

got back and have loads of laundry to do." But that would require doing something, too, so I guess I've just lied. "And I have tons of shopping to do, and—"

"You can have all the time you need when you get back," Shelley says.

I kind of like the sound of that. That will give me ample time to perfect nothingness. "You say they have wildfires going on?"

"Yes. Just north of San Diego. Nowhere near where you're going."

I am never going to write that book on nothing. Hmm. I'd have to do something for it to exist, and the critics would say I'm a hypocrite. "She obviously wrote the damn thing," they'll say, "so she's contradicting herself."

My fax machine kicks into gear, spitting out what looks like . . . yep. It's an itinerary. Shelley is far too efficient for *my* own good.

"Shelley, please. There has to be someone already out there who can do Toby's job." I could randomly pick any name from a Southern California phone book who could do Toby's job.

"Tiana, you're my first choice."

At least I'm someone's first choice.

"I want you to do it," she says. "Your tickets will be at the counter . . ."

I tune her out. Shelley thinks I actually listen to her while she's acting managerial. And it kills me that she has yet to ask even a single question about my return trip to Aylen Lake. It's possible she's simply forgotten I went to interview, um, Evelyn. Maybe I should bring it up, you know, at least so I'll have someone to talk to about Dante.

Hmm. Better not. I'd have to make up more lies. That would require thought, and I don't feel like thinking right now.

After a sleepless, sweaty night (I had dreamed I was alone in a sleeping bag inside a sauna talking to a cartoon Blood Elf Rogue named Lelani), I sleep all the way to crappy LAX, rent a crappy car, and head for number four's crappy beach bungalow, cursing every crappy California driver I can. I intend to get numbers four and seven done before lunch today, and I know I can do it. I mean, they can't have anything to say. They're *real* celebrities.

While number four's crappy bedmate/girlfriend/slut-for-the-day/whatever sunbathes topless on a deck off a dump of a bungalow facing the Pacific in Manhattan Beach, number four complains about his last two crappy action-adventure movies that were "directed by a fucking idiot fool moron." Um, I want to ask him, if you knew the first movie was crappy, why'd you sign on for the second with the same fucking idiot fool moron director? I don't, though. I don't want to make this man upset. He has an unintelligent temper. A few years ago, he threw his cell phone at one of New York's finest outside a club in Manhattan (how ironic). The phone shattered into a million pieces on impact with the cop, yet number four attempted to punch him out anyway. A Taser reduced number four to a sniveling ball of moronic goo, the entire incident ended up on YouTube and *Entertainment Tonight,* and the cop probably hasn't had to pay a cover charge at any club in Manhattan since.

Unfortunately, number four is easy on the eyes, and he is what *Personality* thinks is what *America* thinks is sexy. Five questions and ten minutes are all I need. The pictures take longer. Bedmate Bimbo Bitch wants to be in the picture. She rises and I swear her breasts make a *boing* sound as they leap into the air.

"It'll be *so* hot," she tells him, pressing those silicone fun bags against his back.

"It's not about you," he tells her.

She backs off, her fun bags reinflate, he cracks a smile, and I take the picture.

Done.

I find the infamous number seven on location in a studio getting his face painted, er, made up. He has very large pores and unusually nasty onion breath. He spends most of the interview spouting invectives against the war in Iraq. "We shouldn't have ever fucking gone there, okay?" is his most intelligent quote. He plays an idiot on *Don't Go There* and has most of the funniest lines, but none of what he's said about the Middle East will make it into *Personality*. I draw little curlicues and put beards on smiley faces while he rants, a speck of white spittle growing ominously in one corner of his mouth. I know Shelley will cut the antiwar quotes and say that he's "politically active and outspoken on contemporary issues." That will probably be why *Personality* thinks he's sexy.

He tells me that he's leaving this "fucking idiotic" show at the end of the "fucking idiotic" season for a "fucking" career on the big screen. I almost tell him he'll be stuck in moron roles for the rest of his *fucking* life, but I don't want to take the three hours it would require to *fucking* explain it to him.

"To get out of the box," he says, cutting the shape of a TV with his hairy-knuckled hands, "I have to think *outside* the box. You get me?"

I want to encourage him to think, but I think that might get in the way of his career.

Once he's fully painted (his makeup artist had to work for Earl Scheib), he drags me to the set and has me take fifty pictures of him sitting on a couch in various poses. After the first five, I fake pushing any buttons.

I did like the couch. At least the couch had character.

"How'd I do?" he asks at the end of the interview, that

white fleck of spittle looking dangerously like a pimple about to explode.

I want to lie and tell him he's an ass, but I'm afraid he'll take it as a compliment. "Fine," I say, shielding my eyes from the—damn, that's a boil. Ew.

Done.

Instead of checking into my crappy hotel room, I drive cursing to crappy LAX and book a crappy flight to Seattle, where number eight is filming yet another crappy David vs. Goliath–type coming-of-age jock movie. I'm sure it will get crappy reviews. While waiting for my flight, I call Shelley, who can't believe I've already finished two interviews.

"That was *quick*," she says. "You are amazing."

Whatever.

From the plane, I use the crappy plane phone to call number eight's publicist, who puts me on hold while he "reaches out" to number eight. The accountants at *Personality* will hate me for the phone bill, but I don't care. When the publicist comes back on, he says, "He can give you a twenty-minute window."

Whatever.

As misty-minded as the Seattle weather, number eight has even *less* than nothing to say about anything, which could be some sort of record for Hollywood. Maybe I should get him to write the preface to my book on nothing. Shoot, he could probably write the whole thing. Hmm. I'd have to get him a big box of crayons and some primary school ruled paper, you know, the kind of paper with dotted lines to guide his letters. Then, we'll get some safety scissors and cut and paste what he writes to make the book. . . .

A former star volleyball player at UCLA, number eight has rugged good looks, a disarming smile, a cleft chin, and dimples, but that's about the only thing busy and working about this man's head.

"What is the secret to your success?" I ask.

"I've just been successful," he says.

I rephrase the question. "*How* have you been so successful?"

"Successfully," he says, and he says it seriously.

I . . . kid . . . you . . . not.

I want to hit him with a left hook to get his two brain cells on speaking terms. "Would you say you're riding a wave of success?"

He smiles. "Oh, yeah. It's been quite a ride on the waves of my success."

It's like pulling teeth. I write down the quote I *fed* to him. It's just dumb enough to make someone in America think it's sexy.

"Tell me about the movie you're shooting."

"Well, it's about this guy who has a kid, and the guy was, like, all-world and stuff in sports, and the kid is, like, a total dork, you know?"

I nod. I know a total dork when I see one. I will be taking his picture shortly.

"What about your character matches your personality?" I ask, frowning inside because I have ended my question with a five-syllable word.

He stares at me.

I give him a simplification. "How are you and your character alike?"

"Oh. Well, we're both, um, buff, and athletic, and like, all into healthy stuff."

How, like, totally, like, unquotable.

And stuff.

I take several pictures of him walking a rocky beach barefoot, his pants legs rolled up, his feet and ankles blindingly white, his long surfer's hair flapping in the breeze. He then gets it in his head to jog away from me.

"Keep taking pictures," he says, "I want you to get my best side."

His ass *is* about the smartest part of him, so I take lots. Shelley will rejoice. When he comes back, he's pouring sweat, bent over and out of breath. "Got a cigarette?" he asks.

I . . . kid . . . you . . . not.

On the flight back, I compare these three "leading men" to Dante, and Dante kicks the living shit out of them. When it comes to action and adventure, Dante throws bombs while number four makes them—and often. When it comes to being genuinely funny, Dante is good with the jabs and gibes while number seven just *looks* funny. And when it comes down strictly to backsides, Dante is *smokin'* while number eight plainly smokes too much.

And they all precede Dante on the sexy-man list.

Someone in editorial is a fucking idiot fool moron.

Chapter 27

Weeks drift by, cold November weather drifts in, and I drift about my business.

And the assignments I get generally suck.

Shelley assigns me a series of "Where are they now?" pieces, stories designed, in many cases, to resuscitate and resurrect the dead, I mean, former stars' careers. It is my job to return child stars and other former celebrities to the collective American consciousness. I will first have to remind readers why these people were once celebrities.

That's usually the hardest part of the assignment. *What were we thinking?* I wonder as I struggle. *What the hell made them special?*

Second, I will detail their falls, meteoric or not, into obscurity. The police blotter and court records usually do the trick here, though I actually have to dig for information on others. Like Dante, they just simply evaporated into oblivion.

Finally, I will update our readers on these former celebrities' current situations. I'll only have to use my camera for this part. Once our readers see them as they are now, they'll go back to the original question: *What were we thinking?*

I go to Miami and interview a former one-hit wonder rapper who now works in a video store stocking shelves and recommending Woody Allen films. No one asks for his autograph now, but he says, "They all want to see me do my dance." I ask him to show me, and he does, flapping his arms while marching in place. That was a *dance*? It looks like a man trying to fly. Those pictures—in heart-wrenching sequence—will accompany his story.

I rent a car and drive up to Stamford, Connecticut, catching up with a former model-turned-infomercial spokesperson. At sixteen, she was the "it" girl, appearing on billboards, magazine covers, and commercials for designer clothes, expensive cars, and weight-loss products. Now she hawks acne creams. Supremely articulate with a doctorate in physiology, she says she doesn't miss the glamour and the glitz at all. "I get to eat now," she says. I take a picture of her eating her way into a size fourteen. Her eyes are still skinny.

I fly into Lubbock, Texas, where I interview a former NFL rookie of the year who blew out a knee his second year in the league. After some brutal rehab in the off-season, he returned only to blow out the other knee in training camp. Undaunted, he returned to the University of Texas, received a BA in history, and now teaches middle schoolers the history of the great state of Texas. He hobbles terribly and still uses a cane as he continues to rehab the other knee, but it's a proud hobble. "Sometimes I think I get more respect now than when I was in the NFL," he says. I take respectful shots of him and his students, who really love this guy. Shelley chooses to run the one of him hobbling on his cane instead. I send him a letter of apology, but he takes it in stride, sending me the nicest e-mail: "It's okay. Come back in a year, and you can take pictures of me running."

I take a taxi out to Flushing to interview one of the many redheads who played Annie on Broadway. She's still giving shows at twenty-one, and she's still using "Tomor-

row" to make a buck today. The folks in the audience at
Flushing House didn't seem to mind. "I love to see their
smiles," she says. "I love it when they sing along." I get
several shots of her removing her red wig. We should get a
few letters to the editor for those.

I go to Harlem and interview a misunderstood rapper,
one of the first to curse on CDs before Tipper Gore and her
warning labels. "I got no air time after that," he tells me. "I
had to go underground. I had to be a voice crying from the
wilderness." He shares some of his serious poetry with me,
and it is fantastic. I suggest he get these poems published
in a collection. "Can't make a buck with poetry," he says.
"But music moves in cycles. One day my words will be
righteous again." I include a section of a poem in my piece:
"love is soft as sunrise, simple as sky, silent as silk, solemn
as sea"—Shelley cuts it. The shot of him in his Kangol is
one of the best shots I've ever taken, the lighting and background just right. Naturally, Shelley chooses the one I take
of him flashing ancient gang signs against a graffiti-covered
wall.

My last "Where are they now?" piece takes me to Des
Moines, Iowa, where I interview a former famous twin.
While her sister wallows in fame and swallows too much
alcohol—two DUIs in the last few months—this twin leads
an ordinary life. She didn't go Ivy League, instead attending the University of Iowa and earning an art degree. "I
like being married," she says, tending to her two kids (ages
seven and three) while pursuing her painting dreams. "I
like having the whole picket fence, dog, and stay-at-home
experience. It's where I belong." She certainly seems content, smiling confidently at her professor husband in the
original shot. When Shelley cuts him out and inserts the
other twin in his spot, it makes it look as if content twin is
looking up to and envying the crazy twin.

I have to write so many apology letters to these people.

All of these former stars had fame thrust upon them at early ages. Some couldn't handle it and had no backup plan. The world simply left a few behind. Yet others have thrived out of the spotlight, succeeding like the rest of us in spite of everything. Of all the interviews I've done for *Personality,* these were the saddest and yet most interesting to me.

It is such a shame I only have respect for former celebrities. I like them because they're just like me now.

Throughout these travels, I've been doing a lot of reading, mainly of interracial romances. These are new to me, and I'm surprised there are so many out there. Like any other books I read, I like some and I don't like others. I like the ones that only mention race and get on with it, letting the cover pictures do most of the "racial" work. Okay, I think to myself while looking at the cover, they're different. So what? All people are different. All relationships are different. Tell me a good story about these two. Entertain and enlighten me.

I'm finding that I don't like books that focus solely on race and the "jungle fever" aspects of it all. Yeah, the sex can get red hot, though sometimes the sex scenes read more like an anatomy class lecture. I get the feeling the authors believe the sex is hot *only* because of the contrasts. Back in the day, that might have been normal because interracial sex was taboo, but in today's multicultural society that just doesn't seem realistic to me. Constant conflict, contrast, and jungle fever are *not* good bases for lasting relationships. I prefer interracial romances that transcend race and just tell a good story of a strong man and a strong woman getting together and getting it on. These kinds of books, however, depress me some. Dante and I were strong people, we got together, we got it on, and now we've gone our separate ways. I wish our ending were as happy as the endings I've been reading.

Some days, depression gets the best of me, and I take

the F Train out to Coney Island, walking the barren board-walk, taking pictures of unmoving rides, floating through the New York Aquarium, and walking the beach. The desolation consoles me somehow and says, "Hey, your life isn't half bad." Isn't that what Lawrence Ferlinghetti has been trying to tell us? That life is only "a Coney Island of the mind"?

I also get hot dogs from Nathan's when I'm there. I may be depressed, but I'm not crazy. You can't go all the way out to Coney Island and not get a Nathan's hot dog at Surf and Stillwell. It's un-American. If I didn't get a cheese dog smothered in chili, Krinkle Cut fries, and a large fresh-squeezed lemonade, I'd feel like a traitor to my country.

All this doing nothing is making me fat. I don't quite fit in the skinny little mirror near my dresser, my pants whine, and my tops pop off—buttons, usually. After thinking about joining Gleason's for eighty dollars a month and quickly discounting that idea—I'd be too embarrassed to work out in front of all those hard bodies—I get on the Internet and create a gym right here in my space.

It doesn't cost as much as I thought it would. Shoes—forty-two dollars. Adidas. Not my brand, but they were on sale. A pipe-metal speed bag and heavy bag platform—two hundred dollars. I don't want to scar my exposed ceiling in any way. An Italy Country Pride Everlast heavy bag—a hundred. It's solid white with red and green accents. Italy Country Pride Evergel and regular boxing gloves—seventy-five dollars. With the Evergel gloves, I won't need to wrap my hands at all, and they fit inside my regular gloves like, well, gloves. A six-piece Everlast speed bag set and a jump rope—seventy dollars. For five hundred, the cost of six-plus months at Gleason's and maybe only a few months at fancier gyms, I have my own boxing gym.

Having a place where I can lose some of my pity-party blubber in secret—*priceless*.

I don't know why more women don't do this kind of workout. I use every muscle in my body, don't have to use a big inflated ball, don't have to listen to anorexic women tell me to "feel the burn, ladies," and I don't have to buy expensive shorts, sweats, or tops to "be seen." I estimate that I burn over five hundred calories an hour. I'd have to do over ninety minutes of low-impact aerobics to get the same results.

On the wall next to the metal platform, I posted the Virgil quote that assaults you at Gleason's Gym—with some minor changes:

NOW, WHOEVER HAS COURAGE AND A STRONG, COLLECTED SPIRIT IN HER BREAST, LET HER COME FORWARD, LACE UP HER GLOVES, AND PUT UP HER HANDS.

I have put up my hands a *lot*.

I rise at four-thirty every morning now, put on some sweatpants, and get right sweaty to the glorious sounds of Andrea Bocelli, a blind Italian tenor who has the most sensuous voice. I still listen to Smokey Robinson (and all of his Miracles) and Johnny Mathis, and I occasionally throw in some Sinatra. Besides the obvious benefits of working out, getting up at four-thirty allows me to take a longer shower and rush less afterward. I don't feel guilty all day about not working out or grouse at work about *having* to work out *after* work. I have no extra clothes in a gym bag to schlep around, I have no chance to go home sweaty or tired, and I get to bed at a reasonable time. At four-thirty, even in Red Hook, the world is asleep, peaceful, and serene. I don't need a psychologist, psychiatrist, maharishi, spiritual guide, therapist, counselor, guru, or personal trainer to make me feel better about myself, and cleaning

up sweat on hardwood is a breeze. Some days I work out so
hard I fog up my window.

I have an intense workout.

After all, I had a good teacher.

I work out for fifteen four-minute rounds. I jump rope
for six rounds, *resting* in between each round. I ain't crazy.
I hit the heavy bag for four rounds, not resting at all between rounds. There's just something cathartic and therapeutic about slamming your fists against a big heavy target
and hearing the *pop* and the *pow*. Besides, I have to get
back at my neighbors somehow for all their nocturnal hammering, cutting, and sanding. And, it releases a lot of the
sexual tension that has built up in my body since . . .

I can't get that man out of my head. I've divided my life
into two parts: BD (before Dante) and AD (after Dante). I
miss him.

End of whiny, pining interlude.

And now, back to boxing.

I do the speed bag until I can't hold my arms up any
longer (about two rounds), shadowbox in front of the mirror for two more rounds, and do as many crunches and
push-ups as I can, ending it all with more jumping rope.

My sweats fell off me the other day while I was shadowboxing.

It was cool.

On my legs. Since the window fogged up, I kicked the
sweats away and finished my workout in my underwear.

That was kind of hot, you know?

I'm not the kind of girl to measure myself or even weigh
myself—I'm too old to care much about that kind of thing
anymore. I take me as I am, and I think I've dropped at
least fifteen pounds. I stare down at three inches of space
between the top of my pants and my hips, and I have to
wear a belt. My breasts bounce around in every bra I own
except my sports bras. My booty is tight, muscular, and,

well, it's still out there. No amount of sweat and bounce is going to diminish what heredity has given me. What I like most is my stamina. I can take stairs, run for the train and the bus, and even jog through Red Hook without losing my breath.

I am alive, and I feel *good*.

I stand naked in front of the mirror after every shower and pose. I have cuts. I have abs. I have perky breasts. They don't go *boing*, but they are definitely at attention. I have calves. I have biceps and triceps. I even have tighter skin around my jaw line. I will never become anorexic Evelyn, but let me tell you something—I am one fiercely sexy *corpo provocante* now.

I'm also into saving money like a bandit for some reason. I know, I spent money on my little gym, but when I think of how much I will save in the end by *not* going to a gym, I feel right thrifty. Instead of getting a fancy coffee from the Coffee Den, I make myself a commuter cup of Red Rose tea every morning. I was amazed to find these wonderful tea bags at Fairway Market one morning, and I bought up every box and bag I could. I have yet to find authentic Chelsea buns like the ones Red fried up that morning, but I will. I even cook fish filets on occasion, using Red's "secret" recipe. I checked out Fulton Fish Market but found no smallmouth bass. What a letdown.

But I feel stronger, I feel healthier, I'm more fiscally responsible, and I am damn sexy.

Sigh.

Maybe I'm ready for a real relationship for the first time in my life.

I've noticed other men noticing me more and more. At first, it was subtle. You know, the casual stare, the shifting eyes as I walked through Rockefeller Center. Now that I'm a *scultura* in perpetual motion, I see men racing to share an elevator with me, often riding to the wrong floor. They make pains to sit near me on the bus. They hover near me on the subway. They pause when I pause in front of windows on Broadway. Most are decent looking, but none of them has Dante's eyes. None of them has that penetrating stare of his.

None of them is Dante.

After you've been with a god, you can't simply settle for mere mortals, right?

For the longest time, nothing, and I mean nothing, excited me except my workouts. Okay, it's exciting for men to ogle me, too, but now that I'm in physical shape, I like myself again. My mind occasionally crashes, but twenty minutes on the heavy bag brings me back to life.

I actually go places now. I take pictures just to take pictures: of the waterfront, of children playing, of folks on the subway, and of people picking through fruit and vegetables in front of Fairway Market. I even use the self-timer to take a picture of me fishing on the Valentino Pier, sending it to Dante at the P.O. box in Virginia, "Catch any big ones lately?" written on the back. I don't know if he opened it or not. I hope he did.

And I hope he didn't start a fire with it afterward.

I do my best not to limit myself to Red Hook. I attend Knicks games, hearing my own voice's echo most nights. I even go to the Jimmy V Classic at the Garden to watch unpaid premier basketball players throwing down dunks and hitting three-pointers. The Knicks should watch *them* play. I frequent the Lyceum Theater again, seeing old classics like *A Streetcar Named Desire* and *On the Waterfront*.

I am alive again.

Oh sure, I still want Dante Lattanza with a passion I've never had before. My solution isn't the greatest, but it helps. I bought the *Heavy Leather* DVD. I've watched Chapter 9 more than once a night for the last three weeks. Sometimes three times if I'm really horny. I slow the sparring scenes down and zoom in on Dante. Sometimes I shadowbox with him. At one point, though, Dante looks directly at the camera, at *me*, with those eyes of his, and I . . .

Whoo.

It's quite a boxing workout.

Speaking of boxing, I've watched HBO's *Countdown to Washington-Lattanza II* twice. I was, um, hmm. I, uh, I turned down the sound the first time and kind of, well, got intimate with the TV screen whenever Dante was on and then . . .

You get the picture. Luckily, I have a widescreen TV and heavy-duty shades on my window. The lip marks come off the screen easily with a little Windex.

I turn the sound all the way up for a live ESPN feed of today's press conference. Tomorrow night, they'll weigh in, and both of them will probably gain ten to fifteen pounds by fight time, turning them into light heavyweights.

Dante is clean shaven (sigh . . . I kind of liked the beard) and wears a nice dark blue suit. He could be a *GQ* model without even trying to pose. He just has such a presence, an aura of power around him.

Meanwhile, Tank sports a black suit with gold chains, a large lion medallion where a tie should be, his fingers and his mouth filled with gold. He has no presence. All he has is bling, a shiny bald head, and a blond goatee.

Oh, and the championship belt. Almost forgot. He's had that for ten years.

I turn up the volume just in time to hear a question that makes me cringe:

"Champ, what do you think of your opponent fighting for love?"

Tank smirks. At least I think it's a smirk. He has so much bling in his mouth it could be a grimace of pain. I'll bet his gums bleed all day.

"Only a dumb *<bleep>* fights for love," Tank says,

adding a "heh-heh" for bad measure. ESPN must have the feed on a five-second delay. Tank said MF. Shame on him. That's such a nasty word.

"It is the *best* fight there can be," Dante says, Red sitting beside him. "It is the *only* fight worth having."

"Attaboy, Dante," I whisper. "Shut the MF up." What? I didn't say the whole word. *Pericolosa* women can say "MF."

Tank stands and points at Dante. "Old man, you are full of *<bleep>*."

Dante doesn't stand, and instead of facing Tank, he smiles at the reporters. "I am not full of *merda*. I am full of love."

The reporters laugh, and so do I. Dante cursed in Italian, and ESPN didn't catch it. I've been learning Italian from a site on the Internet. I'll never be fluent, but I know all the curse words. I say *palla* (bullshit) and *idiota* (asshole) often, especially when I'm watching the refs make *palla* calls against the Giants or some *idiota* takes the last seat on the F Train.

Tank points into the audience at . . . Evelyn. "That her?"

Evelyn looks like a twig. Some of my lamps have more meat on their bones than she does.

Dante doesn't respond.

"Don't go there, Tank," I whisper. "You're already an MF. Don't become a *merda*."

"How you doin', mama?" Tank says.

He went there. *Idiota.*

"Baby," Tank says, showing all of his bling, "after I put this fossil back in the ground where he came from, you can love me long time."

There is no laughter this time.

I expect Dante to leap to his feet, but he only rolls his eyes. "At least I fight for something important."

Tank smirks for real this time. "C'mon, Danny Boy. In

the end, you fight for money, just like me. You ain't no better than me."

Dante is nodding to himself. He whispers something to Red, and Red's eyes pop.

Uh-oh. Something's about to happen.

"We will make it winner takes all then," Dante says, and all hell breaks loose. A million camera flashes go off. Red closes his eyes, and so do I.

"What?" Tank says the same time I finally find my voice to yell *"Che?"*

Dante stands and waits for the pandemonium to die down. "Winner takes all. Put it on paper, and I will sign it."

Nobody moves a muscle until Dante whispers something to Red, who pulls out a crumpled . . . That *has* to be a receipt for something. Not the receipt, Red. Get a real piece of paper. I'm sure it will fetch a bundle on eBay, but . . .

Oh. It's just a pen.

Dante takes the pen and pulls the fight poster off the podium. I have half of one hanging near my mirror. Dante's half. It has smooch marks on it. Dante writes rapidly and hands the poster to Tank, who reads it and shakes his head, Tank's entourage of seven or eight Tank clones surrounding him and shaking their heads, too. What a bunch of bobble-heads!

"You're crazy as a *<bleep>*, Danny Boy, but I'd be crazier than a *<bleep>* not to take this deal." Tank signs the poster with a flourish.

Dante offers his hand across the podium.

"Nah, Gramps," Tank says. "You gonna need that hand to wipe up your own *<bleep>* after I wipe up the ring with your *<bleep>*."

The press conference ends with Tank and company leaving in a pack.

Oh . . . my . . . God!

Winner takes all. We're talking at least seven figures

here, probably *eight* if enough folks watch replays of this press conference and order pay-per-view.

"Fighting for love *and* winner takes all," an announcer says from his perch at the ESPN studio. "What's your take on this, Harry?"

Oh, *merda.* It's the dreaded Harry, halting and consti-pated deliverer of clichés other clichés get tired of hearing. "It could be (pause) the fight of the century (*pregnant* pause), if it gets past (pregnant and *way* overdue, the-baby-is-*crowning* pause) the first round."

"So you think it's going to be a quick fight."

"To paraphrase Tennyson," Harry says, reaching *deep* into nineteenth-century Victorian freaking England for a cliché tonight, " 'Tis better to have loved and lost (they've already cut the umbilical cord, Harry, and the child is teething) than never to have *boxed* (the kid has a driving li-cense, Harry) at all."

What . . . the . . . crap?

Harry has never boxed a *single* millisecond in his life, yet there he is, giving so-called "expert" analysis on box-ing. What a bunch of *palla!* If I ever need surgery, I'm not going to go to a doctor who has merely *watched* one thou-sand operations. I'm going to the doctor who has actually *done* some successfully. More boxers need to go into broadcasting to squeeze out these Tennyson-quoting, con-stipated, hairless men with spewing pimples for mouths who call themselves experts. Maybe Dante could be a box-ing analyst after he finally retires. I know I'd tune in to hear what he had to say.

Okay, okay. I'd tune in just to hear his voice.

And to kiss my TV.

I get online and go to a Las Vegas Web site that promises live, up-to-the-minute odds updates. I'm just curious. It isn't as if these odds have anything to do with the ultimate out-come. Last night, Dante's numbers looked grim. With only a $100 bet, I could have won $1,400 if Dante won on Saturday. I would have had to bet $750 on Tank just to win $100. The numbers for the fight to go the distance were off the charts, most predicting a Washington knockout before the *fourth* round.

But not now.

Dante's $1,400 drops to $250 before my eyes, Tank's $750 tanking to $210. I know this is a simplification, but Dante went from a 14–1 underdog to a 5–2 *challenger* in a matter of minutes. Now, the odds are almost even for the fight to go into the tenth round.

A half an hour later, Dante's $250 falls to $125, and Tank's $210 drops to $105, the fight all but guaranteed to go the distance.

The fight, then, is almost dead even according to the odds makers.

Dante says, "I fight for love," and Las Vegas doesn't blink. Dante says, "Winner takes all," and Las Vegas gets nervous, dropping Dante from a 14–1 underdog to a 5–4 *contender* in thirty minutes.

I wish I had bet $1,000 yesterday. When Dante wins— and he *will*—I would have won $14,000, enough for almost seven *years* of riding the New York Water Taxi. But now that I'm in shape, I won't need to be "carried" to work. I can do that all by myself now, whether on a bike or on my own two legs. It's only ten miles.

Hmm. I may need a bike. Twenty miles a day? One *hundred* miles a week? Over five *thousand* miles a year?

I'll get a bike.

Fighting for love and winner takes all. Amazing. It's all so elemental. Why do you fight? For love. And if you win, you take it all. Simple. All sports should be this simple.

But . . .

There's just something fundamentally wrong about this. What is so wrong with fighting for love? I know, I know.

I used to think it was cheesy. But now I don't. The odds should have been much lower *before* Dante said, "Winner takes all." Maybe I can write an article that makes light of all this *palla*.

Sì.

Maybe I can write an article that will repair some of the damage I've done to Dante.

I smile.

Sì.

An op-ed piece. I'm good at those.

And coming from the mean ol' wench who said Dante was washed up all those years ago—and written by the *itch* who revealed he was fighting for love in the first place—the *Times* will have to publish it. They'd have to. And maybe Dante would read it.

Sì.

The *Times* would run it Saturday, the day of the fight.

Sì.

But if I'm going to fight all this *palla*, I'm going to need some *munizione*. And where in New York can anyone find plenty of ammunition?

Brooklyn.

Andiamo!

Chapter 28

I have a *merda*-load of work to do today.

After calling in sick ("I feel so"—*cough*—"lousy, Shelley"), I go to Carroll Gardens and find Dante's old house. It's easy to find. The neighborhood has decked it out with Italian flags and signs proclaiming, "Dante will take it all!" and "Dante Fights for Amore!" His old house is red brick with a single black steel door, black bars on the windows, and *no* graffiti on its walls. Carroll Gardens is taking care of its own. Freshly planted zinnias flank the stoop. This is where Dante began. This is where Connie Lattanza hung out and shot the Italian breeze. This is where skinny Dante took off from every morning to escape Franco the *bravaccio*.

I'll bet this brownstone would cost a million or more now. What a world we live in.

I foot it down to Monte's Venetian Room, where Connie once worked. I don't know what I'll find, but I'm hoping to find some of Dante's oldest fans. Monte's is on the "shores" of the Gowanus Canal, which supposedly contains bodies from decades of mob hits. No one "swims with the fishes" in the Gowanus Canal, though. There are few fish evolved enough to survive the three hundred *million* gallons of raw filth that runs off into it every year. I try to envision the average hit man eating, say, some antipasto, looking out at the spot where he dumped Mickey "the Mouse" Ratatouille, plastic bottles and condoms floating above the very spot.

I can't envision it. Not eating antipasto. Scungilli, maybe.

The great John Huston directed scenes from *Prizzi's Honor* a few feet from where I sit in a curved, shiny red booth, a mural of Venice surrounding me. I order a plate of cold antipasto and an espresso from Vincent, a short, dark-featured man with a high forehead and a shoulder-length gray ponytail.

"First time?" he asks with a slight Italian accent.

I guess not many black women come in here, especially alone and before the lunchtime rush. "No. Yours?"

He smiles. "Just making conversation." He stands there, nodding slightly to the plate of antipasto.

I sample some cheese and an olive. "Nice."

"You know," Vincent says, "Capone used to eat here, as did Frank Sinatra."

I had noticed a LeRoy Neiman print of Sinatra as I came in. I had also noticed an indoor, working phone booth. You don't see them much anymore.

"And Sammy Davis once entertained from midnight to eight AM here," Vincent says. "Let me know when you want the cheesecake." He points to a sign. "It's heavenly to the taste."

"Really?" I ask. Just making conversation.

"It is made with ricotta cheese, not cream cheese like those other *fessi* make it," he says. "It has to be ricotta. After I sprinkle it with confectioner's sugar, you will just die."

"That's why it's so heavenly, huh?" I say. "People die from eating it."

He laughs. "If one has to go," he says, shrugging, "then dying from cheesecake is not such a bad way to go."

I look at the antipasto plate, and it's a meal in itself. "Perhaps another time," I say.

Vincent looks around. "Are you looking for someone?"

I blink. "No one in particular. Why?"

He shrugs. "I don't know. You look like a lady who is looking for someone."

"Well," I say, pulling out my press credentials, a plastic ID card with a pre-sexy woman picture of me on it. "I'm a reporter for *Personality* magazine."

"You don't say."

I do say. "I'm actually looking for anyone who knew Dante Lattanza from the old days."

Vincent grins broadly and sits across from me. "I know Dante from when he was just a little boy." He drums the table with his fingers.

Yes! I pull out my notepad. "Mind if I take some notes?"

"Not at all. What is it you want to know?"

I sketch Vincent on the notepad—in words. I can't draw for *merda*. I write, "Vincent is an old-school, fuggedaboutit kind of guy, receding gray hairline, ponytail, crooked nose, dark eyes." I smile. "First, I'll need your name."

"Vincent Baldini."

I write it down. "Did you know Dante's mother?"

"Sure, I knew Con," Vincent says. "That's short for Connie. Nice lady. Great in the kitchen. Not good. *Great*. The bread she made—*squisito*. She was so hard to replace. Lung cancer. A terrible thing."

"What is your earliest memory of Dante?" I ask.

Vincent rubs his hands on the table. "Con brought him in, set him on this very table." He taps it for effect. "We all looked after him while she worked. A skinny boy, not tough looking at all, but now he will be the champion again, I assure you. Tomorrow night he will reign again. What's your name again?"

"Christiana Artis."

Vincent looks past me to the mural of Venice. "Artis, Artis. I've heard that name before." He focuses on me. "Did you used to work for the *Times*?"

His smile has left Monte's.

"Um, yeah. But now I work for *Personality.*"

His eyes become little slits. "You used to cover boxing some for the *Times*, right?"

Once again, someone is interviewing me. "Yes."

He snaps his fingers. "You're the one who wrote those articles about Dante being washed up."

"That was a long time ago, Vincent," I say quickly. "I don't believe that now."

Vincent sits back, his lips tight. "But you also wrote the fighting-for-love article in September, right?"

I nod. Vincent is very well informed. "But like I said, I've changed my mind about Dante completely. I'm working on an op-ed piece to run tomorrow—"

Vincent pushes back his chair. "Shame on you. Shame!" He shakes a fist in my face. "You do not have to leave a tip. But I will give you one." He puts his bushy eyebrows inches from mine. "When you don't know what you're talking about, don't speak." He walks away.

I look at my antipasto, a sardine eyeing me. *"Che?"* I say to the sardine.

The sardine doesn't blink.

I drop a twenty on the table and leave, my espresso unsipped, my lips zipped, the sardine still staring.

Oh, that went well. I find someone who knows Dante from when he was just a little boy, and what happens? *My* past, not Dante's, ruins the interview. Lovely, just lovely.

I then hike over to Gleason's Gym to see Johnny Sears,

Dante's old trainer. He would have to have something nice to say. Dante was his meal ticket for close to fourteen years.

Every fighter training inside Gleason's stops throwing, skipping, or lifting for a deliciously long beat as I stride up to the main ring, where Sears is barking instructions to two skinny kids no older than twelve. I glance around at all these sweaty men and a few women, and they go back to work.

Nothing much has changed about Gleason's since Granddaddy first brought me here twenty-five years ago. The Everlast banner still hangs, red paint is still peeling, the floor is still scarred and scuffed, the mirrors still need cleaning, the duct-taped heavy bags still sway and groan, and everything is still dark, damp, and sweaty.

"Where you from, *Sports Illustrated*?" Sears asks, his face haloed under the harsh glare of the fluorescent lights. "Chin down, chin down!" he yells at the kids.

"Um, *Personality,* actually," I say. "Just doing a follow-up on Lattanza."

Sears rolls his eyes. "Time!" he yells. He turns to me. "You takin' pictures, it'll cost you."

"No pictures today." Gleason's charges photographers by the hour just to take some pictures.

"All right," Sears says. "You got a minute." He crosses his arms.

"What do you think of your old prodigy?" I ask.

"I hope to Christ Dante wins," Sears says, "but I swear to Christ that he hasn't got a prayer."

That quote won't run, even in the *Times*. "Lattanza's body is solid granite."

Sears waves a towel at me. "And so is his head. I read about his new training. He thinks he's gone old school. A tennis ball? Swimming? Eating fish? *This* is old school.

This is where he should be, not running around the woods in Canada."

It's what I used to think, too, but . . . "He says he's in the best shape of his life."

He rests both hands on the top rope. "Shape is only one thing. He should be sparring real boxers, not his own skinny kid or an over-the-hill cook. Who's he kidding?"

Should I tell him about the third sparring partner he had . . . ? Nah. She's not even in Dante's weight class anymore. "I've talked to Red, and he says Lattanza spars less to protect his hands, knees, and head."

"Lady," Sears says, softer this time, "Dante is in over his head. There'll be nothing to protect him from Tank Washington tomorrow night. Nothing. It will be a bloodbath, and I'll have to wear a raincoat."

A decent quote, but I'd never run with it. Sears is another dead end. I close my notebook. "Will you be at the fight?"

He nods. "Got an up-and-comer on the undercard. I'll be there."

One last try. "Do you think Lattanza can go the distance?"

Sears shakes his head. "I got reservations at Il Campanello for nine-thirty. What you think?"

I go home, defeated and almost humiliated. Isn't there *one* person who believes in Dante the way I do? I'm sure DJ does, but even Red didn't look or act too convinced up in Canada. If I had actually found a couple Dante-crazed fans, maybe ones who had sent him their bloomers, no one would take anything they have to say seriously.

I sit in front of my laptop and begin typing, hoping that by the end of this piece, I'll have some peace.

After several starts and stops, I realize I can only write this one way.

I can only write it from the heart.

Dante Lattanza, a man from Brooklyn, is fighting for the middleweight championship tonight against what some say are impossible odds.

And for whatever cynical reasons, people have a problem with Dante Lattanza's claim that he is "fighting for love."

I was the writer who broke this story two months ago, and I have a problem with this.

In sports today, there are athletes who are problems. They use steroids, HGH, and other performance-enhancing drugs. They have to return Olympic medals. They lose their titles. They serve long suspensions. Some are even banned for life or go to jail. They hold out for more money than they're worth. They get into bar fights. They beat their wives. They demand to be traded. They use injuries as excuses for failure. They whine, moan, and groan if they don't get the ball, the "rock," or more playing time.

These are problems.

"Fighting for love" is *not* a problem.

Dante Lattanza is *not* a problem.

Lattanza gives back to the community, contributing money to Give a Kid a Dream at Gleason's Gym. "There is a new generation of tough Brooklyn kids out there that could be champions," Lattanza says. "They are already running the streets. I'd like to make sure that running counts for something."

Lattanza has his priorities in order. "I fight to put food on the table, for a place to live," Lattanza says. He fights so his son will consider him a hero. So what if he also fights for love? Dante Lattanza is a pure athlete who is self-motivated to train in the way his body and mind know best. If love is his motivation, who is anyone to judge?

What motivated Branch Rickey to bring Jackie Robinson to the Dodgers? Was it love? Was it financially motivated? Was it a cynical move to get more blacks into Ebbets Field?

No. It was the right thing to do.

What motivated Ted Williams and many, many others to fight for their country instead of a pennant during World War II? Was it love of country? It wasn't the money.

It was the right thing to do.

Every four years this nation gathers athletes from sea to shining sea to compete on the world stage. Is it love? It can't be the money.

It's the right thing to do.

In the wise words of Vincent, a waiter at Monte's Venetian Room who has known Lattanza since he was a little boy: "When you don't know what you're talking about, don't speak."

To those who believe Dante Lattanza's fight for love is a good thing, I say, "When you *do* know what you're talking about, *speak*."

I'm speaking today for Dante Lattanza. I'm listening to what he has to say:

"I fight for love," Lattanza tells us. "It is the only fight worth having."

I sit back from the laptop and breathe deeply. It says what I want it to say. I wipe a tear. There's my heart right there on that screen. There's my heart, Dante. Damn if you don't still have it.

I cut and paste the piece into an e-mail addressed to Mel Butler, my old editor at the *Times*. I quickly dial him, and knowing he is a busy man who likes to multitask at multitasking, I don't let him get a word in edgewise when he answers.

"Mel, Christiana Artis. I have an op-ed piece on Saturday's Lattanza-Washington fight, runs about four hundred words, has to run Saturday or else. Think you could run it by Phil posthaste ASAP for me? I'm e-mailing it to you now." I send the e-mail.

"Hello, Tiana, how are you?" Mel asks.

"It's Christiana now," I say, "and that has to be my byline for this one. You get it yet?"

A moment later, he says, "Got it. Give me a moment to read it, Christiana."

I count to ten. He should be done now. "Have you shot it to Phil yet?"

"Just did," Mel says. "Give him time to read it, okay?"

I growl. "Phil reads slowly and you know it."

"So he's thorough, okay?" Mel says. "Op-eds are his babies."

I have to know. "Did you like it, Mel?"

"I wouldn't have sent it to Phil, Christiana."

Shoot. Twelve years I worked for the man, and I never got a single compliment. This is as close as I've ever gotten.

"Has he replied yet?" I ask.

"Christiana, you know—"

Silence. "Mel?"

"Phil likes it," Mel says.

Yes! "No cuts?"

"Straight through," Mel says. "That has to be a first."

Double yes! "Mel, I don't know how to thank you."

"Yes, you do," he says. "Come back to work for me."

I owe him this much. "I'll think about it, okay?"

"Hmm. Right."

"I will, Mel."

"For how long?" he asks. Mel is no dummy.

"I'll call you."

"After the fight, right?" he says. "I know you're going."

Mel is still giving me deadlines. "Next week, Mel, I promise."

"You better, and you know why?"

I have no idea why. "Why?"

"Because it's the right thing to do," he says.

He got me. "Thanks a million, Mel."

"Call me," he says, and he hangs up first.

I do a little shadowboxing after that, bouncing around my space throwing uppercuts.

I feel good.

I just hope it's not too late.

Chapter 29

The next morning I run down Van Brunt to the Fairway Market to pick up a copy of the *Times,* squealing when I see my story ("What's Wrong with Fighting for Love?") and my byline (by Christiana Artis). As soon as my key hits my door, I hear the phone ringing.

Maybe it's Dante. *"Buon giorno."*

"You were certainly busy on your sick day," Shelley says.

I sigh. "Sure was." While I probably should have run the whole op-ed thing by Shelley before I did it, it's really none of her concern. What's she going to do, fire me for writing a piece for no pay?

"You know," she says, "if you had written it for *Newsday,* I wouldn't be so nervous. You aren't thinking of leaving us, are you?"

The idea has been bouncing around in my head a lot, ever since I took the job at *Personality* in the first place. My work at the *Times* had burned me out, I needed a break, and *Personality* wanted me. I thought it would simplify my life, and it has. However, I am learning that I thrive on complications. If I'm not struggling, I'm not really living.

The sheer grind of walking through Carroll Gardens to Monte's and then to Gleason's and back to Red Hook was a rush. I talked to real people about real issues, issues that interested *me*. I wasn't on assignment and talking to fake people. Although I didn't get but one decent quote in five hours of interviewing (and had a rude sardine staring at me), I felt alive as a writer, as a person.

"Say something, Tiana, you're making me nervous," Shelley says.

I check my caller ID. She's not calling from the office. Hmm. I can't sit around here all day waiting and watching the neon clock. I have to go-go-go somewhere so I don't go-go-go crazy before tonight's fight. I could go to the office and . . . Hmm. What can I do? I could do some research on Dante's father. That could take a while. And after that, I can simply change and walk to the Garden. I open my wardrobe and select a tasteful white blouse and black slacks, laying them on the bed and plugging in my iron.

"Tiana? You there?"

"I'm here." Let's see, these will go in a garment bag, and I can pack my curling iron and makeup in my laptop case. "Shelley, I've been thinking. You have to give me more hard news, more investigative assignments. It's what I'm built to do."

"How in-depth can you go with celebrities?" she asks.

"Indeed," I say, and I let that hang in the air. I'll need walking shoes *and* dress shoes. Hose? It's supposed to be cold. Knee socks and dress shoes? Who'll know?

"What are you saying, Tiana?"

"It's *Christiana* from now on, and I'm saying that I don't want to interview another celebrity as long as I live. I only want to interview real people from now on."

"Like who?"

I sigh. Shelley probably doesn't know any real people,

besides me, that is. I begin ironing. "Like doctors and researchers on the cutting edge of a cure for a disease."

"You want to interview nerds?"

I sigh. "Nerds are people, too, Shelley. You don't complain when Jerry fixes your computer, do you?"

"You'd write about computer geeks, too?"

She's never going to get it. "I want to write about heroes like firefighters and cops. Like soldiers, nurses, and EMTs. I want to write about unlikely heroes. Hometown heroes, ordinary people. You know, people our readers can actually identify with. And I wouldn't have to go far. There are plenty of real people around here, over seven million the last time I checked."

"You're going back to the *Times,* aren't you?" she asks.

"You're missing the point, Shelley. I thrive on reality. At times when I was doing the 'where are they now?' stories, I was swimming in reality. I love reality. I guess I didn't know it until I left the *Times* and started hanging out with the beautiful people."

"You don't like the beautiful people?"

"No." I put the blouse on a hanger and hang it on the doorknob to the bathroom.

"Why not? They seem to like *you.*"

Not all of them. "They aren't real, Shelley. They might have been once, but . . ." I start ironing the slacks. "I want to do stories about that kid who grew up with nothing and is somehow making it despite the odds." I think about Granddaddy and the sacrifices he made to raise me. "I want to write about the kid who grew up without parents, the kid who was raised by her granddaddy, the kid who worked two jobs to get through Columbia and become a relative success. *That* kid."

"You know anyone like that?"

I nearly scorch my slacks. "That person is *me,* Shelley."

"You want to write your autobiography?"

I don't respond.

"Why didn't you say so? You have a few weeks of vacation coming up, right? You could knock it out then."

"Once again, you're missing the point." I slide the slacks onto a hanger, hooking the hanger inside the hanging bag. "I was speaking hypothetically. Not rags to riches. Rags to *respectability*, that kind of story." I think of Dante. "Like the kid who grows up without his daddy, learns to box, loses his mama at eighteen, wins the world title, loses the world title . . . You see where I'm going with this?"

"You're talking about Dante Lattanza, aren't you?"

I start gathering my tools of destruction—my curling iron, brush, and hair gel—and shove them into my laptop case. "I'm talking about anyone in America who had a tough start and is kicking ass now. Folks. We still write about *folks* at *Personality,* don't we? Aren't *folks* the very people we're trying to reach? Aren't *folks* in our demographic? There's only so much unreality regular folks can take. Witness the explosion of reality shows on TV."

"Oh, those are so fake."

Only a fake person would think a reality show was rigged. Some of them *are* cheesy, don't get me wrong, but there's something warm and human about them that's missing from so much else on TV or on the silver screen. "We'll talk about this on Monday, okay? I'm getting ready to go in to the office."

"What for?"

Time for a little lie. "I wasn't sick yesterday and I feel guilty." Not. I just want to push my office computer to the limit and work some phones. It'll be hard to reach anyone on a Saturday, but that's half the fun of the grind I miss so much.

"So you're not thinking about quitting?"

"Monday, Shelley," I say, stripping and turning on the

shower. "We'll talk Monday. I'm getting in the shower now. Bye." I drop my cell phone into the sink. It seems to belong there. I may leave it there forever.

But I won't. I still have ten months left on my two-year contract.

Freshly showered and wearing jeans and a white fisherman's sweater under the *pericoloso* leather jacket Dante bought me, I take the New York Water Taxi to Pier 11, splurging and catching a taxi from there to Rockefeller Center as the December skies gray up with snow clouds. My building is almost empty, a few folks scurrying here and there, none of whom I recognize—or want to. When I get to my office, which I have barely used in the last year, I shut the door and go to work.

"I'm going to find you today, Mr. Lattanza," I say.

There isn't much to distract me in this room. Pictures of Red Hook I had planned to hang last February lie propped against walls. A brand-new mini stereo with the tiniest little speakers still sits in its original box in front of the green tinted window looking out on the Avenue of the Americas. Except for a coffee mug that—ew—still contains something hockey-puck-like, there's nothing on this desk but a computer. I type in my password—"RedHooker"—and I'm on.

I begin my search from what I know. Detectives usually follow the money, right? The last money job I know Dante's father had was in the military. He went to Vietnam. Many of these records are now in the public domain. He should be easy to find.

I first make sure Dante's daddy isn't already dead. It's a lot easier telling a child that daddy isn't coming home than telling a child, "Your daddy's dead." I sometimes wish Granddaddy had told me exactly that about my parents. There is no one named "Lattanza" listed on the Vietnam Wall, but that doesn't necessarily mean he came back from

Vietnam. I then research the database for the DPMO (Defense Prisoner of War/Missing Personnel Office) and find there isn't a Lattanza who either had been a prisoner of war or was still missing in action in Vietnam. Man, that war ended over thirty years ago. You'd think we could account for every one of our soldiers by now.

I jot that possible story on a notepad. Why is it taking so long? Are there any unlikely heroes out there still searching for our boys? Why haven't we accounted for every single soldier who served in Vietnam?

I know calling the Department of Defense is a waste of time. I'm not next of kin or any kind of kin to Dante's daddy, and it will most likely take a series of Kafkaesque forms to fill out over several months to get any kind of decent information. Besides, it's Saturday. I'm sure they're working with a skeleton crew there. I hate hearing, "Call back on Monday." I don't want the runaround today, so I Google "military records," and Military.com pops up first and promises a database of twenty million names.

Hmm. In order to use this database, I have to join. I could lie and say I am military, but luckily, I can join with no service affiliation. I can't get past a second screen unless I type in my employer. I smile and type, "*Personality.*" That ought to confuse someone at Military.com.

I'm in.

I explore every branch of the service for anyone named Lattanza. I scroll through the army. Nothing. The navy. Nothing. The air force. Nothing. Therefore—

A *Daniel* Lattanza, E–4, is listed under the marines, unfortunately with no home address other than the state of New York. Though it doesn't narrow down my search much, that makes sense. He enlisted in or was drafted out of Brooklyn. What's an E–4? I do a side search and find Daniel Lattanza was a corporal.

I pop "Daniel Lattanza" into Google and get nothing.

Merda.

On a whim, I put "Danny Lattanza" into Google, and a Vietnam Web site for the Second Battalion, Ninth Marines appears first on the screen. Yes! "Hell in a Helmet" tops the welcome page, but I don't see any immediate reference to Danny. On the navigation bar I see "2/9 Members." Clicking that, I'm taken to a page of names with city, state, year, and some e-mail addresses.

I scroll through the command page. Nothing. Oh, yeah. He was a corporal. He wouldn't be on this page.

I scroll through Echo Company. Nothing.

I scroll through Golf Company . . .

There he is!

I'm good at this *merda.*

Lattanza, Danny "Boy"   Langley, BC 68–69

There's no e-mail address listed after his name, but that's okay. There are other ways, and I know them all. Danny "Boy" Lattanza is in Langley, British Columbia, Canada, or at least he was when this list was updated in . . . June of *this* year.

I'm close. This list was updated only six months ago.

Before checking where Langley is, I go to the 2/9 picture gallery and scrutinize four years of pictures from reunions, all held down in Arlington, Virginia. There are plenty of group shots in front of the Iwo Jima statue, the Vietnam Wall, and the Smithsonian. Many of the pictures aren't captioned—

There he is.

Though seriously graying, I'd recognize that hairy man anywhere. The caption reads, "Danny Boy and wife, Li." The woman next to him is half his size and has long gray hair and . . . Asian features. They sure seem happy.

Danny Boy and Li.

Okay, um, I'm not one to jump to conclusions—*much*—but this looks like . . . I don't know what this looks like. He brought her home with him? He gets out in '69 and brings her . . .

Think, Christiana.

Okay, he's married to Connie, but he brings Li home, and Connie finds out?

Dante said he never came home. He made that clear. Maybe Danny Boy hit the States and took off for Canada with Li, where they shacked up until Connie died sixteen years later? That doesn't make sense.

Maybe Danny Boy married Li in Vietnam or Canada, and no one checked to see if he was already married to someone somewhere else.

Or he lied and said he wasn't married.

I surf off to WhitePages.ca where I find a D Lattanza residing at 19967 96th Avenue in Langley, a far eastern suburb of Vancouver. Though I plan to call Danny Boy's phone number, I want to make sure I have all my ducks in a row. I plug his address into Google and see "Li's Convenience Store" listed as a business about 13.2 kilometers north of Langley.

Danny Boy has a business named after his Vietnamese wife, and I'm about to get deeply into his business. I dial the number.

"Li's, Danny speaking."

He certainly has the same timbre to his voice that Dante has. "Mr. Lattanza, my name is Christiana Artis from *Personality* magazine, and I'm doing a follow-up article on middleweight boxer Dante Lattanza."

Danny Boy doesn't respond right away. "What's that got to do with me?"

Everything, DB. The key to getting people to say something they *don't* want to say is to beat around it steadily until they get tired of the suspense. "Weren't you married to Connie Tucci of Carroll Gardens, Brooklyn?"

"What's this about?"

Evasive, are we? I had better hit him with what I already know. "You served in Vietnam from 1968 to 1969 in Company G of the Second Battalion, Ninth Marines."

I hear a heavy sigh. "That was forty years ago. Look, I've got work to do, so if you don't—"

"I've just talked to Red," I interrupt. I had noticed that "Red" (no last name) was the 2/9's Web site administrator. It's only a partial lie. I *have* been reading his site. "You attended a reunion in 2003 in Arlington with your wife, Li."

"Red certainly has been running his mouth."

Not exactly confirmation, but pretty darn close. "So all of this is true."

"Look, like I said, that was a long time ago."

My fingers are getting sweaty. It is now time to swing dat hammer! "Are you Dante Lattanza's father?"

"No."

Withdraw hammer. Either he's in denial, or . . . "No?"

"No. I am not Dante Lattanza's father."

Either he's in *deep* denial, or . . . "Was Connie pregnant when you married her?"

"No."

If I had the marriage record, I could make absolutely sure. "Then how do you know—"

"I know, all right?"

This seems to be a touchy subject for Danny Boy. "Well, do you know who Dante Lattanza's father is?"

No answer.

"Any suspicions?"

"Why is this important?"

There are so many good reasons why this is important. A boy needs his father, right? A child needs a parent in his life. "Dante is fighting for a world title tonight. He's a public figure. I'm planning to write his biography, and this is vital information." Well, I can always *plan* to write it, right?

"Look, I don't know what you want from me."

So reluctant! "When and where did you marry Li?"

Silence.

"Did you marry her in Canada?"

"No."

"Did you marry her over in Vietnam?" Duh. He had to. They wouldn't have let her just traipse along with him on the government tab unless they were married.

"Why is that important?"

That's not even a definite maybe! "Mr. Lattanza, I can easily get copies of *both* of your marriage certificates if you don't want to cooperate with me. Then all I have to do is check the dates to see if they overlap." Yeah, right. Getting those marriage records from Vietnam won't be easy. Finding military records that may not even exist, even if he had a military wedding, will certainly tax me, too. The 2/9 chaplain might know, right? I'll have to look him up, too.

After another lengthy pause, Danny Boy says, "Can you keep Li out of this? She's been through enough hell in her life."

Danny Boy would make a great politician. I can't get him to confirm or deny anything. Swinging dat hammer: "You were married to two women at the same time, weren't you, Mr. Lattanza?"

"Look," he says, his voice quieter, "if I tell you what I know about Dante's father, will you leave us out of this? We have a life here. We have grown kids and five grandkids. I've been here forty years, you understand? I have a life here. People know and respect me."

"Mr. Lattanza, I can't guarantee that I'll keep you two out of anything I may write."

"Ask at Cammareri's."

Che? "It's closed down now."

"Really? That's a shame. Then ask at Monte's."

I was just there yesterday! "Who do I talk to?"

"Talk to Vincent."

Goose bumps creep up and down my legs. Vincent, my waiter?

"Vincent Baldini?"

"Yeah. That's him."

Geez, Vincent was staring me in the face with Dante's eyes *the entire time*! "Vincent Baldini is Dante's father?"

"I have customers. It's a Saturday. We're very busy."

Still not exactly confirmation, but is that fear I hear in his voice? Sadness? "Is there anything you'd like me to tell Dante?"

"Just that . . . Ah, geez. Tell the kid I'm sorry, all right?"

I need more than that. Dante will need more than that. "Aren't you at least a little proud of him?"

"Yeah," his voice becomes a whisper. "I'm proud of him. I have ten scrapbooks full of that kid. I gotta go."

Click.

If I ever write Dante's biography, I will have to go out to Langley, British Columbia, to visit Danny Boy, his wife Li, their children, and his five grandchildren. Danny Boy can't be evasive if I'm standing in his store with a camera.

All this means I can't just call up Vincent and expect him to cave. I need to grill him face to face, so that if he lies to me, I'll be able to tell.

I am, after all, a *giornalista*. A liar can spot another liar.

I have to make sure he's working, so I call Monte's, hoping someone else will answer.

"Monte's," a female voice says. "This is Liz."

I try to sound Italian. "Is Vince there?" I sound ridiculous.

"He won't be in till one," Liz says. "Wanna leave a message?"

I check the time. *Perfetto.* I can get there by one-thirty, no sweat. "Nah. I want it to be a surprise. *Ciao.*"

This is the fun part of the grind. The chase is the adrenaline rush that fuels the grind and makes the wheels move swiftly.

Now look who's being pretentious! The chase is, simply, a rush.

But I'm in no hurry. I don't have to be at the Garden until nine. Since technically I'm working on a story for *Personality*—I mean, it *could* run in the magazine one day—I can have all my transportation and meal expenses paid. Instead of taking a taxi all the way to Monte's, I call Dial 7 Car and Limousine Service, mainly because it's the only phone number for a car service in my cell phone. I arrange for them to pick me up at one.

Then I wander the halls looking for a hammer and some nails to hang my pictures. I don't find any, as if I thought I could. Who brings a toolbox to *Personality*? That would be too real.

I take this as a sign. It will be so much easier packing up my office if I leave those pictures where they are.

A black Lincoln Town Car (how nice!) picks me up, and I'm off to Monte's in style. "To Monte's," I tell the driver.

"Yeah?" He turns and smiles at me. "You know you've got me for two hours, right?"

"Right."

"And, well, the food at Monte's is *magnifico*."

My driver knows Monte's. I thought he sounded Brooklyn. "What the hell. You can eat, too."

He nods. "I'll cut you a break on the rate."

I smile. "Fuggedaboutit," I say with a giggle. "It's on the company's tab."

He pulls away from the curb. "It's going to be a be-*you*-tiful day."

My driver, Paolo, who I find out lives in Queens but misses Brooklyn "to death, swear on my mothah," opens the door for me at Monte's. I tell the hostess—Liz—to give him whatever he wants, and he zips off. She leads me to a booth, and I wave off the menu. "Just tell Vincent that Christiana's here."

Vincent strolls over eventually and sits across from me. "Saw the *Times* this morning. You trying to butter me up or what?"

I'm not only going to butter you up, I'm going to get you to admit you're Dante Lattanza's father. "I talked to Danny Lattanza today."

Liz brings me an espresso. "You didn't drink yours yesterday, you know," she tells me, and she fades away.

Vincent nods slightly. "So you talked to Danny."

"Yeah."

"How's he doing?"

"Fine." I sip my espresso, looking at him over the rim of the cup. "He had a lot to say."

"Yeah? I'll bet he did. Danny Boy could talk."

Liz brings me a cold antipasto plate. "You hardly touched it yesterday," she says. Vincent waves her away.

"So, you know why I'm here," I say. I have to get Vincent to say it. He has to say it.

"What'd Danny Boy say?" Vincent asks.

I savor a hunk of salami. "He said to ask at Cammareri's. You ever work there, Vincent?"

He blinks. "A long time ago. So what?"

"I told him Cammareri's was closed, and then he said to ask at Monte's." I smile. "Is there anyone other than you who works here now who used to work at Cammareri's?"

"Just me. Again, so what?"

The indirect approach isn't working. Since I'm in Monte's, though, I have to swing a tiny, red-velvet-covered hammer. "He said to ask at those two places about who Dante's real father is," I whisper. "He said to ask you."

Vincent doesn't blink. "Oh."

I have missed playing cat 'n mouse so much! If it weren't such a serious subject, I could say I'm actually having fun. It is *so* much better to be the cat.

"Why would he want me to ask you, Vincent? What do you know?"

Vincent motions for Liz. "Liz, a glass of wine, please."

"Oh," I say, "no thank you."

"Go on," he says to Liz. "It ain't for you. It's for me."

Hmm. Stress. Drinking on the job. "What do you know, Vincent?"

Liz brings him a glass, and he downs half of it. "I . . . I know a few things."

"Such as?" I don't show my claws yet, but they're ready to strike.

"I know that Danny isn't Dante's *papino*."

Confirmation from another source. Good. "So . . . who is?"

He takes another gulp. "I can explain. You see—"

"Are you Dante Lattanza's father?" I interrupt. My claws are now out and in shredding mode.

He finishes the wine and slides his fingers around the base. "Well, it's like this." He looks up at me but doesn't speak.

"Yes?"

He leaves his seat and slides next to me in the booth. "He is not to know," he whispers. "Dante is never to know. It was his mama's dying wish. I never asked Con why. Con was very clear. She did not want the shame to follow him."

Though I think I know, I have to ask, "What shame would follow him?"

He sighs, adding a little shrug. "She was not married to the man who was the father to her child."

"And she knew?"

He nods.

"You two had an affair."

He nods again. "I did not plan to." He runs his hands through his hair. "Ah, Christ, we were just kids. Danny and Con were just kids when they got married, right out of high school. They were crazy. Who does such a thing anymore?"

He's trying to get us off the subject. I ain't biting. "Tell me about the affair."

"Why should I?"

I shrug a little, trying to mimic him. "Better me than the *Times*. When Dante wins and I run with what I know, who knows who'll be coming through that door." I feel like the Godfather. "I'll tell you what. You tell me everything, and I'll keep whatever you don't want out from getting out. *Capisci quello che sto dicendo?*"

He blinks. "You speak Italian?"

"Per certi versi." I smile. "I still have a lot to learn."

"You sound"—he bobs his head side to side—"authentic."

"Grazie." I want to tell him that my first teacher was the best, that my first teacher was his son. "Was Danny at boot camp when your affair occurred?"

"No. Danny was up in the city at a Yankees game with some friends of his, and we were here working late. The Yankees win, we have more people, you know? The Yanks trashed the Red Sox that night, and we were still here at three-thirty. Con was . . ." He shakes his head. "I always loved her, always. We were both lonely. This is a romantic place. We were just two dumb kids. You understand?"

I don't need any more details. Dante Lattanza was conceived at Monte's, just off the Gowanus Canal. Even the most despicable journalist wouldn't print this.

"When did Danny find out?" I ask.

He closes his eyes. "I think Danny always knew. One look at Dante and he didn't see his eyes or his nose or his jaw. I saw myself. Danny didn't say nothing about it, but he knew. He knew, all right? Dante was scrawny, like me. Danny was huge. Anybody could see it." He opens his eyes and sighs. "And then . . ."

"Then what?"

"You are not writing anything down."

I tap my temple. "I have a great memory. Then what?"

"I wrote Danny a letter while he was over there. I felt so guilty. He was my friend."

Whoa. "You wrote a letter and *told* Danny you were Dante's father?"

He nods. "Not the bravest thing I've ever done. I should have told him to his face. He would have . . . I like my nose the way it is, all right?"

I like it, too. "Did Danny write back?"

He shakes his head. "I don't blame him. That kind of thing. I don't know what I would have done."

This is so sad! "How did Connie take it?"

His eyes widen. "Con was *infuriata*. 'What you tell him for?' she says. Her English was not so good. 'What about Dante? What if he finds out?'" Vincent rubs at his eyes. "I had no words for her. When Con was angry, there was no use trying."

I think I would have gotten along fine with Dante's mama. Oh sure, we would have argued nonstop, but . . . I like what I hear about this woman.

Maybe not the conceiving of her son in a restaurant part, but . . .

"When Danny didn't come back," Vincent continues, "Con made up this story. It wasn't really a lie. She tells

Dante he's not coming back, don't ask about him, don't worry, I'll take care of you, we don't need him."

"After Danny was gone for so long, did you ever, I don't know, want to marry Connie?" I ask.

He nods vigorously. "I wanted to marry her, but . . ." He flattens his hands on the table, and they're Dante's huge hands. "Con was still *infuriata*. So many times I almost told Dante, so many times I hugged him, kissed him, gave him advice about the ladies, slipped him some money for Con, for new gloves, for new shoes, for money to spend any way he wanted."

This is depressing. Vincent was an arm's length or less from his son, and his son didn't know his father was kissing and hugging him.

"It's good to know Danny's alive and well," Vincent says. "I was always worried he was, you know, dead."

"Danny's married."

"Yeah?"

"He owns a store in Canada."

"Yeah? He always talked about being his own boss. Danny never liked working for nobody. He got any kids?"

I nod. "All grown, and he has five grandkids. He provided for them, huh?"

Vincent's body jerks. "So did I. You think Con could afford that place of hers without some help? I helped. All my tips went into that place or to Dante's gear. I tried paying for his college classes, too, but Dante was already pro then and could afford them on his own. I begged him to let me help with Con's funeral, but he said he had everything covered. He was stubborn as Con was."

I agree. "Did you still continue to see Connie?"

"You think I didn't want to? Con was beautiful. She was . . . so frail, like a china figurine. I wanted to, but I couldn't." He tattoos the table with his fingers. "Carroll Gardens talks. All those stoops. All those women yakking day and night. I was her friend instead. I was Dante's friend, too."

Unfulfilled. I know just how he feels. I'm only Dante's friend, too. "How do you think Dante will react when he finds out?"

"You are going to tell him?"

I shake my head. "I won't tell him, Mr. Baldini. In fact, I won't write a single word about any of this."

"Bene." He looks at me. *"Grazie."*

I can fully swing the hammer now. "But you will. And soon."

He nods. "I should. I will. The next time I see him."

"I'm gonna hold you to that."

"I should have done it a long time ago," he says, stealing and eating one of my olives. "I wish I could be at the fight tonight."

"You won't be there?"

He shakes his head. "I have to work a double shift. We are never busier than when Dante fights. I have not missed a fight of his in New York until this day, and this could be his greatest moment. Monte's letting us get the pay-per-view, though. I will watch." He touches my hand. "Christiana, I am sorry for all my rudeness. I don't want you to think I am a *boia.*"

I blink.

"I don't want you to think I am a jerk."

I smile. "Vincent, I think you are a good *boia* down deep."

He smiles. "You make the jokes."

I squeeze his hand. "You are his father. I understand how protective a father can be. Dante is just as protective of your grandson, DJ. And trust me, I am fully on Dante's side now."

"Bene. He is a good boy."

"And he'll make a good son."

Vincent nods. "What you wrote I said in the *Times*. I meant that when I said that."

I nod. "And I meant it more when I wrote it." I point to a spot behind the bar. "You should put that on a sign, too. 'When you don't know what you're talking about . . .' "

"Don't say anything," Vincent says. "I like the way you turned it around, too." He looks at his hands. "You're his friend, right?"

"Yes."

"You think you could maybe . . . bring him and DJ here one day?"

I would like nothing more than to be sitting next to Dante here! "I'll try."

"Bene. Molto bene."

"But when he wins tonight, I'm sure he'll be very busy," I say.

He pats my hands. "You will bring him here. You have *coglione*."

I don't know if that is a compliment. "What do I have?"

He weighs something invisible in one hand. *"Coglione."*

Oh. *Those*. "Um, thank you." I think.

He shrugs and smiles. "I mean it in the nicest way. Dante is wise to have friends like you." He looks around. "Just go easy on him with your writing from now on. *Mio dio,* you have a mean way with words."

I stand. "I mean what I write, Vincent. If it just happens to *be* mean, so be it."

He groans. "So glad you no longer write for the *Times*."

I lean down and whisper, "I'll be going back to the *Times* next week."

He drops his head to his chest. *"Coglione."* He shakes his head, rubbing his chin on his chest. *"Dio santo!* I hope he wins."

I lift his chin. "He will win, Vincent. He has to. He's your son."

My driver, sated and not smelling of alcohol—I check—returns me to the office, and I pay him one hundred twenty dollars. He hands back a twenty. "Whenever you need a car, and you're going to Monte's, ask for Paolo Mancini. Do not ask for Paolo Olivera. He does not appreciate fine dining as I do."

"Grazie."

In my barren office, I reconsider the last year working for *Personality*. I've had every so-called "story" handed to me. I've been "handled" by publicists and agents. I've met people I wouldn't even share a cab with on the coldest and rainiest of days. I've taken posed pictures of celebrities posing as people. I've been to surreal places with other-worldly views and have met surreal *people* with other-worldly views.

I need to put my feet back on the pavement. Just talking to Vincent sealed it. I've been blindly going through life in so many ways, writing spoon-fed stories that didn't challenge me or give me a real reason to work hard. Other than my interlude with Dante, this past year has had less drama, fewer surprises, and much less danger than the *quietest* year I spent at the *Times*. I've been leading a soft and sweet marshmallow existence, but I've eaten so much of it I'm feeling sick.

I'm sick of puff pieces. I'm sick of fake people. I'm sick of the surface-ness of life. I know that's not a word, but it should be. The world is not hunky-dory. Celebrities cannot save the planet no matter how many hybrid Hummers they own. Celebrities cannot solve the world's hunger problems with one concert. Celebrities cannot stop terrorism with one movie. Celebrities cannot save rain forests they've never seen nor fully understand AIDS without seeing its many victims up close. They claim to be environmentally conscious, but are they conscious? Do they really know how 99.99% of the world really lives?

An actress *plays* the part of a crackhead or a waitress. An actor *plays* the role of a tough cop or heroic firefighter. They only play at reality, then go home and lead extraordinary lives. And how does *Personality* reward them? By giving them a glossy cover for surviving their *first* year of marriage while millions of real couples survive many years more.

Do I respect their gifts? Sure. I can't do what they do nor would I even want to try, because I'm too busy living. Celebrities are too distant from the very people they're trying to depict. How can they ever provide realistic portrayals of people they've never been or met? Sure, I identify with some of the characters they play, but again—it's only play. Someone yells, "Cut!" when things get too intense or dangerous. Stars get to replay scenes that don't go well. I only get to replay them in my mind or relive them in my fantasies. We the people don't have their luxuries. No one yells, "Cut!" when someone cuts us off in traffic or butts ahead of us in line. No one gives us a do-over when the police pull us over, we miss the train, or we write or say something we shouldn't have written or said. No one provides us a stunt double when the building we work in crashes to the ground. No one makes us look beautiful every morning or makes dresses especially for us. We the people have to work at it. We the people have to be real all the time.

It's time for me to be real.

I call and leave a message with Mel. "I'll be in your office Tuesday." I have to use Monday to clear out of my office and turn in my keys and credentials. It might even be a Monday in New York that doesn't suck.

I am going to resign and go back to the *Times*.

Typing a letter of resignation takes me about a minute:

Dear Shelley:

I quit. Sorry. I'll clear out of my office on Monday morning.

Thank you for all your advice.

Christiana Artis

PS: Yes, I have a job at the *Times,* and no, I won't need a reference from you.

I print it out and slide it under Shelley's door. Hmm. The cleaning staff might toss it. For good measure, I paste my resignation into an e-mail and send it to Shelley. Then, I get ready for the fight, curling my hair in the bathroom.

I start humming "My Way" and pose for the mirror.

I'm almost myself again.

It feels good.

When I hit the doors to the street for what will be the *second* to the last time ever, I say, "Brooklyn has left the building."

Chapter 30

Taxis creep past as I walk through a world lit up by rainbows down Sixth Avenue to Forty-second Street. The year's first snow filters through those multicolored lights turning Times Square into a land of magic. I duck under some Kodak screens in front of the Marriott Marquis on Broadway and call Red's cell phone.

"Girl," Red says, "you and your mouth show up at the worst possible times. HBO cameras are filming me taping Dante's hands as we speak."

I look up at the Astrovision screen on the Reuters Building and see Red taping Dante's left hand, a cell phone pinned to Red's ear by his shoulder. "Red, I see you. I'm in Times Square watching you on TV."

"I'm kind of busy here," he growls.

The ten-foot-tall Red's lips move just a tick slower.

This is so surreal. I must be having an out-of-body experience. "Just give Dante a message for me."

"You tell him, but talk fast." Red hands the phone to Dante on the screen.

"Are you here?" Dante asks.

Just to hear his voice after all these months . . . And I'm

seeing him speak to me. I have to get a video phone. Oh. And so does he. Hmm.

"Christiana?"

He said my name! I have fully left my body and am floating over Times Square. I'm jaywalking in the air!

"Christiana?"

Any lip-readers in Times Square would have "heard" my name! "Um, I'm not there yet, Dante. I should be there soon. I'm watching you talking to me on the big screen in Times Square." I notice a man leaning in toward my phone. "You're, um, huge," I whisper.

The eavesdropper leans even closer, and I back away.

"Good!" Dante says. "Thank you for sending me your picture. Did you catch anything that day?"

"No." I'm in Times Square talking about fishing with a boxer. Only in America. "Red Hook fish don't attack like Canadian smallmouth. You have any luck in Virginia?"

"Nothing like what you caught."

My eavesdropper is getting even closer. I step completely away from him and stand close to the Marquis. "I just wanted to say good luck."

"*Grazie.* I read the *Times* this morning. *Saggia*. Finally, I say to myself, an honest writer with heart."

"*Grazie.*" Whoo. I'm starting to sweat. "Keep jabbing, okay?"

"I will. *Ciao.*" He hands the phone to Red and makes a fist with his left hand, flexing his fingers, and smiling directly . . . at me. Okay, he's smiling at thousands of other people in Times Square and millions of people around the world, too, but . . .

That smile was for me.

The eavesdropper clears his voice loudly. "Were you just talking to Dante Lattanza?"

He seems harmless enough, both his gloved hands where

I can see them, one hand clutching a camera like the *turista* he most likely is.

"Yeah," I say, and I start walking.

"No kiddin'," he says, falling in step beside me. "Dante 'Blood and Guts' Lattanza." He points to the screen where Red is taping Dante's right hand.

"Yeah. He's a . . . he's a good friend of mine."

The man smiles. "Well, what do you know? I guess it's all or nothing tonight, huh?"

"Yeah." I start to move more quickly down Broadway.

The man walks a few paces behind me. "No disrespect, but I bet with my head. My money's on Washington."

I stop and face him. "You wasted your money."

He shrugs. "Hey, I hope Lattanza kicks his ass seven ways to Sunday, but . . ." He shrugs again.

I look up at the snow drifting down. "I hope he wins, too."

The man fades into the crowd, and I fade into a little pity party as I walk. I haven't had one of these in quite a while, and I really should be feeling good about my life. I mean, I realized I was working at the wrong place, and I quit before it was too late. I know I'll have a job at the *Times* on Tuesday. I also found Dante's daddy, and though it's up to Vincent to reveal himself to Dante, at least I had the *coglione* to start the process. I am in the best shape of my life. I am more of a *corpo provocante* than I've ever been before. Men are looking hard at me even now as I walk confidently wearing a *pericoloso* jacket.

But I'm walking alone. *Merda.* I'm walking alone.

If Dante wins, I lose. I know he's going to win. He'll go back to Evelyn, and I'll restart my life at the *Times*. Fresh starts all around.

And then I'll really be alone.

I turn down Seventh Avenue, hoping the scenery will change my mood. This is such a magical place with all its magical lights and magical snow. Tonight New York is miraculous. New York is be-*you*-tiful.

Back to the pity party.

Okay. If by some miracle, let's say Dante loses. Geez. It hurts my heart just to think that. But let's just say, all right? He doesn't go back to Evelyn, he's heartbroken again over this woman, and he'll go into hiding from the press, especially the woman who alerted the press to his "fighting for love" claims in the first place. . . .

I lose again.

One little problem.

I love him.

I even told him to his face, and there were times his eyes told me that he loved me. He said he believed that sex could only come after love, and we had lots of sex. Yes, he's hot and the sex was hotter, but I actually want to be friends with Dante for the rest of my life. Yeah, he makes my heart flutter and all my naughty bits tingle, but I liked myself when I was with him. I was busy with him. I didn't just get busy with him. He let me be a woman.

I've always wanted a man like that.

And I not only love him.

I like him.

That in itself is an earth-shattering and priorities-rearranging statement.

I like him.

I know how Lelani feels. I *like* Dante Lattanza. I like who he is. I like what he represents. I love all that granite, mind you, but behind his granite is a truly likable man.

I've been wearing the cross under my blouse for so long I sometimes forget it's there. I pull it out and kiss it, saying a little prayer:

"God, make it end in a draw. Maybe then I'll have a chance."

Chapter 31

A t the Garden, I wait in line like so many others who only show up for the main event. I am, after all, a New Yorker. The line moves a millimeter at a time, so I call Red again to pass the time.

I am such a pest.

"Christiana, it's getting close to go time," Red says.

"I know," I say. "I'm stuck in line, and I'm bored. What'd you feed him today?"

"What's that got to do with anything now?"

"Just humor me, Red, okay?" I say. "My granddaddy said that on the day of a fight a boxer needs to eat steak, but never well done."

I hear him sigh. "He ate a salad with Italian dressing, a nine-ounce T-bone steak, which I grilled *medium,* buttered toast, and a fresh fruit cup. Wanna know what he drank, too?" Red sounds stressed.

"I know you're taking good care of him, Red, I just worry, you know? What's he doing now?"

"He's praying in the mop closet."

A closet is as good a place to pray as anywhere else, I

guess. I flash back to his closet of a room. I was praying there, too. Praying he wouldn't stop.

"Is the door closed?" I ask.

"Yep."

"So he can't hear you, right?"

"I don't think so."

"I love him, Red." I fight off a tear. "I really love him."

"I know you do," Red says softly. "Does he know?"

"I told him once months ago, but I'm not sure he remembers. Don't let him get hurt, okay?"

"I won't."

"Ciao."

The second I close my phone, I hear an old woman's voice in my ear. "I couldn't help overhearing," she says.

I turn and see an ancient black woman in a flashy silver dress. "Yes?"

"You know something I should know, honey?" she asks.

I hope to God that this isn't Tank Washington's mama. "Dante Lattanza is going to win tonight."

She wrinkles up her wrinkles. "You've been drinking, huh?"

I shake my head and smile. "Tank Washington is going down hard tonight." I notice others listening. "Twelfth round," I say louder. "Knockout."

Mrs. Wrinkled Wrinkles cocks her head. "And just how do you know this?"

I put my hand on my heart. "My heart tells me."

Mrs. WW rolls her eyes and several others in the crowd laugh. "Child, I ain't bettin' on *your* heart."

"Bet on Dante Lattanza's heart then," I say brightly. "His heart is *huge*."

Once I'm inside the Garden, I follow the crowd down to the ring while an undercard bout between two boxers I don't recognize goes on to occasional noise. There are so many celebrities in the crowd. I see Sugar Ray Leonard schmoozing with Sylvester Stallone, the mayor chatting with Robert De Niro, the Raging Bull himself. Is that Martin Scorsese? It has to be. No one has an eyebrow like that. That can't be Chris Tucker shooting the shit with Mr. T. When will Mr. T change his chains? Oh sure, Donald Trump is here, conferring with the Golden Boy Oscar De La Hoya and Rosie O'Donnell.

Oh yeah. Don King is here. Whoop-de-do.

I push down my own hair, just in case.

I notice Evelyn seated near the red corner wearing a flashy golden dress, her hair and makeup absolutely *perfetto*. I'm glad I'm subdued. As much as I want Dante all to myself, I do not want anyone to recognize me tonight.

Except for Dante, of course.

As I check my ticket, I feel a hand grabbing my arm.

I turn and see Lelani wearing a slinky, exquisitely clingy black satin dress and high heels only skinny-footed people can wear.

I hug her hard. "It is so good to see you again!"

She pulls me to an empty seat a few rows behind Evelyn. "You're sitting with me. Red always gets an extra ticket in case Dante's father shows up."

She has no idea how soon that might be.

Lelani looks at my ticket. "Girl, you would have been sitting on Washington's side."

This is very cool. "Lelani, I'm so nervous. I mean, I've watched a bunch of fights, but I never . . ." I sigh. "I never loved the guy fighting before, you know?"

"I knew you were in love with him," Lelani says.

"When?"

She wrinkles up her little nose. "Oh, I suppose it was the second you stole his fish."

"I didn't steal his fish. I asked for it."

"That's when I knew," she says. "You two were playing eye-tag the whole time, too."

She noticed. Was I that obvious?

"Hey," she says, "don't be nervous yet. It's going to be a while. Dante will come out to some Italian song, the crowd will go crazy, and once the fight starts, you won't have any time to be nervous."

"I don't know. My stomach is tumbling."

She takes my hand. "Let me walk you through this. On the way in, Dante will smile at and hug every person he can, whether they want him to hug them or not. He'll pose for pictures. He'll hold babies. He'll kiss grandmas with more facial hair than he has."

"As if he's running for office?"

She nods. "Yeah. Like that."

Dante for president? I'd vote for him. Dante for mayor . . . Sure. Maybe Dante can fix the MTA.

"Ten minutes will pass before he gets into the ring." She smiles, her eyes looking shady. "It may last longer than the fight."

"Don't say that."

She squeezes my hand. "I meant it in a good way."

"Oh." Dante knocking out Tank early? That would be a miracle.

The crowd roars. We look up in time to see one of the unknown fighters biting the canvas and the ref counting him out.

Oh, geez. Now my stomach is in my left ear and my eyes are blurry. I hope my vision clears by the time they clear the ring.

"Lelani, I haven't been to a fight in a long time," I say. "Does Dante have anything special planned for his entrance? Other than the hugging, kissing, and posing?"

"Dante is so boring, Christiana," Lelani says. "Once in the ring, he'll do his four-corners routine, go to the center, bow four times, smile at the world . . ."

I tune her out because I am feeling something incredible inside me, something even more magical than walking through the snowy rainbows out on Broadway. Something mythical.

Yes.

Something mythical is going to happen tonight. Something more mythical than that day on the outcropping when I held hands in the sunset with Dante. It's almost primal. Boxing is primal. All of this—the ring, the crowd, the lights—is primal, deep, heroic. Dante is like an ancient hero about to slay the monster. He's Beowulf about to slaughter Grendel. He's Gawain about to fight the Green Knight. All the signs dancing behind and around me proclaim it: DANTE WILL WIN IT ALL!!! DANTE FIGHTS FOR LOVE! LATTANZA FOR PRESIDENT. Italian flags wave nonstop, Dante's fans really putting their hearts, their very souls into their shouts, those signs, those waving flags. They love him. They're not fair-weather fans. They truly love him.

And so do I.

My hands can't stop shaking I love him so much.

Few people love Tank Washington. They respect him, yes, but only for what he can *do*. Thousands here tonight love and respect Dante for who he *is*.

Dante is a hero.

Dante is *my* hero.

"Christiana," Lelani says, "you're crying."

I wipe tears I hadn't noticed from my cheeks. "Just losing myself in the moment."

Another roar. A song begins. Goose bumps. It's Smokey Robinson's "Being with You."

More tears.

The entire Garden stands and begins singing.

Whoo. Now my legs won't stop shaking.

"Since when did Dante like Smokey Robinson?" Lelani asks.

Did he play this for *me*? Man, I need some tissues. "I, um, I told him I liked Smokey on our way to town that day. I never thought he'd play one of his songs." What does this mean?

While Lelani sings the chorus, I stand on tiptoe to see Dante, but there's no way I can see over all these people.

"He usually plays some extremely loud opera music on his entrance," Lelani says, swaying. "This is nice. What's he trying to do, get Washington's fans to cheer for him instead?"

I am cheering so loudly inside right now!

Smokey's voice fades, and a full band kicks in with Dean Martin crooning, "Ain't That a Kick in the Head."

Oh, this is too much! Everyone is smiling! Everyone is singing! My head is spinning! This song is so be-*you*-tiful! There he is.

Oh, my heart.

He is one huge smile. He's a moonbeam. He's a . . . he's a slice of eaten watermelon. He squints and dances with DJ at his side in front of Red and the cut man, who's bald and wears a paper halo for a hat. The cut man and Red wear black Everlast jackets, and Dante—

Daa-em.

My naughty bits flutter.

Dante looks so hot in green, red, and white trunks with a matching satin warm-up, its hood flopping side to side as he bounces.

"This is really different!" Lelani shouts as the song ends.

"How so?"

"He usually does some Sinatra."

A man behind us with booze on his breath sticks his head between us. "Yeah, 'My Way' would have been more appropriate. 'And now, Lattanza's end is near, and soon his face will be bloody for certain . . .' "

Lelani stares him down. "Kiss off, ya bum."

The man jerks back. "You two ain't Washington fans?"

I wave my hands in his face. *"Mi scusi? Hai un febbre? Non importa, non importa. Idiota."*

The jerk sits.

"You've been busy," Lelani says.

I bite my lower lip. "Dante rubbed off on me."

"I'll say."

I look up at the ring as Dante rolls over the top rope, the crowd roaring even louder. *"Andiamo!"* I shout.

"Um, Christiana," Lelani whispers. "You just asked that drunk if he had a fever."

"I did?"

She nods.

"Oh. I thought I was asking if he was high."

She waves a hand in front of her nose. "But he is."

I watch Dante do his four corners, his arms raised. I watch him stand in the center of the ring and bow in four directions. I watch him commanding that ring, commanding the attention of the Garden, commanding the attention of the entire world, BROOKLYN stitched proudly into his belt.

I also see him wink in my direction.

Damn. My hands and legs had just calmed down, Dante. Give a girl a chance!

He winks at me *again*.

A few heads in front of me turn and look at me.

"That was new, too," Lelani says.

"What was?" I say coyly, fighting to keep my hands from flying off my body.

"The wink. Must be the lights."

I smile. "You *are* jaded, Lelani."

"Yep," she says. "I sure am."

"Andiamo!" I yell, and the heads in front of me turn away.

They're just jealous that a real man didn't wink at them. *Twice.*

Chapter 32

Tank makes Dante wait for five minutes, but Dante doesn't seem to mind. He looks so *good*. He's had a nice haircut and a shave. His body says, "Warrior."

My body says, "Warrior princess needs warrior prince."

I should have had a soda. I must be sugar deficient.

A driving bass beat fills the Garden. Here we go. I hope Tank doesn't—

He's rapping.

I can't even watch.

The beat is hot, but the words he's spouting are completely unintelligible. I hear whispers of "Hell Razah" floating around me. Hell Razah, who used to be Heaven Razah (real name Chron Smith), is from Red Hook, and he's rapping along with Tank. Traitor.

"Dante's entrance had more class," Lelani says.

I agree. Everyone warms up in his own way, I guess, and Tank is sweating profusely by the time he enters the ring, points at Dante, and slides his right glove under his neck.

Dante only smiles.

Tattoos cover Tank's arms, back, and—ew—the back of his bald head. That blond goatee does nothing for him. He wears a black T-shirt, black and white shorts past his knees, white gloves, and black shoes. His entourage holds up his belt, flashing bling and generally being annoying.

And after Tank loses, those fools will have to go get *real* jobs. Ha! Welcome to Burger Barn. Can I take your order, yo?

The lights dim. A spot hits Michael Buffer in his signature tuxedo. My stomach settles down, but my heart thumps loud enough for everyone to hear.

"Let's get ready to rumble!" Buffer roars.

Andiamo.

Let's do this.

"First in the red corner, weighing in at a rough-and-ready one hundred and fifty-eight and one-half pounds, wearing the tricolors of Italy . . ."

The crowd roars. I am deaf.

"With a spectacular record of fifty wins against only two losses, all fifty wins by way of knockout, fighting out of Aylen Lake, Ontario, Canada, originally from Carroll Gardens, Brooklyn, New York . . ."

Another roar. I am dizzy.

"The challenger and former WBA middleweight champion of the world, Dante 'Blood and Guts' Lattanza!"

I cannot hear.

I cannot see.

I am crying.

I feel the love for this man, and I feel love for Red, for DJ, for Lelani, for those around me, even the boozy jerk behind me.

Something mythical just *has* to happen tonight.

When Buffer introduces Tank, the Garden is *much* quieter. Boo-birds in the cheap seats shout all sorts of interesting curse phrases. I'll have to translate them into Italian later.

Meanwhile, Dante and DJ are in his corner, just . . . talking. They're just shooting the breeze moments before

Tank starts pounding Dante's gentle face. Red removes the warm-up. That's what I'm talking about. Dante's rippled abs have sprouted more ripples. Red removes the cross, and Dante kisses it.

I pull mine out and kiss it, too.

"Superstitious?" Lelani asks.

"A little," I say. I kiss the cross again for good measure.

They receive their instructions from the referee in the center of the ring, I hear "Touch 'em up!" from the referee, and Dante bounces back toward me.

Another wink.

Mythical.

Yeah.

This is going to be mythical.

Brooklyn is in the house.

Ding!

Tank charges from his corner, so much stronger, so much quicker, so much more talented than Dante, but Dante slips to the side and throws out *five* consecutive jabs.

He's using his jab.

Lelani says what I'm thinking: "He's using his jab!"

Dante listened to me.

"He's actually boxing!" Lelani shouts.

He's dancing. He's dancing as he danced with me, as if he's just out there shadowboxing up in Canada, kicking up dust and mirroring me.

"He's actually not getting hit for a change," Lelani says.

Dante isn't putting a dent in Tank, but at least Dante's cut man isn't going to get arthritis tonight.

Lelani grabs me. "This is so exciting!"

I can't speak. I'm watching an Italian matador at work. He's bobbing. He's weaving. He's circling. He's jabbing, sliding, pivoting, and turning. I want to shout, *"Olé!"*

Ding!

"He won that round," I whisper to Lelani.

"You don't win rounds by dancing and throwing a few jabs," she says.

I don't reply. Dante's waiting. He's watching. Those eyes . . .

He listened to me. He is actually following my advice. What does that mean? Whatever it means, it is working so far. I look up toward the ceiling. Thanks, Granddaddy. I was always listening to you, especially when you didn't think I was.

The rounds roll by with much of the same, Dante the matador versus Tank the bull. Dante's jab pops Tank's face with increasing regularity. It snaps out like a hammer, and Dante follows it with crisp rights to the body. Dante's chopping wood. Tank can't get inside and resorts to throwing haymakers over the top. I cringe at every bomb Tank throws, but Dante blocks them without backing up, snapping that hammer jab in Tank's confused and frustrated face. Tank resorts to some "rough stuff"—low blows, hitting on the break, holding and hitting, leading with his forehead—and the referee has to warn him constantly to "knock it off, champ."

I hear people all around me complaining. "This isn't the fight I came to see!" they shout. "Where's the left hook?" the drunk behind us mutters. "I came to see the left hook!"

After round ten, I am as sweaty as Dante is. I've been throwing little jabs and right crosses, doing a boxing "chair dance" for ten rounds. At least my hands have something to do. My legs and feet have yet to stop running in place.

Lelani turns to me. "Why isn't he throwing the hook, Christiana? What's he waiting for?"

I want to tell her what I told him, but she might not believe me. Her man, Red, is Dante's trainer, not me. "Maybe he's waiting for the right moment. The right time."

"But he's running out of time," Lelani says, obviously as flustered as Tank has become. "Tank's throwing the heavier punches."

I smile at her. "And here I thought you'd become jaded by boxing."

She grabs my hand. "Not tonight. Dante *has* to win. He just *has* to."

"I know that."

She shakes her head. "For another big reason."

Another reason? "What?"

"I'll tell you later."

From the opening bell of the eleventh round, the fight really begins, and the noise is deafening. Tank and Dante stand toe to toe in the center of the ring, the proverbial "phone booth," punching the living hell out of each other. It's almost a repeat of their first fight, and the folks around me stand and shout. They are so fickle. Both boxers are taking punishment now, sweat and blood flying.

But I can't look away.

Dante's face puffs up, his eyes becoming slits, and it's magnificent, utterly, truly *magnificent*. Blood streams from both of their faces, cuts open and ooze, the white parts of their trunks turning pink. Tank Washington bleeds. He's human after all. Their arms fly faster than even a computer can count, and I swear I can feel the sweaty breezes from their punches. And when the Garden's famous bell rings at the end of the eleventh round, a primal, joyous roar shakes the building.

I can't just sit here.

Without a second thought, I move down our row saying *"Scusi!"* to all the toes I'm stepping on, bumping into Johnny Sears, Dante's old trainer.

"I never woulda believed it," he says.

"You're late for your reservation," I say, but I don't have time to chat, old man.

I rush to Dante's corner where Dante sits on the stool, smiling, his high cheekbones bruised, his nose bloodied,

the cut man working on his nose and eyebrows simultane-
ously.

Red merely gives Dante some water while DJ rinses
Dante's mouthpiece.

Why is no one saying anything? This could be Dante's
final round for the rest of his life!

I guess it's up to me.

I have to put my mouth into Dante's life one more time.

Chapter 33

"**W**in this round and you'll win it all," I say, perched on the ring apron. I notice a microphone taped to the post. Geez, I'm on pay-per-view. Millions of people just heard me say that. Do I care? Hell, no!

"I am behind on points," Dante wheezes.

"What fight are you watching?" I say. "You're up one round at least!"

"He needs a knockout," Red says.

DJ nods. "*Papino,* you need to put him down."

Dante nods, a dribble of blood dropping off his chin. "Yes, Christiana. He must go down. *Fare non preoccupazione.* Do not be afraid. No matter what happens, Christiana, DJ, Red, *fare non preoccupazione.*"

The referee appears. "Seconds out." He stares at me. "Hey, she ain't official."

I ignore him. "What are you going to do?" I whisper to Dante.

Dante winks at me. "I am the teacher."

Every square inch on my body bursts into goose bumps, tears rolling down my face.

Now millions of people have seen me cry.

I am a *mess*.

Dante rises to another impossible roar while Michael Buffer says, "Let's give these two warriors a Madison Square Garden round of applause!"

As if he needed to say that.

I look around me and don't know what to do. I do my best to avoid Evelyn's eyes, but I can't help it. I can't read her eyes. Why isn't she jumping up and shouting? Red tugs my elbow and helps me off the apron, placing me in a chair next to the post with DJ.

"Can he do it, Red?" I ask, wiping my tears.

"He's *been* doing it," Red says. "He's already set it up. Just hope we have enough time for him to finish it." He puts his nose in my ear. "No coaching, now. We have to be quiet or he can be disqualified."

"I know how to be silent, Red," I say. I doubt anyone could hear me anyway above all this noise.

They touch gloves again, and Tank dives in a millisecond later with a crushing right to Dante's jaw. Dante's red, white, and green mouthpiece sputters to the canvas.

My heart drops into my stomach.

Dante falters, hits the ropes, his hands clawing in the air in front of him. Tank crushes him again, this time with an uppercut, and Dante rolls toward his corner where Tank pummels Dante's body again and again and again.

Please do something! I shout in my head.

Then Dante turns his head toward me as Tank hits that gentle face.

Dante winks.

His eyes are clear.

He is the teacher.

My goose bumps have sprouted goose bumps.

Red grips my arm. "That sly old fox," he says.

"He is the teacher," I barely whisper.

"What?"

Dante wobbles out of the corner toward Tank, his legs looking like mine probably looked that day he hit me. Tank throws several rights and lefts followed by a devastating left uppercut. Tank unleashes an arcing right—

And Dante leaps aside and pounds Tank flush on the jaw with a cannon of a *right*, a howitzer, a, well, a runaway *tank* of a punch!

Tank staggers left.

I squeeze the hell out of DJ's arm.

Dante leaps to the other side, showing that *pericoloso* left hook. Tank raises his right to block it, and Dante uncorks another brutal right flush on Tank's jaw.

I am now squeezing the hell out of Red's arm.

Tank's legs wobble, then stiffen, as if he's walking on hot sand with stork legs, his hands limp against his sides.

Tank . . . is . . . *toast!*

Dante pulls a right uppercut all the way from Carroll Gardens and drives Tank's jaw up through his nose. A hard left to the ribs, a blistering right to the chest, and—

There's the hook, and it's a green, white, and *red* hook, you son of a—

Tank's down.

Tank's down!

"He's not getting up!" Red hollers, hugging DJ and me.

"Class," I say, as the Garden shakes, the roars echoing all the way to Brooklyn. I smile. "Class is dismissed."

I can't shout anymore.

I can't make a sound.

The noise is so deafening that I'm deaf.

I see Dante, his hands up and ready for battle, waiting in the opposite corner looking not too much different from that little boy in that baggy T-shirt and billowing shorts, flashbulbs blitzkrieging the ring.

I'm blind.

I'm deaf.

I'm mute.

The referee counts it down along with the crowd.

The referee waves his arms and raises Dante's right hand.

Victory.

He did it!

I can't believe I'm crying. I can't believe I have any tears *left* to cry!

I cannot move as I watch only DJ running into the ring to embrace his *papino*. I look at Red, and he's weeping, both his large, dark hands gripping the bottom rope. I turn to see Evelyn, and she seems to be muttering to herself.

Oh yeah.

Evelyn.

I watch DJ removing Dante's gloves while camera crews spill into the ring. A gold blur then sneaks past me into the ring.

Evelyn.

Oh no.

Oh no, no, no.

I don't want to see this!

Chapter 34

I turn to run, God only knows where, but Red grabs me. "Wait, Christiana. Don't go. It ain't over yet."

"Che?"

"The fight ain't over yet, Christiana," he says. "Stick around."

"But, Red, I—"

"Stick around," he says again. He holds both my shoulders. "I think you're gonna like what you see."

Dante embraces Evelyn, and the crowd roars. My legs buckle and I try to run, but Red holds me still.

"Just wait, Christiana."

Dante smiles and kisses both of her cheeks. He motions to DJ, and it looks like they're having a family conference, not that I would know anything about that. My heart slows a little, but then Evelyn kisses Dante on the cheek, the crowd roars, and I try to pull away from Red.

"For the last time, Christiana," he says, "be still."

I start to cry again. Granddaddy used to say that to me all the time.

Then DJ throws Dante's gloves over his shoulder and escorts Evelyn off the canvas, his arm around his mother.

What just happened?

The crowd is quiet, even restless.

Then Dante motions to me, smiling.

Dear Jesus! I know I don't talk to you like I should but . . . Dear Jesus!

Why can't I move? I wanted to move a few seconds ago.

"You're on, Christiana," Lelani says in my ear. I didn't even know she was standing next to me!

"Lelani, Red—"

Red lets go of my shoulders. "I know you'll keep him happy," he says, his voice hoarse, tears streaming from his eyes. He hugs me. "I knew there was something . . . something *good* about you. Take care of our boy, okay?"

"You're leaving?" I ask.

"Retiring," Red says with a smile. "Gonna open up a restaurant in Brooklyn Heights. You'll never have to pay."

"Yes, she will," Lelani says. "I want big tips." She waves a ring at me. "I am surprised you didn't notice this."

"I'm sorry, Lelani, I—"

"You were focused on your man. I understand." She kisses Red on the lips. "I really do. *Ciao.*"

Camera crews, reporters, and even Harry surround Dante, but he's still beckoning to me. I roll onto the apron and under the bottom rope, standing jelly-legged and almost out on my feet by the time Dante pushes through the cameras and takes me into his arms.

Another roar.

Flashbulbs like lightning.

"Dante, are you sure?" is all I can manage to say.

"*Sì,*" he says. "You are done ignoring me."

I hug him hard. "I will never ignore you again."

I'm sure we're confusing the hell out of these people. I mean, I'm not the woman they think he was fighting for.

Or was I?

Was I?

"Dante, were you fighting for me?" I ask.

"Yes."

This is unbelievable. "The whole time?"

He smiles. "No. Not the whole time."

I have to know when. I have to know when . . . when he fell in love with me. "When did you decide that you . . . when did you decide to fight for me?"

He kisses my forehead. "It did not happen all at once. From the day we met, I liked you. You impressed me. I am not easily impressed. Then you hurt me but I forgave you. I told myself, Dante, you cannot forgive this woman. But I did. You came many miles to tell me to box, not fight. Use your jab, you said. It worked, yes? Then you send a nice picture, one I did not burn, and this morning I read the most amazing article. You wore me down. You worked my body and my heart. I could not resist."

Here come the tears.

Harry the Human Cliché thrusts the microphone into Dante's face and says something stupid like, "How's it feel to be champion again?"

Dante takes the microphone from Harry and taps it. Nothing. "I want everyone to hear," he says to Harry.

Harry goes to the ropes and makes the request. Dante taps the microphone, and huge booms thunder into the Garden. The crowd quiets.

"I have fought . . ."

The crowd goes crazy again.

Dante waits until the noise dies down. "I have fought my last fight."

"No!" howls through the Garden. Amazing. Fifteen thousand New Yorkers just had the same thought I have.

"It was a good fight, yes?" he says.

They cheer.

"It was a good fight. But . . ." He smiles at me, and I get all gooey inside. "It is time to retire. I want to be able to breathe and think when I am old." He pulls me closer and looks into my eyes. "I have won this match for love."

I am lost in his eyes, and I hope no one but Dante ever finds me.

"Love for you, Christiana."

Fifteen thousand people ooh and ahh. I'm glad I'm wearing pants and this jacket. My goose bumps would cut everyone around me to shreds.

"I do not have a ring for you yet, Christiana." He looks around me. "Is *this* ring big enough for you?"

My heart can't possibly get any bigger. "Yes," I say softly. "Yes."

Applause.

"All this canvas, the ropes. It is hard to wear."

Laughter. I'm crying again. He kisses a tear away.

"Are you *sure* you want to retire, Dante?" I ask.

The Garden folks don't want it to happen, shouting, "Don't retire! Keep fighting!"

Dante smiles at the crowd. "I am sure. I want a daughter to train. We will help her be champion."

"Yes." A daughter. A family. What I've always wanted. What I've always needed. What I had until I was two but can't and don't want to remember. What I had with Granddaddy and can never forget. For once in my life, sadness won't be able to hurt me anymore.

For once in my life, I won't be alone.

"I will still fight, though," Dante says.

The Garden becomes silent.

He winks at me. "Christiana, I will fight you for the remote control. I will fight you for the covers. I will fight you for the right to cook in my own kitchen. I will fight for air when we . . ." He raises his eyebrows.

Have you ever heard a thousand catcalls? Now imagine a thousand *New Yorkers* making them. It's a good thing this fight was pay-per-view. HBO will have to edit this part for the replay next weekend.

"I will fight you when we work out together and make our daughter," Dante continues. "I will fight to hold back my tears when we are married and when I hold my daughter for the first time."

I am having this man's baby, and we are making *her* tonight.

"We can get married here, yes?" he asks.

Laughter.

"Are you kidding?" I whisper.

He hugs me fiercely. "See, we are fighting already. It is the sure sign of a healthy marriage. Whatever fights you get into, make sure they end in a tie." He kisses me deeply to glorious applause. "Making up is a good workout, too."

Dante gives the microphone to Harry.

Harry fluffs his hair and says, "Okay, champ, how does it—"

"No," Dante says. "No interview. It was not put in my contract because I was not supposed to win. I do not have to talk to you."

"But—"

"No. This interview is over." Dante guides me to the corner, waving at the crowd. He picks me up and puts me on the top rope, gripping my legs tightly. "Our interview is over, too."

Say what? "*Che?* What interview?"

"The interview I have been having with you since I met you," he says. "The interview that began the very second I saw you in that boat taking my picture. This is the last interview I will ever give. You were a hard interview. So temperamental."

My mouth drops open. "Me? You . . . you . . ."

He puts his forehead on mine. "What? You think I do

not have *giornalista* skills? I have, as they say, mad skills, yo. I was interviewing you almost the entire time."

This can't be, can it? "Oh, no, you weren't."

He nods. "Think back. You will see. It started on the dock when I was only the thirteenth sexy man."

I can't believe this.

"That night I let you take fish from my plate, and later, I let you take my heart."

"You . . . let me?"

He winks. "I have better defense than you think." He hugs me. *"Andiamo,"* he says. "I must say thank you to New York one last time."

We move to the center of the ring and wave, yelling, *"Tante grazie!"*

After one final bow, it takes a phalanx of New York's finest to get us through the throng into the dressing room, paparazzi taking shot after shot of me.

Little old me from Red Hook, the little girl with no parents, the little girl who learned how to box and ended up with a boxer.

I am a story waiting to happen.

I'll never write it. I mean, who would believe it?

I get a scary thought. I'm a celebrity now. I wonder if they'll ask me to say anything wise.

Nah.

They know I'll make sense. They won't quote me. Wisdom doesn't sell magazines.

I lean on Dante's legs as he sits on an examination table in the dressing room unraveling the tape on his hands. We're waiting for the ringside physician to check him out, and it's taking forever.

"Where is Red?" Dante asks.

This might be hard for him. "You don't need Red anymore."

"He is my friend," he says. "I will always need him. I love his cooking."

I tell Dante about Red's restaurant.

"Brooklyn Heights." He smiles. "No wonder he was on the phone so much the last two weeks. He even sneaked off with Lelani. He said they needed some time together. *Bene*. It is about time the world tastes his cooking. We will go there often."

I pout. "I *can* cook."

He puts his hands on my shoulders. "We will cook together, remember?"

"Yes." I crawl up on to his lap and kiss his puffy cheeks. "You dropped your left, Mr. Lattanza."

He shrugs. "Bad habit. But I had to bleed a little to make the lesson I taught real."

"He'll want a rematch."

He captures me with those eyes. "I no longer do rematches, Christiana. No more rematches. Never again."

That's when I, um, suck the life out of him. I know his lungs are empty after that kiss.

"Where is that doctor?" I complain.

"Tank is hurt." He looks toward the mop closet. "We do not have to wait out here, do we?"

In the closet, the only light floats up from the sliver of a crack at the bottom of the door. While a mop handle gets fresh with my booty, I wander my hands all over him.

"This has been so . . . so . . . myth-magical," I say.

His hands are wandering, too. "It is not a word."

"It is now," I say. "I may have it trademarked."

He puts his hot hands under my sweater. "What does it mean?"

"It's what love is," I say, almost out of breath. "Love is full of myth and magic. Myth-magical."

He massages my back. "It is a good word. I will use it in my book."

I lean back. "*Your* book?"

"*My* autobiography."

I smile, not that he can see my smile. "And who taught you how to write?"

"No one," he says, massaging lower and lower. "I can talk. I can type. Therefore, I can write."

I tap his cup with a knuckle. "It's not as easy as all that, Mr. Lattanza."

He slides his hands between my underwear and slacks. Ah. My booty is happy again. "What?" he says. "You jab at the keys using your left more than your right."

"Che?" Oh, that feels so good.

"The keyboard," he says. "The left hand does most of the work. I have made a study of this. I have a good left hand. Therefore, I will be a good writer."

I take that left hand and move it around my slacks to a very special, very needy, seriously wet place. "You have a good left hand, Mr. Lattanza. And now, if you'll be so good as to drop it a bit lower . . ."

"You tell me to keep my left up, and now you tell me to put it down. You have a hard time making up your mind, Christiana. We will have to work on this."

I put his finger under my underwear. "Drop it, okay?"

His finger starts to stroke me. "But now that I have dropped my left, you will hit me."

Oh yes. "As hard and as fast as I can."

For the rest of my life.

Chapter 35

We didn't get married in the Garden, though Dante actually looked into the possibility. "It will only cost two arms and one leg," he told me.

That wasn't going to happen. I need all his appendages, especially his arms.

We were married a month later at Christ Church in Cobble Hill, where a *Sopranos* wedding scene was filmed a few years ago. We didn't have all of HBO's cameras, and it snowed, reducing our guests to, oh, about *eight hundred*, most of whom we didn't invite. Several even waved Italian flags in the back pew. *Personality* sent a photographer, and we ended up with a nice spread a few pages after an exclusive picture of megacouple's latest adoption.

Oh well.

We prepared to honeymoon in Jamaica, but a nor'easter cancelled our flight. Neither of us felt like leaving the Crowne Plaza near JFK—in Jamaica, *New York*—and I couldn't have lasted the flight without messing with him or him with me anyway, so . . .

I can't tell you much about the Crowne Plaza except to say that room service was nice, punctual, and very discreet.

We, um, we tore it up, and we didn't even use the bed all that much. We shooed away housekeeping for days—except when we needed more towels. We did this sauna thing with steam in the bathroom. . . . Oh, and the carpeting was exquisitely plush. Not a single rug burn.

It was, um, really beautiful in Jamaica that time of year.

Mr. and Mrs. Red and Lelani Gregory (I was her maid of honor!) have opened an intimate little restaurant in Brooklyn Heights called Red's Lelani. It's not a boxer bar or sports bar, either, though a poster of Dante and me hugging in the ring is the first picture you see in the waiting area. Red's Lelani serves Italian-Polynesian food.

"Occidental Continental," Red calls it.

Lelani calls it "Poly-talian" and "Ital-esian."

The critics call it "ridiculously superb . . . rambunctiously appealing . . . and the perfect blend of the boot and the islands."

Food critics. Always ridiculously and rambunctiously ransacking the thesaurus.

Red's Lelani, which has a decent view of Governors Island and the Statue of Liberty from its upper outdoor seating area, is doing well.

"You would not believe how many amazing things Red can do with pineapple juice," Lelani told me on our first visit. "We're even going to bottle and sell his barbecue sauce."

The atmosphere at Red's Lelani is not Poly-talian. "No tiki torches, hula girls, mug shots, or Italian flags here," Lelani says. "This is *our* joint."

Instead, a miscellaneous mix of their lives provides the décor, including several round cards, plenty of handmade furniture from Barry's Bay, Hawaiian Tropic calendars, and wonderful photo and poster collages of the old Brooklyn Dodgers.

Yeah. I donated my shrine to them as a wedding gift.

Red cried. I know he and Granddaddy would have been the best of friends.

Lelani turned the actual stool Dante used during his last fight upside down and uses it to hold the menus.

There's some poetic justice in that.

Dante told me much later about the secret deal he'd made with Evelyn a full *month* before the fight. "We both knew we could not start over. There was no magic, no fire. So, we made a deal. We agreed that when I won, I would retire and train DJ at Gleason's every summer."

He and *Eve*lyn (I can now say it without stumbling) made a compromise that day, something Dante said they had never made in their marriage. So far, she's kept her part of the bargain, allowing DJ to stay with us *without* her popping in unannounced for a visit. Since my Red Hook "space," as Dante called it, was too small for the three of us, Dante bought me a house.

A real house.

I do not live in some moronic realtor's idea that a four-family quadra-plex is a house.

After selling his property in Virginia, Dante used the money from that sale and money he already had to buy us a house in South Slope near Prospect Park. It has sea blue clapboard with shiny hardwood floors. A fireplace to snuggle in front of is just off a huge kitchen where we battle for counter space nightly. The house had already been totally renovated, so all we had to do was move in. Three large bedrooms and two full baths fill the top floor. I have my own *real* bathroom for the first time in my life! Red took one look at the kitchen and pronounced it "gourmet." The master bedroom has a deck, which overlooks our private garden, not that we ever, um, look down at the garden when we're, um, "working out." Dante is converting the English basement into a recreation and workout room using my old "gym," and I *sometimes* let him work.

There's just something so extremely sexy about a man hammering a nail. I just can't explain it. I mean, he's good with his hammer, and I love him to nail me.

What's a girl to do?

I love seeing the love and respect our neighbors give him. Dante is just a regular guy, a typical homeowner, chatting up the Donatello family next door. "I've been away from Brooklyn too long," Dante says. "I am no longer homesick."

South Slope isn't exactly Red Hook, but at least I have my own dirt, my own flowers, and my own tomatoes to tend in my *own* yard.

Our summer houseguest DJ is undefeated (12–0) as an amateur, and miracle of miracles, he actually boxes. I've, um, been whispering for him to use his jab more when Dante isn't paying attention. It's working.

"He is a boxer!" Dante shouts at Gleason's Gym. "He does the opposite of everything I teach him! Teenagers! Whatyagonnado?"

DJ wins easily because he has mad skills, and we're hoping he'll be invited to the next Olympic trials.

"When you make the team," Dante tells DJ, "you will represent Brooklyn, not Syracuse."

"I can be from both places, Dad," DJ says.

"No. Only Brooklyn. Brooklyn gave me heart. Brooklyn will never disappoint you."

It has been difficult dealing with the fanfare surrounding DJ's famous name. He prefers "Dante Lattanza Junior" now, which totally solidifies his bond with his legendary father/ trainer. So many reporters want to talk to Dante instead of DJ, but Dante sets them straight. "It is DJ's time, not mine," Dante tells them, avoiding their cameras. "Talk to him. It is his turn to be a legend."

Dante is still a little vain, but he has every right to be. I have had many legendary nights with that man. Oh, and mornings. And occasionally, when we work out through the night *and* the morning, during the daylight hours, too. Hmm. Just about any time, really. We like to "work out" together.

Evelyn has given her mouth a workout, too. She has been a guest on all the talk shows, and I mean *all* the talk shows. She swapped pet stories with Ellen (after agreeing with Ellen that I was a "gold-digging opportunist"), traded recipes with Oprah (as if Evelyn ever cooked!), and gave health tips to Matt Lauer (as if he really needed any). We heard she's filming some cable show where a woman whittles ten men down to one over the course of several weeks. It's going to be titled *Left in the Ring,* and the promos are already running: "She expected a ring but was left in the ring. She's the one the champ didn't choose. . . ."

Nauseating.

Even though I'm nothing but a gold-digging opportunist to Evelyn, I hope she does find a nice man. For all her queenly ways, she is a lady who deserves a gentleman.

Dante has been doing some color commentary for HBO, and he's a whole lot more insightful than any of the other *non*boxer analysts are. Here's an exchange from the other night:

Jim:	*Thornton threw some wicked lefts to Jackson's ribcage that round.*
Dante:	*They took my breath away, too. Those hurt. Those let you know you are alive.*
Harry:	*Pain is gain, eh?*
Dante:	*Pain is* pain, *Harry. Pain hurts. Body shots do damage.*
Harry:	*But those kinds of punches don't often score points on the judges' scorecards.*

Dante: *Land enough of them, and you can send*
            everyone home early. The judges' scorecards
            won't matter.

Harry: *Well, I think Thornton is spending too*
            much time chopping wood.

Dante: *Chopping wood? He is shattering cartilage.*
            He is breaking bones. He is lacerating liver.
            He is bruising lungs. Jackson will be peeing
            blood for days.

As I said, Dante is colorful.

And more popular than ever. We can't go anywhere without someone asking for his autograph. And Little Italy? Fuggedaboutit. He'll never have to pay for another meal there as long as he lives. He gets at least two pairs of underwear in the mail every week, and I love wearing (and not wearing) all those pairs of underwear for my sex god, my *dio del sesso*. The ones that fit. I won't wear thongs, bloomers, or ones with another woman's name stitched onto the crotch.

I cannot nor will I ever complain about all the money we have because he "took it all," and Dante makes sure we use it wisely and for good causes. We still only have the Land Cruiser, and it just exceeded two hundred thousand miles. We auctioned off Dante's gloves, trunks, boxing shoes, mouthpiece, and even his protective cup (!) to raise money for lung cancer research (his charity) and the fight against domestic violence (my charity). It is so amazing what people will bid for used, sweaty boxing equipment.

The cup received the highest bid.

It, um, sits in a box Dante doesn't know about. It's in the attic. Shh. Don't tell.

That's the beauty of a silent auction.

I quit working for *Personality,* but I didn't quit writing. Mel is letting me freelance for the *Times,* and I love it.

I . . . love . . . it.

I get to talk to real people all day.

I'm also writing Dante's biography. Okay, okay, *we* are writing it. Dante can actually turn a nice phrase in English every now and then, and the editing sessions are hotter than hot. I have to dry out my keyboard some days. We already have a publisher (Little, Brown) and a contract with lots of zeroes.

Now if I can only find the time.

You see, we have our hands full in a big way.

Dantiana "Red" Lattanza arrived last month, all nine pounds, nine ounces of her.

"She will be a heavyweight for sure," Dante says.

Dante thinks we conceived her in the mop closet at the Garden. I think we made her in Jamaica, New York. No matter who is right, Dantiana will have an interesting story to tell her friends when she grows up.

Not that we'd actually ever *tell* her these details. I was made in a mop closet? I was made in Queens?

I don't want to scar my child for life.

Dante has already started training her to be a southpaw. "Keep your right high, higher . . . *bene,*" he says as he boxes her with his pinkies. "You will move like *seta,* like your silky mama. Protect yourself at all times, don't stop jabbing, *tenere provare.* When the time is right, you come out swinging like your mama."

He's also giving her advice on boys: "If you love a bad boy, he will make you cry. A good boy will never make you cry. You must find a good boy. Your mama will help you. She can tell."

And I can. I have a good boy. His name is Dante.

I didn't tell Dante about Vincent, but one cold snowy

night, Vincent came through. On a visit to Monte's, Dante kissed Vincent on both cheeks before sitting, and it brought tears to Vincent's eyes. Mine, too. I handed Dantiana to Vincent so he could hold his granddaughter for the first time. It was myth-magical, and Vincent wept. Dante saw Vincent's tears, my tears, and my eyes moving from him to Vincent.

"No," Dante said.

I could only nod and say, "Yes."

Dante, my Dante, my gentle, gentle man, didn't weep or even tear up. He stood, took Dantiana from Vincent and handed her to me, then hugged his father as his *son* for the first time in his life, right there during happy hour at Monte's Venetian Room, looking out over the suddenly beautiful Gowanus Canal.

Another myth-magical moment.

I didn't mind the bursts of Italian those two shared for the rest of the evening, their voices so much alike that they blended into one sexy Italian voice. Dantiana's eyes went back and forth between them. She's going to be at least bilingual, maybe more. She has her father's eyes.

Once Dantiana is asleep, Dante and I talk, argue, and make up every night. I used to think that relationships were interviews that never ended. Now I know different.

Marriage is the interview that never ends.

I'm so glad I decided to interview him. . . .

"Do not lie to these good people who are reading this book," Dante says, trying to delete the previous sentence. "I was the one interviewing you from the very beginning. Type that."

"No," I say.

He lifts me from this chair and slides into it, turning me to face him. He looks over my shoulder while he attempts to type. "I will fix this," he says.

I start to grind on him, unbuttoning my red, white, and green flannel shirt. I look behind me to see what he's typed so far, and I laugh because I only see a question:

"May I interview your corpo provocante now?"

Acknowledgments

I'd like to thank the following folks for their help in the creation of this novel:

*Stephanie and Giuseppe Spalino for checking and correcting all the Italian words and phrases in this novel. Italian is a tricky, regional language. Any mistakes in this text are my own, not theirs;

*Mike Riddle for knowing how to spell a certain actress's name, listening to me rant about the current state of boxing, and helping me to live "in the balcony";

*Greg Redd (a real-life master chef) for his recipes, puns, and friendship;

*All the residents (you know who you are) and staff at Camp on Craig for their encouragement;

*My agent, Evan Marshall, and editor, John Scognamiglio, for their support, care, and insight;

*My wife and sons for giving me many moments to cheer for them over the years.

She's had celebrity, isn't hurting for money, and is living peacefully single in Charlotte, North Carolina. Still, Sonya Richardson can't resist starring on a hit reality dating show to give America a taste of what a real black woman is like. And this former pro athlete is breaking all of "Hunk or Punk's" rules, refusing to bling-up like a diva, and tackling whatever high-octane drama her suitors have in store. But one contestant is throwing Sonya off her game. He's surprisingly kind, way too easy to spill her secrets to—and giving her the kind of hope she hasn't felt in a long, long time . . .

Widowed former pastor John Bond knows he's the show's "designated white guy," expected to fail every challenge and be gone in a month. He also knows he has to take risks to change his lonely life and find love again. The odds may be against him, but Sonya's honesty and resourcefulness are inspiring him to do whatever it takes to stay in the running, win her heart . . . and prove their dreams can be a reality.

**Please turn the page for an exciting
sneak peek of J. J. Murray's
A GOOD MAN
coming next month from Kensington Publishing!**

"Bob, we're in serious trouble."

"What's wrong now, Larry? We have the mansion rigged and most of the Crew moved in, don't we?"

"We're short one Nubian princess and one white guy."

"What? I thought we had our princess under contract! I thought it was a done deal! Where is she?"

"She bailed on us and took a gig with Survivor instead. More exposure, she said. They start filming on Wetang Island off Indonesia next week. Wetang! What a name!"

"They chose Indonesia? Are they insane? After all the earthquakes, terrorist attacks, tsunamis, and volcano eruptions?"

"It does add to the element of danger."

"But we begin filming next week, Larry! Did you call the other semifinalists?"

"I did. One's doing Big Brother as their token woman of color. One got a nice part in Tyler Perry's next Madea movie, and our last hope decided to play Lady Macbeth in a community theater production of Macbeth in Racine, Wisconsin."

"She chose community theater in Racine, Wisconsin, over reality TV? What was she thinking?"

"*Lady Macbeth* is a plum role, even if it's in Racine, Wisconsin, in January."

"You offered all of them more money, right?"

"Of course. I almost doubled it. Still no takers."

"They're insane! They get to stay in a multi-million-dollar mansion for free, eat for free, wear clothes they couldn't possibly afford in real life, go on all-expenses-paid dates to interesting places and restaurants they couldn't even get reservations for, and get fifty grand on top of all that, not to mention all the exposure they can use to make even more money later."

"It is indeed strange. I guess some women just don't know what's good for them."

"What about the surfer, what was his name, Rip?"

"Rip is out surfing in Australia. I called him, and he said, 'The waves are wicked rad sweeet Down Under this time of year, bro.' That was a direct quote. I assume he's riding barrels and cutting sick off South Stradbroke Island as we speak."

"I hope a shark tears his legs off. He wouldn't have lasted past the second episode anyway."

"And we would have needed subtitles for him. He spoke surfer."

"Geez, Larry, what are we gonna do? Are we still getting hits from the Web site?"

"A few strays here and there, but no white guys. We'll spam the Internet until we find another one."

"And now we're reduced to spamming for contestants. Why'd we call the show *Hunk or Punk?* No one wants to be a punk."

"It rhymes, and our advertisers love the name."

"I liked *Beefcake* or *Cupcake* better. Even *Hero* or *Goat* would have been better."

"*The focus group chose* Hunk or Punk."

"*I hate focus groups. They're inherently stupid, and they eat too many doughnuts.*"

"*But our T-shirt sales are picking up.*"

"*Our what?*"

"*We've been selling reversible* Hunk or Punk *T-shirts. When you want to be a hunk, you wear the hunk side out. When you want to be a punk, you wear the—*"

"*I get the concept, Larry,*" Bob interrupted. "*But what good are T-shirts if there's no show? What are we going to do?*"

"*I'll handle it, Bob. You just make sure the mansion is ready and the Crew is prepped and primed to be hunky and punky.*"

"*But where are we going to get a Nubian princess on such short notice? And where will we find a white guy who's willing to be humiliated on national TV?*"

"*Bob, this is America. There's always some woman who thinks she's a princess. Look at Bristol Palin. And there's always a white guy who likes to be humiliated. Look at Al Gore.*"

"*Oh, yeah . . .*"

Chapter 1

It started with a phone call from Sonya Richardson's publicist.

"Sonya, how's it going?"

I haven't heard from Michelle Hamm in five years, Sonya thought. "Fine, Michelle. How have you been? A better question is *where* have you been?"

"I expected only to leave you a message."

Sonya sighed. Michelle was infamous for not answering her questions.

"I am so surprised that you answered, Sonya," Michelle said. "It's ten o'clock on a Friday night. Why aren't you out with your bad self?"

Because I don't have a "bad self" anymore, not that I ever had a bad self. "I lead a quiet life now. You know that."

Just me in my suburban Charlotte, North Carolina, home on my suburban couch in my suburban great room, watching my new flat-screen TV bought at a suburban electronics store. Wow. This is the first phone call in days that hasn't asked me for a donation. Hmm. Michelle's on the line. I may be donating my time somewhere soon.

"Let me guess," Sonya said. "There's some WNBA function I just *have* to attend."

"Nope," Michelle said. "WB is doing a new show called *Hunk or Punk*."

She's calling me to discuss what's going to be on TV. "And what does this have to do with me?"

"You're single."

She has to remind me. Ten hard years in the WNBA, playing for two Olympic teams, traveling around the world several times, taking mission trips to Haiti and New Orleans in the off-season. I had no time for a man. I barely had time for myself.

"What's your point, Michelle?" *I have my own TV shows to watch.*

"They're looking for a strong, attractive, literate, intelligent black woman just like you."

"No, they aren't. Not on shows like that."

"They *are*. Wouldn't you like to have twelve hunky men fighting over you?"

"No."

"The actual word is 'woo.' These men are going to 'woo' you on national TV."

Woo? Noo. "And you thought of me?"

"I could only think of you, Sonya."

"Gee, thanks. Um, *you're* still single, aren't you, Michelle?"

"Yes, but I am not—"

"And you're strong, attractive, literate, and intelligent, right?"

"Of course, but I don't look anything like you. I'm thick in some spots and much thicker in others. Some spots I haven't *seen* in years, not even with a mirror. You're cute. You probably still have some baby fat. Unless you've let yourself go."

"No, I'm still in shape." *I just don't have anyone to ad-*

mire my shape except me. "What makes you think I would go on TV to find a date?"

"Are you married, shacking up, or dating anyone now?"

"No." *Loneliness is next to godliness. Most of the time.*

"Are you even trying?"

"No."

"Then maybe you *have* to go on TV to get a date."

Sonya shook some cobwebs from her head. "That makes no sense."

"Sure it does. It ain't happenin' with what you're doing now, right? Why not roll the dice and see what happens and get *paid* to do it at the same time."

Because I don't need *it to happen!* "Look, I'm not hurting for money, and I don't need a man, okay? I'm happily single." *And my couch needs me to keep it warm. My remote control whimpers when I'm not around. My TV sighs whenever I don't turn it on.*

"C'mon, Sonya. No one is *really* single and happy. If it weren't for my cat and an occasional hookup, I'd be miserable. Why don't you live a little? Go on the show. Let your hair down. Have some fun for a change."

I've never had much hair to let down. "No."

"Well, look at it another way. Do we really want another diva with an attitude representing us on TV? This is our chance to show America a *real* black woman for a change."

Now that *is tempting. I am sick of what's on TV for the most part. Reality shows are often faker than regular shows. It's why I watch Animal Planet and* Man v. Food *just about every day. Those are real shows. I mean, who doesn't want to know what parasites are living inside the human body? And who doesn't eat? And sometimes the shows seem to overlap. I'll be watching something about tapeworms on Animal Planet, and then I'll wonder if the host for* Man v. Food *has a tapeworm that helps him eat so much. How many shows can do that overlap?*

"Earth to Sonya."

"I was just thinking about . . ." *I can't tell her I was thinking about tapeworms.* "I was just wondering why you think I'm a real black woman."

"You're a success story without the extensions, the attitude, and the diamond-studded fingernails. You grew up in Jersey as an orphan in the 'hood, got raised by your saintly grandmama, you were the first in your family to graduate college, your college team won the national championship twice, you were an all-American in college three times, your team made the NCAA tournament all four years you were there—"

"I know my bio, Michelle," Sonya interrupted. "What's your point?"

"You're not only beautiful—you're actually interesting, unlike a lot of the beautiful people on TV. If I were the average American couch potato, I'd want to get to know you better."

"*I* am a couch potato." *And loving every lazy minute of it.* "Couch potatoes are not interested in the lives of other couch potatoes." *If there were a market for it, it would already be on TV.*

"Sonya, you are the ultimate role model for black women. TV needs you."

TV needs me about as much as I need TV. Wait a minute. I need TV, mainly to help me sleep. Does that mean TV needs me to help other people sleep?

"Michelle, please listen," Sonya said. "I am not a role model. I played ball. I earned my living playing with a ball. That doesn't make me—"

"You're a role model," Michelle interrupted. "Little girls looked up to you."

Right. I'm too short for them to look up to me. "And I'm forty. Those shows are for much younger women. I don't have a chance of being a Nubian princess." *Who thinks up that noise anyway? Nubian princess? Why not Nubian* queen? *TV is always downgrading black women.*

"Forty is the new twenty."

"Not to a twenty-year-old," Sonya said. *Or to a forty-year-old with a reluctant knee, elbows that pop for no reason, and toes that rarely warm up.*

"You could be glamorous, you know."

"My glamorous days are over." *Not that I had any in the first place. When they put makeup on me for those WNBA calendars, I felt like a clown.* "Don't they have an age limit for shows like that?"

"You just made the cutoff."

How nice. "Thank you for thinking of me, really, but no thanks."

"Um, I already sent in a few of your old headshots and your bio."

Sonya shot off the couch. "What?"

"And the producers are *very* interested in what they've seen. They want to meet with you soon. As in, as soon as you can get to LA. That kind of soon."

The witch! "You already signed me up?"

"It's what I do, right? And I didn't exactly sign you up. I just sent a few pictures and your bio. No harm in that."

"Michelle, you haven't really been my publicist for the last five years," Sonya said. She turned on her TV and tuned it to The Food Channel, muting the sound. "And Michelle, those headshots have to be at least ten years old."

"They're actually fifteen years old."

Geez, I was still a kid! "But that's not how I look now. You're misrepresenting me."

She's still misrepresenting me. She tried to paint me as some "bad girl from Jersey" back in the day to increase my salary, as if being "fierce" would put more people in the seats. No one bought that mess. Nike wouldn't have signed me to represent their shoes if I were a "bad girl" from anywhere.

"I'll bet you haven't aged a day."

I have aged many *days, and a few more during this conversation.* "Michelle, I have several body parts heading south, I have wrinkles, my evil knee cracks—"

"And all of that can be fixed or hidden," Michelle interrupted. "They are *really* interested in you, Sonya. They are willing to pay you a lot of money to take the role."

The what? "The role? I'm playing myself, right? How is that a role?"

"You know what I mean. You'll be playing the role of the woman in waiting, the role of the damsel in the castle waiting for her knight in shining armor, the role of—"

"The desperate middle-aged woman afraid of dying alone," Sonya interrupted. *Ouch. That hurt to say. It must be somewhat true if it hurts me like that.*

"It's funny you should mention desperate, Sonya. The producers actually sounded desperate when I talked to them."

"So let them remain desperate. I'm not desperate."

"You're a beautiful woman alone on a Friday night."

"And I'll be a beautiful woman alone on a Saturday night, too." *And on Sundays and Wednesdays, I'll be a beautiful woman getting my prayer and praise on in church.* "I like my life, Michelle. I like quiet. I didn't know how necessary quiet was to me until I had some quiet. Silence is indeed golden. You know I didn't like all that noise and hype. I never liked doing post-game interviews or have any microphones jammed into my face or cameras following my every twitch. And now you want me to go on TV for what, months? That's not me at all. You *know* this."

"Well, um, I already told them that you were interested in doing this show."

Sonya snapped off the TV. She had already seen the host of *Man v. Food* eat the five-pound burrito. "You told them I was interested before you even tried to get *me* interested?"

"Well, if they weren't interested in you being interested, I wouldn't have called you to check on whether you were interested or not."

Her logic still escapes me. "So what if they're really interested. *I'm* not interested."

"But, Sonya, the money is ridiculous, more than your first year's salary for the Comets."

"I told you. I'm not hurting for money."

Because I'm not hurting for common sense and I actually learned something from my business administration classes at the University of Houston. I lived like a nun for ten years in the league before splurging on this house and the Maxima outside. The interest from the money I earned and invested wisely during my playing days keeps me living comfortably.

"I told them you'd consider twice that," Michelle said.

"What?"

"And they said fine. They said fine, Sonya. See what I said about desperate?"

And this makes me feel . . . less homely for some reason. They're willing to pay old me double. "They doubled the money?"

"One hundred thousand dollars."

Whoa. They are seriously desperate. Who can afford to throw that kind of money around these days?

"At least think about it," Michelle said.

"Oh, I'll think about it." *For about a minute. This is not gonna happen.*

"It could be fun, Sonya."

"It could be stupid, Michelle."

"Not with intelligent you as the star."

"I don't want to be a star." *I was the point guard, the player who made everyone* else *look good.* "I'm middle-aged now. I'm past my need for attention."

Okay, who am I kidding? I would love to have the attention of a good man, but not the smothering kind of attention. The remote belongs to me. This couch belongs to me. My space belongs to me. But to have twelve men pawing at me? At the same time? I'd have a football team and *the coach after me.*

"Do this for us, Sonya. Do this for all us thirty- and forty-something sisters who don't have hot men or any men in their lives for that matter. Be our shining example in these dark times. Be our Nubian princess."

"Michelle, you're tripping."

"It's part of my job description."

Sonya laughed. "I am *not* saying I'll do this, but if I did, how long would this show last exactly?"

"You're thinking about doing it?"

"I said *if* I did."

"The show will last for approximately six months to a year."

Geez. Movies don't take that long to film. "I don't know. Those guys will be so young."

"You don't look your age at all, Sonya. And that could be the big secret they reveal at the end. That's how these shows work, you know. Our Nubian princess has been hiding something from you hunky punks. She's actually old enough to be your mama!"

Not funny.

"Remember that *Penthouse* playmate on *Momma's Boys* a few years ago?"

"No." *They don't have* Penthouse *playmates on Animal Planet.*

"The ratings for that show went through the roof when she revealed that secret. Oh, yeah, she got dumped and vilified on all the entertainment shows right after that, but the ratings were fantastic."

But I'm her opposite. "I doubt I'd be good for ratings."

"Why?"

"I'm *good,* Michelle. I'm a Christian, remember?"

"You never let me forget, Sonya."

"And I'm boring. I am a home-girl homebody. And if I revealed my true age to the man I eventually chose, he would dump me in a heartbeat, and I'd look foolish."

"Oh, one can only hope! Then you could do *another* show! Dumped by a punk, she's back to win her hunk. It will make TV history."

Michelle is a seriously damaged woman. "You're kidding, right?"

"No, and that would almost be better. You'd be on TV for up to *two* years and we could easily clear half a million—or *more* with endorsements and appearances."

We. She said "we." Michelle must be hurting for money. I stopped paying her a long time ago. "Two *years* of that foolishness? That's insane. If I did do it, I know I wouldn't last more than six months." *Why does it sound as if I'm talking myself into this? Why am I still talking to Michelle at all? Is part of me actually intrigued by this?* "And when the younger guy dumps me in the end, that's it. No sequels."

"Oh, you never know. The man you choose might *like* cougars. And you played for the Lady Cougars in college, too."

"Once upon a time when *both* of my knees worked, Michelle." Sonya returned to the couch, digging her feet under the cushions. "I can't believe you told them I was interested."

"You could have been a movie or a TV star and you know it. You still could be. Look at all the older women out there raking it in. Halle Berry, Vanessa Williams, Regina Hall, Nia Long, Kimberly Elise, Tyra Banks, Angela Bassett, Sanaa Lathan, Vivica Fox. Every one of them is forty or older. Older women have staying power. You think the Kardashians will look that good in their forties?"

I don't think they look that good now. "Who cares about the Kardashians?"

"See, you're already sounding like a diva."

Me? Never! "That's not the life I wanted after basketball, and it's not the quiet life I crave."

I want only what God wants. I have always wanted that, and I hope I've done Him proud. I wouldn't have had all that injury-free success in the WNBA without His almighty help. "How does she keep doing it year after year?" those so-called basketball experts asked. Hard work, dedication, and the God in me. So what if I haven't been fruitful and multiplying. Not every woman has to be married with children to be fulfilled.

"Michelle, I don't think this show is right for me."

"It's *perfect* for you."

"Nothing is perfect except the love of God, Michelle."

"Okay, okay, I'll level with you. I, um, I already sort of . . . *okayed* the contract. All you have to do is sign it."

Sonya nearly threw her remote control across the room. *I can't believe I thought about throwing my remote control across the room. How would I function?* "You just . . . sort of . . . *okayed* the contract."

"Um, yeah."

"You can't do that!"

"I already did it."

"Not without my permission!"

"True, but it was actually kind of easy. Just a few strokes of a pen. I hope I spelled your name right."

"I don't even pay you anymore." *She forged my signature! This is not happening!* "But they haven't even met me yet!"

But why aren't I just saying no and hanging up on her?

Why am I still even talking to Michelle? What is it about being a Nubian princess that is keeping my interest? Okay, I've never been one. Not many people have. I'm sure there's something psychological about all this, but I'd have to be crazy to go on this show!

"They *need* you, Sonya. Their first choice took a spot on *Survivor* instead."

"And that's a show I might actually *like* to do. It's athletic, outdoors, a challenge. *This* show, I mean, where's the challenge? All I have to do is kick guys off until I'm left with one man, right? Where's the challenge in that? I could probably do it on the first episode. I am good at saying no, and I'm sure I could say it eleven times in less than thirty seconds!" *Only I'm not saying "no" now. Nubian princess Sonya. It has a nice ring to it.*

"Sonya, they are so desperate that they're willing to fly you out to LA, pamper you to death, and do whatever it takes to make you happy."

Sonya rolled her eyes. "But I'm happy right now." *Oh, that wasn't very convincing.* "I *am* happy, Michelle." *And I've always thought that people who say they're happy usually aren't happy at all.* "In fact, for them to *keep* me happy, they'll understand if I *don't* do this."

"When's the last time you kissed a man?"

Geez, stay with the conversation. She's so random.

"Sonya, when's the last time you kissed a man?"

Middle school? But that was a boy. "I don't remember."

"I didn't think you would. When's the last time you even talked to a man?"

High school? Those must have been the days. I wish I could remember them. "I don't need a man. A man is too much trouble." *But how would I know that? I haven't been with any man long enough for him to give me any trouble. Maybe that's why I'm so happy.*

"On this show, the men come to you, and you decide

who stays or goes," Michelle said. "I would give *anything* for that kind of power. I would give up Starbucks forever if I could have that power for even one day."

That is a lot *of power. Michelle practically lived in Starbucks when I was in the league.* "Michelle, there has to be someone else out there who *craves* that kind of attention. I'm not that person."

"Your last date was seventeen years ago—today."

It was? Seventeen years ago? Geez. Who was the president? "How do you know that?"

"I'm your publicist. I write stuff down. I update your bio. You remember who it was with?"

No clue. "Who was it?"

"Archie Freeman."

"I went out with him?" *What was I thinking?*

"Girl, I rest my case. You can't even remember your date with the then NBA rookie of the year and future league MVP. You two made such a cute couple."

Archie's now playing ball in China because no one in the NBA can afford him or his failed drug tests anymore. Or the arthritic knees that keep him out of thirty games a year. "I didn't remember the date because it wasn't memorable." *The man had the nerve to call me "Ma." He said it was like calling me his "boo." Right. He just wanted me to be another one of his baby mamas.*

"Sonya, what are you wearing right now?"

There she goes being random again. "What does this—"

"Sonya," Michelle interrupted, "*what* are you wearing?"

"Sweats and a T-shirt." *No socks. Old, comfortable house slippers. No makeup. A hair tie. Drawers. Standard outfit for watching shows on The Food Network.*

"Who are you with?"

"No one." Sonya turned on the TV. "Oh, I'm with the big guy on *Man v. Food.* He is a trip. Last night he put away seven *pounds* of seafood." *Where does he put it all? He's not that big. I'll bet he has huge calves.*

"And you're okay with that?"

No. Watching a man eat too much for my amusement is lamer than lame, but I get so many cool recipes this way. "I'm not saying that I'm interested, all right? I'm just saying that I'll think about it. Please don't tell them I've agreed to this foolishness."

"I won't. But they're on a timetable."

And so am I. My time is my time. Sonya sighed. "What would I have to do next?"

"Go to Instant Talent dot com and answer a few questions."

"What kind of questions? Didn't you send them my bio?"

"Your bio doesn't answer *these* kinds of questions. Promise me you'll answer them."

"I promise."

"And promise you'll consider this opportunity carefully."

"Carefully *and* prayerfully."

"I'll call you tomorrow. Bye." *Click.*

That was rude.

Sonya booted up her laptop, which was always waiting a foot away from her on the lounge chair next to the couch, and got on Mozilla Firefox, her favorite Web browser because it was uncomplicated. In moments, she was staring at:

To see if you qualify for *Hunk or Punk*, answer the questions on each page.

Question 1: How tall are you?

Five-seven. That was in my bio.

What is your hair color?

Black with a few mean grays. I am so tired of plucking them, and they're right at my hairline, too.

What is your eye color?

Hazel. It isn't light brown. It's true hazel.

What is your ethnicity?

African? African American? Caribbean? All three? But I can only mark one. African American.

What is your body type?

Athletic? Yeah, right. Lean muscle? Not as lean as it was ten years ago. I guess I'm "Slim." But where's "Thick" or "Big-boned" or "Stacked"? I thought they wanted a black woman for this show.

What "body apparel" do you have?

As a freshman at the University of Houston, I added a tiny cougar cub tattoo to my arm. It's faded to a birthmark-looking thing now. I have pierced ears but nothing else. I am so not the right person to be a Nubian princess.

Thank you for your time. Please attach a recent photo and type a daytime telephone number in the box below. Click the "Make Me Famous!" button below to submit your answers, photo, and phone number.

Michelle already gave them my picture and I am not giving out my e-mail address.

Sonya hit the "Make Me Famous!" button, the screen went blank, and then she saw:

Thank you for your time. Please attach a recent photo and type a daytime telephone number in the box below. Click the "Make Me Famous!" button below to submit your answers, photo, and phone number.

"I don't have a recent picture, and you can't have my e-mail address," she said to the screen.

She clicked the button again.

Thank you for your time. Please attach a recent photo and type a daytime telephone number in the box below. Click the "Make Me Famous!" button below to submit your answers, photo, and phone number.

"Geez." She sighed, and then she smiled. "A recent photo. They don't specify what *kind* of photo." She browsed the Web until she found a cute baby cougar, right clicking and saving it to her hard drive. She typed "youcanthavemyaddress@noway.com" and "1-800-000-0000," attached the baby cougar, and hit the "Make Me Famous!" button.

Thank you for submitting your answers. We will contact you if you've made the cut.

Don't call us, we'll call you. She laughed. *I don't know how.*

On a whim, she checked her e-mail in-box and found a message from WB:

Congratulations, Sonya Richardson! You are a finalist for "Hunk or Punk"!

What? I didn't even give my correct e-mail address! And so soon? They are seriously desperate.

She checked the time on the e-mail. *Were they sitting there waiting for my answers to arrive in LA? They only had about a minute to look at my answers. Creepy. But how'd they know it was me? I shouldn't have sent the baby cougar. That was a dead giveaway.*

Please click below to view our eligibility requirements:

Sonya clicked, and another Web page opened on the screen.

All applicants must sign statements acknowledging that they have read, understand, and will comply with all of the eligibility requirements of *Hunk or Punk:*

1. Employees, officers, directors, and agents of . . .

That is a long list of companies. It's a wonder anyone in California can even go on these kinds of shows. I've only ever had one employer in my entire life, and that was the Houston Comets, and they don't even exist anymore.

2. Applicants may not presently be a candidate for any type of political office and may not become a candidate from the time the application is submitted until one year after first broadcast of the last episode of *Hunk or Punk.*

So if I wanted to be president, I couldn't run right away because I was on this show? That sounds un-American. This must be another part of the Arnold Schwarzenegger rule.

3. All applicants must be U.S. citizens or resident aliens living in the U.S. or foreign citizens who can travel without restrictions to and from the U.S. and have a passport valid for one year following the submission of the application and must be able to obtain any visas and/or documentation required to travel without restrictions to and from the U.S.

I know my passport is in this house somewhere. I haven't used it since the Sydney Olympics. I looked young in that passport picture, too.

4. All applicants must be at least twenty-one years of age.

I'm forty. Wait a minute. They wanted people twenty-five to forty, but everyone has to be at least twenty-one? You mean there may be some guys younger than twenty-five trying to pass for twenty-five? Geez, I will be as old as some of their mamas!

5. All applicants must be single and not currently involved in a committed intimate relationship, which includes: any marital relationship (whether or not the parties are separated or currently in the process of divorcing or annulling such marriage); any cohabitation relationship involving physical intimacy; or a monogamous dating relationship more than two months in duration.

I definitely qualify there. I've been single all my life. At least they can't drag any of my old boyfriends onto the show to talk smack to me or dish any dirt about me. Unless they fly in Archie from China.

Sonya shuddered. *God, keep Archie in China, okay?*

6. Applicants must never have been convicted of a
   felony or a misdemeanor or ever had a restraining order entered against them, either of which
   were based in whole or in part on the commis-
   sion of one or more acts involving moral turpitude
   or violence, as defined by the producer.

*Maybe that's why they can't find any true divas to do
this show. "Moral turpitude" . . . "restraining orders" . . .
"violence." But this means my suitors, no matter how hard-
core they look or act, are going to be a group of squeaky-
clean men. Fakin' the funk, that's all it is. Maybe I am the
right person for this show.*

All applicants understand that participation in *Hunk
or Punk* may expose applicant to the risk of death, serious injury, illness, or disease, and/or property damage.

*Death? Illness? Disease? Property damage? Romance
can be that dangerous? Lord Jesus, thank You for sparing
me all that so far. Oh, WB, you make it sound so fun. Sign
me up right now!*

7. Applicants must also be willing and able to participate in physical activities such as skydiving,
   snow skiing, ice-skating, parasailing, water skiing,
   and rollerblading.

*That is definitely not a list for women of color. I've never
done any of these things. I may have gone roller-skating
twice in my life. Snow skiing? Please! Paying hundreds of
dollars to go rushing down an icy mountain at eighty miles
an hour and ending up wrapped around a tree is not my*

idea of a good time. I ain't that crazy. Skydiving might be fun—once.

8. Each applicant understands that the producer may disclose any information contained within her application to third persons connected with *Hunk or Punk* and to compile information about applicant's private, personal, and public life, personal relationships with third persons, confidences and secrets with family, friends, significant others, including without limitation: physical appearance; personal characteristics/habits; medical treatment/history; sexual history; educational and employment history; military history; criminal investigations, charges and records; personal views and opinions about life, the world, politics, and religion.

What could they find? My lifetime stats? Boring. Maybe the specific shoes I wore for Nike. A knee injury that sidelined me for five games and keeps me limping around on cold days now. I usually keep my opinions to myself. I've been a member of St. Mark AME over in Pineville for eight years. There's really nothing that they could ever find that—

Sonya lost feeling in her hands.

No. That's . . . No. That was a long time ago. They couldn't find out about that. Only two living people know about that, and I'm one of them.

She said a quick prayer and continued reading.

9. Each applicant understands that if chosen as a Nubian princess on Hunk or Punk, she may be audio- and/or videotaped twenty-four hours a day, seven days a week by means of open and

hidden cameras, whether or not she is then aware that she is being videotaped or recorded, and that such recordings may be disseminated on television and/or all media now known or hereafter devised, in any and all manner throughout the universe in perpetuity.

The universe? Who are they kidding? As if we're going to mail boxed sets of the show to another galaxy to market reality TV. Then the aliens will know for sure that there's no intelligent life on this planet. I used to be on camera all the time. I was watched by millions during the Olympics, but I don't miss that kind of attention at all.

10. Applicants understand that use or revelation of personal information and recordings may be embarrassing, unfavorable, humiliating, and/or derogatory, and/ or may portray her in a false light. Each applicant agrees to release, discharge, and hold harmless WB from any and all claims, including claims for slander, libel, defamation, violation of rights of privacy, publicity, personality, and/or civil rights, depiction in a false light, intentional or negligent infliction of emotional distress, copyright infringement, and/or any other tort and/or damages arising from or in any way relating to the submission of an application, participation in the selection process, participation in *Hunk or Punk*, the use of the personal information or recordings, and/or the use of the applicant's name, voice, and/or likeness in connection with *Hunk or Punk*, or the promotion thereof in all media now known or hereafter devised.

Way to cover thy backside, WB. How could they portray me as anything but what I am? I am what I am. And if they even attempted to humiliate me, I'd walk out. I mean, unless they found out about . . . No. That was over a quarter century ago. Long past history, and those records are sealed. And they better stay sealed.

11. Any applicant who has appeared on any prime-time television reality show such as *Survivor, Big Brother, The Apprentice, elimiDate, The Amazing Race, American Idol, Extreme Makeover, America's Next Top Model, Rock of Love, The Real World, Make Me a Supermodel,* etc. . . . or is involved in the current production of any such television show must disclose such information in her application and may, at the producer's sole discretion, be deemed ineligible to participate in Hunk or Punk.

I have heard there are people out there who make a profession of being on reality TV. That's scary. I'd get worn out saying, "Look at me!" all the time. They must be too afraid to live their lives outside of the spotlight. That's so sad. Their lives only have meaning if they can rewind it and relive it. Do I really want to join them? I suppose if I do find the man of my dreams, it would make telling people how we met much easier. "Wanna know how we met? Pop in that DVD and fire up some popcorn."

12. All applicants must authorize the producer to conduct a background check, which may include a credit check, a military records check, a criminal arrest and/or conviction check, a civil litigation check, a family court litigation check,

interviews with employers, neighbors, teachers, etc.

Who could they talk to? All my coaches? They'd only have good things to say. I played the game, and I played the game the right way at all times. I practiced hard, made all the right sacrifices, and stayed true to the game. I respected the game. My teachers in high school would have good things to say, too, even my professors. I earned that degree in business administration. I wasn't one of those scholarship athletes who used her star status as an excuse not to do assignments or go to class. But would the producers go back to when I was a teenager, too? They don't seem that thorough, I mean, they're pretty much accepting me sight unseen from the jump.

13. An applicant who is selected as the Nubian princess may be required to undergo physical and psychological examinations and testing and meet all physical and psychological requirements as set by the producer.

They give psych evaluations, too? Let's see. First question: "Do you want to be on this show?" Oh, yes! "Then you're crazy." If I pursue this thing to its completion, I just might become crazy.

14. The Nubian princess must be available to travel and participate in *Hunk or Punk* for selected days over a six-month period for one year following the submission of the application, and to participate in taping additional materials and in promotional activities for selected days thereafter upon the producer's request.

Huh? "Selected days over a six month period for one year." That makes no sense whatsoever. Does it mean that about half of my time I'll be taped? They better not put cameras in my bathroom and bedroom. What is my business is nobody's business, no matter what the contract says.

15. A Nubian princess must agree to live, participate, and cooperate with the other individuals and the producer during the taping of *Hunk or Punk*. A Nubian princess must be able to travel for long periods of time, be adaptable to various living situations, and enjoy participating and living in close proximity with others of varied background and experience.

I traveled for four years with my college team and ten years with my pro team. If I can survive a dozen women on long road trips for a total of fourteen years straight, I can survive anything. But a house full of men? Yuck. So what if they're hot men. Still yuck. A normal man makes a mess. A hot man would make a hot mess. And if they're younger, hot men, I'll probably be picking up their drawers. More yuck.

16. Applicants understand that the eligibility requirements may be changed, modified, or amended by the producer in its sole discretion from time to time.

In other words, if I'm not attitudinal enough or "black" enough or "diva" enough, they may try to put words in my mouth or make me do things I wouldn't normally do. That ain't happening. May the words of my mouth and the meditations of my soul be acceptable to You, oh Lord, my

*strength and my redeemer. I'm definitely gonna be praying
every other breath during this thing.*

Click below if you agree to these terms.

Sonya shrugged and clicked. "Here goes nothing."